The Queen's Maries
A Romance of Holyrood

by

G. J. Whyte-Melville

The Queen's Maries
A Romance of Holyrood

by G. J. Whyte-Melville

ISBN: 978-93-64288-05-7

Published by

DOUBLE 9 BOOKS

2/13-B, Ansari Road
Daryaganj, New Delhi – 110002
info@double9books.com
www.double9books.com
Tel. 011-40042856

ABOUT THE AUTHOR

G. J. Whyte-Melville (1821-1888) was a notable British author known for his novels and works of fiction, particularly those set in the context of military and adventure. His writing reflects his experiences and interests, often focusing on themes of heroism, military life, and adventure. Some of his notable works are **"The Interpreter: A Tale of the War"** (1867): One of his most recognized works, this novel offers a detailed portrayal of military life and espionage during wartime. **"Katerfelto: A Story of Exmoor"** (1860): A novel set in the English countryside, showcasing Whyte-Melville's skill in depicting rural life and adventure. **"Satanella"** (1868): A novel featuring elements of romance and intrigue, set against a backdrop of political and social drama. **"The Gloved Hand"** (1865): Another example of his engaging storytelling, blending romance with adventure and mystery. G. J. Whyte-Melville's contributions to literature are notable for their detailed and engaging portrayal of military and adventure themes. His novels remain of interest for their historical and narrative depth, and his ability to blend romance with adventure has earned him a place in 19th-century British literature.

Whyte-Melville passed away on November 7, 1888, but his works continue to be appreciated for their vivid storytelling and exploration of themes related to heroism, duty, and military life.

CONTENTS

'Yestre'en the Queen had four Maries—
The day she'll hae but three—
There was Mary Beton, and Mary Seton,
And Mary Carmichael and me.'

CHAPTER I

'Turn back, turn back, ye weel-fau'red May,
My heart will break in three;
And sae did mine on yon bonny hill-side,
When ye wadna let me be!'

Many a smiling plain, many a wooded slope and sequestered valley adorns the fair province of Picardy. Nor is it without reason that her Norman-looking sons and handsome daughters are proud of their birth-place; but the most prejudiced of them will hardly be found to affirm that her seaboard is either picturesque or interesting; and perhaps the strictest search would fail to discover a duller town than Calais in the whole bounds of France. With the gloom of night settling down upon the long low line of white sand which stretches westward from the harbour, and an angry surge rising on the adjacent shoal, while out to seaward darkness is brooding over the face of the deep, an unwilling traveller might, indeed, be induced to turn into the narrow ill-paved streets of the town, on the seaman-like principle of running for any port in a storm; but it would be from the sheer necessity of procuring food and lodging, not from any delusive expectation of gaiety and amusement, essential ingredients in a Frenchman's every-day life. And yet Calais has been the scene of many a thrilling incident and stirring event. Could they speak, those old houses, with their pointed gables, their overhanging roofs, and quaint diamond-paned windows, they could tell some strange tales of love and war, of French and English chivalry, of deeds of arms performed for the sake of honour, and beauty, and ambition, and gold—the four strings on which most of the tunes are played that speed the Dance of Death—of failures and successes, hopes and disappointments, the ups and downs, the ins and outs, the cross-purposes, the hide-and-seek, that constitute the game of life. In that very house, over the way yonder—with its silent courtyard, in which the grass shoots up vigorously between the stones, and from which to-day nothing more unusual issues than an old peasant woman in a clean cap, carrying a young child with a dirty face— slept, perhaps, the loveliest woman the world ever saw, a widow, while yet a bride, a queen while yet a child, on her way from one royal throne to take possession of another. Yes, here she lay the night before she quitted her dear France, never to see it again; the bright, the beautiful, the beloved, a very rose amongst all the flowers of the garden, a very gem amongst all the gold and tinsel that surrounded her, the link in a line of kings, the pride of two countries, the fairest of God's creatures—Mary, Queen of Scots—here she lay, with life and love and hope before her, and slept, and dreamed not of Fotheringay.

It was a chill autumn night. Beyond the walls a rising breeze moaned fitfully over the dreary flats. The ebbing tide murmured as it receded, returning, and yet returning, as though loth to leave that comfortless expanse of wet level sand. A few drops of rain fell from time to time, and though a star struggled out here and there, the sky became momentarily more obscured. It was a gloomy night out at sea yonder; it was a gloomy night here on shore, dismal, foreboding, and suggestive of farewell.

But within the town, bustle and hurry, and a certain amount of confusion, not unmixed with revelry, imparted considerable life and animation to the hours of darkness, scaring indeed some of the quiet householders, and rousing the echoes in the narrow streets. Horses, picketed in the market-place, stamped and snorted and shook their bridles; spurs clanked on the pavement; steel corslet and head-piece flashed in the light of torches held by bearded men-at-arms, looking doubly martial in that red glare. Here might be seen a dainty page in satin doublet, with velvet cap and feather, elbowing some sturdy groom who was bearing a cuirass home from the armourer's, or leading a charger to its stall, and inquiring, with all a page's freedom, for the lodging of his lord, to receive, probably, an answer neither respectful nor explanatory, but productive of a stinging retort—for in those days the pages of a great house were masters of all weapons, but especially of the tongue. There might be observed a group of peasant-women, in clean hoods and aprons, with baskets on their heads, lingering somewhat longer than was absolutely necessary to exchange with harquebusiers or spearmen those compliments in which the French imagination is so prolific, and which the French language renders with such graceful facility. Anon, a lord of high degree, easily recognised by the dignity of his bearing, and the number of his retainers thronging round him with arms and torches, passed along the streets, exciting the curiosity of the vulgar and the admiration of the softer sex; while more than one churchman, threading his way quietly homeward, dropped his 'Benedicite' with gentle impartiality amongst the throng. The blessing was usually received with gratitude, though an exception might occur in the person of some stalwart man-at-arms, large of limb, fresh-coloured, and fair-bearded, who returned the good man's greeting with derision or contempt. These reprobates were invariably well armed, and extremely soldier-like in their bearing, to be distinguished, moreover, by their blue velvet surcoats, on which St Andrew's cross was embroidered in silver, and the peculiar form of their steel-lined bonnets, which they wore with a jaunty air on one side the head. Something, also, of more than the usual assumption of a soldier might be traced in their demeanour, as is apt to be the case with the members of a *corps d'élite*, and such the Archers of the Scottish Body-Guard had indeed a right to be considered both by friend and foe. Although in the service of His Most Catholic Majesty, many of them, including their captain, the unfortunate Earl of Arran, were staunch Protestants; and at that rancorous period, the supporters of the Reformed Church did by no means confine themselves to a silent abnegation of the errors they had renounced.

One archer, however, a young man with nothing peculiarly striking either in face or figure, save an air of frankness and quiet determination on his sun-burnt brow, acknowledged the benediction of a passing ecclesiastic with a humility that excited the jeers of two or three comrades, to which he replied with the quiet simplicity that seemed to be a part of his character, 'An old man's blessing, lads, can do neither you nor me any harm,' and proceeded on his way without further remark or explanation; while the manner in which his rebuke was received by the scorners themselves, denoted that he was at least a person of some consideration and standing in the *corps*. Elbowing his way through a gaudy crowd, consisting of the Marquis d'Elbœuf's retainers, who were accompanying their master in his attendance on his royal niece, and certain satellites of the House of Guise, for the duke and duchess, with Cardinal Lorraine, had already escorted the Queen of Scotland thus far upon her journey, our archer turned into an *auberge*, already filled with a mixture of courtiers, soldiers, pages, men-at-arms, and other officials, and seating himself at a small deal table, coarse and clean, requested to be served, in a tone of impatience that implied a vigorous appetite and a long fast. While the host, quick, courteous and smiling, bustled up to him, with napkin, trencher, and some two feet of bread, the archer removed the bonnet from his brow, and, looking around him, nodded to one or two acquaintances with an air of considerable preoccupation, ere he subsided into a profound fit of abstraction, which, to judge by his countenance, proceeded from no agreeable theme.

He was a man of less than thirty summers, sufficiently well-built, and of ordinary stature, with no peculiar advantages of person or bearing that should distinguish him from any other gentleman-private of the Scottish Body-Guard. His arms, indeed, were scrupulously clean and of the best workmanship; for when a man's life depends daily on the quality of his blade, such details become a matter of course; and if his apparel were a thought more carefully put on, and of a more precise cut, than that of his fellows, this distinction seemed but to arise from that habitual attention to trifles which is the usual concomitant of energy and readiness for action. A sloven *may* be a brave man, and a capable; but if the machine is to remain in good working order, every screw should fit to a hair's breadth, and a coat of varnish over the whole will not detract from its efficiency. Our archer, then, was well but not splendidly dressed; nor would his face more than his figure have attracted the attention of any casual observer. Nine men out of ten would have passed him by unnoticed. A woman would have been first puzzled, then interested, perhaps eventually fascinated, by the quiet repose of that stern, calm brow. It was a face of which the expression was many years older than the features. A physiognomist would have detected in it resolution, tenacity of purpose, strong feeling, repressed by habitual self-control—above all, self-denial and great power of suffering.

For the rest, his complexion, where not tanned by the weather, was fair and fresh-coloured, according well with the keen gray eye and light-brown hair of his Scottish origin.

The archer's meditations, however, were soon put to flight by the agreeable interruption of a well-served supper (for, indeed, prior to those days, as old Froissart will bear us witness, the French excelled in cookery); and after the first cravings of appetite were appeased, he emptied a cup of red wine with a sigh of considerable satisfaction, then returned to his platter with renewed vigour, and filled his goblet once more to the brim.

'Good wine drowns care,' said a laughing voice behind him; 'and Cupid himself cannot fly when his wings are drenched. Ho! drawer, quick! Another flask of Burgundy, and place me a chair by my pearl of Scottish Archers, till he tells me what brings him here eighty leagues from Paris, unless it be to mingle his tears with the salt brine of the accursed Channel that bears our White Queen[1] from the shores of France.'

[1] Mary was called '*La Reine Blanche*,' because she mourned in *white* for her first husband, Francis II.

An expression of pain shot rapidly over the archer's face as he greeted the speaker with a cordial grasp of the hand; but he answered in the deep steady tones that were habitual to him.

'A man may have despatches to carry from the constable to his son; and d'Amville is not likely to overlook a soldier's delay on such a road as this, where there are as many horses as poplar trees. I could take the Montmorency's orders yesterday at noon, and be here to supper to-night, without borrowing the Pegasus you ride so recklessly, my poetical friend.'

The other laughed gaily; and when he laughed, his dark eyes flashed and sparkled like diamonds.

'My Pegasus,' said he, 'needs oftener the spur than the rein; but who could not write verses, and sing them too, with such a theme before him? Listen, my friend. I am to sail to-morrow with them for Scotland. Heaven's blessing on d'Amville that he has selected me to accompany him! Nay, we are appointed to the Queen's galley; and Mary will take at least one heart along with her, as loyal and devoted as any she can leave behind.'

He checked himself suddenly, and a sad, wistful expression crossed his handsome brow, whilst the dark eyes dimmed, and he set down untasted the Burgundy he had lifted to his lips. Something in his voice, too, seemed to have enlisted the archer's sympathy, and he also was silent for a moment, and averted his looks from his companion's face.

After a while he forced himself to speak.

'I must return,' said he, 'in two more days. Is it true they embark without fail to-morrow? Is there no danger from the ships of England? Is Her Majesty well accompanied? Doth the household sail with her? Ladies and all?'

'The Maries, of course,' replied the other, answering only the last question, which he reasonably considered the most interesting to his listener; 'and right glad they seem to be to quit this merry land of France for that cold bleak country where I hear music is scarcely known, and dancing interdicted as a sin! I marvel much at their taste. To be sure, they accompany one who would inspire the wildest savages with chivalry, and make the veriest desert a paradise! Ah! when was such a garland of beauty ever trusted to the waves? The Queen and her satellites! One lovelier than another, but all paling before her. A bumper, my friend! on your knees, a bumper—a health to the letter M! nay, pledge me one for each of the four, and a fresh flask for the Queen—for the Queen!'

Again the speaker's voice sank to a whisper, and the archer, who had ere now recovered the usual indifference of his demeanour, proceeded to do justice to a toast which could not, according to the manners of the age, have been refused, and which, in truth, for reasons of his own, he was by no means loth to pledge. The table at which they sat, however, was by this time surrounded by the different frequenters of the *auberge*, for the archer's companion, no other than the poet Chastelâr, was too well-known and popular an individual in the gay circles of France to remain long unnoticed, where so many of her nobility were congregated. Young, handsome, and well-born, his romantic disposition and undoubted talents had rendered him an especial favourite with a people who, above all things, delight to be amused, and with whom enthusiasm, whether real or affected, is generally accepted as an equivalent for merit. To look on Chastelâr, with his long dark curls and his bright eyes, was to behold the poet-type in its most attractive form; and when to beauty of feature and delicacy of mind were added a graceful figure, skill in horsemanship, as in all knightly exercises, great kindliness of disposition, and gentle birth, what wonder that with the ladies of the French Court to be in love with Chastelâr, was as indispensable a fashion as to wear a pointed stomacher, or a delicate lace-edging to the ruff? And Chastelâr, with true poet-nature, sunned himself in their smiles, and enjoyed life intensely, as only such natures can, and bore about with him the while, unsuspected and incurable, a sorrow near akin to madness in his heart.

As gallant after gallant strode up to the table at which the two friends sat, the conversation became general, turning, as such conversations usually do, on the congenial themes of love and war. Again and again was mine host summoned for fresh supplies of wine, and the archer, whose recent arrival from Paris made him an object of general interest, was plied with questions as to the latest news and gossip of the capital. Richly-mounted swords were laid aside on the coarse deal table, cloaks of velvet and embroidery draped the uncouth chairs, gilt spurs jingled on the humble floor, and voices that had bandied opinions with kings in council, or shouted 'St Denis!' in the field, were now exchanging jest and laugh and repartee under the homely roof of a common wine-shop.

Even the Marquis d'Elbœuf, the Queen's uncle, a lord of the princely house of Guise, and Admiral of France, joined with a sailor's frankness in the gay revel, and taking a seat between Chastelâr and the archer, questioned the latter as to his late interview with the constable, and the well-being of that distinguished veteran, a soldier of whom every man in France was proud.

'And you made sail with the despatches the moment you were out of his sight,' observed the marquis. 'I'll warrant, you made a fair wind of it all the way to Calais, for the Montmorency brooks no delay in the execution of his orders. How looked he, my friend?—and what said he? Come tell us the exact words.'

'He looked like an old lion, as he always does,' answered the archer, simply; 'and he said to me in so many words, "These letters must be in my son's hands within eight-and-forty hours. I can depend upon you Scots. May the blessing of Our Lady be upon you, my child. And now, Right— Face! and go to the devil!"'

The Marquis laughed heartily.

'He loves your countrymen well,' said he, 'and with reason. I have heard him swear the bravest man he ever saw was a Scot.'

A murmur of dissent, if not disapproval, rose around the table, and many of the Frenchmen present bent their brows in manifest impatience; but the marquis, who had his own reasons for wishing to be well with the Scottish nation, and whose frank nature brooked no withdrawal or modification of his opinions, struck his hand on the board, till the cups leaped again, and repeated in loud tones—

'A Scot!—yes, gentlemen—a Scot. And I know why he said so—for I too was present at the boldest feat-of-arms even the constable ever witnessed; and so was my modest friend here with the cross of St Andrew on his breast—only he was but a stripling then, and had hardly strength to hold his pike at the advance. A health, gentlemen! Do me reason. To the memory of Norman Leslie, Master of Rothes! one of your difficult Scotch names. Norman Leslie, the bravest of the brave!—Will you hear the story?'

'Tell it, marquis!' was repeated on all sides, and cups were set down empty on the board, as many an eager warlike face turned towards the Admiral of France.

'It was at Rentz, then,' proceeded d'Elbœuf, 'where the old Emperor out-generalled *us* as completely as we outfought *him*, and the two armies were almost within bow-shot of each other. We resembled a couple of angry dogs that are not permitted by their masters to fight. A clear slope of some two or three hundred paces divided us, and the German light-horsemen came galloping out to skirmish, tossing their lances in the air and bantering us. There must have been, at least, a hundred of them within a pistol-shot of our lines. The blood of Frenchmen soon boils up, gentlemen; but we had no orders to engage, and I, for one, kept my men-at-arms in hand, for the king was commanding in person, and Condé, and the constable, and the Duc d'Anguien were present, and likely to visit any breach of discipline with severe reproof. Ah! they cannot thus interfere with us at sea; but I ground my teeth at intervals, and thought, if the order would only come, what short work we would make with the German dogs.

'Norman Leslie, however, had come up after the council was over in the king's tent, and so, I suppose, fancied himself free to act. He had but half a score men with him at most; but he formed them into line, and charged up the hill into the thick of the enemy. It was a noble sight to see him, gentlemen, in his coat of black velvet, with its broad white crosses, and his burnished armour, with a red Scotch bonnet on his head. How he drove that good gray horse of his a dozen lances' lengths ahead of his following! He rode through and through the Germans as if they were a troop of children at play. We, in the lines, I tell you, counted five of them go down before his lance broke. Then he drew his sword, and though they shot at him with musquetoons and culverines, we could still see the red bonnet glancing to and fro, like fire among the smoke. At last they detached a company of spearmen to surround him, and then striking spurs into his horse, he came galloping back to our lines, and rode gallantly to salute the constable in the centre. As he kissed his sword-hilt, the good gray fell dead at Montmorency's feet. Alas! his master followed him in less than a fortnight, for though the king sent his own leech to dress his wounds, brave Norman Leslie was hurt in so many places, that it was out of the power of leech-craft to save him. What say you, gentlemen? a bolder feat-of-arms than that was never attempted by a soldier, and it was executed by a Scot! What say you of a man that would ride through an armed host single-handed to fetch away a laurel leaf?'

The archer smiled, and bowed low at this flattering tribute to his nation.

'I might return your compliments, marquis,' said he, 'had we not a Scotch proverb which implies "*Stroke me, and I will stroke thee.*" And yet it is but fair to say I have known a rougher ride than even Norman Leslie's taken for a silk handkerchief, and by a Frenchman.'

'A silk handkerchief! a lady's of course,' said one. 'A love-token!' exclaimed another. 'Undertaken in deliverance of a vow,' suggested a third. 'Done by an Englishman for a wager,' laughed a fourth.—All had some remark to make except Chastelâr, whose colour rose visibly, and who looked distressed and ill at ease.

'A handkerchief of the softest Cyprus silk,' insisted the archer in his quiet expressive voice, 'and rescued by the very man to whom I this day presented his father's letters. And yet it is no wonder that the constable's son and a Marshal of France should be a brave man. I tell you, gentlemen, that I saw d'Amville at the head of a band of Huguenots sorely pressed, and outnumbered by his countrymen of the Catholic faith, so that he had but one chance of retreat in placing a rapid stream betwixt himself and his pursuers. As he was facing the enemy, whilst the last of his followers entered the water, a handkerchief dropped unnoticed from beneath his corslet. He discovered his loss, however, as soon as he reached the opposite bank; and dashing once more into the stream, under a murderous fire, charged through the press of men-at-arms to the spot where it lay, dismounted, picked it up, and cut his way back again to his own troop. There was blood on the handkerchief when his page unarmed him that night; but I think it was the blood of the bravest man in France.'

'And the handkerchief?'—cried several voices. 'Whose was it?' 'Who gave it to him?' 'Happy the lady who owned so true a knight!'

The archer smiled once more.

'Nay, gentlemen,' said he, 'it was no love-token after all. But the marshal is the soul of loyalty as of honour. There was an M and a crown-royal embroidered on the margin. It belonged to the White Queen—to her whom France is to lose to-morrow for ever.'

'What a theme for the minstrel!' exclaimed d'Elbœuf gaily. 'Chastelâr! canst thou hear and be silent? Awake, man! drench thy brain with Burgundy, and improvise us some stanzas!'

The poet looked up with the air of one who shakes some painful burden off his mind. He put his cup to his lips, and answered gaily enough.

'Not on that theme, marquis, at least to-night. Is it not the eve of our departure? And can there be merriment for France when she thinks of all she is to lose on the morrow? Nay, gentlemen, if you must have a song, let it be a lament. Let France mourn the absence of one whose like she may never hope to see again.'

Seats were drawn nearer the table; the guests' faces assumed an air of interest and expectation. Through the open doorway might be seen the humbler servants of the household crowding eagerly to listen. Chastelâr looked around him well-pleased, and sang, in a rich mellow voice, the following stanzas, after the model of his old instructor, the celebrated Ronsard:—

'As an upland bare and sere,
In the waning of the year,
When the golden drops are wither'd off the broom;
As a picture when the pride
Of its colouring hath died,
And faded like a phantom into gloom:

'As a night without a star,
Or a ship without a spar,

Or a mist that broods and gathers o'er the sea;
As a court without a throne,
Or a ring without a stone,
Seems the widow'd land of France bereft of thee.

'Our darling, pearl, and pride!
Our blossom and our bride!
Wilt thou never gladden eyes of ours again?
Would the waves might rise and drown
Barren Scotland and her crown,
So thou wert back with us in fair Touraine!'

Amidst the applause which followed the notes of their favourite, cloaks and swords were assumed, reckonings were discharged, farewells exchanged, and laughing, light-hearted gallants streamed up the dark street in quest of their respective lodgings. Soon each was housed, and all was quiet ere the first streaks of dawn rose upon the sleeping town, and the cold bleak shore, and the dull waves of the brooding Channel.

CHAPTER II

'Farewell! Farewell! How soon 'tis said!
The wind is off the bay,
The sweeps are out, the sail is spread,
The galley gathers way.

'Farewell! Farewell! The words, how light!
Yet what can words say more?
Sad hearts are on the sea to-night,
And sadder on the shore.'

Twenty-four hours had elapsed since Chastelâr sang his farewell song in the little *auberge* at Calais.

He now stood on the deck of a large galley, manned by a sturdy crew of rowers, whose efforts, however, were but little assisted by the light airs that blew off the shore. The ample sail would fill at intervals, and then flap idly against the mast. The measured stroke of the oars seemed on that wide expanse of water to have but little effect in propelling the labouring craft, and the companionship of a corresponding vessel at some quarter of a mile distance proceeding at the same rate, and in the same direction, neutralised all appearance of locomotion. A bright moon shone down upon the Channel; and the coast of France, still at no great distance, was distinctly visible in her light. Comparatively little way had been made since the galley's departure, nor did her course bear her in a direct line from the shore. The rowers also had flagged somewhat in their usual efforts. Rank upon rank, these brawny ruffians chained to their heavy oars were accustomed to labour doggedly, yet effectually, under the stimulus of the whip. To-night, however, a gentle voice had interceded even for the rude galley-slaves, and while they enjoyed this rare respite from over-exertion, many a foul lip, that had long forgotten to form anything but curses, writhed itself into an unaccustomed blessing for the fair widowed Queen of France. Yes, what a strange companionship in that dark hull, having indeed nothing in common but the thin plank that was equally the hope of all! Down below, forcing her through the water, men who had almost lost the outward semblance of humanity, whose hearts were as black with crime as their bodies were disfigured with the hardships of their lot; men whom their fellows had been forced to hunt like wild beasts out of the society of their kind, and to keep chained and guarded at an enforced labour worse than death; and seated on deck within ten paces of these convicts, a bevy of the fairest and gentlest of the human race, a knot of lovely maidens chosen for their birth, and beauty, and womanly accomplishments, to surround a mistress who was herself the most fascinating of them all, the very pearl of her sex, Mary Stuart, Queen of Scots.

Chastelâr, leaning against the mast, gazed aft upon the deck, and listened to the talk of Mary and her maidens as they chatted together in the freedom of that unrestrained intercourse which the Stuarts have ever encouraged with their household. It was pleasant to hear the women's soft tones mingling with the plash of the water, and the flap of the empty sail; but there was one voice of which every note thrilled, even painfully, to the poet's heart.

Mary was reclining on a couch that had been prepared for her against the taffrail of the vessel. Though the tears were still wet upon her cheek, and a fresh burst was imminent every time she looked upon the coast, she could yet force herself to speak gaily, and strove to keep up the spirits of her maidens with that charm of manner which never failed her at the very worst.

'And where is our Duenna?' said the Queen, archly; 'I have scarce seen her since the hour we embarked, when she walked the deck with her head up and the port of an admiral. D'Amville yonder, studying his charts as if he were in unknown seas, instead of the ditch that divides France from Britain, could scarce have looked more seaman-like.'

The young lady she addressed, a provoking specimen of the saucy style of beauty, with mischievous eyes, the whitest of teeth, and an exquisite little foot that was always conspicuous, laughed most unfeelingly in reply.

'Your Majesty should see her now,' she said. 'I shall never call her proud Mary Beton again. She is below, in the darkest corner of the cabin. She has buried her head in the cushions. She is ill. She is frightened, and her velvet dress is creased and tumbled, and stained all over with sea-water!'

'You cruel child,' said the Queen, good-humouredly. 'Mary Seton, you are incorrigible. But we must send down to succour her, poor thing! Ah! it is only a heart-ache like mine that makes one insensible to all other sufferings. Mary Hamilton is too susceptible—she will be ill also; but you,

Mary Carmichael, you have a kind disposition and a ready hand. You will not laugh in her face like this saucy girl here; go down and succour poor Beton. Give her our love—tell her she will yet be well enough to come and look her last with us on the dear land of France.'

The young lady whom she addressed rose at once from her occupation, which, like that of her mistress, seemed to consist in gazing steadfastly at the French coast, and with a graceful reverence to the Queen, departed on her errand of consolation.

As she passed Mary Seton, the latter's quick eye detected a few drops, it might be of spray, upon her cheek. The Maries could sympathise with their Queen's regret in leaving a country that had been to them a pleasant home; and a woman's sorrow, as we all know, while it is more easily cured, is also more easily excited, than that of the sterner sex. Mary Carmichael's was not a disposition to give way to unavailing grief; above all, was one in which the instinct to conceal strong emotion predominated. With much kindliness of heart and real good-nature, she was yet somewhat intolerant of weakness in herself and others. Brave and self-reliant, she could make small allowance for timidity or vacillation even in her own sex; and had either mental or bodily pain been able to extort one exclamation of suffering from her lips, she would have been bitterly ashamed of it a moment afterwards. To look on her clear blue eyes, her finely-cut and regular features, her smooth brow, and determined mouth and chin, determined and uncompromising, despite of red lips, white teeth, and dimples, you would have decided that the one drawback to her attractions was the want of that yielding softness which is a woman's greatest charm. '*On aime ce qu'on protège;*' and the haughty beauty who humbles while she conquers, little guesses how a man's rude heart warms to the gentler suppliant, who clings to him, and trusts in him, and seems to say she has but '*him* in the world.' Masses of soft brown hair, and a rounded outline of form, feminine and symmetrical, somewhat redeemed Mary Carmichael's appearance from the charge of *hardness*. Altogether she gave the gallants of the French court the impression of a woman whom it would be difficult to like a *little*, and hazardous to like *much*. So what with the danger of her charms, and her own dignified and reserved demeanour, she had received less admiration than was due to the undoubted beauty of her face and figure.

While she goes below to succour her friend, who is suffering from sea-sickness, we will give some account of the four ladies of honour, commonly called the Maries, who waited on the Queen of Scots.

Mary Stuart herself, with all her predilections in favour of France, a country in which she spent the few tranquil years of her disturbed and sorrowful life, never suffered her connexion with Scotland to be weakened or neglected. She kept up an active correspondence with her mother, Mary of Guise, who held the reins of government with no inefficient hand in that country, till her death. Many of her household were Scotch. She showed especial favour to the archer-guard, all of whom were of Scotch extraction,— favour which, over-estimated and misunderstood by their captain, the heir of the house of Hamilton, was, perhaps, the original cause that 'turned weak Arran's brain.' She gave such appointments in her household, as were nearest her person, to the Scotch nobility; and she chose for her own immediate attendants, four young ladies of ancient Scottish families, whose qualifications were birth, beauty, and the possession of her own Christian name. 'The Maries,' as they were called, accordingly occupy a prominent position in the court-history of the time; and as their number was always kept up to four, several of the oldest families in Scotland, such as the Setons, the Flemings, the Livingstones, &c., had the honour of furnishing recruits to the lovely body-guard. At the time of her embarkation for Leith, the Queen was accompanied by a very devoted *quartette*, as conspicuous for their personal attractions as for their loyalty to their sovereign. It was even rumoured that the faithful maidens had bound themselves by a vow not to marry till their Queen did. Be this, however, as it may, not one of them but might have chosen from the flower of the French Court, had she been so disposed. Nay, gossips were found to affirm that many a warlike count and stately marquis would have been happy to take any one of the four; only too blest in the possession of a Mary, be she Mary Beton, Mary Seton, Mary Carmichael, or Mary Hamilton.

A short sketch of each, at the commencement of our narrative, may serve, perhaps, to prevent confusion, and to elucidate the actions of some of the humbler characters in our drama. We are of honest Bottom's opinion that it is best 'to call forth the actors generally according to the scrip. First say what the play treats on; then read the names of the actors; and so grow to a point.'

We will begin, then, with the eldest of the four—the lady who, with her head buried in cushions, was groaning afresh at every lurch of the creaking galley, and who suffered despondently, refusing to be comforted.

To-day it is scarcely fair to bring her before the public. Yesterday she might have been seen to the greatest advantage, for Mary Beton was one of those people who seem to have been placed in the world for the express purpose of wearing full dress. The most romantic imagination could not have associated her with homely duties, *déshabille*, or dishevelled hair; and the Queen used to observe, laughingly, that he must be a bold man who could venture to ask her hand for a galliard, and contemplate the possibility of disarranging a fold of her robe, even in that stateliest of measures.

And yet she was handsome, too, in a cold, unfeeling, haughty style. She had large handsome eyes, and a large handsome figure, and large handsome hands, which she loved to display. She was perfect in all matters of court *étiquette*, in which it was impossible to find her tripping, and would have died rather than 'bate one of the accustomed ceremonies with which she delighted to glorify her mistress and herself. When she stood behind the throne with the Queen's gloves in her hand, she was the admiration of all chamberlains, grand carvers, seneschals, and such court officials, so unmoved and dignified was her bearing, so scrupulously rigid her demeanour, so completely did she sink the woman in the maid-of-honour. And her disposition corresponded with her lofty manners, and her fine, well-dressed form. Less unfeeling than careless of all matters that did not appertain directly or indirectly to the court, she neither seemed to seek nor to afford sympathy for the petty vexations and annoyances which a little *coterie* of women is pretty sure to find or create for itself. None of the Maries ever went to her for advice and assistance, only for instructions and commands. Though but little their senior, she was always considered and treated as a kind of lady-superior by the other three, and even the Queen used to call her jestingly 'The Duenna,' and vowed that she never felt so unlike a Stuart as, when after some trifling breach of court *étiquette*, she encountered the tacit rebuke of Mary Beton's grave, cold eye.

If she *had* a weakness, it was ambition. If there was any one road that led to her heart, it must have been through the portals of a palace, along tapestried passages, between lines of bowing lackeys, with a gentleman-usher at each turning to point out the way. She wrapped herself in the folds of a majestic decorum, and paced along the journey of life gravely and disposedly, as if it were a minuet.

What a contrast to laughing, roguish, Mary Seton, that Will-o'-the-wisp in petticoats, who flitted hither and thither amongst the courtiers, and pervaded every apartment of the palace with the air of a spoiled child whom nobody ventured to thwart or to chide. White-headed statesmen, grave ambassadors, ponderous in the double weight of their sovereign's dignity and their personal appearance, iron-handed warriors, and haughty cardinals, all acknowledged the influence of the bewitching little maid-of-honour; and it seemed that the most devoted of her slaves were those whose years and station afforded the strongest contrast to her own.

The constable himself, the famous Montmorency, from whom the faintest gesture of approval could have lured every brave man in France willingly to death, would follow her about like a tame dog, and Cardinal Lorraine, churchmen though he were, would have entrusted her with state secrets that he scarcely ventured to whisper to his own pillow. She might have done a deal of mischief if she had chosen, that lively, laughing, little maiden. Fortunately she was thoroughly good-natured—so heedless that she forgot in the afternoon everything that was told her in the morning, and had, moreover, not the slightest taste for mystery or political intrigue. It would be difficult to say what was the especial charm people found in Mary Seton. Her features were irregular, and her figure, though exquisitely shaped, of the smallest. Dark eyes and eyelashes, with a profusion of light hair, gave a singular expression to the upper part of her face, whilst a mischievous smile, disclosing the pearliest of teeth, completed all the personal attractions of which she could boast. It was, indeed, one of those *haunting* faces, which, once seen, make an unaccountable impression, and which, if ever permitted to engrave themselves on the heart, do so in lines that are not to be obliterated without considerable pain. There was something *piquante*, too, in her continual restlessness. Even here, on shipboard, she could not be still for five minutes together. She had already pervaded the whole vessel from stem to stern, above and below, nor was her curiosity satisfied till she had personally inspected the poor galley-slaves, returning to the Queen, brimful of the private history of the two or three greatest criminals amongst them, with which, according to custom, she had made herself familiar, ere she had been an hour on board. Her mistress, though in no merry mood, could not forbear being amused.

'I believe,' said she, 'that you would rather work, chained to an oar, like these poor wretches, than sit still.'

And Mary Seton replied, demurely—

'Indeed, madam, idleness is the parent of evil; and, doubtless, even at the galleys, my good behaviour would soon raise me to be captain of the gang.'

A pair of dark eyes, that had hitherto been fixed on some object amidships, were raised in wonder to the laughing speaker, reproachful, as it were, of her levity at such a time; and Mary Hamilton's beautiful face, paler and more beautiful than ever in the moonlight, seemed to take a deeper shade of sadness as she resumed the occupation in which she had been interrupted with an unconscious sigh. Sitting at the Queen's feet, she was ready, as usual, at the shortest notice, to fulfil her mistress's wishes; but the latter remarked, with concern, that her favourite maid-of-honour had been silent for hours, and that the novelties incidental to their situation had failed to rouse her from the abstraction in which, of late, she had been habitually plunged. It grieved the Queen's kind heart, for, though she loved the others dearly, perhaps she loved Mary Hamilton the best of all; and it was no wonder. Beautiful as she was, with her large solemn eyes and her black hair, framing the oval of a perfect face, pale and serene like an autumn evening, with her tall graceful figure and womanly gestures, there was yet an undefinable charm about Mary Hamilton that seemed independent of all outward advantages; as though she must still have been lovable, had she been old, ugly, and deformed.

It is a melancholy, nay, a morbid sentiment which bids us feel in all exceeding beauty something akin to sorrow—and yet, who will deny the uncomfortable fact? Perhaps it arises from the longing after perfection which appertains to our immortality. Perhaps it is but the hopeless consciousness that our ideal can never be attained. At least the feeling exists; and in Mary Hamilton's beauty, doubtless, the melancholy element predominated. It did not make her the less beloved, we may be sure; and the black-eyed maid-of-honour was worthy of the attachments she kindled wherever she was known. A kinder heart than hers never beat beneath a bodice. Wherever she heard of a sorrow, however trivial the cause, she was there to soothe. Utterly unselfish, she was ever ready to sacrifice her own will, her own amusements, her own advantage, to the lightest wish of another. And although the very sentinels at the palace-gate blessed her for her beauty, as she passed through, she seemed the only person about the Court who was insensible to her own attractions. Gentle, yielding, trusting, and enthusiastic, here was a woman ready prepared and bound, as it were, for the sacrifice. Need we say the victim could not fail to be offered up?

Meanwhile, the galley strained and laboured on. The dripping oars fell with measured cadence on the water; but the land-breeze, dying away towards midnight, refused to second the efforts of the rowers, so that the distance from the French seaboard appeared scarcely to increase. The Queen evinced no intention of going to rest. Reclining on deck, she kept her eyes fixed on the cherished land she was so loth to leave, and inwardly longed for a storm, or any other contingency, that should drive them back into port, and give her a few more days' respite from her banishment.

Probably so unwilling a journey was never taken to claim a crown; and yet Mary was accompanied by many good friends, and true affectionate relatives, and loyal subjects, all anxious to see her securely established on the Scottish throne. Another galley of like tonnage accompanied her with a portion of her household, whilst two ships of war furnished an escort, by no means unnecessary, for Elizabeth's friendship was little to be relied on, and England, as usual, commanded the Channel with her fleet.

On board the Queen's own ship, d'Amville had taken the personal command, and studiously refrained from indulgence in the society of his charge, lest her fascinating conversation should have seduced him from his seaman-like duties. D'Amville, too, had long since yielded to the charm of that beautiful face, which only to look on was to love, and worshipped the Queen of Scotland with a devotion as touching as it was chivalrous in its hopeless generosity;—d'Amville, who sat now in the small dimly-lighted cabin, with his charts before him, and pressed to his bosom the Cyprus silk handkerchief of which we have already heard—the one treasure prized by that loyal, manly heart—the guerdon for which he gave up ambition, and comfort, and even hope. Truly there are strange bargains driven in love, reminding us of our traffic in beads, and brass, and tinsel, with naked savages—a few inches of silk, a half-worn glove, a thread of soft hair, in exchange for the noblest efforts of body and mind, the best years of life, perhaps the eternity of an immortal soul! Not that the coveted prize is reserved for such adoration. Alas! that it should be so. Rude hands pluck down the fruit that fond eyes have gazed on for so many sunny hours in vain, and the Sabine maiden loves her Roman bridegroom none the less that he carried her off by sheer force of manhood, not, perhaps, entirely so reluctant as she seemed.

Chastelâr had been standing motionless for a considerable period, leaning against the mast, apparently wrapped in meditation. At a signal from the Queen, however, his whole bearing altered, his face lighted up, and in an instant he was at her side. Mary Hamilton changed her position somewhat restlessly, and Mary Seton, rejoicing in the capture of a fresh listener, immediately took upon herself to communicate the commands of her mistress.

'Fair sir,' said the laughing maid-of-honour, 'although you are certainly an ornamental object, measuring your stature yonder against the mast, you will be more useful here, at Her Majesty's feet, to give us some information as to the progress of our voyage. Doubtless you are in Monsieur d'Amville's confidence, who seems to think himself relieved of all care of us, now he has got his unprotected charge fairly out to sea.'

'Hush! madcap,' said the Queen. 'And do you, Chastelâr, go below and inquire of our courteous commander whether by to-morrow at daybreak we shall, indeed, have lost sight of our beloved France. Already the beacon off the harbour is low down on the horizon, and the weather seems thickening to windward. Ah! the next lights we see will be on the bleak shores of Scotland—a dark, sad voyage, indeed, with a dreary termination!'

The poet bowed low and retired to fulfil the royal commands, whilst the Queen, leaning her white arms upon the bulwark, gazed longingly towards the shore. Tears coursed each other down her beautiful face, as she murmured forth her unavailing sorrow in such broken sentences as these—

'France! France! my own beloved France! I shall never see you again. Country of my adoption! country of my love! Ah! it is sad to step at once, like this, from youth to age; it is cruel to feel still young and hopeful and capable of happiness, and to know that the bright days have departed from us for evermore. Poor Dido! you too gazed, in your agony, upon the sea, as I look ever towards the land; and your fond heart ached as mine aches now, and broke at last, as mine, I feel, will break ere long. My case is worse than yours; you had at least your home and country left, though you lost your Trojan love that the sea gave you, and the sea took back again!'

Whilst she spoke, she felt Mary Hamilton's cold lips pressed against her hand. The kind heart, alas! itself not wholly ignorant of sorrow, could not bear to witness the sufferings of its mistress. Her other maid-of-honour, however, took a livelier view of their position, and was not slow to express her dissent.

'Nay, madam,' said she; 'Dido gave up a throne for a bonfire, as I have heard your Majesty relate, whereas you are but losing sight of that faint beacon over yonder for the certainty of a crown. Besides, are there not Trojans in plenty where we are bound? What say you, Mary Hamilton? we need not look long for an Æneas a-piece, without counting those we take across with us. Listen, there is one of them singing even now.'

Mary Hamilton felt her face burning in the darkness, though none could see her blush; and indeed, whilst her companion spoke, the Calais light sank beneath the black line of the horizon. As it disappeared, Chastelâr's mellow voice was heard, rising above the rush and ripple of the water and the jerk of the massive oars.

'What need have we of beacon sheen
To warn us or to save,
With the star-bright eyes of our lovely Queen
Guiding us o'er the wave?

'What need have we of a following tide?
What need of a smiling sky?
'Tis sunshine ever at Mary's side,
And summer when she is by.

'Her glances, like the day-god's light,
On each and all are thrown;
Like him she shines, impartial, bright,
Unrivall'd, and alone.

'Alone! alone! an ice-queen's lot,
Though dazzling on a throne;
Ah! better to love in the lowliest cot
Than pine in a palace—alone!'

As he concluded, the singer approached Her Majesty with the information she had sent him to seek.

Softened by her sorrows, influenced by the time, the scene, the devotion of her follower, feeling now more than ever the value of such kind adherents, what could Mary do but reach him graciously the white hand that was not the least attractive of her peerless charms? And if Chastelâr pressed it to his lips with a fervour that partook more of the lover's worship than the subject's loyalty, what less was to be expected from an overwrought imagination, and a susceptible heart, thus brought in contact with the most fascinating woman of the age? And the Queen drew away her hand hurriedly, rather than unkindly, with a consciousness not wholly displeasing, and Mary Seton looked discreetly into the far distance, as though there was something unusually interesting in that dull expanse of sea. And Mary Hamilton, clasping both hands tightly to her heart, leaned her head against the bulwark, and said nothing; but rose, as if intensely relieved, when an increasing bustle on board the galley, and a general movement amongst its inmates, denoted some fresh alarm, and the necessity for increased watchfulness and exertion.

It was even so. Their consort, holding a parallel course at no great distance, had caught sight of the English cruisers, who, whatever might be their orders from 'good Queen Bess,' were as much mistrusted by d'Elbœuf in his command of the Scottish Queen's little squadron, as by d'Amville who took her own galley under his especial charge. In those days the sea and land services were not so distinct as now.

Signals were exchanged between the two galleys to make all possible speed, and the slaves, grateful for Mary's interposition on their behalf, laid to their oars with a will, in a manner that could never have been extorted from them by the lash. As there was but little wind, they soon increased their distance from the English men-of-war, who, however, came up with and captured one of the French ships containing the Earl of Eglinton and the Queen's favourite saddle-horses. Mary herself, nevertheless, escaped their vigilance, and an increasing fog soon shrouded the little convoy from its pursuers.

Thus in darkness and danger, too ominous, alas! of her subsequent career, Mary Stuart sped on towards the coast of Scotland, leaving behind her the sunny plains of her beloved France, as she left behind her the bright days of her youth,—days that she seemed instinctively to feel were never to dawn for her again through the storms and clouds that brooded over the destinies of her future kingdom.

CHAPTER III

'Oh! 'gin I had a bonny ship,
And men to sail wi' me,
It's I wad gang to my true love,
Sin' my love comes not to me.'

About the same hour at which the galley bearing Mary Stuart and her fortunes, eluded, in the increasing darkness, the vigilance of the English cruisers, an archer of the Scottish Body-guard, with whom we have already made acquaintance, might have been seen pacing to and fro on a strip of white sand adjoining Calais harbour. After a long day of labour and excitement, preparatory also to a ride of some two hundred miles on the morrow, this midnight walk was perhaps the least judicious method of passing the hours sensible persons devote to repose. Our archer, nevertheless, continued it with a perseverance that denoted considerable preoccupation, pausing at intervals to gaze wistfully on the sea, and anon resuming his exercise, as if goaded to bodily effort by some acute mental conflict.

In honest truth, like Sinbad the Sailor, he was oppressed by a metaphorical Old Man of the Sea, that he could not get rid of, although in his case the unwelcome equestrian had assumed the form of a prevailing idea, connected with a young woman instead of an old man, and resembling Sinbad's encumbrance in no particular except the tenacity with which it clung.

Reader, it is worth while to go to the Pampas to see a Gaucho lasso and mount a hitherto unbroken horse. How the animal, conscious of his degradation, fights and rears and plunges, wincing from the cruel spurs to rise at the maddening bit! How his eye dilates and his nostril reddens, and his whole form contracts with mingled fear and rage! Shaking his head wildly, he dashes ere long into a headlong gallop, and becomes stupefied to discover that, even at his fiercest speed, he bears his tormentor along with him. Subdued at last, he bends his neck to the hand that has tamed him, and experiences a new sensation of increased power and confidence in submitting to the master-will. So is it with a manly, resolute nature, when it first feels the influence of another's existence on its own. There is a certain charm, indeed, in the novelty of the sentiment, but there is also surprise, apprehension, and a strong disposition to oppose and crush the unaccustomed usurpation. After many an unavailing struggle, the conquered must, however, submit to the conqueror; and, like other slaves, he loses the desire for liberty with the consciousness of incapacity to be free. Use in time renders him perfectly docile and broken-in; at last he is perfect in all the paces of the *manége*, and carries one rider nearly as pleasantly as another. He is a useful hack now, but the mettle of the wild-horse has left him for evermore.

Our archer was in the first stages of his tuition. He was, so to speak, only lately caught and mounted. We can but wish him a merciful rider with a kind heart and a light hand!

Walter Maxwell, for such was the name in which he stood enrolled on the list of the Archer-guard, was the younger son of an old Scottish family, possessed of an unblemished pedigree, considerable territorial possessions, and a sad lack of broad pieces. Then, as now, the upper classes in Scotland, with many noble qualities, were cursed with a morbid desire for the shadow rather than the substance of wealth. In Queen Mary's days, the pound Scots represented in value the shilling English. In Queen Victoria's, the laird on one side the Tweed, with his few hundreds a year, would fain make believe that his possessions equal those of the squire on the other, who owns as many thousands. His difficulties, his shortcomings, his meannesses originate in this, the paltriest of all ambition, that would make his shilling look like half-a-crown. Frugal and industrious as are her peasantry, prosperous and enterprising as are her yeomen and traders, probably the gentry of Scotland are at this moment more oppressed with difficulties than the parallel class in any other country under the sun.

In the time of which we write, the Scottish nobility were afflicted with the same unfortunate tendencies. There was then even more of display abroad and less of ease at home; whilst the unsettled state of the country, compelling every baron to entertain as many feudal retainers as he could arm and feed, helped to drain their resources to the very dregs. Violence and intrigue, political as well as private, were naturally resorted to by those who had no other means of replenishing their empty purses; and what with old feuds strictly entailed, and new differences perpetually arising, Scotland could only be likened to some huge cauldron, in which a thousand different ingredients were boiling, and the scum perpetually rising to the surface.

In such a state of things there was not much provision for younger brothers; and as the somewhat heathenish doctrine, not yet eradicated, then prevailed of considering individuals simply as links in a line, and postponing all personal claims to those of that great myth—the family—it may easily be imagined that the younger sons of a noble Scotch house had small cause to congratulate themselves on their aristocratic lineage.

Walter Maxwell might consider himself fortunate that he had the shelter of the old tower at home until he had arrived at the strength and stature of a man—that he was permitted to feed at the same board, and enjoy the same pastimes as his elder brother, the heir—that he might follow to her grave with a son's decorous grief the mother who had doted on her youngest—and that his share of the family possessions was not limited to its name, but included a right to breathe the moorland air round the old place till he had attained his fifteenth year. Perhaps, after all, he inherited his share of the patrimony. He gained health and strength, and good manhood, on its broad acres. He learned to back a horse in its meadows, and fly a hawk on its hills, to swim in its dark loch, and to wield a blade within its walls. Perhaps, in bequeathing him an iron constitution, a vigorous frame, and a courageous heart, the old lord had done enough for the golden-haired child who used to come running to him after supper, and pull his gray moustaches, and climb merrily upon one knee, whilst the heir occupied the other.

At fifteen Walter Maxwell went out upon the world. A year after, he was the youngest gentleman private in the French king's Archer-guard. Many a dame in Paris would turn round to look again on the blooming youthful face—almost a child's still—so pleasing in its contrast with that manly form, clad in the showy armour of the guard. The Duchess of Valentinois herself had desired to have the young boy-archer presented to her; and it is to be presumed that Diane de Poitiers, a lady of mature experience, was no mean judge of masculine attractions. A word from the woman he so adored was sufficient to interest Henry II. in the Scottish recruit, and Walter Maxwell was more than once selected for duties demanding discretion as well as fidelity and courage. All these qualities were, indeed, in constant request at such a court as that of the French king. At a more advanced age, the young soldier had also distinguished himself in the disastrous affairs of St Quentin and Gravelines, where the French suffered serious defeats; and it was but the consistency with which he remained steadfast to the Protestant religion that stood in the way of his rapid promotion. He was a favourite, too, with his comrades for his courage and soldier-like bearing beyond his years, as well as for the indefinable attraction of those buoyant spirits which, like the bloom of youth on the cheek, seldom outlast maturity.

During the reign of Henry II., that chivalrous monarch, notwithstanding his severity to the Protestants, and the prevalence of their religion amongst his Scottish Archers, placed the most implicit confidence in his body-guard, riveting their unshaken loyalty with many favours and immunities, till they walked the streets of the capital objects of admiration and envy to the very grandees themselves. Perhaps the warlike Henry was of opinion that a soldier's religion need not interfere with his obedience; and, indeed, too many of the Archers might have made the same answer, that some two centuries and a half later the old grenadier of the Empire gave on a question of doctrine to the Pope, — '*Et de quelle religion es tu, mon fils?*' asked his Holiness of the grim sentry who kept the door that led into the awful presence of Napoleon I. '*Je suis de la religion de la Vieille Garde,*' replied the veteran, with an astounding clatter of his musket, as he 'carried arms' to the Pontiff. We take leave to doubt if the Protestantism of the Scotch Guard often stood in the way of Henry's commands to his favourites.

But the evil day dawned at last. In the pride of his manly beauty, and the vigour of his warlike frame, the king of France rode gallantly into the lists, to break a lance in sport for the bright eyes of his ladye-love. On his helmet he wore the colours of Diane de Poitiers. And the duchess herself, looking down from the gallery, felt her heart leap with pride in the noble appearance of her royal lover. What shall we say of Henry's infatuation for this seductive woman, nearly twenty years his senior, himself the husband of the most accomplished lady in Europe, for Catherine of Medicis was notoriously as wise as she was beautiful? What, but that it is folly to argue on the wilfulness of the human heart, and that the most untoward and ill-advised attachments are apt to prove the strongest and the most fatal. The king loved her madly, and was not ashamed to avow his passion openly in the sight of France. Walter Maxwell attended the sovereign as one of his squires, and bore a knot of the same coloured ribbons on his bonnet.

And now the trumpet sounds a flourish, and the king, raising his vizor, calls for a bowl of wine, and without dismounting, quaffs it with an ill-concealed gesture of courtesy to some one in the gallery—then, a perfect horseman, he backs his charger to his post. Opposite, like a statue sheathed in steel, sits his antagonist, the captain of the Archer-guard. A proud man to-day is Gabriel, Earl of Montgomery, for the Scottish peer has been chosen to break a lance with the French king, in presence of two royal brides and their bridegrooms! There is a hush of pleased expectation and interest over the whole assembly; only the Duchess of Valentinois turns pale with ill-defined apprehension. She feels the value of her last love, wildest and dearest of all, lawless though it be. It was but this morning the king told her in jest, he should not close his vizor lest she might not recognise him; and she had chidden him, half playfully, half in earnest, for the insinuation. She would know that warlike form she thinks in any disguise—and the colour mounts again to her face as she catches his last glance, while he settles himself in the saddle, and lays his lance in the rest. He has not closed his helmet, after all! She will chide him seriously, though, to-night, for his selfish carelessness of danger. Again the trumpet sounds, and the lances shiver fairly in mid-career. Firm and erect, the king reaches the opposite extremity of the lists; then, swaying heavily in the saddle, falls in his ringing harness to the ground. The Queen and her ladies rushed tumultuously into the lists. Catherine de Medicis has a *right* to succour her husband. Diane de Poitiers, sick and faint, loses her consciousness in a swoon. She is scarcely noticed, for all are crowding round the king.

Alas for the gallant monarch! Alas for the bold man-at-arms! A splinter from Montgomery's lance has entered the eye through the unclosed helmet, and penetrated nearly to the brain. Ere twelve days elapse, Catherine de Medicis is a widow. Francis II. has succeeded to the throne, and Mary Stuart is Queen of France.

The favour of the Duchess of Valentinois was no passport, we may fairly suppose, to the good graces of the queen-mother; and although Walter Maxwell retained his appointment in the guard, his hopes of advancement perished with the death of his royal patron. Such disappointments, however, though they press heavily on an enthusiastic spirit, are lightly borne by such a temperament as Maxwell's. His disposition was naturally calm and unimpressionable beyond the average. He possessed the rare quality of seeing things as they were, and not as he wished them to be. Above all, he had that quiet confidence in himself which could wait patiently for an occasion, and seize it without hurry or agitation when it arrived. Moreover, he had been brought up in the stern school, that turns out the most finished pupils, after all. Poverty and hardship give their lessons for nothing; but men remember them better than Latin and Greek. We may be allowed to doubt whether all George Buchanan's classic lore and pedantic periods were as well worth acquiring as Maxwell's aptitude to saddle, shoe, and groom his own horse, cook his own rations, burnish his own corslet, and keep his head with his hand.

Changes also took place in the Scottish Guard. The Earl of Arran, heir to the house of Hamilton, was appointed to its command, and already that eccentricity began to manifest itself which was fostered, at last, into madness, by the sunshine of Mary's unconscious smiles. Arran chose to alter the discipline, the accoutrements, and the whole system of the *corps*, and such interference with their old habits was by no means relished by its members. During the short reign of Francis II., Mary Stuart's sympathies with her countrymen, and knowledge of their customs and prejudices, checked many a proposed innovation that would have created open dissatisfaction; but when she became a dowager Queen, and Charles IX. succeeded to the throne, the archers found themselves curtailed of many of their privileges, and no longer looked upon as what they considered themselves—the *élite* of the French army. Seeing, however, that, like the famous '*gants glacés*' of a later period, they had earned this position by constantly volunteering for all dangerous duties, they might well be uneasy at the prospect of forfeiting a distinction it had cost so much hard fighting to attain.

It was during the short eighteen months of Mary's reign as Queen of France, that our archer, in virtue of his office, was brought in contact with the fascinating sovereign and her court. That he became the devoted adherent of his royal countrywoman is not to be wondered at; but in Maxwell's consistent loyalty to the Stuart there lurked a deeper feeling of interest than he liked to allow even to himself; an interest that he could not but connect with another Mary attached to the person of her mistress. The Queen, as is well known, was a daring and skilful horsewoman; a masculine accomplishment, by the way, that many womanly natures acquire with great ease. Perhaps, as its chief art consists in ruling by judicious concession, they have learned half the lesson before they get into the saddle. As a natural consequence, Mary was passionately fond of the chase, and followed it with a degree of recklessness somewhat discomfiting to her less courageous or worse-mounted attendants. In fact, she sustained more than one severe fall without its curing her in the least of her galloping propensities.

It fell out on one occasion, near the Castle of Chambord, whither the court had repaired for this princely recreation, that our archer was in attendance on Mary and her *suite* at the moment the stag was unharboured, and, with a burst of inspiriting music, the hounds were laid on. The Queen, as was her custom, went off at a gallop, outstripping her attendants, and followed, at unequal distances, by the whole cavalcade. Walter Maxwell, on a clambering, Roman-nosed French horse, was plying his spurs to keep within sight of the chase, when a faint scream of distress, and a young lady borne past him at a pace that showed she was run away with, diverted his attention from the pleasures to the exigencies of the moment. Though the animal beneath him was neither speedy nor active, he managed, by a skilful turn, to reach her bridle rein, and so, guiding her impetuous horse into an alley that diverged from the line of the chase, succeeded in stopping him before his own was completely exhausted. While the young lady did not, in the least, lose her presence of mind, she was naturally a little discomposed and a good deal out of breath. Nevertheless, she thanked her preserver with frank and graceful courtesy, avowing, at the same time, in very broken sentences, her inability to control the animal she rode.

The confession was tantamount to a request that her new friend would not leave her. The most determined Nimrod could scarcely have abandoned a lady who thus placed herself under his charge, and Walter Maxwell, with his passionless exterior, had a good deal of that manly generosity in his composition, which warms at once to the unprotected and the weak. Instead of toiling after the whole company, then, on a tired horse, behold him riding quietly through beautiful woods, by the side of a young lady, whose peace of mind seemed to depend on his keeping his hand on her bridle rein.

People soon become acquainted when thus associated. Mary Carmichael, with a colour much heightened from a variety of causes, and her rich brown hair disordered by her gallop, had never looked prettier in her life; whilst a glance or two shot at her protector from under her riding-hat satisfied her that he was a gentleman of good nature and lineage, also that she had remarked him more than once before, when fulfilling his duties as a guardsman about the court. Before they had ridden a mile, he had told her his name and all about himself.

'A Maxwell!' exclaimed the young lady, whose apprehensions were by this time considerably soothed. 'I ought to have known you for a Maxwell at once. You've got the frank brow, and the ready hand, and the silent tongue of the Maxwells.' Here she checked herself with a laugh and blush, whereat her companion laughed and coloured a little too. 'Why, we are kinsfolk at that rate,' she added, courteously. 'My mother's niece married a Maxwell of the Den, and they are a branch of the Terreagles Maxwells, and so are you.'

'I have left home so long,' answered Walter, gravely, 'I cannot count my kin; and yet I will take your word for it. I should think the better of myself,' he added with a smile, 'to have a right to call you cousin.'

The archer rarely smiled; when he did, his usually stern features softened and lighted up almost into beauty. The change was not unmarked by the maid-of-honour.

'A Carmichael never failed a kinsman,' said she, and her voice shook a little, while her soft eyes gleamed;—'or the old tower would be looking down still upon Dumfries, and there would be more than a blackened arch, and a few mounds of grass standing by the hearth-stone, where my father once received King James. Well, Sir Archer, you have done a cousinly deed for me at least to-day.'

Perhaps she expected he would make some acknowledgment of his good fortune in the opportunity, but Maxwell rode on in silence. A French gallant would have overwhelmed her with eloquence, and few men but would have hazarded a few compliments, however trifling. She scarcely seemed offended, nevertheless. Her mute companion was absorbed in a brown study, thinking how well she looked in her riding-gear. It may be that her woman's intuition told her as much.

Presently a burst of horns in the distance announced the direction of the chase. Mary Carmichael's steed pricked his ears, and showed symptoms of insubordination once more. Walter's grasp was on the bridle in an instant, and the rider thanked him with a grateful smile.

'The ready hand!' she said, laughing. 'Was I not right in saying you inherited the gifts of your family?'

'It must excuse the silent tongue,' he answered. 'I am no squire of dames, and you ladies of the court must needs look down on the unpolished soldier. And yet his silence may offer more of respect and regard in its humility than the loudest professions of admiration from those who have never been taught to say less than they think, and think less than they feel.'

'And receive twice as much in return,' she replied, in a very low voice, and averting her face from her companion as she spoke. Then she put her horse into a quicker pace, and ere long they met and joined a party of the courtiers returning from the chase.

After this, though they saw each other but seldom, and had no more rides together, there was a sort of tacit understanding between the two. Nobody remarked that if Walter Maxwell was on guard, Mary Carmichael's manner displayed more animation, and her dress was, if possible, more becomingly arranged than usual. Nobody remarked that one of the archers, more than any of his comrades, displayed unusual readiness in volunteering for all duties that brought him near the Queen's person, and never seemed so contented as when riding in her escort, or mounting guard at her door. Yet it was true, notwithstanding; and, although not a word had been exchanged by these young persons of a more explicit tendency than those we have related, there had yet sprung up between them one of those mysterious affinities, that in this world of ours lead to such troublesome results.

It was not till Mary Carmichael had sailed for Scotland in the *suite* of her royal mistress, that it occurred to Maxwell he was losing time and opportunities by remaining in his present service at the court of France. He wondered it had never before struck him so forcibly, that the Archer-guard no longer occupied its proud position in the land of its adoption—that its privates were no longer so well born, its drill so exact, nor its discipline so perfect as in the days of its old commander, Montgomery—that Arran was a weak-minded enthusiast, who would finish by disgusting both officers and men—and that Charles IX. was already beginning to look coldly upon them, and depriving them, one by one, of the privileges by which they set such store. Then his patron, Montmorency, was getting infirm and worn out; and with the constable's demise, adieu to his hopes of advancement in the service of France!

Mary Stuart, too, in her new kingdom, would need all the stout hands and loyal hearts that she could muster. It was clearly the duty of every Scotchman to rally round the fair young queen.

Ere our archer had concluded his midnight walk, he had made up his mind; and as he posted back his long ride to Paris, the following day, he resolved to claim his dismissal from the French king, and to seek his fortune once more in the land of his birth.

CHAPTER IV

'We are the boys that can wrestle and ride,
Empty a saddle, and empty a can,
Keeping the rights of the border side,
Warden to warden, and man to man;
Never another go welcome here
As the lads of the snaffle, spur, and spear.'

At the time of which we write there were few worse places wherein to be benighted than that wild district on the borders of England and Scotland, appropriately called the 'Debatable Land.' Bleak and barren, on a gusty evening late in autumn, a less desirable locality for the traveller could scarcely be imagined; and he must have been a hardy adventurer who would not have preferred the dirtiest corner of the smokiest hostelry to the uncertain track that led through its morasses, especially on a tired horse. Such was the reflection uppermost in Walter Maxwell's mind as he marked the dusky horizon becoming more and more indistinct, and calculated the diminishing chances of his reaching the Castle of Hermitage, where he had hoped to find rest and refreshment with his kinsman, James Hepburn, Earl of Bothwell, and, doubtless, in that country where horses were so easily come by, a fresh mount to take him northward on the morrow. No longer an archer of the Scottish Guard, Maxwell was on his way to Edinburgh from the English seaport at which he had landed in returning from France. With his reputation as a soldier and his family connexions, he had little doubt but that he would be welcome at Holyrood; and indeed, had it been otherwise, an indefinable attraction, that he would not have confessed, seemed to draw him irresistibly towards the Scottish capital.

During the whole of his journey, however, by land and sea, his destination had never seemed so remote, nor the likelihood of his reaching it so small, as at present.

'Hold up, you brute!' said Maxwell, as he felt if the straps of his corslet were secure and his sword loose in its sheath, whilst his poor horse took that opportunity of floundering on its head.

'Hold up! If you fall you'll never get up again; and unless mine host's directions were inspired by beer and brandy, we must be a good way off Hermitage yet. Happily the moon is rising every minute. Well, you were a good beast this morning, though you're not worth your four shoes now!'

While he spoke, he patted the poor animal on the neck, and, as if encouraged by the caress, it pricked its ears and mended its pace of its own accord.

Maxwell was too old a soldier not to be on the alert in such a situation: it was with a feeling more of annoyance than surprise that he heard the tramp of horses advancing at a rapid pace over the sounder sward he had left behind him; and whilst he shortened his reins and hitched his sword-belt to the front, it was but with a dogged consciousness that, though he meant to fight to the last, he was sure to get the worst of it, outnumbered, and on a tired horse.

He had, however, the caution to halt on the far side of some broken and boggy ground; so that the new comers, whom he now made out to be but two, must attack him at a disadvantage, if they intended violence; and he thought how he could best separate them, that they might not both set on him at once.

The horsemen, however, halted immediately they caught sight of him, and the foremost called out in a loud, frank voice, undoubtedly English in its tone—

'Is it friend or foe? A man must be one or other in the Debatable Land!'

'Friend!' answered Maxwell confidently, adding, as an earnest of his sincerity, 'Keep near the big stone, or you'll go in up to your girths!'

Following his advice, the horseman and his attendant, who appeared nothing more than a simple domestic, emerged upon sound ground. The former was admirably mounted, and although his dress denoted the gentleman rather than the soldier, he sat his horse with the ease of a skilful cavalier.

Maxwell made out also in the moonlight that he was perfectly armed, wearing both pistols and rapier, and carried a small valise, with somewhat ostentatious care, on the saddle in front of him.

'Friend!' he repeated, bowing ceremoniously, as he brought his horse alongside Maxwell's, 'foes are more plentiful in this district on a moonlight night. We may meet some gentlemen hereabouts who would give us anything but a "Highland welcome." As we are going in the same direction, by your good leave we will travel together. Union is strength; although,' he added, glancing at the other's tired horse, 'haste is not speed.'

His manner was courtly, or rather courtier-like, in the extreme, and Maxwell saw at a glance he had to do with one of the porcelain vessels of the earth; yet there was a conventional tone of indifference, a something of covert sarcasm, and implied superiority in his voice, that jarred upon the franker nature of the soldier.

They rode on, however, amicably together—the attendant, a burly Southron, apparently by no means easy either in mind or body, keeping close behind his master. The latter was bound, he said, for Hermitage, which he hoped to reach before midnight, and he seemed to treat his new companion with a shade more deference when he learned that Maxwell was a kinsman of the redoubted Earl of Bothwell.

Some men have a knack of extracting information without affording any in return, and this faculty appeared to be largely possessed by the well-mounted traveller, who, while he conversed with the ease and freedom of a thorough man of the world, dropped every now and then a leading question that denoted an insatiable and unscrupulous curiosity.

The Scotch have generally an insurmountable dislike to being 'pumped,' and Maxwell, whose shrewdness soon perceived his new friend's intention of subjecting him to that process, resented it by an increased reserve, which subsided ere long into an almost unbroken silence.

They rode on for some time, accordingly, interchanging only an occasional remark—the stranger accommodating his horse's pace to that of his new acquaintance, whilst his servant jogged painfully along behind him, suffering obviously from abrasion, the curse of unpractised riders, and seeking relief, as well by sighs and groans, as by fruitless changes of position in the saddle. The moon shone out brightly, and its light enabled Maxwell to examine the face and figure of his comrade.

He was a spare man, of less than middle age, with the marks of good breeding apparent in his thin, sharp features, and small feet and hands. His figure, though too angular, was sufficiently graceful; and his face, though pale, bore the clear hue of a healthy and enduring constitution;—although he would have been a well-looking man enough, but for the restless expression of his small gray eyes, which peered from under the straight thick eyebrows with a vigilance amounting to suspicion, and the thin, firmly-compressed lips, a little drawn in at the corners, as if by an habitual sneer.

Maxwell, accustomed, in his warlike life, to judge of men at a glance, found himself vaguely speculating on an exterior beyond which he could not penetrate. The shaven lip and cheek denoted a man of peaceful profession; but the finished horsemanship, the hanging of the sword, the readiness with which his hand sought his pistol-holsters, savoured of the soldier. Again, his thoughtful brow and worn face might well become some distinguished scholar or man of science; but the tone of his conversation, and the levity of his bearing, contradicted the supposition that he could belong to the 'wise ones of the earth.' He seemed conscious, too, of his new friend's observation, and more inclined to court than shrink from it, as if priding himself on the impenetrable reserve, with which he could combine an appearance of extreme cordiality. The restless eyes, however, were not still for an instant; and the soldier, in the midst of his speculations, was equally startled and shamed by the observation which aroused him, and proved that the civilian's vigilance had been far more active than his own.

'I thought so!' said the latter, speaking in quiet, rapid tones. 'There are night-hawks abroad, as usual, in this cursed wilderness. Did you not see the glitter of a head-piece over the height yonder? Now, if these are jackmen out on their own account, you and I will have to trust to the speed of our horses, which is doubtful, and our knowledge of the locality, which is negative— this poor devil will have his throat cut to a certainty.'

Even at this disagreeable juncture, the man spoke in a bantering tone, as it were between jest and earnest. His servant, a stout, able-bodied fellow enough, regarded his master with a ludicrous expression of dismay.

'Your horse is fresh, and looks like a good one,' answered Maxwell, somewhat contemptuously; 'keep round the shoulder of that hill, and you will find a beaten track that leads to Hermitage. At least, so they directed me. Mine is tired; I *can't* run; so I *must* fight. If I arrive not by daybreak, you will know what has become of me, and can tell the Warden he should keep better order on the Marches.'

The other laughed outright.

'A sharp pair of spurs are no bad weapons on occasion,' said he; 'but I am much afraid I must trust to other friends to-night.' He laid his hand on his holsters, and continued, 'Those fellows will come in again in front of us, and I had rather face every outlaw in Britain, from Robin Hood downwards, than turn back into the wilderness. Let us halt for a minute. I can hear the tramp of their horses even now.'

As the three drew up under the shadow of some rising ground, they could distinctly hear the gallop of horses and the clatter of arms on the other side of the acclivity.

'There are half a score at least,' observed Maxwell, with increasing animation. 'You are quite right—they want to intercept us in the pass yonder. What say you, sir? Shall we pay them in steel or silver? for metal they will have. Can your servant fight?'

'Like a devil,' answered the other, 'when it is impossible to run away; and, faith, he'll be between two fires to-night, for I can hear a body of horse in our rear as well. What say you, Jenkin? Had you not rather be lying drunk in the filthiest gutter in Eastcheap than make your bed here on the heather, with a rough-footed borderer to pull your boots off, and an Armstrong's lance through your body to make you sleep well?'

The man gave a sulky grunt in answer. He was evidently irritated at the heartless levity of his master, but he looked all the more dogged and resolute, and seemed likely to fight till the last. The night wind, too, bore on their ears the tramp of a body of horse behind them; and it was simply a question whether it were not better to charge through those in front, and take their chance.

After a hurried consultation, they agreed to ride steadily forward to the pass, at a good round pace, yet not fast enough to convey the idea of flight. If their enemies were there before them, they must charge without hesitation and try to cut their way through, the Englishman remarking with grim sarcasm, that 'the Warden was likely to have a good appetite if he waited supper until his guests arrived.'

As the three wayfarers neared the pass, the dusky forms of their enemies were already drawn up in its shadow; and a shot, fired at Maxwell, which cut the ribbon from his sleeve, sufficiently denoted their intentions. A voice, too, from the midst of the little black mass was heard to exclaim, in more polished language than might have been expected —

'Dead or alive, Rough Rob! take the man in the centre, and let the others go free!'

'Thank you,' observed the Englishman, who occupied that position between his servant and Maxwell, adding, through his set teeth, 'I shall owe you one, whoever you are, and pay it before I've done with you, or my name is not Thomas Randolph!'

Maxwell heard the promise, but had no time for astonishment at thus finding himself the companion of Elizabeth's ambassador to the Scotch court under such uncomfortable circumstances, inasmuch as a grim borderer, on a tall bay horse, was already within lance's length of him, and in another stride his own tired animal was rolling on the heather, and he was defending himself as well as he could on his feet.

Two or three shots were fired, the flashes from the pistols and musquetoons lighting up the faces of the combatants, as they rode to and fro through the skirmish. With the exception, however, of Mr Randolph's first shot, which made 'Rough Rob's' good gray mare masterless, the fire-arms did little damage, save rendering three or four of the horses perfectly unmanageable.

As Maxwell shifted his ground, and traversed here and there, parrying with his sword the thrusts of his adversary's long lance, a tall man rode up to him, and shouting, 'A Carmichael!' seemed about to cut him down; then, as if perceiving his mistake, he checked his raised arm, and turned upon Mr Randolph, whom he attacked with considerable energy, shouting his war-cry, as though from the force of habit, once more.

The latter defended himself valiantly, but notwithstanding the assistance of his servant who fought with the cool intrepidity of an Englishman in a difficulty, he had too great odds to contend with, and must have fared badly, had not assistance come from an unexpected quarter at the very moment when honest Jenkin fell from the saddle with an awkward knock on his pate from the back of a Jedwood axe, running his assailant through the arm, however, as he went down.

Mr Randolph's bridle had already been seized, and the valise torn from his saddle by the tall man who seemed to command the party. Both Maxwell and the ambassador were now surrounded and nearly overpowered, when two more horseman, followed by a numerous troop of cavalry, came galloping up from the rear, and charged into the *mêlée*, with a violence that made a clean breach through the outlaws. One of them, a gigantic borderer, with a broad, good-humoured face, rolled Maxwell's antagonist, horse and man, to the ground, knocking the rider down again with the butt end of his lance, when he strove to rise; whilst the other, a tall cavalier magnificently accoutred, turned Mr Randolph's horse courteously out of the press, dealing one of his assailants a buffet, that must have cut him in two, had it not been mercifully delivered with the flat of the sword, and rebuking the others in a voice of authority that all seemed to recognise. Indeed, a cry of 'the Warden! the Warden!' was by this time passed from lip to lip amongst the outlaws, and horses' heads were already turned, and spurs plied to seek safety in flight. For the third time, too, to-night, Maxwell heard the name spoken which kindled so many recollections in his breast. Disembarrassed of his enemies by the rescue that arrived so opportunely, he noticed the Warden ride rapidly up to the leader of the band, and say in a low voice, '*You* here, Carmichael! for shame!' after which, the other turned rein, and galloped off at the utmost speed, accompanied by all his followers save two, one of whom was dead, and the other disabled. It struck him also that the pursuit was not nearly so vigorous as might have been expected from the rescue, and that the Warden appeared far more anxious to pay every attention to Mr Randolph than to take vengeance on those who had attacked him. The latter had never lost his *sang froid* during the encounter, and was, if possible, more self-possessed than usual at its termination.

'Your Scottish welcomes, my Lord Earl,' said he, 'are hearty, though rough. I never was more glad to see your lordship. It is fortunate for us all, except this gentleman, whose acquaintance I regret to have made so inopportunely, that you came to-night somewhat further than the drawbridge to meet your guests.' As he spoke he pointed to the dead body of 'Rough Rob,' which was lying at his horse's feet.

'Who is it?' asked Bothwell of his henchman anxiously, ere he replied to the courtier; and the gigantic horseman who had rescued Maxwell, dismounting, turned the dead man's face to the moonlight.

'It is but "Rough Rob,"' replied he, carelessly, after a brief examination of the corpse. 'A likely lad too, though he was a kinsman of my ain. Ay, Rob, thou'rt out of the saddle at last, man; but I would like weel to ken wha's gotten the gude gray mare.'

'Secure the other rascal,' said the Warden, turning his horse's head homeward. 'Let Dick Rutherford and two more jackmen bring him on in the rear. Help Mr Maxwell to his horse, some of you, and leave that carrion to the crows.'

The cavalcade was now set in motion, Bothwell and Mr Randolph riding together in front; the former, after a hasty greeting to his kinsman, appearing to devote his whole attention to the ambassador. Maxwell, whose relationship to the Warden made him an object of interest to the jackmen, came on in the rear at a slower pace, for his horse was now completely exhausted. He was, however, accompanied by the borderer who had rescued him, and who seemed to have taken a great fancy to him for his swordsmanship.

Dick Rutherford, or, as he was more commonly called, 'Dick-o'-the-Cleugh,' set much store by that cool courage which he himself possessed in no common degree; and as he looked on every hand-to-hand encounter in the light of a pastime, at which he was himself a first-rate performer, so he could never withhold a certain amount of facetious approbation from any other skilful player at the game. He was, at this period, the Warden's henchman or principal man-at-arms, and would have followed his chief to the death, for Bothwell had the knack of winning the hearts of his retainers by a rude cordiality and boisterous frankness akin to their own.

The Warden could drain a deeper cup, back a wilder horse, and couch a heavier spear than the rudest of his jackmen; his fine manly person, great strength, and soldier-like bearing, fascinated while they controlled these savage natures; and whatever deep designs may have lurked beneath this frank exterior, James Hepburn seemed to have no ambition beyond the reputation of being the boldest borderer on the Marches. He would ride alone, or attended only by 'Dick-o'-the-Cleugh,' through the worst of these lawless districts, and the latter was never tired of detailing the hand-to-hand encounters with freebooters, in which the Warden had come off victorious. Dick, too, was an adept in all the intricacies of his profession. He could follow a trail like a bloodhound, fight like a demon, and drink and ride like—a borderer. With all this, his great strong body contained a soft heart, and an inexhaustible fund of good-humour.

After looking at Maxwell in silent admiration for a space of five minutes, he began—

'I would ha' wagered a hundred merks now that there wasna' a man in Scotland could ha' kept little Jock Elliott at half-sword like that; and he on his white-footed gelding with his long lance in his hand. Jock will no' hear the last o' it from me in a hurry. I trow he's found his match o' this side Teviotdale, brag how he may!'

'You know him, then?' asked Maxwell, somewhat surprised to discover such an intimate acquaintance with an outlaw on the part of the Warden's henchman.

'Know him?' repeated the other; 'he broke my head at Bewcastle market only yesterday was three weeks; but I'm thinking, I'm even with ye now, Jock, my man! All in good part though,' he added, 'for little Jock Elliott's a canny lad, and a far-off cousin o' my ain.'

'*Little* Jock Elliott!' observed Maxwell in return. 'Why, he looked to me nearly as big a man as yourself.'

'It's a name he got when a boy,' answered the borderer, 'to know him from his brother, big Jock Elliott, that's gone to his rest. Ye see they were all Elliotts and Armstrongs that were in the slack[2] the night, *forbye* "Rough Rob," and he was a Rutherford,—more shame till him that let himself get guided that way by a Southron!'

[2] The pass.

'I heard another name too,' said Maxwell, whose curiosity was thoroughly aroused. 'Who was the tall man that seemed to be the leader of the party? the man that rode by me just before you struck in so opportunely, and shouted, "A Carmichael!" when he drew his sword.'

'Oh! it would be just one o' the Carmichaels that happened there by chance,' replied Dick, with an expression of hopeless stolidity overspreading his broad countenance; and Maxwell, seeing it would be useless to question him further on that subject, turned the conversation to the more congenial topics of horses and weapons, and the advantages and disadvantages of the new-fashioned musquetoon. In this manner they journeyed on in rear of the party till the dark towers of Hermitage loomed against the midnight sky, and the clatter of the drawbridge, as it was lowered, together with a considerable bustle inside the walls, announced that preparations were being made for their entrance.

Bothwell and Randolph, who had been riding at the head of the party, halted at the postern until the rest came up, and the former proceeded to muster his troop once more ere they crossed the bridge. Maxwell remarked that the prisoner had escaped, but as no one else seemed to take any notice of the circumstance, he discreetly held his tongue. Whilst the gates were being opened, and the drawbridge secured, operations which occupied a considerable time, Bothwell welcomed his guests formally to his 'poor tower,' addressing himself, as before, more particularly to Randolph.

'I regret much,' said he to the latter, 'that your duty compels you to be in the saddle again to-morrow at daybreak; but he who serves a Queen, as well I know, must never flag for an hour in his zeal. It shall be my care to provide you with a proper escort, and my own henchman shall accompany you to Edinburgh.'

Randolph thanked the Warden courteously.

'Your kinsman,' said he, 'will perhaps accompany me. He, too, as he tells me, has urgent affairs in the capital, and I could not wish a stouter escort if I carried a king's ransom along with me.'

Maxwell accepted the offer eagerly, notwithstanding the earl's hospitable objections; and Bothwell, as they turned to cross the drawbridge, once more expressed his sorrow that the English ambassador should have been attacked within his jurisdiction.

'I must take yet stricter order with these knaves,' said the Warden; 'there are too many broken men still in the Debatable Land who get their living by what they can lift. Your valise is gone, but that we can easily replace. I fear, however, that it contained something more valuable than wearing apparel. Despatches probably for the Queen, and—and—Lord James, Her Majesty's half-brother?'

Mr Randolph could not repress a sneer.

'Certain letters,' he answered, 'indeed there were, of no great value to those knaves, if, as your lordship seems satisfied, they are illiterate freebooters who cannot read. I have a few more here,' he added, pointing to a packet that peeped from his boot; 'and, indeed, the only one of importance is written in a cipher with which I myself am unacquainted. Your lordship need not, therefore, be uneasy about the safety of my despatches.'

Bothwell looked considerably put out, though he strove to mask his annoyance under an affectation of great cordiality; and Randolph, as he followed him into the castle, seemed hugely to enjoy the discomfiture of his host.

CHAPTER V

'She could whisper, and smile, and sigh,
Pleading, flattering, ... so can the rest;
But oh! the light in her roving eye
Would have wiled the babe from its mother's breast.'

The Queen of Scotland was fairly settled in her own palace of Holyrood. We must now shift the scene to the royal presence-chamber in that picturesque old building. It is a lofty and well-proportioned apartment, of which, however, the small windows and thick walls denote that it was originally constructed with a view to purposes of defence. It is hung round with a quaint and elaborate tapestry, more curious, perhaps, than tasteful, representing various incidents in the heathenish history of Diana; whereon the goddess bares her knee and draws her bow, to the discomfiture of her rival's children, with mythological effrontery. Beautiful oak carvings adorn its massive chimney-piece, and its panelled roof is richly emblazoned with the armorial bearings of a line of kings. The floor, instead of being strewed with rushes, is carefully waxed and polished, a foreign innovation which has already excited some displeasure amongst the graver courtiers. Such furniture as the room contains is heavily gilt and decorated. The sovereign's chair of state seems to blaze with embroidery and cloth of gold. It is a right royal apartment, not unworthy of the company by which it is occupied.

To-night the Queen holds one of her state-receptions, and around her person are gathered the flower of the Scottish aristocracy. Many a bold baron who spends half his life sheathed in armour, walks none the less stately to-night that he has donned satin doublet and silken hose, that his brow is bare of its steel head-piece, and he carries his plumed bonnet in his hand. Many a dame of clear blue eye and dazzling fairness scans with critical glance every fold of the royal drapery, and watches if she cannot catch and appropriate another grace from her Queen. They are thronging round her now, for the dissensions which shall mar her unhappy reign are as yet only in the bud. Each may expect some fresh boon from a new sovereign, and the baron's ambition to become an earl is just as eager, and probably twice as unprincipled, as the varlet's to become a page, or the page's to become a squire. Even thoughtful Lord James, the Queen's half-brother, the lay-churchman, the soldier-statesman—the staff on which she leans, little dreaming it can ever break in her hand and pierce her to the quick—has forgotten his sister in his sovereign, and wears on his calm sad face an unusual expression of deference to-night, because of prospective advancement and his promised earldom of Mar, and the broad lands and additional title of Moray, to which he hopes it may lead. He has taken his stand on the right of the Queen's chair, and Mary whispers to him ever and anon as she requires information concerning her new subjects; although, with the tact of her family and her own kindly acuteness, she has already mastered the names of most of them, and has even gained the good-will of more than one rugged baron by a happy question regarding his old gray tower or his favourite horse.

But amongst many eager countenances, of which, with all their different expressions, each wears a family likeness of curiosity and expectation, it is touching to observe the chivalrous face and the lofty bearing of the Maréchal d'Amville, who has come to bid farewell to his Queen and his ladye-love. With all the polish of a courtier, with all the pride of a soldier, and with that dignity of manner which noble natures, and these alone, acquire from a hopeless sorrow bravely borne, d'Amville kneels before her who was Queen of France in the sunny days that seem to have shone so long ago. Many a weary year has he knelt in spirit before that magic beauty which he now feels he looks on for the last time. He never expected for a moment that his wild hopeless love could win him anything but sorrow, yet he grudged it not, nor strove to conquer the idolatry for which he was prepared to pay its cruel penalty,—he is paying it even now. Kneeling there to kiss the white hand that reaches him a letter for her kinsfolk in France so gently and so gracefully, looking up once more at the face that will haunt him to his grave, and feeling that none but himself will ever know his folly or its punishment; and that she, its object, smiling so frankly upon him, little guesses how gladly he would give her his blighted life, then and there, at her feet.

But, gentleman and soldier as he is, none can guess his heart by the unmoved brow, the unshaken voice, and the scrupulous deference with which he pays his homage. Gracefully he insists on the reception he will meet with in France, as bearing the latest news from her who was the pleasure and the pride of the whole kingdom, and his own good fortune in having been permitted to accompany her and see her safely bestowed on her Scottish throne. Mary can scarcely keep back her tears at the allusion; but, with so many jealous eyes around her, well she knows she must play her part at any cost, and she gulps them down with an effort.

'Farewell,' she says, 'my brave protector and pilot; be assured Mary Stuart never forgets a friend. You will advise the Guises of my welfare and happiness. You will tell the French court and the French people,' she added, drawing herself up and speaking in a louder tone, so as to be heard by all, 'that you left me on a royal throne, surrounded by the bravest and the most loyal nobility in Europe.'

A murmur of applause went the round of the circle at this spirited declaration, and Lord James gave the Queen a glance of mingled surprise and approval.

As d'Amville rose from his knee and retired, Chastelâr, who followed in the train of the Maréchal, passed before the Queen to make his farewell obeisance. The poet's face wore an expression of determination foreign to its usual character; but it was observed by one who watched its every turn, that he never lifted his eyes above the hem of Mary's robe. She inclined her head graciously to him, nevertheless, and he passed into the outer circle, and was soon conversing lightly with the maids-of-honour and other of the courtiers.

It chanced, however, that the Queen had forgotten some additional message for her kinsfolk, with which she intended to charge d'Amville, and ere he had reached the door, she wished to call him back. The first person whose eye she caught happened to be the Earl of Arran, who had taken up a position opposite Her Majesty, and seemed to observe her narrowly.

Not unwilling to pay the house of Hamilton every compliment in her power, Mary beckoned the Earl to her side and charged him with her commission. Arran's wild eye flashed fire at the proposal!

'I will obey your commands, madam,' said he, rudely, 'though there be pages enough in the gallery to send after a French adventurer. It seems that France had better come to Holyrood and abide with your Majesty once for all.'

His tone was so loud, and his bearing so excited, that the bystanders gazed in astonishment on one another and on the Queen.

Mary looked surprised, almost scared for a moment, and then flushed with displeasure; but her sweet temper soon prevailed, and she answered gently,—

'Nay, cousin, you shall do my bidding yourself as you have always done. Have not you and I reason to look back upon the days we spent in France as the happiest of our lives? Youth comes but once, my lord, and we shall neither of us ever be so light-hearted again.'

The unfortunate nobleman trembled from head to foot, and turned deadly pale. He seemed about to indulge in some frantic outbreak, which he repressed with an effort; then with writhing lip and dilated nostril, he strode towards the doorway, the courtiers making way for him as he passed with looks of astonishment and alarm.

Lord James, glancing at Morton, put his finger to his brow and shook his head gravely. The grim Douglas laughed his ghastly laugh, and with his hand on the haft of his dudgeon-dagger, muttered something about 'blood-letting' and 'melancholy,' that, had he been the physician, would have boded no good to the patient; and Arran, rushing tumultuously through the gallery to cool his brow in the night air, reappeared in the Presence no more that night.

It seems to us there is a strange, sad moral in the history of this beautiful Queen. Probably the gift that women most desire, beyond riches, wisdom, even virtue itself, is a power of fascination over the other sex; and this dangerous charm must have been possessed by Mary to a degree that in the days of Greece and Rome would have been attributed to supernatural influence. With all her advantages of rank, talent, and education, this very quality, so far from adding to her happiness, seems to have been the one engine which worked her own destruction, and that of every kindly heart that came within her sphere. Few of the other sex could look upon Mary without an inclination, at least, to love her; and how many, like high-minded d'Amville and poor half-crazed Arran, had cause to curse the day when first they felt the spell of that sweet face, apparently so unconscious of its power! Of all the eminently beautiful women the world has seen, Mary Stuart wrought the most of wreck and utter ruin with the kindliest disposition and the best intentions. Dalilah, we have never doubted, was a heartless sensualist, covetous only of pleasure and gold. The Phrynes and Aspasias were, probably, finished courtesans, with whom the affections were but instruments necessary to a profession of which they were thorough mistresses. Cleopatra, like a royal voluptuary, grudged no price for her desire; and in her love of conquest, blazoned forth and made the most of her rich southern charms. *Marguérite de Valois* knew and cultivated her resplendent beauty with the diligence of a devotee and the scientific aptitude of a Frenchwoman. But the Queen of Scotland alone seems to have been half ignorant and wholly careless of those advantages which women most prize and cherish; seems to have regarded her loveliness as little as the flower its fragrance, and to have gone about frankly and freely dispensing her dangerous notice with the innocence of an involuntary and unconscious coquette.

It is notorious, that even the lower animals acknowledged the influence of this captivating nature. Dogs attached themselves to the Queen with their brave fidelity, from the instant they came into her presence. She loved to dress her own hawks, and was pleased to boast that she could reclaim the wild bird of the air with greater facility than the most experienced of her falconers. Horses that fretted and chafed under the boldest cavaliers, would bend at once to the gentle hand of the royal equestrian, and carry her with safety and docility. The brute yielded gladly, as though proud to contribute to her happiness; and man looked and longed and grieved, and did his best to make both himself and her miserable.

Of physical beauty there is no question that she possessed an extraordinary share—perhaps more than any woman of that or any other age. Like her mother, she was of lofty stature and peculiar dignity of bearing, whilst she inherited from her father an exact symmetry and the most graceful proportions. James V., though he made bad use of his physical advantages, was one of the comeliest and best-limbed men in his dominions. Mary's hand was a model for a sculptor, whilst every gesture and every movement of her body was at once womanly and dignified. But it was the Queen's face that riveted the attention, and fascinated both sexes with its entrancing loveliness. Other women might be beautiful; other women might have had the same smooth, open brow, the same chiselled features and pencilled eyebrows, the same delicate chin and white full neck and bosom—ay, even the same long, soft hazel eyes, and rich dark chestnut hair; but where was the woman in Europe whose glance, like hers, raised from under those sweeping eyelashes, found its way straight to the heart; whose smile seemed at once to entreat and to command, to extort obedience and bestow reward, like sunlight penetrating the coldest object and warming and brightening all within its sphere? Yes, there was many a beautiful woman in France and Scotland, not to mention such fair dames at the English court as did not fear to provoke the displeasure of 'good Queen Bess' by too engaging a deportment or too becoming an attire; but there was only one Mary Stuart, as many an aching heart in steel-clad bosom was fain to confess to its cost.

And yet on that fair face was often to be remarked an expression of melancholy, as though produced by some vague foreboding of evil, such as cast a shadow over the countenances of so many of the Stuarts.

Even James V., though he could revel with the noisiest, and sing many a merry stave of his own writing, amongst which

'We'll go no more a roving

By the light of the moon,'

is not the least suggestive and poetical, bore on his brow this mysterious presage of evil, although it was perhaps more apparent, as well it might be, in the pensive lineaments of his descendant, the first Charles, and the surpassing beauty of his peerless daughter, Mary Queen of Scots. Was it this that the soothsayer meant, when Mary of Guise took her beautiful child, then a mere infant, to the famous Nostradamus, and bade him cast her horoscope, and fortell her destinies? The sage looked on the blooming face, turned so artlessly towards his own, and announced in his deep grave tones, 'There is blood on that fair young brow!'

Through her happy childhood in the peaceful islet of Inch-ma-home—through her graceful youth, spent with the daughters of France in the quiet retreats of Amboise and Fontainebleau—through her early wedded life and short supremacy, as through her widowhood, when the *Blanche Reine* was the darling and pride of the French court, this shadow of evil never left her. It pervaded her turbulent reign in Scotland, her many reverses, her cruel injuries, her disheartening defeats, her dreary captivity. Perhaps it never faded from her brow till the glory of death shone over it, in the hands of the headsman at Fotheringay.

Mary looked round her courtiers in dismay at Arran's extraordinary conduct. The sad expression was more than usually apparent on her fair forehead: she whispered a few words to her brother, who seemed to be her refuge, as was natural, in her difficulties, and Lord James, darting another glance at Morton, quitted the apartment with his usual staid impassive air.

Then the Queen, rising, broke up the circle by which she was surrounded, and pacing through the room, addressed herself by turns to the different nobles present, and was observed to be more than usually condescending to the Earl of Morton, as though some instinctive prescience bade her deprecate, as early as possible, the hostility of that fierce uncompromising nature.

The Earl's grim countenance relaxed into a smile that added to its natural ghastliness, as she passed; and Secretary Maitland whispered to Lord John Stuart that—

'The Douglas was in a courtly mood to-night, and reminded him of the lion in George Buchanan's elegy that was led by the lady in a silken chain;' to which the gay prior of Coldinghame, contemplating a shapely leg he loved well to display in a galliard, replied with a light laugh—

'I never mistrust the lion so much as when he shows his fangs,' alluding to the prominent teeth and unshapely mouth of the redoubted Earl.

'Nor I the Douglas so much as when he hides his claws,' answered Secretary Maitland; and the two passed gaily on to take part in the amusements and revelry that once more enlivened the walls of old Holyrood.

CHAPTER VI

'She waited not for guard nor groom,
But stepp'd into the hall:
Around her were the four Maries,
Herself the rose of all.'

It is not always in the immediate presence of royalty that there is the most enlivening conversation, or the greatest amount of gaiety about a court. Although the Queen of Scotland was the essence of good-humour, and when in comparative privacy encouraged to the utmost freedom of intercourse and absence of formality amongst her attendants, yet on an occasion like the present, in a gathering of the great nobility of her kingdom, it may easily be imagined that an unusual amount of decorum and restraint was observed throughout the circle which actually surrounded their sovereign.

At a short distance, however, from these graver seniors were grouped the Maries, in the splendour of their courtly dresses, and the bloom of their own intrinsic charms. The young ladies seemed to have completely recovered whatever ill effects may have been produced by the hardships of a sea voyage, and their plumage, like that of certain tropical wild birds, appeared the sleeker and more variegated for the storms through which they had passed. We would fain possess the pen of that eloquent writer who describes in our morning journals the weekly recurring changes of Parisian fashion, with a fidelity not to be surpassed by the superlative gossiping powers of Brantôme or Pepys, and a touching earnestness that never stops short of enthusiasm, and often amounts to poetry; then would we detail the tasteful costumes of this seductive quartette with an accuracy that should make the ladies' mouths water, and every hair on the head of the family stand on end. We would depict in glowing language their several robes of orange and violet and courtly *cramoisie*—the stately fall of their folds, the delicate edging of their lace, the trim defences of the jealous ruff, and rich embroidery on the shapely glove. We would not 'bate a pearl, nor a tress, nor a flounce, till the dazzled reader should count every stitch of needlework on the attire of these sumptuous damsels. But we must leave such visions to younger and keener eyesights, satisfied to take for granted the radiance of the Maries from the admiration they excited, and the compliments that were paid them by all.

As Chastelâr followed the Maréchal through the outer circle, he lingered for a few minutes amongst the maids-of-honour, to take his leave of the ladies with whom of late he had been so closely associated. It would have been amusing to mark the different effect his farewell produced on each individual of the four.

Mary Beton, half-a-head taller than her companions, magnificent in dress and deportment, received his salutation with the dignity of an empress accepting the homage of a vassal.

Mary Seton laughed in his face.

'Farewell!' said she, with mischief gleaming from her eyes: 'Farewell! our fellow-sufferer and Prince of Troubadours. As you are never likely to cross the seas again, be sure you take back with you to France nothing but what belongs to you. None of the hearts of us unfortunate maids-of-honour, for instance. They are prized in Scotland, I can tell you; and the Maries want at least as many as they have got amongst the five of them, you may be sure!'

'And suppose I leave my own instead,' answered Chastelâr, laughing, yet at the same time colouring—an embarrassment not unmarked by Mary Hamilton, who shot one eager glance at him, and turned her eyes away, blushing too; 'suppose I must return to France, fair mistress, a loser by the exchange?'

'We'll have the palace swept and searched for the missing article,' she answered, gaily. 'I think I can promise you that the one who has got it won't keep it. There, you needn't look so shocked, Mistress Beton! You can't guess which of the Maries has robbed our poor poet so mercilessly. It's a sweet name, Mary, is it not? But don't forget it rhymes to "vary." And so, good luck to you, Chastelâr! and fare you well!'

'*Souvent femme varie, fol qui s'y fie,*' answered the poet, forcing a laugh, though a less acute observer than any one of the four might have noted that he was distressed at the turn their conversation had taken, and that the wilful girl's shaft had been shot home. 'Adieu, Mistress Carmichael,' he added, as she, too, in her turn frankly bade him farewell; and then he passed on to Mary Hamilton, and paused for an instant, irresolute, before the dark-eyed maid-of-honour.

She did not offer him her hand as the others had done. She never lifted her looks to his face. Pale as she usually was, she turned paler than ever, and her cold, distant bearing would have almost seemed to infer that she was offended, and that her greeting was extorted from her as a duty of ceremony, rather than springing from the free impulse of friendship.

And yet he knew it was not so. Though scarcely so quick-sighted on such matters as women, even men have an intuitive perception that they are beloved. In either sex the consciousness produces a kindly feeling towards the worshipper, and it seems hard to deny a few gentle words where so much is ungrudgingly bestowed. Mistaken compassion! Perhaps the fiercest efforts of hate would be less cruel than this ill-judged lenity. It is like hanging out the beacon where it shall guide the bark on to the quicksand. It is like Varney counterfeiting Leicester's whistle to lure Amy Robsart to destruction. When people pass spurious money in exchange for sterling gold, they find themselves ere long in the felon's dock; but there is no law to punish the coiner who stamps a few false words with the royal die of truth, and pays them away unblushingly, for all the happiness and all the welfare of the poor fool he deceives.

'You are going back to France,' said Mary Hamilton, with a wonderfully composed countenance and steady lip. 'It is your home—I wish you joy of your return.'

'Nay,' answered Chastelâr, his voice softening while he spoke. 'You know how happy I have been in Scotland. How devoted I must always be to this court and this country. I must follow d'Amville to Paris for the present, but the one hope of my life will be that I shall soon return.'

He spoke truly enough; he even hoped the royal lady then employing all the fascinations of her manner on Morton and his kindred, might hear his last words and give him one responsive glance to carry with him into his banishment. In this he was disappointed. The Queen, seated at some distance from the group, and surrounded by her barons, was for the moment 'every inch a Queen,' and Chastelâr passed out of Holyrood, with Mary Hamilton's 'farewell' warmer and more hopeful since his last words, to warn him (could, indeed, warning ever profit in such cases), that, in stretching for the rose he would never reach, he was trampling the poor violet ruthlessly beneath his feet.

She seemed in better spirits, too, after he was gone, although silent and inattentive to the surrounding gaiety, a distraction not unnoticed by Mary Beton, who believed herself officially answerable not only for the dresses and deportment of her three companions, but for the thoughts and sentiments of their inmost hearts.

'I have told you twice,' she said at length with an offended air, 'that the Queen rides out to-morrow for the hawking after early mass, and that you and Mary Seton will be in attendance. You will wear the sad-coloured riding gear passamented with silver, and French hats—but neither of you seem to heed me.'

'She is thinking of a French head, rather than a French hat,' laughed incorrigible Mary Seton; 'but indeed I have listened to you even more attentively than usual. Ah! Mistress Beton, what would I not give to possess your careful forethought and common sense! *You* never neglect anything—*you* never forget anything. The Queen trusts you with her state-secrets, and when you carry her work to her in the Council-chamber, even Maitland and Morton look upon you as if you were one of themselves. Why are you not weak and giddy like me, or pensive and sad like Hamilton, or absent and haughty like Mary Carmichael has grown of late? Look at her yonder holding the Queen's train as if *she* were the sovereign, and our beautiful Mistress the maid-of-honour!'

Mary Beton smiled, not displeased at the adroit flattery of her junior. She did indeed pride herself on two especial qualities—utter impassibility, and scrupulous attention to details.

'I am somewhat older than the rest of you,' she said, bridling her handsome neck within her handsome ruff, 'and I have learned to avoid all pleasures and interests that take my attention from my duty. I am always responsible and always employed. I have no time for the follies that seem to afford the rest of you so much amusement.'

'And yet you would become them well,' said the other, coaxingly. 'Come, now, be persuaded to play Diana in the next *masque*. I will dress your hair myself, and the gallants all vow you are fitted for the part both in person and character. Handsome and stately and cold.'

'That is exactly why I do not care to join in it,' replied the elder lady, with increasing cordiality, for no daughter of Eve was ever yet insensible to flattery, even when ugly and repulsive and old, whereas Mary Beton could boast considerable attractions. 'I tell you, my dear, it is better to keep out of temptation. You envy me my self-command, you say, and I repeat to you it is a quality I possess because I am heart-whole and free.'

'But so am I,' interposed the girl, vehemently, 'and so are we all, I suppose, in reality, for the matter of that; and yet it is possible that our time maybe coming too,' she added, reflectively. 'Ah! Mistress Beton, I shall see you some day with a lover as stately as yourself, perhaps. What an imperial pair you will make!'

Mary Beton looked by no means displeased. The smile on her handsome face partook of a meaning expression not devoid of triumph, as though the contingency were neither very remote, nor wholly disagreeable; but, of course, the less she felt it to be unalterable, the more emphasis she laid on her denial.

'Never!' she exclaimed, strenuously. 'I am surprised, my dear, at your thinking for an instant of such an absurdity. I never saw one yet, to my fancy, that I could like better than another.'

'Nor I neither,' echoed Mary Seton, eagerly; adding, in a voice of unusual gravity, and with a wistful expression on her countenance rarely seen there, 'I think if I did, it would be an unlucky day both for him and for me!'

Even while she spoke an unusual stir in the ante-room heralded the approach of some distinguished stranger who was to be received with more than ordinary ceremony. In such cases the Queen's ladies gathered round their mistress as in duty bound, although at other times it was Mary's practice to retain but one of them in the immediate vicinity of her person, and to permit the rest to mingle in the general circle, amusing themselves in their own way.

The duties devolving on 'the Maries' were, indeed, much to their liking, and might well be called a 'labour of love.' They vied with each other in passionate adoration of their mistress, whose sweet temper and generous disposition never failed to gain the hearts of all those who came about her person. If there was a charm in all the Stuarts which won blind devotion from their associates, what must have been the fascination that surrounded the gentlest and loveliest scion of that illustrious race!

The Queen of Scots was a thorough *gentlewoman*, in the noblest and fullest acceptation of the term. That she lacked firmness where her affections were involved, and promptitude of action where her safety was threatened, what is this but to say that she was a woman and not a hero? Courage, both the masculine spirit that braves mortal peril, and the feminine fortitude that can sustain suffering and sorrow, she proved that she possessed on more than one stricken field, in more than one dreary house of humiliation and bondage. On both these chivalrous qualities the last scene of her life drew largely, and Bayard himself, the bravest of the brave, could not have faced death more nobly than did Mary, the fairest of the fair. Yet with all this she was exquisitely sensitive of the feelings of others; she could not bear to give pain; she hesitated to remonstrate, and could scarcely bring herself to chide. The regulations of her household, to the carrying out of which the Queen herself attended with housewifely care, prove the regard she entertained for the personal comfort of her domestics.

The allowance for the table of her ladies and maids-of-honour was the same as that of their sovereign. If the reader is curious to see the bill of fare for a royal dinner in the sixteenth century, the following are its contents:—

'Four soups, four *entrées*, a piece of "beef-royal" boiled, a loin of mutton, and a capon; of roast meat, one neck of mutton, one capon, three pigeons, three hares, and two pieces of fat meat. For the dessert, seven dishes of fruit, and one of chicory-paste, one gallon of wine, one quart of white wine, and one of claret; eight rolls of bread.' The latter item appears as if this plentiful supply were a dinner for but eight people. Probably, however, the remains of the feast furnished forth the inferior tables. A characteristic memorandum appears at the same time directing that the Queen's ladies, including the Maries, shall have the same diet as their mistress.

Mary Carmichael was in attendance on Her Majesty, and holding the royal train during the conversation we have detailed. It was broken off abruptly by the stir in the ante-room.

'This must be the English Ambassador!' exclaimed Mary Beton, drawing herself up to her full height, and assuming her most frigid air of *étiquette*.

'He has come back sooner than he was expected, and I wish he had stayed away altogether,' observed Mistress Seton, on whom Randolph had made no favourable impression during their previous acquaintance, for the latter had held Elizabeth's credentials at the court of Holyrood from the Queen of Scotland's first arrival, and had been absent to receive personal instructions from his own sovereign but for a few weeks.

'What is the matter with Mary Carmichael?' whispered Mistress Hamilton, anxiously, as the three young ladies glided into their places behind the Queen. She might have spared herself the question, for almost ere it was spoken the agitation which caused it had disappeared; and although, when Randolph entered the presence-chamber, Mary Carmichael had started, turned very pale, and dropped the royal robe from her hand, ere he had advanced three paces, her colour had returned somewhat higher than before, and she was fulfilling her duties more scrupulously than ever, with an unusual expression of cold indifference on her fair and haughty face.

CHAPTER VII

'For though I was rugged and wild and free,
I had a heart like another man;
And oh! had I known how the end would be,
I would it had broke ere the play began.'

As Mary Stuart stood forward to welcome Elizabeth's ambassador to her court, many an eye dwelt on the face and figure of the Scottish Queen with enthusiastic admiration. Though dressed in the mourning which she still wore for her first husband, the dark folds of her robe did but enhance the brilliancy of her complexion, and, whilst even the spotless ruff did not detract from the fairness of her neck, the whitest hand in Europe hung like a snowdrop against the black volume of her draperies. Even Randolph, cynic though he were, could not repress a thrill of delight as he approached so beautiful an object, though the sentiment uppermost in his diplomatic heart, had he put it into words, would probably have been as follows:—

'It is lucky my mistress cannot see you at this moment, or she would hate you more cordially than ever, and my task would be even more difficult than it is!'

He made his obeisance, nevertheless, with the cool assurance and easy grace of a practised courtier. The Queen received him with a cordiality that she seemed anxious should not be lost on the bystanders.

'A messenger from my loving cousin,' said she, 'is always welcome; how much more when he comes in the person of our old and esteemed friend Mr Randolph.'

The ambassador answered in a few well-chosen words for his sovereign and himself, dropping once more on his knee and craving permission to present an autograph letter and a costly ring from Elizabeth to the cousin whom she never saw. Mary received them both with expressions of unbounded delight, and the shrewd bearer, judging from his own experience and his own heart, argued that there must be no small weakness concealed under so much affection, and that it was unnatural for one woman to be so fond of another, unless she felt herself uncomfortably in her power.

Mary questioned him of his journey.

'You have had a long ride,' said the Queen, 'and we can but give you a rude, though hearty, welcome. A long ride and a dangerous, for indeed the borders of both countries are not so quiet as we could wish, or as we hope to render them before many months are past.'

Randolph answered with ready tact—

'It is to the Queen of Scotland's servants I owe my safe arrival at Holyrood. Permit me to recall to your Majesty's recollection an archer of your old Scottish Guard.'

With these words he drew Maxwell forward and presented him to the Queen. Randolph was a good-natured man when it cost nothing, and, moreover, it was a part of his profession to make a friend wherever it could be done at a small outlay. Mary received Walter Maxwell with the utmost condescension. Had she followed her own impulse, she would have shaken him cordially by both hands and bidden him a hearty welcome, for the sake of old times and the memory of her dear France; but monarchs must not give way to impulse, and indeed are better without such weaknesses as affections and associations. So he knelt low before her and kissed her royal hand, the while Mary Carmichael seemed to have discovered something so engrossing in the skirt of her mistress's robe, that she never lifted her eyes from the embroidery with which it was adorned.

'And how fared you in the wild Border-land?' resumed the Queen, 'the land of moss and moor—of jack and spear—a pleasant district if you want to breathe a horse or fly a hawk; but, as our loyal burghers say, bad to sleep in for those who would pull their boots off when they retire to rest.' The Queen spoke of the border as though it brought agreeable associations to her mind, and indeed she dearly loved the open plain and the free air of heaven.

'Had it not been for your warden, Madam,' answered the courtier, 'I might have slept in my boots till the day of judgment. This gallant archer and myself would scarce have had a tale to tell, if the Earl of Bothwell did not take to spur and snaffle as kindly as the wildest freebooter on the marches.'

'How so?' inquired Mary, the colour mantling to her cheek, and her eye sparkling with animated interest. The Queen was a Stuart to the marrow, and loved well to hear of a gallant feat of arms.

'Why, thus, Madam,' replied the ambassador. 'Ere the moon had been up an hour, we saw ourselves beset by a party of some ten or twelve horsemen, who occupied a pass in front of us, and as we were but three, I leave your

Majesty to judge that my feelings as a man whose trade is rather peace than war, were by no means agreeable. My companion, I may observe, was all for fighting, without counting.' He spoke, as usual, in a tone that might be either jest or earnest; also, as usual, nothing within the range of his eye escaped him. He noted the Queen's interest. He observed Mary Carmichael look up for an instant, and resume the study of her embroidery with a heightened colour. He caught Mistress Beton in the fact, examining his own person with an air of dignified approval that amounted to admiration; and it was not lost upon him, that while Lord James looked more anxious than common, others of the circle exchanged glances of deeper meaning than his plain tale would at first appear to warrant. All this he saw without seeming to see, and made a note of his observations.

'And you charged them and cut your way through!' exclaimed the Queen, with head up and flashing eyes, like some beautiful Amazon, clenching her slender hand the while as though it held a sword.

'Charge them, your Majesty, we did perforce, for it was more dangerous to go back than forward; but the cutting seemed more on their part than ours. The situation, too, was ridiculous enough, had a man been in cue to laugh!' resumed Randolph, in the same dry sneering tones. 'My comrade's horse was rolling on the heather, and he defending himself, like a second St George, on foot. My servant, saving your Grace's presence, a beef-fed knave from Smithfield, roared and plunged about like a baited bull, till he received a *coup-de-grâce* that would have cracked any skull but a Londoner's, from a useful instrument that my Lord Bothwell tells me is called a Jedwood-axe. Whilst I myself, vainly endeavouring to protect person and property, was forced to abandon my valise, and turn all my attention to the defence of my own head.'

'And they robbed you of your despatches!' exclaimed Lord James, interrupting the narrator with ill-concealed anxiety, while three or four nobles glanced at each other with looks of covert triumph and amusement. 'Indeed, Madam,' added the future Regent, recovering himself with an effort, 'these outrages are insupportable; they must be promptly punished and put down!'

'And they shall be so,' answered Mary, drawing herself up proudly, 'if I ride through the "Debatable Land" myself in corslet and head-piece, as my fathers did before me. Alas! I fear steel harness is the most fitting attire for a Scottish Queen.—But you have not told us how you escaped,' proceeded she, turning to Randolph with marked courtesy, and a softened manner. 'You were rescued, were you not, at your utmost need, by our warden?'

'The Earl of Bothwell did, indeed, come riding in like a whirlwind,' replied Randolph, 'at the very moment when I had resolved that my last sleep must be that booted one to which your Majesty's citizens have such a rational objection. If the Warden of the Marches be chosen for his prowess in single combat, there never was a better selection! Man and horse went down before his lance without a struggle, and his very war-cry seemed to act upon the freebooters like the shriek of a hawk on a wisp of wild-fowl. Faith, they took to their wings like wild-fowl too, where it was hopeless to follow them, and I rode home to supper at Hermitage without the slightest wish to cultivate a farther acquaintance with that portion of your Majesty's domains.'

The Queen laughed as he concluded. She had listened with obvious interest to the Englishman's account of the skirmish, and seemed in heightened spirits when it was over. She beckoned to Mary Beton, and whispered in that lady's ear, who retired from the circle, and presently returned, followed by a page, bearing a small gold cup, richly chased and decorated with precious stones. It was filled with wine, and Mary put her own lips to it ere she offered it to Randolph.

'You will pledge us,' said the Queen, with her sunny smile; 'and when you drink to a lady, sir, not a drop must remain in the cup. If you examine it, you will see that its sides are ornamented with lance heads and trophies of arms. Will you favour Mary Stuart by keeping it in remembrance of your rough ride and the dangers you affronted in her service?'

Randolph bowed to the ground. He knew and appreciated the value of such a compliment, and whilst he saw in the giver's frank countenance and cordial manner the sincerity of her good-will, his heart never smote him for the double part he was expressly sent there to play.

The Queen's curiosity did not yet seem, however, to be thoroughly satisfied, and she questioned the ambassador with considerable minuteness as to the appearance and bearing of his foes. Randolph's answers were marked by his usual tone of covert sarcasm; but she elicited no more from him than he had already detailed, save that the valise which he had lost contained in reality no papers of importance, or, indeed, any papers whatever, except a few private memoranda of his own—an announcement which seemed to clear Lord James's brow from a load of care, while it created obvious disappointment on two or three other anxious faces.

The truth was, that Randolph, faithful to his own Queen in the faithless part which he enacted to another, was the bearer of certain instructions to Lord James, which were very different in tenor from the cordial letter he was charged by Elizabeth to deliver to her cousin. There was even yet a strong Catholic party about the court, to whom the possession of these despatches would have been an inestimable windfall; no less, indeed, than a foundation for a charge of treason against the Queen's Protestant half-brother.

The attack, then, on Randolph and his companion, was prompted by nobler names than the Armstrongs and Elliotts, who lived by rapine on the borders; but their schemes had been baffled by the wily Englishman, who fought like a demon to preserve the valise, of which he was, in reality, utterly careless, and by that means led his assailants to believe that, in carrying it off, they had become possessed of a valuable prize.

'I am charged by the Earl of Bothwell,' said Randolph, at the conclusion of his narrative, 'to present his unalterable duty to your Majesty. His lordship, not satisfied with extricating me from the sloughs of the "Debatable Land," has sent his own henchman to conduct me safely to the capital.'

Mary started perceptibly, and the colour she could not entirely repress rose faintly to her cheek. Well did she know that her warden was thoroughly devoted to her interests, and that, in whatever intrigues he might be mixed, Bothwell's loyalty was unshaken to his Queen. Perhaps she may have already asked herself whether it did not partake of that devotion which shed a halo over the days of chivalry. At all events, his sending his own henchman to the court, denoted some more than usual necessity for communicating with his sovereign; and Mary prepared to take her measures accordingly.

At that unhappy period, when not a day passed without the hatching of some plot, the development of some intrigue—when every man's hand was against his neighbour, and noble preyed upon noble without scruple or remorse—even the Queen was obliged to remember that jealous eyes were on the watch for her every movement, and to practise dissimulation where dissimulation was alike unsafe and unworthy.

She turned to Mary Seton, who had been listening with an appearance of great amusement, and gave her some directions in a low voice, that even Randolph's quick ear could not overhear.

The young lady curtseyed and withdrew, first casting a glance of considerable meaning at Mary Carmichael, who replied to it, by assuming as unconscious an air as was compatible with the red spot that burned in either cheek.

Walter Maxwell now found himself in the presence of the lady whom he had been determining so many long weeks that he would forget, and to see whom once more he had consistently abandoned his profession, and undertaken a long journey by sea and land. As is usually the case, the moment he had looked forward to, hardly repaid the anxiety of expectation. The maid-of-honour's greeting was formal in the extreme, betraying a degree of coldness that seemed almost to argue aversion; and he was, of course, fool enough to be hurt and angry, instead of pleased and triumphant. Whoever saw a woman accost the man she loves with half the cordiality she displays to the merest acquaintance? On the contrary, she receives his greeting with a reserve that to any one else would be positive rudeness; and even when alone with him, preserves, for a space, a certain embarrassment in her womanly shame and fear, lest she should betray the tenth part of all she feels.

Mary Carmichael was no exception to the rule of her sex. In fact, she possessed more than her due share of that pride which, when brought in contact with a kind nature, produces so much sorrow, and with a proud one so much dissension. Although the Queen, who was again seated, had dismissed her from her duty as train-bearer, and she was at liberty to converse with all the freedom a crowded assembly permits, she could think of no more pertinent remark to make to her admirer than the following:—

'You have brought us news from the French Court, Master Maxwell? Is it as gay as it used to be? I wonder you had the heart to leave it.'

There was something in her manner that repelled and irritated him.

'I came to serve my Queen,' he replied, stiffly, and in a tone as cold as her own. 'Our sovereign knows how to appreciate loyalty, and does not forget her old adherents in the short space of a few months.'

'Our sovereign would welcome a lapdog if it came from France, I think,' replied the other, indifferently, utterly disregarding the future suffering her insincerity would cause herself. 'Our sovereign has already expressed her satisfaction at seeing you, and would probably give you a yet heartier greeting if you could inform her of the latest fashions in head-tire and farthingale. We are far behindhand here, you see, in these barbarous regions!'

She spoke with an assumption of levity so unlike herself, that he was disgusted as well as angry; and, indeed, it was somewhat unjust that the maid-of-honour should thus revenge upon him her own confusion at his appearance.

'I am no silk-mercer,' he answered, rudely; 'nor have I travelled so far to bring a lady the colour of a ribbon.' And with a swelling heart and a feeling of pain he could not have believed possible without experiencing it, Walter Maxwell turned away, and lost himself amongst the crowd of surrounding courtiers.

Far different was the conversation carried on at the same moment by that courtly pair, the diplomatic Mr Thomas Randolph and the stately Mistress Mary Beton. The former, with his keen political foresight, had lately been reflecting that a close intimacy with at least one of the household, would open a fertile channel for information regarding the Queen's private thoughts and doings, such as would be invaluable to him in his present capacity as confidential agent to Elizabeth. He had also observed the admiration which his late appearance had obviously elicited from the senior maid-of-honour; and he had no more scruple in deliberately proceeding to make love to that austere damsel than he would have had in putting her to the torture, had the latter process, rather than the former, been the most effectual way of gaining her confidence.

Mary Beton was not insensible to admiration. She was a woman, and, with all her magnificence of deportment, consequently inherited the propensities of her sex; but she would not have appreciated indiscriminate homage; and the dish to please her palate, if we may so speak, required to be elaborately dressed and seasoned, and sent up on a silver trencher at least.

To have won Mr Randolph's good opinion, however, was a conquest of which any lady might be proud. The ambassador's high position, his invariable assurance and self-reliance, his thorough knowledge of the world, and sarcastic readiness of tongue, had rendered him an object of considerable interest to the dames of the Scottish court. They exaggerated, as women will, his influence, his talents, his successes—diplomatic as well as social—and the favour with which he was regarded by the English Queen. They quoted him, they talked about him—above all, they were a little afraid of him; and the latter sensation possesses an indefinable charm for the venturous tendencies of the female character.

Mary Beton was startled to find how gratifying to her self-love were the attentions of the English courtier.

It was difficult to say by what subtle process he led her to infer that he took pleasure in her society. Every word he said might have been proclaimed unblushingly by the Lion-King-at-Arms. And yet before Randolph had spoken a dozen sentences to Mary Beton, he had dexterously led her to infer that she was the only woman in that crowded assemblage whom he considered worthy of his notice; that their ideas were sympathetic, their tastes similar, and that a mutual alliance must necessarily be established between them.

To-night he confined himself to a few adroit questions respecting the costumes in a proposed *masque*; and Mary Beton answered them with a freedom far different from her usual reticence. All he wanted was to pave the way to her confidence; and he was the last man to scare the steed by showing the halter while he proffered the corn. So he took his leave as soon as he saw he had made a favourable impression, and went his way cheerfully to sup with Morton and Maitland, leaving Mistress Beton in a most agreeable frame of mind, with her head, at least, an inch higher than usual.

We must now follow Mary Seton as she glided stealthily away from the presence to fulfil the Queen's whispered command.

With an expression of more than usual intelligence on her saucy features, that active damsel hurried through the ante-rooms and galleries, and along certain dark stone passages, which she threaded with the confidence of one to whom these intricacies were familiar, till she reached a small vaulted apartment, from whence emanated a prevailing odour of beef and ale, denoting it to be the buttery. Spur and steel scabbard clattered on the stone floor of this resort, and rough voices might be heard jeering and pledging each other with a rude cordiality proportioned to the extent in which, as the Scotch say, '*The malt got above the meal.*'

A grave individual in black, however, presided over these festivities, and could always keep order by the summary process of refusing to draw more ale. This official started to behold the white figure of the maid-of-honour standing in the doorway; but Mary Seton, with a finger on her lip, simply said, 'Lord Bothwell's henchman;' and the seneschal, interrupting that personage with the black jack of ale at his lips, brought him into the dark stone passage, and confided him to the radiant messenger before he was aware.

Dick Rutherford, though his faculties were of the keenest on a moonless night in Liddesdale, was somewhat confused on this his first visit to Holyrood; nor were his intellects necessarily brightened by a huge repast of beef, washed down with strong ale, after a long ride and a fourteen hours' fast.

Once in the passage, he thought he was dreaming. A vision of loveliness in shining array, whose head reached to about the middle of his corslet, accosted him with hasty frankness.

'You left Hermitage this morning?' said she, laconically.

'At daybreak,' answered the borderer, scarcely reassured by this accurate knowledge of his movements.

'You have a letter from the warden for the Queen?' proceeded the damsel.

'A letter!' repeated 'Dick-o'-the-Cleugh,' his Scottish caution coming rapidly to the rescue. 'I'll no say but there might be a bit parcel, or such like. If I've no lost it by the way,' he added, doubtfully, and feeling the while under his corslet for the safety of the packet.

Mary Seton's little foot stamped impatiently, whereat the giant started in his boots. She turned upon him quite fiercely.

'A jackman does not lose a Queen's packet,' said she. 'If he does, he may chance to lose his own head. Follow me!' And she flitted on through the dark passages, turning at intervals to see that she was followed by the astonished borderer.

Presently they climbed a narrow, winding stair. After ascending several steps, the maid-of-honour stopped, opened a door, and pushing aside some heavy folds of tapestry, bade her follower enter, warning him not to strike his head against the low doorway.

'Dick-o'-the-Cleugh,' dazzled and confused, found himself in a very small and brilliantly-lighted apartment. The roof was high; but the room itself was scarcely large enough to contain six or eight persons. A table prepared for supper, and laid for two, occupied the whole space between the window and the ample hearth, on which a wood fire blazed and crackled cheerfully. The borderer's gaze was riveted at once by the gold plate on the supper-table, richly chased, and bearing the crown-royal on its burnished surface.

Mary Seton could not forbear a smile at his astonishment.

'This is somewhat different from the head of a glen in Liddesdale,' said she, with a ringing laugh. 'Thanks to my good-nature, you have now seen a Queen's chamber. Give me your packet, and get you gone!'

While she spoke, she ran her eye over the athletic figure of the borderer, magnificent in its size and strength when seen in that small apartment, and well set off by his warlike gear.

'What a fine man!' thought Mary Seton, as she scanned him. 'And oh! what a good face, and how unlike a courtier!'

But on 'Dick-o'-the-Cleugh's' honest countenance might be seen an expression of great perplexity. In the first place, he was a good deal charmed, and not a little stupefied, by the beauty of his guide; in the next, he was extremely apprehensive of an immediate apparition of royalty; and, lastly, he was embarrassed how to refuse anything to the most fascinating young lady he had ever yet set eyes on. Nevertheless he answered stoutly, though deferentially—

'My packet must be delivered into the Queen's ain hand. You're no the Queen hersel', I'm thinking, though well you might be, my bonny lady, for I never saw the like o' ye.'

The tone of admiration in which he spoke was so obviously involuntary as to be flattering in the extreme.

Mary Seton looked pleased, and continued more graciously—

'I spoke to prove you. You can be faithful to a trust, can you? What is your name?'

'They call me Dick Rutherford,' he answered; 'but in Liddesdale I'm "Dick-o'-the-Cleugh." Ask the Liddesdale lads if I'm to be trusted! But I'm havering. The like o' you will never set your bonny foot in Liddesdale, nor ask tidings o' the like o' me.'

Dick spoke almost despondently for a moment. He brightened up though at her reply.

'A brave man and an honest is the noblest of God's creatures. I believe you to be both. Although,' she added, mischievously, 'they're scarce enough at Holyrood, there are a good many more brave men than honest on *your* side the country, or I've been misinformed.'

Dick was on the eve of entering into an elaborate defence of his kindred, and an explanation of border probity, which could not but have been edifying, when he was interrupted by the entrance of the Queen herself, about to sup, after the fatigues of the day, private and quietly, with her kinswoman the Countess of Argyle.

The borderer was now completely overwhelmed. Nevertheless, he delivered his packet with an honest simplicity, in favourable contrast to the manners of most of her ambassadors; and Mary Stuart acknowledged its receipt with a few gold pieces, and dismissed him with her pleasantest smile.

His previous conductor guided him back till she landed him in the court of the palace; and although 'Dick-o'-the-Cleugh' possessed to the full the loyalty of his countrymen, and a borderer's devoted admiration for womanly beauty, he had no distinct recollection of the sovereign's countenance, so completely was it effaced from his memory by her bewitching maid-of-honour.

Poor Dick! Many a long day afterwards his honest heart ached when he thought of that memorable night, recalling the merry eyes and the sunny hair and the dazzling figure of his fascinating guide. Brave, simple 'Dick-o'-the-Cleugh!' He had better have been up to his neck in the softest moss in all Liddesdale.

CHAPTER VIII

'But had I wist, before I kist,

That love had been sae hard to win,

I'd have lock'd my heart in a case of gowd,

An' pinn'd it wi' a siller pin.'

It was the anniversary of the death of Francis II., and Mary, whose attachment to her youthful husband evinced itself by a scrupulous respect for his memory, had ordered a dirge to be performed in the Royal Chapel at Holyrood for the repose of his soul. The sacred edifice had been appropriately hung with black; nor was any accessory neglected that could enhance the gloom of the scene. Carpenters had been employed for some days previously in preparing the mournful display; and a good deal of murmuring and discontent had arisen both in the court and city at the proposed ordinance. The *Godly*, as the Protestant party somewhat presumptuously termed themselves, mistrusted this return to papal ceremonials, and made no secret of their dissatisfaction.

Mary, however, tolerant as she was of opposite opinions, always remained staunch to the ritual in which she had been brought up, and spared no pains to carry out with due pomp a solemnity which she esteemed essential to the occasion.

The morning broke gloomily, when the Queen, attired in deep mourning, and attended only by Lady Hamilton, entered the chapel for early mass. Her lovely face looked paler than usual under the veil of crape which shaded it, and there was an expression of something more than sorrow, of annoyance and apprehension, on its lineaments. Perhaps she was thinking of her brief reign in France, not long enough for a sovereign to discover the many troubles and anxieties that line a crown. Perhaps she was recalling the adoration she had been used to receive from the excitable French people, and contrasting it with the gloomy brows and ominous mutterings she had already encountered amongst her new subjects.

Mary had been but a few weeks on the Scottish throne, ere she became aware that even her beauty and her bereavement were not sufficient to cover the *odium* of her religion in the eyes of these northern zealots, and that Protestantism might esteem it a duty both to God and man to insult a helpless woman because she was a Catholic Queen.

As she passed slowly up the aisle with weary step and downcast air, followed by her maid-of-honour, it may be that both the women were longing wearily for that rest which they came here to seek—glad to be relieved, if but for an hour, of the burden which at some future time they should cast down at once and for ever—almost wishing that the time was come, and the journey over, and the resting-place at hand.

And now the anthem swells and sinks and fills the echoing aisle; and the crimson light streams through the deep-stained windows on chiselled font and sculptured cross and monumental marble, while the tones of the choristers rise and fall like the song of angels speaking of hope and peace and pardon for the penitent—wailing in their celestial sorrow for the loved that yet are lost for evermore.

In that flood of harmony the Queen bathed her wounded spirit, bidding it contemn the reefs and rocks that beset its earthly course as it floated, if but for an instant, towards the eternal shore; and Mary Hamilton, joining in the tide of prayer and praise, forgot her hopes and fears, her tottering happiness and earthly misgivings, while she felt that there was yet in store for her a home of endless welcome, a joy that no uncertainty could poison, a love no falsehood could take away.

Prosperity goes to church, as well it may, to return thanks for the benefits it has received; to fulfil, as it were, its own part of the compact by which it flourishes; to acknowledge its advantages and to entreat their continuance; then it walks back into the sunshine in its purple and fine linen, with a pleasant consciousness of debts discharged and duties well fulfilled. Not so its ailing brother, gaunt Adversity. For the latter the temple of God is the temple of refuge, the temple of healing, the temple of consolation; thither it may bring its sores and its sackcloth, without misgivings and without shame; there it is on a level with the proudest, and in unison with the happiest; it drinks from the same stream, and out of the same cup; it returns to its labour and its sorrow, strengthened and refreshed. Though the heart be aching, it is sound and unbroken still; and the storms may pelt their fiercest, it only longs the more to come again.

As the anthem proceeded the Scottish Queen became aware that another voice had been added to her choir, of considerable depth and volume, thereby completing its harmony and greatly enhancing its effect. This organ was the property of an individual whose unfortunate destiny it was to make a far greater stir at the court of Holyrood than became either his talents or his station, and to meet with a fate which his antecedents did not deserve.

In the train of the Count de Moretta, ambassador from the court of Savoy, the Duke of which principality was another unsuccessful suitor for the hand of the Scottish Queen, came a good-humoured little Italian, David Riccio by name, whose especial gifts at this period seem to have been a knack of mimicry, not unusual among his countrymen, and a fine bass voice of great power and sweetness.

These were the qualities that first recommended him to the notice of Mary; and when, in addition to his musical acquirements, she found him quick-witted, ready and obliging, fluent with the pen, and a perfect master of the French language, she promoted the good-humoured, deformed, and diminutive foreigner to the post of private secretary, little dreaming of the construction which would hereafter be put upon so harmless an appointment.

In the meantime Riccio revelled in the exercise of his delightful talent— filling the crape-hung building with his notes of mournful melody—and Mary listened entranced, and forgot for the moment her troubles, her widowhood, and her crown.

But the charms of music, and even the consolations of religion, can but stave off earthly cares for a brief period of repose, after which they are prone to thrust themselves on our notice with a vigour all the more imperative for such temporary respite. When mass was concluded, and Mary, with her maid-of-honour, was about to quit the chapel, she could not but observe how none, save her immediate attendants and personal household, had assisted to form the congregation; how the nobility of her court, with but few exceptions, had remained outside, with a certain ostentatious assumption of dissent from the religion of their Queen. She could not help remarking as much to her attendant.

'Do you not see, my dear,' said she, bitterly, 'how the new religion is disposed to charity and toleration? My Protestant lords will not even join in the devotions of their Sovereign, when she prays for the welfare of her husband's soul. They will not "weep with those who weep," nor "rejoice with those who rejoice," unless it be by Master Knox's permission, and in black cassock and Geneva band. Verily, Mary Hamilton, it is a weary lot to be a woman, but it is a daily humiliation to be a Queen!'

'I know not what a Queen's trials may be, madam,' answered the other, on whose sweet face the halo of devotion had not yet faded away; 'but a woman's sorrows, I fancy, may be too hard for a woman to bear, unless she brings them with her unreservedly and lays them all down here.'

While she spoke she stood near the chapel-door, and the December sun, shedding its rays through the deep red cross of the stained window above, streamed full upon her fair and gentle face. It seemed to her mistress, even then, that she looked like some patient saint, purified by suffering, and bearing the cross of her Master in the red glory of martyrdom.

But such holy thoughts as these were soon driven from Mary's mind by fresh annoyances. On leaving her chapel, and emerging into the courtyard of her palace, the Queen found it crowded by an assemblage of her nobility, whose motley apparel, of the gayest and gaudiest hues, contrasted offensively with her own sad mourning garb. Not one of them had shown sufficient sympathy with her feelings to wear so much as a black ribbon on his doublet, or to doff the plume that flaunted from his rich velvet bonnet. Stung to the quick by such disrespect, Mary determined to meet it by an insult as injudicious as it was unworthy. Halting on the threshold of her chapel, she took not the slightest notice of the salutations offered her by the proudest lords in Scotland, but beckoned to the new singer, whose voice had recently so much delighted her, and giving him her missal to carry, complimented him with marked familiarity on his performance; and so, holding the astonished Italian in conversation at the chapel-door, kept every one else waiting uncovered until she had done with him.

Many a haughty brow was already bent on the unknown stranger. Gray moustaches, that had bristled in the teeth of the English archers at Flodden, were pulled in mingled astonishment and anger; while hands, always too prompt to shed blood, gripped dagger and sword-hilt, as though neither the sacred locality nor the presence of the sovereign would long restrain them from open violence. The first impulse of the Scottish noble was to resent an insult or avenge an injury on the spot. Morton alone, of all the crowd, seemed to experience neither indignation nor surprise. The smile that gave his face so fiendish an expression only deepened and hardened round his mouth. He glanced from the Queen to her ill-chosen favourite with looks rather of amused malignity than offended pride. Morton's will was strong in proportion to his passions, and these, with all their abiding energy, were thoroughly under the control of his hard unfeeling nature. The Douglas was, indeed, one of those who would 'strike sooner than speak, and drink sooner than pray;' yet he only glared on the singer with a kind of comic ferocity, and the poor little Italian shrunk nearer his protectress with a prophetic horror of the hard-featured earl.

Bidding Riccio follow in her train, the Queen passed on through the cloisters of the palace towards her own apartments, returning with cold courtesy the salutations of her nobility. The courtiers looked meaningly at each other, and then at the new favourite, who slunk along behind his mistress, bearing her gorgeous missal, in ludicrous dismay. Secretary Maitland, a man whose wits were always at hand, and who could transact more business in ten minutes than the rest of the Privy Council in as many days, approached her Majesty with a huge bundle of papers under his arm, and the Queen, taking them from him without remark, handed the whole at once to Riccio. The secretary ventured on an expostulation.

'They are for your Majesty's *private* information,' said he, deferentially, but in a tone of marked disapproval.

'And I have given them to my *private* secretary,' replied Mary, haughtily; thus hastily and injudiciously confirming the appointment that led to such disastrous results.

'Shall I attend your Grace to explain their contents?' asked Maitland, as coolly as if nothing unusual had taken place.

'When I send for you, sir,' answered the Queen; and even Maitland's assurance was compelled to give way. He could but bow and fall back amongst the crowd.

Some of the nobles were so offended that they quitted the court on the spot; others thought it a bad opportunity to press their respective suits with the sovereign, and lounged off, as it were inadvertently, to their different amusements and occupations—one to fly a hawk, another to try a horse, not a few to break their fast on rich food and strong potations; the while they discussed the gossip of the court, which had received no inconsiderable fillip from the events of the morning.

Lord James walked gravely away to Mr Randolph's lodging. His brother, the gay lay-prior of Coldinghame, mounted his horse to join a merry-making on Leith sands. The Earl of Huntly and the Earl Mareschal departed to prepare an ordinance for the council, discussing, to all appearance, weighty matters of state; yet, perhaps, could their dialogue have been overheard, it related to far less important topics. The courtyard of the palace was almost deserted, and Mary, dismissing her maid-of-honour and the Italian, prepared to take a solitary turn up and down the cloisters, to soothe her temper and compose her troubled mind.

The Queen thought she was alone. It was not so, however; for, from the moment of her leaving the chapel, her movements had been watched by a man concealed behind one of the arches; and no sooner had her attendants quitted her than he emerged from his hiding-place.

Mary started, and almost screamed, as this unexpected figure stepped forth and stood in front of her. Indeed, a bolder nature might have been alarmed at its wild appearance and the vehemence of its gestures.

Pale and haggard, all unbraced, and with disordered dress—but unarmed, even to his sword—the Earl of Arran confronted Mary Stuart with none of the ceremony observed by a subject in the presence of his Queen.

'At last!' he shouted, with passionate vehemence, and placing himself so that she could not pass by him,—'at last I see thee once more. After weary hours of watching by night and day, after danger and difficulty and longing, I see thee once more. No longer the Queen of Scotland, surrounded by her court, and haughty in all the panoply of royalty, but Mary Stuart, the flower of womanhood, the darling of France, and the idol of Arran's heart.'

'What mean you, my lord?' exclaimed the Queen, utterly aghast at this unheard-of proceeding, and hardly knowing, in her astonishment, whether to stand or fly. 'Are you mad or dreaming? I am, indeed, Mary Stuart, and it is not thus I should be accosted by the Earl of Arran.'

'Mad!' returned the unfortunate nobleman, the wild cunning of insanity gleaming from his eye, and pointing with his wasted hand to the palace windows as he spoke. 'Hark ye, madam; they are mad up yonder. Mad from vaults to roof of this accursed building, this stronghold of superstition and Papacy. The Lord James is mad, who would deliver his sister into the hands of the ungodly; the priests are mad, who would withhold her, by main force, from the tidings of salvation; the choristers are mad, singing their unholy dirges for the souls that are gone to perdition. Mary! Mary!'—he changed to accents of wild affection and entreaty—'I alone am devoted to you. The house of Hamilton is the only refuge for the Stuart.'

Mary was constitutionally brave. Her courage began to return as she reflected she was within call of her household and retainers. She had a natural regard, too, for her kinsman; and a woman's pity for the wreck that something within, too truly, told her she herself had made. She tried to quiet the poor maniac with soothing, gentle words.

'Nay, cousin,' said the Queen, 'when have I doubted your loyalty or your honour? Why come to assure me of it at this unbecoming hour, and in this unbecoming guise? You are afflicted, Arran, and ill at ease. Retire into the palace; our own physician shall attend you; the best of lodging and the best of care shall not be grudged to my kinsman.'

For a moment Arran seemed calmer, and once or twice he passed his hand across his brow, as though waking from some troubled sleep, or trying to recall some lost recollection. And, indeed, whilst the Queen kept her eye on him, though he tried hard to avoid her glance, it held him in a certain subjection. No sooner, however, was it withdrawn, than his madness blazed forth once more.

'It is the plot!' he shouted again, as though addressing some imaginary audience, 'the accursed, traitorous plot, that I alone have power to prevent.

Papist and Protestant, rebel and renegade, from the four winds of heaven, they are banded together to carry off my Queen. Listen, madam; on my knees, I implore you to listen.'

He knelt, and clasped Mary's hand in both his own.

'I have discovered a conspiracy to seize your royal person, and to carry you into bondage. Lord James has consented to join in it. The Earls of Seton and Livingstone have signed the bond drawn up by smooth and crafty Lethington, with every name attached in characters of blood, except his own. Morton has promised his assistance; for when was the Douglas out of any scheme of violence and crime? And Bothwell, with his border reprobates, is to put it in execution; but Arran will save his Queen.'

'How say you? Morton? my brother? trusty Seton? and Bothwell, loyal and true? Impossible! You are raving,' said the Queen, now thoroughly alarmed. 'Where shall I turn to? What shall I do?'

'The Hamiltons will rally round the Stuart!' exclaimed the maniac, rising from his knees, and making as though he would seize Mary in his arms.

Before she could call for help, however, he suddenly desisted from his purpose, and placing his finger on his lip with a gesture of caution and a glance at the Queen, in which cunning and imbecility were strangely mingled, moved swiftly and stealthily away.

With the quick perceptions of insanity, he had caught the sound of an armed step approaching through the cloisters; and ere Mary had recovered from her dismay, a tall, warlike figure bowed to its very sword-hilt before her, and she found herself face to face with the Warden of the Marches.

He had been riding all night to reach Holyrood. He had galloped on ahead of the best-mounted of his troop, who were even now rounding the base of Arthur's Seat, as they neared the Scottish capital. In those troubled times there was no lack of excuses for the warden to seek personal instructions from his sovereign, and Bothwell had availed himself of some late misunderstanding with Lord Scrope, the warden on the English side, to obtain an audience of the Queen. With a wild feverish longing for the sweet face, to behold which was fast becoming a necessity of his existence, he had hurried to the presence of his sovereign. And now, when the moment had at last arrived, the colour faded in his bronzed cheek, and he trembled, that strong man-at-arms, like a girl.

Agitated and frightened as she was, Mary recovered herself sufficiently to receive him with becoming dignity. As his stalwart figure bent in homage, and the upturned face, with its manly features and fair short-curling beard, softened visibly beneath her glance, the Queen might well leave her hand in her subject's for an instant longer than the customs of a court required. He looked like a man who had both strength and will to help a woman at her need; and the bold border chief kissed the white hand that lay so gently in his own, with all the devotion of a worshipper kneeling before a saint.

'You are welcome, Bothwell,' said Mary, 'though you come, doubtless, to tell me of fresh disturbances on the border—fresh troubles to harass and perplex the Queen. The true heart and ready hand grow rare at Holyrood, and more and more welcome to Mary Stuart day by day.'

'I am but a plain soldier, madam,' answered Bothwell. 'Your Majesty's need of me is at once my pride and my reward. It is nothing new to tell you that every drop of James Hepburn's blood belongs to his Queen.'

'I believe it,' answered Mary, smiling sadly; 'and yet even Bothwell's loyalty has this very morning been questioned. Nay,' she added, as the Earl started indignantly to his feet, 'I, at least, never doubted you for an instant.'

'I have but one answer to my accusers, madam,' replied the warden, pointing significantly to his sword. 'If a subject questions my loyalty, I can demand the ordeal. If my sovereign suspects it,' he added, with a slight trembling in his voice, 'I can but give her my life to vindicate my honour.'

'O Bothwell!' exclaimed Mary, 'would that all were like you! I have none to counsel me; none in whom I can trust; none to sympathise with me in my loneliness, a widow, and a Queen. To-day, in my bereavement and my affliction,' she added, reverting to the conduct of her courtiers, which had so hurt and irritated her best feelings, 'not one of them had the decency to share in the mourning of their sovereign. Even my warden comes before me in his ordinary attire, but that is fairly excusable when it consists of corslet and head-piece hacked and dinted in my service.'

'Say not so, madam,' answered Bothwell, pointing to a sprig of willow worn in his basnet. 'I gathered yon sprig from the sallows that skirt its bank as I rode the water of Roslin in the misty dawn. I could not forget the day of my Queen's bereavement; and it shall never be told that Bothwell forbore to share the dangers or the sorrows of his sovereign.'

The angry colour that had brightened it all the morning died out on Mary's cheek. She looked at the Earl steadfastly while one might have counted ten, then her lip quivered. She turned her face away, and burst into tears.

CHAPTER IX

'"To arms!" the citizens bellow—"Alack!
These riders are loose in the town once more!"
But a good steel jack, and a friend to my back,
The Causeway I'll keep in the teeth of a score.
For never another can ruffle it here,
Like the lads of the snaffle, spur, and spear.'

We have seen Bothwell in his harness,—the loyal nobleman, the true knight, the Warden of the Marches, and Lieutenant of the Borders in the service of his Queen. A different personage, in truth, from wild James Hepburn, with his father's hot blood rioting in his veins, and his own propensities for evil, encouraged by a strong will and vigorous temperament, acting on a bad education, a weak brain, and a heart with just enough of good in it to make him lonely and unhappy.

Like his father, the profligate Earl Patrick, he was disposed by nature to take a leading part in all scenes of turbulence and strife; unlike that father, his better feelings would sometimes be permitted to influence his policy, and weaken his determination. Earl Patrick seems to have had a happy facility of ignoring all promises, bonds, and even oaths, when their observance became inconvenient, and would have scorned to allow his patriotism to stand for an hour in the way of his advancement. His son, with all his faults, was a Scotchman at heart; and, perhaps, like many another whose fate has served 'to point a moral or adorn a tale,' it wanted but the difference of a hair's breadth, at the right moment, to have made him as good as he turned out evil. Perhaps Bothwell's real sphere was riding his war-horse in mail and plate amongst the wild morasses of the marches. Perhaps he was never so happy as when engaged in hand-to-hand conflict with some daring marauder, a stalwart man-at-arms like himself—lance-thrust and sword-stroke freely dealt and stoutly received with but little ill-will on either side. Whilst his foe was in the saddle he would close with him gallantly, striking fiercely, and shouting, 'Queen Mary!' but, down upon the heather, the adversary of a moment ago became the helpless friend, to be set upon a horse and borne gently to Hermitage, there to be tended carefully till his wounds were cured, when he should be set free at a trifling ransom, to meet and fight it out again.

'Twas a wild adventurous life that of a southern Scottish nobleman in the days of the beautiful Stuart; yet not without its pleasures and its charm. He lived in his old keep, a petty monarch within his bounds, surrounded by adherents who would not scruple to shed every drop of their blood in the service of their chief. Bold, athletic, and self-reliant, he held his sway by the charter of his sword; he gained his revenues by the unfailing influence of 'snaffle, spur, and spear.' For his relaxation, he leapt on a good horse, and cast his hawk into the air, by the side of many a green nook and fresh brawling stream, or holloaed his hounds on the slot of the flying deer, scouring over the moorland, and bruising the fragrant heather beneath its hoofs. For the business of life, the same good horse came round to the door, champing under his steel frontlet, and the men-at-arms mustered on their bonny bay geldings with laugh and jest, and loud anticipations of plunder. The moon glinted coldly on steel jack and burnished head-piece as they clattered off, and the morning sun rose on the troop returning with its booty—driving jaded cattle before them with their long lances—encumbered with panting, footsore sheep—household plenishing on some of the saddles—armour hacked and besmirched—two or three bloody sconces beneath draggled plumes—and here and there a led horse, coming masterless home.

But the life was at least one of manhood and adventure; a good training for a soldier, and an invigorating substitute for the debaucheries in which, under other circumstances, these bold spirits would have been prone to indulge. When a border noble, with his train, rode into Edinburgh, the vintner hugged himself in his snow-white apron, and the canny burgher made his doors fast ere it was yet twilight, and resolved that no shouts for help on the causeway should lure him at night from his chimney corner into the troubled street.

Walter Maxwell, proceeding quietly up the High Street, and ruminating, not too pleasantly, on his prospects, found himself accosted by his new friend, 'Dick-o'-the-Cleugh,' as he was about to turn into his solitary lodging, and get through the evening as well as he could, reflecting on two unpleasant subjects—the continued coyness of his lady-love and his own diminished fortunes, for his employment at the Scottish court was more honourable than lucrative. To be in love usually makes a man unsociable; to be in debt often has a reverse effect. Maxwell, at all events, felt little disposed for an evening spent in his own company.

'I've been the length of Holyrood to see for you!' exclaimed the borderer with a boisterous welcome, 'and here I happen on you like a deer that's ta'en the double when the bloodhound is off the slot. Come away, man, come away; the warden's gotten a grand spread the night, an' I was bid to fetch ye, 'gin ye were in the Queen's presence! And noo', ye'll just gang in wi' me; ye ken we've an awfu' grip, we Liddesdale lads! an' I would like fine to see if ye can drink, man, as well as ye can fight. I'm thinkin' little Jock Elliott's no forgotten ye, Mr Maxwell!' And Dick laughed heartily at the recollection of his first acquaintance with his present companion.

Maxwell professed his readiness to accept the Earl's invitation, and linking his arm in that of the stalwart henchman, proceeded in the direction of Bothwell's lodging, the pair provoking no little ill-will from divers armed retainers in the street, who recognised the cognisance of the Hepburn, and some admiration from the maids and matrons of the Old Town, the latter especially approving of Dick's stalwart proportions and comely, good-natured face.

'Yon's a proper man!' observed a stout dame with her arms a-kimbo, to a dishevelled and dirty lady, emptying a pail of water scarcely more dirty than herself.

'He's no that ill,' replied the other, desisting from her operations to push back her tangled locks, that she might have a good look. 'Lass!' she added in shrill, impressive tones, 'he's a godless borderer. I ken them fine by their 'spauld-pieces.[3] He'll get his licks the night, I'm thinkin', an muckle guid may they do till him! It's no sae saft lyin' on the causeway as doun amang the moss-hags at hame!' After which ill-omened sentiment, she retired abruptly, shutting her door with a bang.

[3] Plates of steel that defended the arm and shoulder.

Honest Dick, however, took no notice of these and other less unpleasant remarks, but strode boldly on, discoursing, between bursts of merriment, on the encounter with little Jock Elliott, an assault of which he seemed to entertain a highly facetious remembrance.

'In here, man,' said he, turning up one of those offshoots from the main street, which is termed to this day 'a close,' and dragging Maxwell after him with obvious glee. 'I ken the place fine by the weather-marks forenent the wa'. It's an awfu' toon this, for a body to lose theirsel'! There's runnin' water too to guide a man,' pointing to a sluggish stream of filth that trickled under their feet; 'but it's no that clear that it is in Liddesdale. Up the stair, man; yer' welcome, nae fears!'

As Maxwell entered the apartment, a long, low room, plainly furnished and crowded with armed men, he was cordially greeted by the earl's retainers, who had mustered in great force. They had seen his hand keep his head, against heavy odds, and they warmed to him at once as a kindred nature. Their meal seemed to be concluded, but the serious part of the entertainment was yet to commence; and large jacks of strong ale, with flasks of wine, standing at no great intervals on the board, denoted ample means of quenching the thirst engendered by a long ride. The warden rose to greet his new guest with frank courtesy, and bade him to the upper end of the room, where he himself sat at a cross table surrounded by the most distinguished of his guests.

Bothwell had doffed his usual attire of steel jack and head-piece; he was now dressed in close-fitting doublet and hose, which set off the strong proportions of his figure to great advantage. Without pretensions to strict personal beauty, the warden had fine features, and a bold, frank bearing, not unpleasing. Though he had lost one of his eyes in a skirmish, the defect was scarcely observable, and the slight scar, left by the wound on his cheek and eyebrow, rather added to the characteristic expression of his face. It was that of a daring, perhaps a reckless man, one who was inured to danger and used to strife; yet was there something soft and even tender in his smile. Flushed with wine, and exchanging broad jests of the coarsest with his laughing guests, he looked a fitting leader in a revel or a charge; and yet a close observer would have detected a hollow ring in the loud laugh, a false note in the jovial strain, a capability for better things than feasting and fighting, and a self-accusing consciousness that it was lost and thrown away.

The mirth was at its highest. If Bothwell was splendidly dressed, his costume was but sombre when compared with that of his princely guest, the Marquis d'Elbœuf, who shone with satin and jewellery in all the florid brilliancy of French decoration. If the warden's draughts were deep, and his toasts objectionable, the Lords John and Robert Stuart, the Queen's half-brothers, pledged him freely and out-talked him shamelessly, with a happy mixture of juvenile thirst and royal audacity. When Maxwell took his seat at the upper table, amidst these and two or three more of the wilder gallants of the Court, the wine had circulated freely, and the spirits of the party had risen to that point at which discretion ceases to interfere, and reason begins to discover that she has been all day in the wrong. D'Elbœuf flung himself into the spirit of the scene with the keen zest of his nation. The Admiral of France was the last man to refuse a challenge from friend or foe.

'You shall pledge me in turn, Bothwell,' said he, filling a large silver measure with wine. 'Every man of you shall do me reason. These wild lads, who ought to be nephews of my own, and who drink as if they were grandsons of Charlemagne; Mr Maxwell, there, who has just come in, and must be suffocated with thirst; your huge squire of the body, who might hold a cask; and all your gentlemen riders, rovers on land, as their chief used to be at sea. What, Count Bothwell! We have not forgotten the breeze off shore, and the bold Norwegian coast.'

'Nay, Marquis,' answered Bothwell, filling himself a bumper, 'my Liddesdale lads will drink any toast you please, if they like the liquor. But down on the marches we have a saying that "he who rides in the dark should dismount before daylight," and faith, now that I am on shore, I have forgotten all about the coast of Norway and the wild North Sea, once for all.'

'The toast! the toast!' exclaimed Lord John Stuart. 'Let us have the drink first, marquis, and the tale of the warden's wicked doings afterwards. There's something in this wine that makes a man marvellously thirsty.'

'Waifs and strays!' replied the marquis, holding his beaker above his head. 'Count Bothwell first taught me the rights of an admiral on neutral seas. Pledge me, gentlemen; the toast is quite in your own line.' And d'Elbœuf, laughingly heartily, set his cup on the board—empty.

A dark flush swept over Bothwell's brow. A man does not always like to be reminded of his past exploits, but the company were clamorous for an explanation of the Frenchman's toast, and d'Elbœuf had drunk too much wine to disappoint them.

'We were lying off the coast of Norway,' said the admiral, 'and our host here in his armed galliot, with the Lion of Scotland at the main, was never tired of cruising about in search of adventures. He was Admiral of Scotland, as I of France; but whilst I waited for fortune, I think he followed the jade and grasped her by the hair. Some pirates had fired a village and were carrying off the inhabitants, when your warden here caught the knaves, red-handed, in the bay;—we make short work with these gentry at sea, where ropes are so convenient, and he strung them up to the yard-arm by dozens, like Normandy apples on a tree. The poor captives were too rejoiced to go back to the ashes of their dwellings; but a breeze springing up from the land, our friend here was obliged to make sail, carrying off, inadvertently, two or three trifles belonging to the village; amongst others, a fair girl with blue eyes and golden hair, who had once inhabited the principal house. I was on board the galliot some six weeks afterwards at an entertainment given by our host, where we drank nearly as much wine as we are like to do to-night, and this fair lass filled my cup and emptied her own, nothing loth, as though she relished her wine and her company. "But shall you not send her back?" said I to my host, seeing that she had been already six weeks on board. "Shall you not send her back before her friends lose patience and a complaint is made at Court, and a coil, all for a pair of merry eyes and a wisp of yellow hair?" "Not yet," answered your warden. "Not yet. Do you not know that waifs and strays belong to the admiral?"'

A loud laugh followed d'Elbœuf's explanation. The sentiment was quite in accordance with the company, and the point of his narrative, turning as it did on an act of illegal appropriation, was hugely enjoyed by the carousing borderers.

There were two exceptions, however, to the general merriment. Bothwell looked grave, more sorrowful, perhaps, than displeased; and honest 'Dick-o'-the-Cleugh,' smiting a sledgehammer fist on the table that made the beakers leap again, burst out—

'Puir lassie! It's ill liftin' a bairn from the ingle, or a lamb from the fauld!'

The wine was, by this time, producing its effect on the company. The men-at-arms were beginning to flush and talk thick, descanting, without much regard for listeners, on the merits of their horses and their own prowess, both in fighting and carrying off the property of their neighbours; the latter branch of their profession being obviously esteemed equally honourable with, and the natural prelude to, or consequence of, the former. Even Maxwell's brain was somewhat heated; albeit, he was naturally of a temperament on which wine is slow to take effect, and his late arrival had spared him some of the pledges of the borderers; although, to do them justice, they evinced a most hospitable desire to make up for lost time. Bothwell, too, who had been plunged in gloomy fits of abstraction, and who seemed to rouse himself with difficulty from some engrossing subject of meditation, was now getting as hilarious as the rest. D'Elbœuf was full of smiles and spirits, and scraps of French songs, somewhat wasted on his audience; whilst Lord John, whose ruling passion was of course in the ascendant, proposed gravely to dance a measure amongst the jugs and drinking cups on the table, and actually mounted a chair as the first step towards that difficult performance.

At this juncture, a ray of moonlight streaming through the narrow windows, athwart the glare of lamps and torches, gave a new turn to the impulses of the merry-makers.

'It'll be a bra' night this in Liddesdale,' observed 'Dick-o'-the-Cleugh,' who was given to sentiment in his cups.

'A rare night for a foray!' exclaimed Lord Robert, producing from the interior of his bonnet two or three black velvet masks, such as were then frequently worn in cities by both sexes.

'Shall we have a cruise, admiral?' said Bothwell. 'I doubt not I can find you in vizards, for you and I are both well enough known in Edinburgh to meet fewer friends than foes.'

D'Elbœuf agreed cordially to the proposal. Like his countrymen in general, he was averse to continuous hard-drinking, and a night of adventure in the town was more to his taste than a steady carouse with these inexhaustible borderers. His host, too, appeared in the restless mood of a man who has some secret pain goading him to action. The more he drank, the fiercer seemed to grow the impulse to be doing. When the arch-tempter wants a tool that shall be at once keen and strong, he takes a bold vigorous nature; he humbles it in its own eyes; he wounds it in its best affections; he whispers, 'do to others as *they have done* unto you;' then he tempers it in the furnace of memory, and sharpens it carefully on the grindstone of remorse; finally, he steeps it in rough strong wine; after that, it is fit for anything, and will cut through steel harness and muslin fold with vindictive impartiality.

Masks for the party were soon produced in sufficient number, and these, with their cloaks or plaids, would be disguise enough in the event of the night's amusement growing to a breach of the laws, such being, by no means, an unlikely result. The warden desired his retainers to sit still and continue drinking till his return—directions with which they showed no unwillingness to comply; but as the masked party, brandishing their torches, shouting, singing, and laughing, descended the stair into the close, 'Dick-o'-the-Cleugh' whispered to Maxwell to get his sword and accompany him.

'There'll be mair pows than ane crackit the night, or all's done,' remarked the borderer. 'The warden's no canny when he's crossit. Aince the whingars be oot, I'm no thinkin' muckle o' yon' Frenchman, an' thae wild lads is clean wud wi' drink. We'll be nane the waur o' a decent body like yoursel', Mr Maxwell, just to strike in an' see fair play.'

With the exception of a slight delay in the close, to witness Lord John's performance of his promised hornpipe, the effect of which was somewhat marred by the gutter traversing the pavement, nothing occurred to check the progress of the rioters. Save for themselves, the street lay utterly quiet and deserted in the cold moonlight. The party, linking arms, reeled and swaggered on, followed, at no long interval, by 'Dick-o'-the-Cleugh' and Maxwell, both tolerably sober.

Presently, Bothwell halted at the door of the only house from which lights were shining.

'What say you, gentlemen?' laughed the warden. 'I know Master Craig, the mercer, well. It seems that he is expecting us. Shall we go in and take our rere-supper with pretty Mistress Alison, his daughter?'

'By all means!' exclaimed d'Elbœuf. 'The best dressed damsel that walks the High Street on Sundays. I should know her anywhere by the orange stripes on her farthingale.'

'And the bonniest lass on Leith Sands at the merry-making to-day,' added Lord Robert. 'I little thought when I gave her her fairings this morning, I should sup with her to-night!'

'The neatest foot and the tightest stocking in the Old Town,' said Lord John, 'and the best dancer to boot. Knock at the door, Bothwell, and bid them let us in, in the devil's name!'

Concealing themselves under the wall of the house, the party waited, with much stifled merriment, the result of Bothwell's application for admittance.

His cautious knock was at first unanswered, but on repetition, the light was observed to be obscured at one of the windows, and a female head, scarcely so well arranged as that of Mistress Alison herself, was thrust into the moonlight, the owner demanding, in a guarded whisper, 'What's your wull?'

'Go down and unbar the door,' answered Bothwell, in like tones of secrecy, and pulling his mask carefully over his face. 'We have come to sup with your mistress.'

'It's the earl!' the girl was heard to say, turning round obviously to hold parley with some one in the room; and then another voice whispered in softer tones, 'Is it you, my lord?'

'Why, of course it is!' answered Bothwell, somewhat surprised, nevertheless, that he should be so easily recognised.

'I have expected you this hour and more,' was the reply, as the two figures moved at once from the window.

'The devil you have!' observed the warden, now completely puzzled; 'then why don't you come down and open the door?'

Presently bars were heard to be withdrawn, and the party of rioters, if we may so term them, marshalled themselves in close order, prepared, if necessary, to go in with a rush. The door, however, was only partially unclosed, and the figure of a strapping serving-wench guarded the narrow interstice. She seemed less satisfied than her mistress, and inclined to hold further parley.

'Hoo will I ken it's you?' said she, shading the candle with her large coarse hand.

But the caution was too late. Lord John's shoulder was by this time applied to the door. Lord Robert blew out the candle, and the Admiral of France, with characteristic gallantry and national politeness, stifled the outcry of the astonished damsel in the dark.

The assailants had now gained the body of the place, still keeping their masks on, and with noiseless footsteps they ascended the stair; Maxwell and 'Dick-o'-the-Cleugh,' who had neither of them much stomach for the adventure, remaining at the door to keep watch.

The others turned into a comfortable parlour in which fire and lights were burning, as if to make them thoroughly at home. A delicate little supper, with a flask or two of wine, stood on the table, and a very smartly dressed lady, not without beauty of a bold, imposing style, rose to welcome them.

As Bothwell entered, this gaudy-looking dame seemed about to rush into his arms, but observing that he did not remove his mask, and was accompanied by three or four others, she checked herself, and remained standing in the middle of the room as if not altogether mistress of the position.

The warden, bowing low, advanced to take her hand, and Mistress Alison suffered him to do so, with an expression of ludicrous uncertainty on her handsome face.

'Will you not unmask, my lord?' said she; 'though late, you are welcome, and so are your friends. Why did you bring them with you?' she added, in a troubled whisper.

It was impossible to carry on the deception any longer; and by this time the laughter of the party had been so long smothered as to defy further restraint. With many apologies and courtly compliments and honeyed phrases, interrupted by bursts of merriment, one and all unmasked, disclosing to the bewildered Mistress Alison the features of quite another earl from her expected guest, and of three or four of the wildest gallants at Holyrood, with whom, nevertheless, she was not entirely unacquainted.

One of the most beautiful qualities in woman is her pliant nature, her tendency to adapt herself to circumstances, the readiness with which, in the absence of white bread, she contents herself with brown. Of this amiable facility the mercer's daughter now afforded a striking instance. Bidden or unbidden, *here* were the gallants,—good-looking, amusing, and well-dressed; and *there* was the supper. Mistress Alison did not hesitate long.

'You will not depart without breaking bread,' said she, pointing to the well-covered table, with courteous hospitality.

Lord Robert filled himself a bumper on the spot.

'Pledge us, fair Mistress Alison!' said he; 'a cup of wine will restore the bloom to that damask cheek, paled with the alarm of our sudden arrival.'

The lady drank and smiled. It is but fair to observe that, notwithstanding his lordship's polite fiction, the 'damask cheek' had never paled, nor Mistress Alison lost her presence of mind for an instant. Perhaps she was not entirely unused to these impromptu supper-parties.

Merrily they sat down, heaping their cloaks, and swords, and masks in the corner of the room, their hostess only stipulating against too much noise, and insisting that her guests should not disturb the repose of the honest mercer who slept above.

Mistress Alison seemed tolerably familiar with the private history of her company, and the general gossip of the Court. As she displayed the turn of her round arm, and close-fitting bodice, while filling plates and drinking-cups, she had a jeer, or a sarcasm, or a compliment for each. She congratulated d'Elbœuf on the conquest he had made of her serving-woman, who, never having seen a live Frenchman before, gazed at the admiral open-mouthed. She twitted the two Stuarts with their approaching bondage that should put an end to all such midnight pranks.

'For,' said Mistress Alison, 'in less than a week, ye'll both be dancing in fetters to the tune of "Wooed and married an' a'," and the bonny brides will have gotten the two most graceless gallants in Scotland for their grooms; and as sure as death, I'll see the wedding, if I creep into the palace through the buttery window! Ay, my Lord Bothwell! you're bold riders, you Hepburns; but the bonny lass that thinks to tame wild John Stuart, is the boldest amongst you all. Well, well! it's a good steed that'll gallop till dawn. Once she gets into the saddle, she'll daunton[4] him, never fear!'

[4] Daunton, to tame; or familiarly, to cow—from the French *dompter*.

A loud laugh rewarded this sally at the expense of the young noblemen, who were indeed making the most of their remaining hours of freedom; and Lord John, who was about to marry Bothwell's sister, was so delighted with the conversation, that he took Mistress Alison's hand and proposed that they should dance a measure together on the spot.

But the lady had no intention that her agreeable visitors should remain for too long a period. In the midst of her mirth she had never entirely got rid of a certain air of apprehension, and twice or thrice she had stopped in the middle of a sentence as if to listen. All at once she turned pale, *really* pale this time, and set her goblet down untasted.

'For any sake! my lord,' she exclaimed, with an imploring look at Bothwell, 'go your ways now. I can let you down the back stair. Go your ways, gentlemen, I entreat you, or there will be blood spilt before all's done!'

Already the tramp of feet and altercation of voices had been heard in the street; now the clink of steel fell familiarly on the ears of the guests upstairs. They rose to their feet, and commenced buckling on their swords simultaneously.

'We are, indeed, fortunate,' observed d'Elbœuf in high glee; 'a jovial carouse, a delightful supper-party, and a midnight fray, all without the slightest trouble or inconvenience.'

'For the love of mercy, begone!' pleaded Mistress Alison, pushing them, one after another, to the door. 'For *my* sake, for *any* sake, for *all* our sakes! They're breaking in the door! They're coming up the stair! It's the earl; as sure as death, it's the earl!'

'What earl?' laughed Bothwell, carelessly, and yet curious to know the name of the favoured nobleman, for whom the supper they had just eaten was prepared.

'The Earl of Arran, of course!' replied Mistress Alison, blushing through her tears. 'It's too late now, for their swords are out and their blood up, and the street full of the red-handed Hamiltons! What will I do? What will I do?'

Pending further measures, Mistress Alison covered her head with her mantle and cried piteously.

Bothwell smiled grimly in his beard when he heard the name of Arran. They were none of the best of friends, the Hepburns and the Hamiltons, at any time. To-night, the warden's heart thrilled with a fierce pleasure at the thought of crossing swords with their chieftain's son.

'Draw, gentlemen,' exclaimed Bothwell, putting himself at the head of the party. 'A Hepburn! a Hepburn to the rescue! draw, and follow me!'

Thus shouting, he rushed to the stair-head, followed by his friends, who appeared, one and all, as ready for the fray as they had proved themselves for the feast.

The door had, indeed, been broken open, but the narrow entrance was still filled, and stoutly defended by the stalwart figure of the warden's henchman. Though the odds were fearfully against him, his great strength and familiarity with his weapon had enabled him to make a gallant defence against the assailants, who were closing round him. At the first alarm (and the borderer's quick ear had caught the step of armed men approaching, long before they came in sight) he had entreated Maxwell to return for the assistance of his comrades, who were sure to be found still carousing in Bothwell's lodging. That gentleman used his own discretion in preferring to turn out the city-guard; but of this intention the other was ignorant. 'Dick-o'-the-Cleugh' never doubted he could keep the door single-handed till assistance should arrive.

Thrust and blow and parry succeeded each other with fearful rapidity. The borderer was long of limb and in capital wind; moreover, his heart was as true as the steel in his hand; but three or four to one will beat the best of swordsmen, and he was overpowered at last, and driven back towards the stair.

At this crisis a desperate charge of fresh combatants, led by Bothwell from above, came opportunely to the rescue. It cleared the hall and the door, which was instantaneously closed and barred by the ready-witted serving-woman. Assailants and assailed now found themselves carrying on the combat in the street.

The skirmish became general. The Hamiltons mustered in force, and came swarming to the assistance of their kinsmen. Bothwell's riders, too disturbed from their carouse, arrived by twos and threes, and the superiority of their arms and training made them formidable partisans. Inured, as all Scotchmen were in those days, to blows and bloodshed, strife was the natural element of the borderer, and, drunk or sober, he was always ready for a fight.

The Old Town was soon disturbed from its repose—peaceful citizens leaped from their beds, and ran to the windows; night-capped heads were thrust out into the moonlight, to watch the tumult in the street below, as it waved backwards and forwards in the vicissitudes of the struggle. There was but little outcry; for men's passions were thoroughly aroused, and they were fighting to the death. Sometimes a hollow groan, or a heavy fall on the stones, contrasted dully with the scuffle of feet and the clash of steel. Sometimes a fierce oath accompanied a shrewder blow than common, or a deadly thrust that had been driven desperately home; but there were few shots exchanged, and in the hand-to-hand conflict, the Hamiltons were gradually losing ground.

Once Bothwell succeeded in reaching his enemy, and exchanged a couple of passes with Arran; but the Hamiltons rallied round their chieftain's son, and the warden, grinding his teeth with rage, was compelled to forego his revenge.

Several wounded, and more than one corpse, encumbered the street; the fray was getting serious, and even 'Dick-o'-the-Cleugh' seemed to think it was an affair more of business than pleasure, when the common bell began to toll loudly, and the city-guard, guided by Walter Maxwell, and commanded by no less a personage than Lord James Stuart himself, made its appearance on the scene.

These hardy burghers, well-armed, and confident in the sympathies, and, if necessary, the assistance of the townsfolk, thrust themselves boldly between the combatants; Lord James, on whose thoughtful brow could be traced no more excitement than ordinary, himself striking up the weapons of either party, as he bade them lay down their arms in the Queen's name.

Bothwell had just reached Arran for the second time. The warden's eye glared wickedly and the froth was white on his moustache. Arran, pale as death, and with madness flaring in his looks, struggled to meet his enemy, shouting wildly and incoherently in a paroxysm of insanity.

Their swords had actually crossed when Lord James struck in between. His face was calm and unmoved; nay, there was a lurking satisfaction in his eye, for, to the plotting diplomatist, there is always gain in the differences of the powerful; but to-night it was Lord James's cue rather to stifle than foment such dissensions, and he wished also to stand well with the citizens by quelling a disturbance that had alarmed the town.

'For shame, gentlemen,' said he, beating down their weapons with the sheathed sword. 'For shame! you, Arran, her near kinsman; and you, Bothwell, in whom she trusts. What will the Queen say when she hears of it?'

The red blood faded from the warden's angry brow at Mary Stuart's name, and sinking the point of his sword, he fell back with a look of deep shame and contrition. In his fiercest moments that spell was sufficient to make him docile as a child.

Not so Arran. With a wild shriek of rage, he darted a savage thrust at the peace-maker, that, had it taken effect, might have spared Scotland much bloodshed and Mary Stuart many a tear, for her wily bastard-brother would never have moved again. It was not fated, however, to reach its object; for 'Dick-o'-the-Cleugh's' quick eye caught the movement, and he parried it with a force and rapidity that shivered Arran's blade in pieces, and beat it from his hand. His retainers now gathered round their leader, and forced him from the ground, the unfortunate maniac raving and writhing in their grasp.

Bothwell, too, got his men in order, and withdrew them, submitting patiently to the rebukes of Lord James. It is needless to observe, that on the first appearance of their grave brother, the Lords John and Robert had taken to flight, closely followed by d'Elbœuf, who did not wish to figure as a brawler at his niece's court. The warden alone remained to bear the blame, and, now that the excitement had cooled, he bitterly regretted what he had done.

As he was followed by his henchman, Lord James called the latter back.

'Let me look in your face, good fellow,' said he; 'you have saved my life to-night.'

'The redder's lick is aye the warst in the fray,' answered the other, good-humouredly; 'and doubtless your honour was no takin' notice, and it must have gone clean through ye,' he added, dogmatically.

'You have saved my life,' repeated Lord James. 'I leave no scores unpaid for, good or evil, and if ever the time should come, I shall not forget the debt I owe you.'

But 'Dick-o'-the-Cleugh' shook his head doubtfully. 'I'm no sae dooms sure o' that,' said he, as he strode on after his chief. 'An' I wad like ill to be beholden to a man that could part sic a bonny fray. Oh, man!' he added to Maxwell, who had now joined him, 'what garred ye bring in the burgher-guard? The drink was just dyin' out in our lads, and we wad ha' gotten the grandest ploy I've seen sin' I cam' out of Carlisle jail.'

CHAPTER X

'Away! away! thou traitor strang!

Out of my sicht soon mayst thou be!

I granted never a traitor grace,

And now I'll not begin with thee.'

It was with no agreeable feelings, that Maxwell received a summons to attend the Council at Holyrood the morning after the fray. Ere he had well slept off the fatigues and dissipation of the previous night, he was disturbed by a pursuivant in the royal livery, with the lion emblazoned on his surcoat, who required his immediate presence at the palace, and from whose rigid sense of duty he found it difficult to extort permission to summon 'Dick-o'-the Cleugh' as a witness in his favour.

Maxwell reflected that the borderer's straightforward testimony would serve to exonerate him from any share in the disturbance, except the measures which put a stop to it; and by dint of argument, remonstrance, and a bonnet-piece or two, he succeeded in sending a message to Bothwell himself, who, for reasons of his own, was only too ready to despatch his henchman in reply.

As they proceeded together towards the palace, attended by the pursuivant and four stout men-at-arms, 'Dick-o'-the-Cleugh' could by no means be brought to consider their past broil in the light of a breach of the peace. On the contrary, he esteemed it from beginning to end as the simple and natural consequence of a jaunt to the capital, and was fully persuaded that their present expedition must result in a vote of praise to all concerned.

Yet the borderer's iron nerves seemed affected as they entered the precincts of the Abbey. He was unusually restless, and glanced hither and thither, as though in expectation. Certain female tones in the garden by no means restored his composure; and while Maxwell, with a thrill of offended pride, that was yet longing to forgive, recognised Mary Carmichael's well-known voice, Dick nudged him vigorously with his elbow, and whispered—

'Ye'll hae to speak up for the twae o' us, Mr Maxwell. I was aye dashed wi' the women-folk; an' it's like they'll no let us away the day without gettin' a sight o' the Queen and her leddies. Man, I would like fine to see them in their braws!'

Ere Walter could reply, a gentleman-usher beckoned him silently to advance, while two stout men-at-arms, crossing their axes in front of his follower, gave 'Dick-o'-the-Cleugh' to understand he must wait till he was sent for. Unusual vigilance seemed to pervade the palace. The guard was doubled on the staircase and in the galleries, whilst a strong body of cavalry occupied the court.

As Maxwell's conductors halted at the door of the council-chamber, the former felt his wonted composure sadly disturbed by the appearance of Mary Carmichael, who was crossing from the garden towards the Queen's apartments. She started and blushed vividly when she met his eye, and then, observing him to be under escort, turned pale with obvious apprehension. She stopped, too, as if she would fain speak with him; but after an imploring glance that seemed to entreat his forgiveness, and assure him of her sympathy, hurried away.

So strangely constituted is the human mind, even in those who most pride themselves on their philosophy, that Maxwell felt his heart lighter than it had been for a week, and entered the awful presence of the council without the slightest appearance of dismay; and yet he had not exchanged a syllable with her, had only caught her eye for an instant, and heard the rustle of her garments as she passed. Surely there is some strange magic in our nature that works below the surface, and encircles the bravest and the strongest in its spells.

In the centre of the room, which Maxwell now entered, stood a massive oak table, covered with papers and parchments, prepared for the sign-manual of Mary Stuart. Around it were seated those Scottish noblemen whose turn it was to assist the deliberations of their sovereign, thwarting indeed the free-will, and impeding her resolutions, yet constituting and considering themselves the trusty advisers of the crown.

The Duke of Chatelhérault, in right of his high rank and royal lineage, acted as president; and on his noble brow might be traced an expression of puzzled vexation as he followed in vain Secretary Maitland's rapid and masterly explanation of the business in hand. That astute diplomatist, carrying his colleagues triumphantly with him, was furnishing a brilliant display of rhetorical fireworks, to prove that the measure he now advocated (which had indeed for its object the placing of additional power in Lord James Stuart's hands) was the only possibility of saving the country; and the haughty Hamilton, dazzled rather than enlightened by his eloquence, looked as dissatisfied as a man generally does who is 'convinced against his will.'

The Queen's brother had assumed a modest and deprecating air, as who should say, 'I seek not authority, but only wish rigidly to fulfil the duties that are thrust upon me'—a sentiment he had already expressed to the council when they sat down. The others listened in different attitudes of attention or approval, according as their interests or their convictions led them to agree with the speaker; whilst Mary herself, whose chair was drawn a little apart from the table, looked up from her embroidery ever and anon in the face of her half-brother, with an expression of perfect confidence and affection. Though her noble intellect might detect many a flaw in her secretary's arguments, she was too thoroughly a woman not to be a *dishonest reasoner*; and of all the intriguers who backed Lord James in his efforts at supreme power, none supported him so fearlessly and confidingly as the Queen.

David Riccio sat, so to speak, under her Majesty's wing. His evident favour with his mistress extorted for him a certain outward deference and cold civility from the nobles; but he was already inclined to put himself too forward, without reflecting that the key of a lady's *escritoire* is but a frail weapon to meet a two-handed sword, and a velvet doublet a poor defence against the blow of a dudgeon-dagger.

When Maxwell was admitted, the State Secretary had just concluded his peroration, and was shuffling his papers together on the table with an air of business-like satisfaction. He looked up at this new arrival, however, with calm indifference, and spreading a blank sheet of paper before him, appeared ready to enter at once upon a new affair with fresh energy and attention.

Lord Ruthven, whose temper was none of the sweetest, and whose liking for the warden was of that kind which would fain have had a yard and a half of green turf, and the same measure of cold steel, between them, scowled upon Bothwell's kinsman with all the ferocity of which his stern features were capable—a compliment returned by Maxwell with a stare of undaunted defiance. Morton stole a rapid and sinister glance at the Queen, while his beard curled with his habitual sneering smile. Huntly, Argyle, and the rest, settled themselves into comfortable attitudes, as though the more important business of the morning were now disposed of.

The Duke of Chatelhérault, as the aggrieved person, was the first to speak. With a haughty affectation of indifference, he asked—

'Who is this witness? Is he of gentle birth?'

And being informed by Maitland that he was a kinsman of Earl Bothwell, his Grace replied, indignantly—

'An impartial witness ye have brought before the council! Why not examine the earl himself? if, indeed, he acknowledges any authority but border-law. It is well that the Hamiltons can right themselves with their own good swords.'

Maitland cut short his further objections by desiring Maxwell to proceed with his account of the fray, while the Queen looked up from her work as if about to expostulate, but checked herself with a half-smothered sigh.

Maxwell told his tale simply and frankly. It was obvious that the fray had originated in a brawl begun by the Hamiltons, who had insisted on forcing their way into Mistress Alison's house. Seeing that bloodshed was unavoidable, he had hurried off to alarm the civic guard, leaving the earl's henchman at the door. When he returned, the skirmish, as Lord James could corroborate, was at its height. The henchman could speak to what took place during the narrator's absence; he had craved permission to bring him to Holyrood for that purpose.

His manly, straightforward evidence seemed to make a favourable impression on the council. Maitland looked up from his notes, and, glancing at the duke for approval, desired the borderer to be summoned.

Honest Dick entered the council-chamber with an undaunted front, till he caught sight of the Queen, when he blushed up to his ears, and made a profound and exceedingly awkward obeisance. Then he looked about as if in search of something, and finally stood bolt upright, like a man prepared to be 'shot at.'

'Your name?' said the duke, haughtily.

Dick reflected a few moments, and then answered, with the air of one who makes an admission under protest—

'Dick-o'-the-Cleugh.'

'Your calling?' added the president, severely.

'Just a rider,' answered Dick, after another pause.

The nobles glanced significantly at each other, and Huntly observed, with a smile—

'That is another word for thief in your country, is it not?'

Dick looked extremely demure and unconscious, as he replied—

'Na, it's broken men they ca' thieves on the border—just like Catherans an' Gordons an' that in the North.'

The council could not forbear a laugh, and even the Queen bent over her work to conceal her amusement.

'Faith, Huntly, he shivered his lance fairly against thy breastplate this time,' said Lord Seton; and Huntly, throwing his portly person back in his chair, vowed good-humouredly that the definition was a sufficiently precise one at either extremity of the kingdom.

The borderer's examination then proceeded.

'Was it by your chief's orders that you defended the door in the High Street last night?'

'I took nae orders yestre'en frae the warden,' replied Dick, 'forbye to see to the naigs about our back-coming.'

'Would you have ventured to draw upon the Earl of Arran—upon my son,' asked the duke, 'without your chief's express commands to slay him if you came across him?'

'I ken your Grace fine,' answered the borderer, not very directly, 'seein' you're the grandest nobleman in Scotland; but if yon was the Earl of Arran, an' a' your Grace's blood fight like yon camsteary chiel, I wad like ill to keep the causeway anither nicht frae the Hamiltons.'

'What was the origin of the disturbance?' here interposed Secretary Maitland, seeing that the discussion produced no obvious results. 'Who began the brawl, man, and first bared steel?'

'I could not say,' replied Dick, looking profoundly ignorant. 'I'm thinkin' the stramash was a' in gude fellowship, till his honour here, the Lord James, an' the city guard struck in an' spoilt all.'

'Why, you yourself were at half-sword with a score of them when I came up,' said Lord James, laughing, in spite of himself, at the borderer's coolness.

'Oo! that was just a ploy!' answered Dick, with a grin of delight at the recollection. 'I've seen waur licks than yon gi'en an' ta'en in Bewcastle Markit, just for gude-will ye ken, an' a tass or twa o' brandy.'

'Let him go,' said the duke, 'till we send for him again. It is not against this faithful knave, your Majesty and my lords, that I appeal for justice, but against the Earl of Bothwell.'

Again Morton shot a lurid glance at the Queen, whose white fingers were travelling fast to and fro through her embroidery.

'The earl had entered the house peacefully enough when I left,' began Maxwell, but he was sternly and peremptorily commanded to hold his peace, whilst a whispered consultation was carried on by the chief nobility present, in which Lord James alone took no part.

The Queen, with an angry spot on each cheek, continued to work very fast.

'It is but a part of the plot against Her Majesty's person,' said the duke, after a while, 'a plot which my son himself has discovered, and which on his recovery he will prove on the Earl of Bothwell's body with his blade. Meantime, there lies my glove; if the Hepburn has a friend, let him take it up!'

Maxwell interposed, eagerly.

'To any one of my own degree,' he began—but an imploring glance from the Queen at her brother had roused that statesman from his apathy, and he interfered.

'Take back your glove, my Lord Duke!' said he. 'This is no affair of private brawl, but a matter in which the safety of the crown is involved. My lords, I move for a committee of inquiry on the spot.'

The duke bit his glove through, ere he replaced it on his hand, and then, with moody brow and angry eye, listened in silence to the conference.

'I move that James Hepburn, Earl of Bothwell, be committed to ward till such time as he can purge himself from the charges brought against him by the Earl of Arran,' said Lord Ruthven, after another brief consultation, with a smile of triumph on his pale, gaunt face.

With the exception of Seton and Argyle, who seemed to think the warden was receiving scant justice, and a weak remonstrance from Lord James, which yielded gracefully to the urgency of the case, the council agreed upon this precautionary measure, and it was carried accordingly.

Secretary Maitland made out the warrant for the earl's committal; it wanted but the Queen's signature to become valid.

Mary rose from her chair and drew up her majestic figure.

'Nay, my lords,' said she; 'it is surely unjust to condemn the absent without proof. Let the warden return to his charge on the border. He may render himself at any time, in less than twenty-four hours from Hermitage.'

'You cannot refuse to ratify the deed of your council!' urged Ruthven, fiercely. 'Nay, Madam, you *dare* not,' he added, with growing insolence; and would have said more; but Mary shot a glance at him, before which even his rugged nature quailed.

'Your Majesty's confidence in the earl is greater than that of your advisers,' observed Morton, not deigning to conceal a sneer. 'Already he boasts of his influence over the Queen, and vows that steel gauntlet shall not wrest him from Holyrood, though a white glove can lure him from Hermitage.'

The colour rose on Mary's brow, and her bosom heaved quickly. It was evident the Queen was wavering.

'It is but a measure of precaution,' argued Maitland, in his plausible off-hand tones, spreading at the same time the warrant before his sovereign. 'After all,' he added, 'it may be but a mere brawl about a wench! The Earl of Bothwell has ever been given to such follies overmuch.'

The Queen signed the paper hastily; then threw the pen on the table, and walked in silence from the council-chamber.

CHAPTER XI

'Oh! better for me that a blind-born child
Never a line I had learn'd to trace,
Than thus by a look and a laugh beguiled,
To have read my doom in fair Alice's face.

'And better for me to have made my bed
Under the yews where my fathers sleep,
Calm and quiet, at rest with the dead,
Than have given my heart to fair Alice to keep.'

So Bothwell was committed to ward in Edinburgh Castle, yet was his durance but of a temporary nature, and devoid of the customary rigours that accompany imprisonment. The warden made no effort to escape, although he had a strong party of friends about the Court, and might at any time have created considerable disturbance had he chosen to resist the royal authority; but he bowed his head to the blast with unexpected humility, and a submission, the result of mixed motives. He lived in daily expectation of release by the Queen's own authority. His appointment on the border had not yet been filled up, and Hermitage was still occupied by a staunch garrison who acknowledged no law but their chief's behests. Day by day did the warlike earl, pining, as well he might, for the free breeze on his brow and the swinging gallop of his steed, reflect on the effect which such devotion as his could not fail to produce on the Queen. Danger he had always faced readily for her sake; fatigue he had cheerfully endured; and now he submitted patiently to captivity, because it was Mary Stuart's will. Day by day he expected a pardon, a release, an acknowledgment, a communication, and day by day he was disappointed. 'Hope deferred maketh the heart sick;' but this proverb applies rather to weak natures; in strong, it is apt to make the heart savage. Stung by what he conceived to be ingratitude, irritated by neglect, sore from conflicting feelings, such as rend an ill-disciplined character with pangs to which mere physical suffering is comparative relief, those weeks spent in Edinburgh Castle produced an effect on Bothwell's disposition that after years could never eradicate. Even 'Dick-o'-the-Cleugh,' who remained in attendance on his master, and who was free to come and go at his pleasure, shook his head gravely, and averred that 'confinement was just destruction baith to man an' beast! He would like fine to see the warden ridin' the Marches again wi' the Liddesdale lads at his back.'

But though Dick thus expressed himself, and doubtless meant what he said, he was conscious in his heart that the banks of the Esk and the braes of Teviotdale would never be the same to him again. The brawny borderer had a new interest in life now, strange to say, unconnected with hawk or hound, with morning chase or midnight foray, with axe or lance, or mighty stoups of ale.

Once in the week it was Mary Seton's custom to visit the town of Edinburgh on foot, to make purchases for her mistress and her comrades, of those odds and ends which ladies consume in such wonderful quantities. The wilful little damsel had taken a great fancy to the borderer, as you may see a child sometimes pleased with a huge Newfoundland dog. Such attachments are not remarkable for reciprocity. The biped, half-pitiful, half-amused, entertains a feeble liking for so faithful an attendant; the quadruped wishes no better lot than to serve its little idol slavishly all its life, and die licking its hand. How the child cuffs it and teases it, and makes the noble animal ridiculous, pulling its ears and tail!

'Dick-o'-the-Cleugh' had but one day now in his week instead of seven. He observed, not without inward gratulation, that his attendance on these saints' days, so to speak, was by no means unwelcome; and Mary Seton, on her return to the palace, never omitted to inform the Queen that she had seen Earl Bothwell's henchman, neither did her mistress take her to task herself, nor suffer Mary Beton to do so, for these interviews.

So the strangely matched pair moved along the High Street, and the lady, who, in addition to his other good qualities, had discovered the borderer to be a capital listener, told him the Court news, for the edification of his chief, with considerable volubility.

'We're all in confusion now,' said she, one bright winter's day, as she tripped along the cleaner portion of the pavement with a light basket in her hand, which sometimes as a great favour she permitted her Newfoundland to carry, while that faithful animal stamped contentedly alongside in the gutter. 'The palace is turned inside out. We have got the "new acquaintance" at Holyrood.'

Dick looked as if he didn't understand, and yet did not quite like the information. Something that would have been jealousy in a more presumptuous admirer, shot through his great frame. Had he been physically a retriever, he would have put his tail between his legs.

'I dinna like acquaintances,' said he, looking *down* at her bodily a foot or so; looking *up* at her metaphorically any number of yards. 'Give me friends, Mistress Seton, auld friends, an' no too mony o' them.'

'You wouldn't like this acquaintance!' laughed the young lady, merrily, whereat her companion looked on her admiringly, as one who listens to sweet music. 'He's an acquaintance that would put *you* on your back readily, for as strong as you think yourself; he has overcome the Queen and the household and Mr Randolph and Mary Beton, and all of them but *me*.'

'No,' replied the borderer. He did not the least understand what she meant, but admired her intensely, nevertheless.

'It's the sickness,'[5] at last she condescended to explain, between bursts of laughter at her companion's puzzled countenance. 'There are but two of the Queen's ladies fit for duty at all—Mary Carmichael and me; and she is so occupied with your chief's kinsman, Mr Maxwell, that she couldn't be more useless if she was ill in bed. The Court is as dull as ditch-water, and I shall have to walk up this weary hill to do everybody's business twice a week instead of once; that is the upshot of it.'

> [5] An epidemic that prevailed at the Court, answering to the indisposition which we now term *influenza*, and mentioned by Randolph in his letters to Cecil.

A ray of intense pleasure gleamed on her listener's face at this announcement; but it clouded over a minute afterwards, and he asked with undisguised anxiety, 'If there was no danger for herself?'

The girl could not but feel gratified at his obvious interest in her safety; but she laughed again, and answered, merrily—

'Do you think nobody can be bold who is not six foot high? I fear sickness, I tell you, as little as you fear Lord Scrope, and hate it perhaps more; and yet you have the best of it, too. I had rather face death on an open moor than in closed bed-curtains. I wonder if anybody would miss me much?' she added, more to herself than him, for the grave chord had somehow been struck in her thoughtless character.

He did not answer, and when she looked at him, his face was turned away.

'Do you think they would?' she proceeded, with the pertinacity of a spoiled child. 'Stranger things have come to pass. You might be riding merrily in Liddesdale, whilst Mary Seton was lying stark and cold under the Abbey stones.'

'It would be a dark day in Liddesdale,' was all the answer he made; but he would not let her see his face, and his voice sounded as it had never done before.

A tinge of remorse, such as that which the urchin feels when he takes a bird's-nest, smote almost unconsciously at the girl's heart; yet was the sensation, though pathetic, by no means unpleasant.

She laughed and bantered him more than usual during their walk; but on that day, and indeed every day afterwards till he returned to the border, she suffered him to carry her basket; and the honest retriever, proud of his degradation, followed at her heel, with ever-increasing fidelity and devotion. The bird's-nest was taken now, and it is no use attempting to put such articles back again; moreover, it had been thoroughly harried, emptied clean of its treasures, and all the eggs were in that one basket.

CHAPTER XII

'Oh! is my basnet a widow's curch,
Or my lance a wand of the willow tree,
Or my arm a lady's lily hand,
That an English lord should lightly me?'

Unusual silence prevailed in the lofty hall of Hermitage, and the dinner hour, commonly one of mirth and festivity, arrived with a solemn gravity, by no means welcome to the light-hearted borderers. It was in vain that large joints of beef and mutton steamed on the long tables, and ample baskets, piled to the edge with coarse oaten bread, stood side by side with deep measures of foaming ale below the salt, while a modest display of plate, in which one or two church ornaments were conspicuous, decked the upper end of the board. The preparations, indeed, smacked of good cheer, but the hilarity which promotes digestion was wanting.

The master-spirit, gloomy, morose, and preoccupied, walked to and fro under the stag's antlers, at the extremity of the hall, and no man dared to question or interrupt his meditations.

Bothwell was indeed chafing to the verge of madness. In vain he had submitted patiently to a mock imprisonment at the Queen's pleasure; in vain he had waited till days grew to weeks and weeks to months for some acknowledgment from Mary of the injustice she had done him—some expression of sorrow or sympathy for the loyal soldier and devoted vassal. No acquittal came, no reprieve, no message. Desperate and goaded he had escaped from his confinement at last, and fled to Hermitage, where he now found himself, as autumn waned, in the anomalous attitude of an attainted subject holding a royal fortress, and a warden of the Marches, without the privilege of communicating with his sovereign. It has been truly said that no position is so false as that which entails responsibility without conferring authority, and of this he found himself too keenly conscious. Neither was Bothwell's a nature to submit patiently to a slight. Hot-headed and irascible, with strong feelings and a sad want of foresight, he could act, but he could not endure. At this period he had indeed sufficient reason to feel aggrieved, and he fretted like some wild animal in a cage. It was noon; the guard was being relieved in the outer court. Bustle reigned in the kitchen; two or three old hounds, with wistful faces, licked their lips as they nosed the savoury preparations that emanated from that department; hawks screamed and flapped their wings on the perch; everything denoted the arrival of the most important hour in the twenty-four.

By twos and threes brawny men-at-arms lounged into the hall and took their places at the board. A year ago, shout and jest and schoolboy prank would have been rife at such a moment; the earl's laugh would have been the loudest and his voice the gayest amongst them all; now they watched him pacing silently to and fro, with looks askance. Taking their cue from their chief, the boisterous riders were gloomy as mutes.

Bothwell turned suddenly and summoned his henchman.

'Is the holy man not ready yet?' said he, with something of irony in his tone. 'Ho! bid the knaves bring in the food. Cowl or cassock, rochet and stole, or black Geneva gown, not one of them but comes to corn as kindly as the longest-legged borderer that ever lifted a spear. Bid them serve, Dick, in the devil's name.'

'Nay, James Hepburn,' said a deep, stern voice at the earl's elbow, 'not in the name of the evil one, but in His from whom cometh all good. Bless the food,' he added, stretching both hands over the board which was now spread, and shutting his eyes reverently while he prayed: 'Bless those good things which are the product of thrift and honest industry, and may every morsel turn to gall on the lip, and poison in the breast, that is wrested by violence and bloodshed from the store of the widow and the fatherless!'

'Amen!' ejaculated Bothwell, without pretending to conceal the sneer on his lip, as he took his seat; whilst his retainers, glancing with a comical mixture of respect and astonishment at a man who dared to address their formidable chief in accents of reproach, seemed uncertain how to receive a blessing of such doubtful import on the border. The obvious course was to fall to without further ceremony; and soon the clatter of knives and drinking-horns drowned all qualms of conscience, if indeed such were experienced; 'Dick-o'-the-Cleugh' merely remarking, as he filled his trencher, 'that if all the beef in the larder that was *lifted* behoved to turn to gall, there wou'd be no want o' mustard for a whiley in Liddesdale.'

Evidently putting a strong constraint on himself, the earl proceeded to entertain his guest with marked distinction and courtesy. Indeed, after a time, the stately bearing and obvious sincerity of the man could not fail to produce a favourable effect; and though Bothwell, for political reasons, was disposed to court his good opinion, he could not but confess to himself, that under that black robe and grave exterior, lurked a spirit equal in point of courage, and far superior in energy, perseverance, and force of character, to his own.

Even the rude borderers felt the influence of his presence. Although the name of John Knox was ere this familiar in all men's mouths, through the length and breadth of Scotland, these lawless soldiers, while professing, for the most part, the Reformed religion, which combined in their eyes the intrinsic advantages of freedom, liberality, and cheapness, were at heart wofully indifferent to its tenets, or its obligations. They had thrown off with small compunction the shackles of the Roman Catholic Church; they were not quite so ready, however, to submit themselves to the discipline of that faith which had supplanted it. In all violent and fundamental changes of opinion, the teachers of a new doctrine have to contend with two serious difficulties: the ill-judged warmth of their more zealous disciples, and the convenient indifference of a large proportion of converts, who cannot be brought to see the advantage of dissent, if it is to substitute one form of government for another.

Physically, the great Scottish Reformer appeared scarcely equal to the work he had engaged to perform. His spare frame was indeed sufficiently ascetic to command respect; and his dignified bearing, well set off by the close black gown, with its loose sleeves, which he chose to wear, was not unworthy of the holy profession of which he was so zealous a member; but his stature was low, and his bodily strength proportionate. Nevertheless in his high grave brow, only partially covered by a close black skull cap, there was rectitude, pitiless, indeed, of others' weakness, but equally stern and uncompromising towards its own. The bold features and pale colouring of the face, more remarkable than comely, denoted energy with force of will; and though the mouth was somewhat large and coarse, its expression was firm and daring in the highest degree. His dark eyes, which it was his habit to fix intently on those with whom he conversed, were brilliantly piercing, and in the heat of argument or declamation shone and sparkled with an inward flame. A flowing beard descended to his girdle, somewhat softening the harshness of his features, and imparting a patriarchal dignity to his whole person. There was but little appearance of versatility on his immovable face, and yet John Knox, driven by his zeal into the political stream, had been forced to trim his bark more than once to suit the exigencies of the storm; and it may be that this very consciousness added to the stern defiance of his bearing.

Without attempting to be 'all things to all men,' the Reformer never forgot for an instant the one end and aim of his unceasing efforts, the destruction of papacy in his native land; and if ever he did turn aside for an advantage, or halt for a breathing-space, it was but to gather fresh energies for the great work, and devote himself more unreservedly to its accomplishment. If he was prejudiced, bigoted, and illiberal, he was at least an honest man thoroughly in earnest.

The latter quality invariably wins respect in the rudest, as in the most civilised societies, and even Earl Bothwell's wild jackmen could not withhold an involuntary homage from one whose peaceful profession, while it did not affect his insensibility to physical danger, or his coolness under trying circumstances, was followed out with an energy and perseverance of which their own lawless pursuits afforded no example. The Reformer, too, for all his infirmities, could back a horse and fly a hawk with the best of them. His stirring life had given him habits of activity and daring, whilst the energy of action was not wanting, which is so useful an accessory to a keen intellect. Though he ate sparingly, the preacher's cup was filled and emptied with grave, good fellowship, and he did not disdain to mingle in such mirth as was restrained within the bounds of decorum. There was a spice of quaint humour in his conversation that insensibly excited the attention of the most careless listeners; and though he never so far forgot his sacred office as to descend into buffoonery, he was no contemner of a ludicrous illustration or a harmless jest.

The dinner, nevertheless, progressed wearily. The churchman's presence restrained that wild ribaldry which had been, of late, Bothwell's only attempt at gaiety; and when the jackmen had eaten their fill, and satisfied their thirst, a gloomy silence once more pervaded the old hall.

It was the practice at Hermitage to conclude every meal with the standing toast of 'Snaffle, spur, and spear;' but to-day cups were emptied less cordially than usual to the accustomed pledge, and a long grace from Mr Knox immediately succeeding, it was received by the listeners with more respect than attention. It was a relief to all when the earl, calling for a basin and ewer, dipped his hands, wiped his beard, and rose from table, summoning the Reformer to attend him for a stroll upon the rampart, and whispering a few words to 'Dick-o'-the-Cleugh' as he passed out of the hall.

That worthy received his master's commands with an appearance of intense gratification, which communicated itself, as if by electricity, to the majority of his comrades. Bustle and activity seemed all at once to pervade the castle, and the merriment hitherto stifled and repressed broke forth with renewed violence. The tramp of horses and the clank of steel smote gratefully on ears in which such sounds made the sweetest of music; and when the churchman crossed the courtyard in search of his host, he found it filled by some two score of well-mounted men-at-arms, drawn up in disciplined army, with 'Dick-o'-the-Cleugh' at their head.

The earl was giving his final orders to this leader with considerable energy. He was in a towering passion, none the less unbridled that he was not going to command the expedition himself.

'Were he ten times warden,' the Reformer heard him say, 'he should not drive horses, with impunity, from my side the March. Does my Lord Scrope think that James Hepburn has been superseded at Hermitage? or that I am a likely man to submit to the slight he has endeavoured to put upon me? Faith, not while this arm of mine can lay lance in the rest. If you come across the English warden, Dick Rutherford, you shall cast James Hepburn's defiance in his teeth. Within twenty-one days, alone, or with his following, on foot or on horseback, with spear, sword, or axe, and not more than three English miles from the border, I challenge him to meet me, if he be a man, and "God defend the right!" Have you picked the horses?' he added, abruptly, and turning with a soldier's eye to scan the troop.

'I cast the twa four-year-aulds,' answered Dick, 'an' I waled the soar[6] and the three bays, forbye the white-footed yane, an' I'm ridin' Wanton Willie mysel'. Gin I track the drove to Peel-fell, will I follow them into Cumberland?'

[6] Sorrel or chestnut—next to bay, the favourite colour of the borderers.

'Follow them to hell!' answered Bothwell. 'I will have that gray gelding back if he is stabled in Carlisle. I'll have him from under Lord Scrope himself, if the Englishman never gets across a horse again. What! there is peace between the two countries, more's the pity, or I had been at his castle-gate by this time with all Teviotdale at my back; and so you may tell him, if you can meet with him under steel.'

'They might ha' been ta'en by the Langholme lads,' interposed Dick, whose spirits were rising considerably with the prospect of a foray, but who looked upon the whole affair, nevertheless, as a matter of business combined with wholesome recreation. 'They lifted a score o' runts frae "daft Davie," in Lammas time, an' took the vara' coverlet aff his wife's bed. He saw it himsel' at Dumfries, puir fallow!'

'Nay, nay,' answered Bothwell, 'the Langholme riders do not come down by the score, with dags, and petronels, and St George's cross on their basnets. If it's not a warden-raid, as, indeed, it can hardly be, it has been done by the warden's orders; and he shall answer it to me as sure as I serve Queen Mary! At least, with all her pride, she shall know that Bothwell never suffered it to be lowered an inch,' he muttered between his teeth as he turned away.

'Dick-o'-the-Cleugh' put the men in motion and himself at their head. As they emerged upon the open ground from the gray walls of the square old keep, the slanting beams of an autumn sun gilded the brown heather, and shed a soft lustre over the undulating moorland ere it flashed from the steel armour of the troop. The riders were in high spirits at the prospect of a change from their long period of inaction. The horses snorted and shook their bridles gaily. It was a party of pleasure and adventurous excitement to all concerned, and even now they were anticipating their plunder and jesting about their profits. Only one heart felt more softened than usual under its steel breastplate. 'Dick-o'-the-Cleugh' acknowledged the influence of the mellow sunlight and the balmy breeze. Somehow the very earth and sky seemed to connect themselves with a pair of laughing eyes and a shower of bright hair, with a fairy figure tripping up the High Street, a basket on its arm; or, as he had seen it first, shining like a vision of light in the dark passages of Holyrood, with a voice that used to thrill so sweetly once, that he never heard now but in his dreams. The henchman would have fought like a lion, and yet he felt tenderly disposed towards all living things. He would have met death more cheerfully than ever, yet he seemed only to have learned the value of life within the last few months; another contradiction—but is it not full of contradictions, that engrossing folly in which the true believer is as sure to suffer martyrdom as the false worshipper is to obtain his reward?

The earl and his visitor watched the troop defiling round the base of a low acclivity that soon hid them from sight. As they disappeared, Bothwell turned away with a bitter curse. He scarcely felt as if he had a right to order an expedition on the border in the name of his sovereign; and again Mary's injustice and neglect rankled like a poisoned shaft in his breast. But the earl was in no mood for balancing probabilities or counting cost. The horses that had been driven were his own, and he had reason to believe that Lord Scrope was not ignorant of the theft. This was sufficient to rouse his ire to the utmost, and he had despatched a force to follow and retake them, strong enough to preclude the possibility of failure. It was maddening, though, to be compelled to stay within the four walls of Hermitage, when his retainers were in the field; maddening, all the more that his present false position, as he argued, was owing to a queen's injustice and a woman's ingratitude.

A few short turns upon the rampart, with the soft west wind fanning his brow, restored his composure, and addressing his companion, he professed his readiness to enter at once upon the business which had brought the latter to Hermitage.

The preacher pointed to the surrounding scenery, the waving tracts of moorland bathed in the lustre of an afternoon sun, the cattle feeding securely in the green nooks and pasturage which broke the uniformity of the undulating waste, the yellow patch of cultivation under the very shadow of the keep, and the clear, autumnal heaven above all, pale and serene, and dappled here and there by flaky clouds edged with gold.

'It is not *my* business,' said the preacher, 'nor is it *thine*, Lord Warden, that hath brought me here, but the will of Him who holdeth this glorious universe in the hollow of His hand. It is to do His work that I have ridden through these wastes from dawn till mid-day, and that I must depart again ere set of sun. I charge thee to aid me, heart and hand, in the service of my Master!'

It is the misfortune of earnest men that, in this self-seeking world of ours, they seldom obtain the credit they deserve for sincerity and singleness of heart. Bothwell listened with outward respect, yet unworthy suspicions *would* not be kept down.

'Now for some double-dyed intrigue,' was his inmost thought, 'some plot set on foot by impenetrable Moray, not satisfied with his new earldom, and turbulent Morton, with his own craft added to the recklessness of all his Douglas ancestors, and Maitland, the skilful penman, the subtle diplomatist, wise as the serpent and plausible as the father of lies himself. They would fain make a cat's-paw of rude James Hepburn, for, doubtless, they want a bold heart and a ready hand to aid their schemes, and they send this godly man, half-fanatic, half-hypocrite, to feel if the tool be heated the right temper. I wot they may burn their fingers, one and all of them, yet!' But he only answered, abruptly—

'I believe you are the friend of my house. You will counsel nothing that can prejudice my honour, or my loyalty to the Queen.'

'My great-grandfather, my gude-sire, and my father, have served your family, James Hepburn, for three generations. Ay! served them when their banner was waving in the fore-front of the battle, and the arrows of the English archers were hailing against their harness like a storm from hell. Do you think their blood is not boiling in my veins because I wear a Geneva cassock for a steel breastplate? Do you think if my forebears shrank not to ride through fire and water for the Hepburn, I would fear to encounter death in his defence, much less would tempt him to danger or disgrace? Nay, my lord earl, though the commands of *my* Master are imperative, they will but lead to your aggrandisement in this world, and your salvation in the next.'

John Knox paused and turned a scrutinising look on his companion's face.

The latter plucked a morsel of grass from the rampart, and flung it on the breeze.

'Let us see how the wind blows,' he replied, with a scornful laugh; 'fair or foul, ye can trim your sails to it, all of ye, and I can ride through a storm with the best!'

'Nay!' exclaimed the Reformer; 'the labourer is worthy of his hire; know ye not that the great trial is approaching between the powers of darkness and the children of light? In France, the sovereign and his ministers are determined to stifle the good cause with the strong hand, and even now the blood of saints and martyrs crieth aloud from the very stones in the streets of Paris. The scarlet woman who spreadeth her mantle over the Seven Hills, and waveth her white arms abroad to lure souls to perdition, seducing some with indulgences and driving others to despair with her curse, is battling for her very existence, and that of the reptiles she hath spawned, and who crawl around her feet. Here in Scotland—ay, at Holyrood itself—hath not an image been erected unto Baal? and is not the idolatry of the mass raised weekly by Mary Stuart, whom men call Queen of Scotland, and who is herself a daughter of perdition?'

'Hold!' exclaimed Bothwell, in a voice of thunder, and advancing a step towards the speaker, as though about to hurl him from the rampart. He restrained himself, however, with an obvious effort, and proceeded in a calmer voice, 'It was not to malign his Queen that you sought an interview with the most devoted of her servants?'

Knox saw his zeal had carried him too far. The Reformer, like those whose persuasion he reprobated, was somewhat prone to allow that 'the end justified the means.' He retraced his steps, therefore, as it were, and resumed more calmly—

'Her Majesty must be saved from the influence of evil advisers. Why are her communications with the bloody Guises so frequent? Why is Popish Riccio all-powerful at Holyrood? Why is Bothwell virtually banished, and well nigh attainted for a traitor? But because there is a schism in the camp of the faithful, and a house divided against itself shall not stand.'

'The Queen has, indeed, dealt me scant justice,' answered the earl, musingly. 'What would your employers have me do?'

'I speak for myself,' replied the other, 'or rather I speak the words that are borne in unto me by Him whose servant I am. What shall ye say of a family in which brother is at variance with brother? of an army in which troop falls away from troop, for some petty feud, when the enemy is drawn up over against them in battle array? The nobles of Scotland are gathering to the front for the defence of their souls' liberties, and the boldest spirit amongst them all keeps aloof here at Hermitage because of a foolish brawl with a weak enthusiast who bore him no real ill-will.'

'I will never return to Holyrood,' answered Bothwell, looking wistfully towards the north while he spoke, 'till the Queen sends for me herself and acknowledges her injustice. I will never stretch the hand of reconciliation to Arran till I have dealt him a buffet with a steel gauntlet and a Jedwood axe in its grasp.'

'Nay, nay,' expostulated the Reformer; 'shall the edifice that such as you might rear on the goodly foundation of religious zeal, with the barons of Scotland for your fellow-workmen, crumble away for want of one stone in its right place? Once reconciled with Arran, the house of Hamilton might easily be secured in your interest. I can take upon myself to promise so much, or why am I here to-day? With Moray's good-will, Morton's friendship, the duke's aid, and the favour of the godly throughout the kingdom, who so powerful at court as the Earl of Bothwell? Would it not be well to teach the Queen (for her own welfare) the indispensable lesson that a woman can only rule through the influence of men—by the brain of the wise and the arm of the strong? Would it not be well that Mary Stuart should learn, once for all, that she must look to James Hepburn as her champion and her trust?'

The picture was painted in glowing colours, and set in a vivid light. The temptation to such a nature as Bothwell's was indeed of the strongest. It thrilled through heart and brain, that imaginary victory which should place in his power the option of humbling her to the dust, by whom he felt so aggrieved, or, better still, of foregoing his revenge and enjoying the nobler yet more complete triumph of forgiveness to his Queen. Nevertheless, the feudal feeling of resentment for an aspersion was still strong within him.

'But he accused me of treason,' urged the earl, lashing himself once more into anger, 'would have attainted me before the council as a traitor to Queen Mary, as a rebel who meditated violence on her sacred person!'

'The dream of a madman!' answered Knox. 'You know well that the earl's health has long been failing, that he is of those who are scourged and tormented in the body for the discipline of their souls. In his paroxysms of insanity he is as one possessed, but they leave him like the poor maniac from whom devils were cast out, "clothed and in his right mind." Nay, he did but accuse you of that which he had himself meditated in his madness. The Earl of Arran did indeed entertain a wild project to carry off the person of Mary

Stuart, and immure her in some stronghold at his pleasure. The scheme was that of a madman, and yet might it have been feasible, nevertheless.'

Bothwell started, and turned pale. He could not trust himself to speak. At that moment, wild phantom shapes, that had vaguely haunted him for long, seemed suddenly to assume a distinct aspect of reality. Dropped by an unconscious hand, the seed now struck root, that was hereafter destined to bear such appalling fruit. The offspring of a chance word, a wild and maddening vision took possession of his brain. He looked around at the solid dimensions of his fortress; he counted the gallant hearts within its walls, for whom his will was law; he thought of his friends and following, his resources and his influence, his own daring and his father's brilliant crimes. One desperate cast for the great stake; one bold swoop for the shrinking quarry; a few shots, a thrust or two, a white form borne swiftly away at a gallop, and the sweet face that had been a dream to him all his life might become a reality at last!

Why, even crazed Arran had been man enough to entertain such a scheme, whilst he, Bothwell, was eating his own heart here at Hermitage. Well, stranger things had come to pass. He must watch and bide his time; must be wary, vigilant; above all, must be patient. It was a stirring season. For a bold man *nothing* was impossible.

He replied at last, but cautiously and with reservations. If he joined the Protestant party, agreeing to act with Moray, Morton, and the rest, it must be under certain conditions; if he consented to a reconciliation with Arran, it must be accompanied with sundry stipulations which should be communicated hereafter at greater length. Even Maitland could not have been more mysterious, and the Reformer found himself wondering at the rapidity of a transformation which had changed the wild, reckless, border noble into a cold and scheming diplomatist.

He had attained his object, however, and that was enough for him. With a firm persuasion that he was furthering the good work, he took his leave of the earl, well-satisfied, resisting all hospitable importunities to remain, and even declining the offer of an escort to conduct him in safety through that lawless district.

'My Master will care for me,' said the preacher, as he prepared to leave the castle on horseback when the shades of night were closing in. 'He who has sent me on my mission will provide for the safety of His servant!' And so departed unarmed and alone.

Well might Morton hereafter pronounce over this dauntless nature its well-known epitaph, 'There lies one that never feared the face of man.'

CHAPTER XIII

'Bonny Kilmeny gaed up the glen,
But it was na to meet wi' Dunira's men,
Nor the rosy monk of the isle to see,
For Kilmeny was pure as maiden could be.'

Walter Maxwell was ere this domiciled at Holyrood. Attached to the Queen's household, and devoted to her person, Mary esteemed him not the least trustworthy of those servants in whom she placed implicit confidence. He had accompanied his sovereign on those roving expeditions in which she took so much pleasure, when the beautiful Stuart, worthy to reign over a nation of warriors, would pass entire days in the saddle, traversing her dominions, and making acquaintance with her subjects; or flying her hawk and following her deer-hounds over the wild moorlands, and amongst the romantic passes of her new kingdom. He had attended her in her progress to Aberdeen, that ill-advised journey which, commencing with merriment and festivity, the huntsman's holloa and the cheering notes of the horn, ended in strife and bloodshed and the wild wailing of the coronach, cried by the widows of the Gordon over the flower of their clan.

Maxwell had done good service on that sad day when the waters of Corrichie ran crimson with the Highlandman's blood, and had turned with a brave man's pity from the sickening sight of Sir John Gordon's execution at Aberdeen, performed before the very eyes of the weeping Queen. Gallant, handsome John Gordon! the victim of a political intrigue, who walked to the block with the jaunty step of a bridegroom in holiday attire, and waved his dying homage to his sovereign, a brave soldier and a loyal gentleman to the last.

It is said that Mary fainted at the sight; and, indeed, she never attained the necessary hardness of heart to rule such a turbulent and distracted country as that in which it was her lot to reign.

On more than one occasion Maxwell had proved himself the possessor of a shrewd brain, a silent tongue, and a ready hand. His was that least courtier-like of characters, which yet perhaps thrives best at a court. When all around are selfish and intriguing, each feels well-disposed towards the frank, single-hearted comrade who wishes but to serve his sovereign loyally, and entertains cordial good-will towards his fellows. Monarchs, too, even the haughtiest and most exacting, are disposed to appreciate a blunt honesty that does not shrink from encountering the royal displeasure for the royal advantage, and doubtless find it refreshing from its contrast with the servility to which they are accustomed. It must be like the change from the sickly air of a hothouse to the fresh mountain breeze. Besides, it is so easy to forgive even insolence in those who are wholly in their power; and there is a delicate flattery after all to the lion's forbearance, in the man's temerity, who puts his head in the lion's mouth.

The Queen of Scotland, however, was one of those who, while they attach to themselves irresistibly all who come within their sphere, are, from their own feelings, disposed to think kindly of their immediate retainers, and to reward fidelity and affection as they deserve.

Maxwell found himself in high favour with Mary, and it is not strange that he should have been devoted heart and soul to her interests. He persuaded himself that he was loyal to his sovereign for her own sake, and ignored with considerable determination that Mistress Carmichael had any influence whatever over his sentiments.

That young lady's behaviour at this juncture was of a nature to make an admirer sufficiently uncomfortable. We remember to have heard that there *are* female dispositions on which the exercise of the affections has an irritating tendency, and to whom the dawning possibility of eventful thraldom is as agitating as it is inviting. These wild-birds, albeit they become when tamed the gentlest of domestic fowls, are sadly prone at first to beat their breasts against the cage, also to peck viciously at the caressing hand that would smooth their ruffled plumes. Whether it be that they entertain a feminine delight in any state of sentiment, argument, or fact involving a contradiction, or whether they indemnify themselves, whilst they can, for future docility, we profess ourselves incompetent to state; but the axiom seems to be sufficiently established, that the process of taming is often uncomfortable and hazardous, the result not always to be depended upon when complete.

Mary Carmichael, in addition to her other qualifications, was a devoted Papist; Maxwell, it is needless to observe, a staunch Reformer. Religious feeling ran high at Holyrood. The Romish Church, a zealous advocate for proselytism at all times, has ever been most intolerant when losing ground; and perhaps no bigotry is so blind as a woman's adherence to a sinking faith.

Maxwell could not conscientiously look with approval on Mistress Carmichael's rigid attendance at mass in the Chapel Royal. The maid-of-honour concealed neither her dislike nor her contempt for those who had abandoned the religion of their fathers, and the ritual of their sovereign. This alone was a fruitful source of irritation and ill-feeling between the lovers, if so they can be called; and when we add that the gentleman was of a haughty and reserved disposition, the soul of honesty and frankness, without the slightest experience in the ways of woman, and the lady as wilful, unjust, and self-tormenting as those reasonable beings usually become when thoroughly in earnest, it is superfluous to dwell upon the feelings likely to exist between such a pair, continually brooding over imaginary wrongs, and never for a moment out of each other's minds.

One scene, amongst many, may afford a specimen of the terms on which they stood.

Maxwell was proceeding to the royal apartments with certain papers which had been submitted to Mr Randolph's inspection ere they were returned to the Queen for signature—so anxious was Mary, at this period, to keep well with her cousin of England. Elizabeth's ambassador had taken rather a fancy, in his own selfish, easy way, to his former travelling companion, and though, of course, he would have sacrificed him without scruple, he probably liked him none the less that he could not fashion him into a tool.

As Maxwell traversed the long gallery, Mistress Carmichael was proceeding in the same direction with a basket of winter roses gathered in the Abbey garden, and could not forbear blushing as deep as the reddest of them when she encountered him. Of course she was angry with herself for doing so, and naturally visited the fault on him, arguing, plausibly enough, that if he had not been there it would not have happened; therefore she turned her head steadfastly away and marched on without speaking. Hurt and irritated, he drew aside to let her pass, thus meeting her, as it were, half-way in her desire to avoid recognition. So far nothing could be simpler. If the lady did not wish to be delayed she had only to pass on without further stoppage. She did so accordingly, but by the merest accident, and the most provoking awkwardness, tilted her basket and dropped half her flowers on the floor. Of course he was compelled to assist her in picking them up; for these two were the only occupants of the gallery; so he knelt down and refilled the basket gravely without a word.

'Thank you,' said Mary Carmichael, with the slightest possible tremor in her voice. 'How deftly you have done it, and how much beholden to you I am!—and—and—thank you, Mr Maxwell.'

Here was an opportunity that would have been seized by any other gallant about the court to ask, at least, for one of the roses in reward; and perhaps even Maxwell, though somewhat impatient of such follies, would have been less reserved with any other of the Maries than the one who now stood before him, still arranging her basket, and obviously in no immediate hurry to go away. He waited, however, for her to speak first. After a little hesitation, she pointed to the papers he was carrying.

'Shall I take them for you to the Queen?' said she, and her hand trembled as she extended it towards him.

He took the pretty hand in his own, and she did not withdraw it.

'Mistress Carmichael,' said he, 'I am a plain man, and I hope an honest one. I have not so many friends that I can afford to lose any for lack of courage to ask an explanation. How have I offended you of late? Tell me as frankly as I ask you, and I will take care not to transgress again.'

Her bosom heaved, and her colour went and came.

'Offended?' she replied; 'and me? oh, no! What have I done to make you think so?'

He was still very grave, and a shade paler than before, but his countenance was immovable, and indeed stern. It was a peculiarity of Walter Maxwell that, under strong excitement, his exterior became unusually cold and composed.

'I have thought so for long,' he resumed. 'Perhaps it has distressed me more than you would think possible. I trust I have done my duty as thoroughly as if you and I had been friends; but I have felt that difficulties appeared greater, and hardships less endurable than if our differences had not existed. The breach has widened day by day; ere long, you and I will have learned to hate each other.'

'Oh, no, no!' she murmured, scarce above her breath, but she kept her head bent down, and the tears were dropping fast among the winter-roses in her basket.

He had never let go her hand; he folded it in both his own, and pressed it to his lips.

'Mary Carmichael,' said he, 'since the day we first met in the forest of Chambord, I have wished to be worthy of you, and you alone. I am no woman-worshipper, no smooth-tongued silken gallant, and yet I think there are few things I could not do to please you; nothing, save my honour, I would not sacrifice for your sake.'

A gleam of intense pride and pleasure shone for an instant in her eyes; the next, her face contracted as if with pain, and she looked up scared and wild, through her tears.

'You must not say so—you must not say so,' she exclaimed, drawing her hand away hurriedly, and with a frightened, half-distracted air. 'Let me go now—let me go; I hear the others coming.'

'Is that your answer?' said he, very lowly and distinctly, but with a pale face, and something in his voice that it was better not to trifle with.

She looked here and there, like some graceful wild animal caught in the toils. Footsteps were indeed approaching, and half the flowers were again scattered on the floor.

'You must not say so,' she repeated; but for an instant she placed her hand once more in his with a lightning glance of unspeakable tenderness; 'at least not yet!' she added, and sped hurriedly away.

When she was gone, Walter Maxwell stooped down, picked up one of the roses, and hid it carefully within his doublet. Then he proceeded to his business with a lighter heart and a brighter face than he had carried since he came to Holyrood.

We will follow the young lady to the apartment in which the Maries were accustomed to congregate when off duty, plying their needles with industrious rapidity, and lightening their labours, we may be sure, with the pleasures of conversation.

It was a pretty room, high up in one of the turrets of the palace, overlooking the Abbey garden, and was full of the little elegancies and comforts which women gather about them, or which seem to grow up around, in the most unlikely places, as a natural consequence of their presence. Quaint tapestry adorned its walls, less hideous than are usually those grotesque efforts of industry, and representing pastoral scenes of love-making and simplicity, not devoid of browsing sheep, limpid streams, and fat little cupids flying about in the air. Scarfs, fans, gloves, and needlework were scattered over the room; and Mary Hamilton's rosary of fragrant wooden beads, inlaid with gold, hung from the back of a carved oak chair, of which the cushions were triumphs of embroidery wrought by the maids-of-honour themselves. A portrait of the Queen, in her well-known velvet head-dress and voluminous ruff, smiled above the chimney-piece; and immediately under it was placed an elaborate crystal timepiece, of French workmanship, presented by her mistress to Mary Beton, and reverenced equally as a token of the royal good-will and a marvel of mechanical art. The last-named lady glanced at it with the conscious pride of possession.

'It will be dark in less than an hour,' said she, folding away the corner of a large square piece of embroidery on which herself and two of her companions were engaged; 'we have done enough for one day, and these small stitches are very trying to the eyes. I expect the Queen's summons, too, every minute, for one or other of us.'

'She is writing letters in her cabinet,' answered Mary Carmichael, who had her own reasons for knowing how large a packet had just gone in. 'I could see her beautiful head bending over her table as I came down the terrace steps in the Abbey garden when I brought you in these roses.'

'You haven't half filled the basket after all!' exclaimed Mary Seton, who was busy arranging the flowers about the room; 'and like your sex, my dear, you have taken care to gather plenty of thorns. If I wear a garland of them at the masque to-morrow, as I intended, I shall be a veritable Scotch thistle, not to be touched with impunity; a fitting partner for that masterful border-thief, little Jock Elliot, who cocks his bonnet and sings "Wha dare meddle wi' me?"'

'You have become half a borderer yourself, I think, ever since Bothwell was banished the court,' answered the other, not quite relishing this allusion to the half-filled basket, of which the spoils were scattered in the gallery.

'Poor Bothwell!' answered Mary Seton, with a sigh; 'now that is what I call a *man*! When he walks through the court in his armour, he looks like a tower amongst the other lords. There is not a taller or a more stalwart figure amongst all his riders, proper men though they be, except perhaps that gigantic henchman of his.' And again the damsel sighed, and looked grave for an instant, though she was laughing merrily again the next.

'Is he not coming back soon?' asked Mary Hamilton, waking up from one of her fits of abstraction, and fixing her large mournful black eyes on Mary Seton's saucy blue ones.

'Who? which?' asked the latter, mischievously.

'Why, D'Amville,' answered Mary Hamilton, absently; 'were you not talking of him? He has been more than a year away.'

'D'Amville!' exclaimed the other, with her ringing laugh; 'I hope not! At least if he brings that mad poet in his train, to turn all our heads with rhymes and flattery. Nothing interests you but what comes from France! No, we were talking of Bothwell, stout Earl Bothwell, who is worth a dozen of him. I am sure the Queen thinks so.'

Mary Beton looked up reprovingly, but in vain; the flippant speaker was in her swing, and not to be disappointed of her say.

'I'm sure we've all been dull enough at court ever since Bothwell got into disgrace. And after all, I don't believe he bared steel till the others drew on him first. I *know* the Hamiltons outnumbered his people two to one; and nobody disputes that Arran is quite mad now, or that the duke was always an old goose. I think it very hard that Bothwell should have been made the scapegoat, that I do! and I've always said he hadn't fair play from first to last.'

'Hush!' interposed Mary Beton, gravely; 'the matter was tried in Her Majesty's own presence, before the council.'

'The council were a parcel of intriguers!' vociferated the little partisan, now getting positively vehement. 'The council wanted to get rid of him, because he was the most loyal amongst them all, and they made the skirmish an excuse. Why, I'm sure Ruthven is ready enough with his dagger, and my own dear father cleared the High Street from end to end with his own good sword and half a dozen jackmen before I was born, and the king swore he was quite right. I've heard him say so a score of times. No, no! the council had their own reasons; and I'll never believe but that Englishman was at the bottom of it, though he pretended to be the warden's friend!'

'If you mean Mr Randolph,' said Mary Beton, bridling within her ruff in high disdain, 'you only expose your ignorance of state affairs. What could he have to do with it? or how could the turbulence of a wild border noble affect the Queen of England's confidential minister?'

'Only that I am convinced his red-haired mistress is at the bottom of all the mischief that goes on here,' answered the other, determined not to be put down. 'I believe she hates our dear beautiful angel of a Queen, partly because she's her cousin, and partly because she's been married, and partly because there is nobody like her in this world. I won't abuse Randolph, Mistress Beton, because he admires you hugely, and that shows the man has good taste; but I may say what I like of Elizabeth Tudor, who is no more *my* Queen than I am *hers*.'

The elder damsel looked mollified, though she feebly deprecated the implied compliment.

'These are dangerous topics,' said she, gathering her draperies around her, and rising from her chair. 'It is enough for us to occupy ourselves with our own office, and I cannot conceive why we have not yet heard Her Majesty's summons.'

This lady was of a methodical disposition, and loved to perform her regular duties at their stated times without interruption.

'Those endless letters!' exclaimed Mary Seton; 'and all about treaties and alliances, and the most uninteresting subjects. I declare I wouldn't change places with the Queen to have her beauty and her throne. She is harassed and wearied to death. Dear me! how I wish she would marry, and take some stout-hearted lord to share her troubles and anxieties with her once for all!'

'I'm surprised at you!' exclaimed Mary Beton, now completely shocked. 'It is most indiscreet to talk on such matters, and scarce maidenly even to think of them. Is it that you might follow her example?' she added, in a tone of severe reproof.

'I am not sure but what I should,' sighed the other, and relapsed into silence, which, strange to say, was not broken for the space of full five minutes.

Perhaps the last suggestion thrown out had awakened matter for reflection in the minds of each of the four Maries.

At the expiration of that period, however, Mary Beton remarked that it was getting very dark; and Mary Seton at the same moment proposed that James Geddes, the Queen's fool, should be summoned to make sport for them during the hour of idleness preceding supper.

'I will go for him,' said Mary Carmichael, and, wrapping a plaid round her head and shoulders, hurried out of the room.

James Geddes, who filled the honourable and somewhat lucrative office of royal fool or jester in the palace of Holyrood, was one of those half-witted unfortunates of whom so many may be met with even in the present day in Scotland, and who occupy the intermediate space between sanity and positive imbecility. They cannot be termed lunatics, for they are usually harmless, and even amiable in disposition, showing kindly feelings towards animals, infants, and such helpless objects, and even school-children, if not tormented by the urchins beyond all endurance. They are not idiots, for, although their perceptions may be warped, they are in vigorous possession of their faculties, and indulge, indeed, in a shrewd caustic humour of their own with which few rational beings can compete. Neither can they be called actually in their right mind. Perhaps the Scottish peasant best describes the mental state of such an one when he says, in an explanatory tone, 'Ou! he's just a natural!'

James Geddes, accordingly, was 'just a natural,' and earned his wages, consisting of meat, and fee, a parti-coloured suit of clothes, and a cap and bells which he could not be persuaded to wear, by furnishing unlimited mirth to the royal household, and occasionally a jest that diverted the grave lords in council, and reached the ears of the gentle Queen herself.

Such was the wiseacre, in search of whom Mary Carmichael sped down the winding stairs that led from the Maidens' Tower into the devious passages of the palace. Obviously the most likely place in which to find him would have been the buttery, for it is a kind compensation of nature, that weakness of brain should be accompanied by great power of the digestive organs, and James Geddes could eat as much at one meal as would last a philosopher for a week. The maid-of-honour, nevertheless, passed that well-stored apartment without stopping, and proceeded with a light step and a heaving bosom into the Abbey garden, over which the dew was falling, and the shades of evening gathering fast.

Passing through the flower-beds she had despoiled in the afternoon, and which doubtless failed not to call up tender recollections, the young lady glided like a phantom into the shade of an adjoining orchard, through the branches of which an early star or two were already beginning to twinkle down. Here she halted, and, removing the shawl from her head, peered into the darkness, and listened attentively, though for a few minutes—

'The beating of her own heart

Was all the sound she heard.'

Now, by one of those coincidences which do occasionally happen in real life, especially where certain mysterious affinities combine to produce improbable results, Walter Maxwell was returning from Secretary Maitland's office to his own lodging at the same twilight hour, and although it involved a considerable *détour*, had chosen to proceed through the Abbey garden, and along the corner of the orchard, from which in the daytime he could see the windows of the Queen's apartments and those of her ladies. Walter was no romantic enthusiast, to derive intense pleasure from a mere association of ideas, and yet he paused under the shadow of an old apple-tree, and gazing on the dark mass of building opposite, recalled, with an intoxicating thrill, his interview with his mistress in the gallery. We have, most of us, experienced certain moments in life when we are satisfied to enjoy present bliss, without taking into account the insufficiency of its cause, or the shortness of its duration. We know we are happier than we have any right to be, and we wilfully ignore the consciousness, and refrain from asking ourselves the 'reason why.' Like pride, this state of self-gratulation usually 'goeth before a fall.'

Maxwell's quick ear could not fail to detect the light footstep of his ladye-love as she, too, entered the orchard, and he recognised her, muffled as she was, and in the darkness, as we recognise intuitively those whom we have trusted with our happiness. He sprang forward to meet her.

Undemonstrative and calm as was his character, he would have caught her to his heart, and vowed never to part with her from that moment; but ere he had made one step in advance, a tall cloaked figure, which seemed to come out of the very stem of an adjoining tree, anticipated his movements, and Maxwell, scarce believing his eyes, saw the woman he loved caught in its arms, and disappearing in the folds of that close and familiar embrace.

He had nerve, temper, and, above all, self-command. Though the cold drops stood on his forehead, and a deadly sickness crept about his heart, he had presence of mind to reflect on what he ought to do. In a dozen seconds he had argued the point, for and against, in his own mind, and had come to the conclusion that he was justified in undeceiving himself, at such a crisis, by the evidence of his senses. He remained under the shadow of the old tree and listened, with every organ painfully acute, and every nerve strung to its utmost pitch.

'My darling,' said the stranger, smoothing back the hair from the face, which looked fondly up into his own, 'how late you are this evening! I should have gone without seeing you in five minutes more; but I knew you would not fail me, if you could help it, at our trysting-place.'

'You might be sure of that,' she answered, clinging to him with both hands clasped upon his shoulder. 'Last week, and the week before, I came to the moment. I cannot bear to keep you waiting, or to think of you watching and hiding here like a thief—you that I am so proud of, and so fond of; you on whose arm I would like to hang before the Queen and the whole court, and I dare not even mention your name, except in my prayers. You are cold,' she added, wrapping his cloak across his throat and chest with sedulous affection, 'cold and wet with dew already, and perhaps tired and hungry too, and I may not bring you into the palace, and warm you, and take care of you. Oh! what a life it is!'

He laughed cheerfully, though with caution.

'Always the same,' he said; 'always unselfish and considerate, and thinking of me! Why, you little witch, do you never reflect on what a scolding you would get if you were caught running about like this, in the gloaming, to meet a cavalier under a tree? What would Mistress Beton say forsooth? Strict Mistress Beton! She would vow not a dove would be left in the dove-cote after a while, if such doings were passed over. Do I look like a hawk to harry a bird's-nest, Mary? Am I such a terrible wild young gallant, my pretty one?'

She put her white hand over his mouth. Maxwell saw it in the starlight.

'Do not speak so loud,' she said. 'I am sure you are as incautious as a boy. Indeed, I wish you *would* harry the nest, as you say, and carry me off with you, for I am tired of never seeing you, except by stealth; and then it makes me so anxious and so fretful not to know where you are, or when we shall meet, for weeks and months together.'

'My dear,' he answered, gravely, 'it is in the Queen's service and that of our religion. It must triumph at last, as sure as those stars are shining above our heads. You and I have vowed to devote our lives, if need be, to the good cause. If worst should come to worst, we shall not be separated for long. There are no partings up there, Mary.'

He pressed her tenderly to his side, and pointed to the sky, in which star after star were now glimmering forth.

She drew her hand across her eyes, and kissed him fervently once more.

'I shall be missed,' she said. 'I must stay no longer. It is *very* hard not to see you again for such a time! Well, well, duty before all. And now, have you the packet from the cardinal? What say the Guises to the last communication?'

'They dare not even write,' he answered. 'Though I acted my part well, and looked such a masterful beggar, that even you, Mary, would have flung me an alms, they searched me when I landed at the port of Leith, scrip, wallet, and all; nay, they broke my staff across, lest it should be hollow, and filled with papers—I would I might have done it myself over the knave's pate that could be so wary. No; the despatches must travel by word of mouth; and that is a better trick than even Randolph has learned yet, with all his cunning. Listen, Mary. They trust you, my pretty one, because you belong to me—this is for the Queen's private ear alone.'

Maxwell was a man of honour. He would stay to hear no more. It was enough that his dearest hopes had withered in a breath. That the edifice he had been building insensibly for so long, decking it with all his fancies, and furnishing it, so to speak, with the most precious gifts of his affections, and the warmest feelings of the heart, had crumbled into dust at a moment's notice. He would not, for that, intrude upon another's secrets; and although the delay of a few moments might have placed him in possession of matters that would have insured his own aggrandizement, and enabled him to take a fearful revenge on the two by whom he felt so cruelly injured, yet he stole noiselessly away, placing his hands upon his ears, that he might not, inadvertently, hear another word of their communications.

Where is the man who can consistently shape his conduct upon a train of reasoning independent of his feelings, at least where those feelings are vitally concerned? It never occurred to him that he had no right to listen at all. The question was one of life and death to him, and he felt justified in arriving by any means at a certainty. Such is human nature in the best of us. Principle is principle, and honour is honour, only so long as circumstances are not too overwhelming, or necessity too urgent. Conscience is the only guide who never yet lost his way.

We will not follow Walter Maxwell as he left the Abbey garden for the solitude of his own chamber, never utterly dreary and forlorn till to-night. He had a brave, stout heart, that could strive against any odds, and scorned to flinch from any amount of pain. Perhaps these suffer most in proportion to their strength.

CHAPTER XIV

'And some said this, and some said that,

And our bonnie Queen, she laughed loud and free,

But down on his knees the poor fool sat,

Says, "Never a fool is there here but three!"'

After taking a tender farewell of the cloaked stranger, more touching and affectionate, if possible, than her greeting, Mary Carmichael fled back to the palace like a lapwing. There was no time to lose in securing James Geddes, if she would not have the length of her absence remarked, and she found him, as she expected, drinking a warm posset in the buttery. Like the rest of his class, the fool could at times be sufficiently self-willed and captious, rating his own society at no trifling value, more especially if he saw that it was sought after; and it required no small amount of management to wheedle him into merriment if not so disposed. On the present occasion he refused point-blank to stir from the chimney corner, and it was only by dint of much coaxing, and the promised bribe of a box of French comfits, that Mary Carmichael prevailed on him to accompany her, and bore him off in triumph to the turret-chamber, there to make sport for the Queen's maids-of-honour.

His entrance was greeted by acclamations, which he received with complete indifference. He brightened up, however, when the comfits were produced, and sat down to munch them with an expression of the most perfect satisfaction and vacuity.

He was a stout, middle-sized man, with a long, heavy face, a large mouth, and hanging under-jaw. When he lolled his tongue out, and half-shut his meaningless gray eyes, he looked a being devoid of the slightest spark of intellect; at such times, nevertheless, he was most apt to produce those simple witticisms which served to amuse the court.

Not a word was to be got from him till he had finished the comfits. At length, the last and largest disappeared down that capacious maw; then he yawned, stretched himself, and condescended to observe—

'He would have to bid the ladies farewell, as to-morrow he should take his leave of Holyrood.'

'What shall we do without you?' exclaimed Mary Seton, who took James Geddes under her special protection, and vowed, in her pert way, that he was infinitely more sane than half the Queen's advisers. 'We cannot let you go—you are the only amusement we have!'

'There'll be no lack of fules the morn,' answered James, with a look of comical disgust; ''deed they may call it Follyrood now, with gude cause. Have ye no heard tell of the braw doings in the Queen's Park? Troth, ye'll be able to wale your Joes the morn! Every lass her lad! And they riding mother-naked every man o' them. Na, na; they're no wanting fules at court i' the noo, an' I'll just tak' my foot in my hand, an' turn wise-like mysel'.'

'Why, the masque will only be six against six as usual,' answered Mary Beton, characteristically disposed to take a matter-of-fact view of the proceedings, 'six savages and six amazons. I have seen the dresses; and very complete they are. What is there in that to displease you, James? I thought you dearly loved a festival or a frolic.'

'I'll no gang till I've had my denner,' answered James; 'but I'll no bide at Holyrood, once the trade is overstocked, as it is like to be. I'll just gang my ways to the Border, an' take up with stout Earl Bothwell and muckle Dick. He'll like fine to get word o' Mistress Seton. Troth, if they measure fules by the foot, ye've gotten a grand yane, my bonny doo, to your share; for ye've clean bewitched Dick.'

That young lady laughed and blushed, then frowned and looked cross, lastly peeped into the box of comfits for something to stop James's mouth withal. The latter put on his densest look, and proceeded—

'Ay, the time's no what it was. I mind when me and Jenny Colquhoun was the only fules in Holyrood; forbye the French lassie, that was no worth speaking of, and Robin Hamilton the porter. Set him up! to shut the wicket in my very face last St Andrew's day, and swear he would break my sconce across, if it wasna as toom as a borderer's bonnet. Awbody kens he's a Hamilton, an' the Hamiltons have aye mair hide than horns. Nae offence to the bonny leddy here, that's no mindin' the like o' me. Aweel, there's mair fules than three at Holyrood i' the noo; an' it's time for James Geddes to be packing, when he's the only wise-like body about the place.'

'Then you think we are all losing our wits,' remarked Mary Carmichael, as she made up the wood-fire, lit the silver lamp that stood on the table, and set the room in order, according to her wont.

'Ye'll no find yours in the Abbey garden, I'm thinkin',' replied James, whereat the questioner looked extremely angry and confused. 'I mind a bonny sang that plays—

"I'll wager, I'll wager, I'll wager wi' you,

Five hundred merks and ten."

I'll no tell ye the wager, Mistress Carmichael; I'm only a fule, ye ken; but "I'll wager, I'll wager, I'll wager wi' you," that ye dinna gang oot like a ghaist in the gloamin' just to pu' an apple frae a tree. There's a canny lad wad like ill to jalouse ye kept tryst wi' anither; that's just one mair to the count. I doubt I maun be flittin' frae Holyrood, or we a' gang daft thegither.'

'What does he mean?' exclaimed Mary Beton, all the duenna aroused within her as she marked the fool's cunning looks, and her comrade's obvious discomfiture.

'Hooly an' fairly, Mistress Beton!' exclaimed Geddes, with whom the Queen's principal lady was no great favourite. 'Keep your ain breath to cool your ain brose. Will you grudge the lasses their bit ploy, an' keep back all the Joes to yersel'?

"She wad na hae a Lowland laird,

Nor be an English lady."

They'll no threep that on you, Mistress Beton. Na, na; ye're a true Scotchwoman; an' it's just a spoilin' o' the Egyptians, as godly John Knox wad call it. Troth, ye've made a fule o' a wiser body than yoursel', I'm thinkin'. I'll no grudge Maister Randolph the cap an' bells, but he'll get the fee an' bountith a' gate the like o' him gangs, I ken fine. Aweel! ten fingers an' ten taes, I canna number the fules at Holyrood; for I'm no gude at the countin', and I canna tell mair than a score; but I'll gang my ways to the border the morn, for the trade is just over-stockit.'

'You give your tongue too much liberty,' said Mary Beton, who was considerably displeased at James Geddes's indiscreet allusions, and not disposed to conceal her disapproval. 'You presume on the Queen's good nature. Have a care; if I mention your conduct to the master of the household, you will be taken to the porter's lodge to taste of Robin Hamilton's discipline once again!'

The fool's face grew livid, and an ugly gleam shot from his heavy eye. There was evidently some rancour brooding in his heart against the tall porter, who, it may be, in virtue of his office, had been ordered ere now to inflict corporal punishment on the jester. He fell to cursing the Hamiltons with the unmeaning malevolence of insanity. From the proud duke and his unfortunate son, whose state of mind should indeed have obtained immunity from a fellow-sufferer, to the stalwart gate-keeper, he called down upon all who owned the name every evil that madness could imagine, or hatred suggest, and then, stopping suddenly in his curses, he moved awkwardly across the room to where Mary Hamilton, buried in thought, sat somewhat apart from the rest, and seizing the hem of her garment, began mouthing and kissing it, and wetting it with his tears, in a reaction of feeling which, sustained by one so imbecile, it was pitiful to behold.

As they are given to unaccountable and deep-rooted aversions, to gratify which they have been known to display incredible sagacity and cunning, so these unfortunates are capable of strong attachments, cherished with a morbid vehemence peculiar to their malady. A madman's affection and a madman's hatred are alike to be avoided, since the former is as inconvenient as the latter is dangerous.

James Geddes entertained a devotion for Mary Hamilton which amounted to idolatry, and was never so well satisfied with himself, or so nearly rational, as when employed in some trifling commission for the beautiful maid-of-honour. Also he watched her as you may see a dumb animal watch every look of its owner, and was especially jealous and irritated if he fancied she bestowed too much notice or favour on any one else.

'What is he driving at?' exclaimed Mary Seton, observing that the fool, although with an expression of deep contrition, was now indulging in a series of mysterious winks and signs. 'Ask him, Mary Hamilton. He seems to have some secret understanding with you. Ask him, for pity's sake, my dear; he'll have a fit if he goes on like that.'

But her curiosity was not destined to be satisfied; for at this juncture a page entered the apartment with a summons for Mistress Hamilton to attend the Queen; and that lady departed accordingly, leaving her half-witted adorer in a state of woeful penitence and discomfiture. Crouching among the embers in the hearth, he hid his face in his hands, rocking himself to and fro, and 'crooning,' in a sing-song voice, a succession of broken unintelligible sentences. From these fits of dejection the ladies knew it was impossible to arouse him.

The Queen was seated at a massive oaken writing-table, on which she was heaping together a quantity of letters and papers when Mary Hamilton entered. A single lamp shed its light upon her fair brow, which seemed to-night heavy with an unusual load of care. Her features wore the languor of mental fatigue, and even her attitude denoted the listlessness of one who is wearied by too much thought and study. She had been writing to her cousin of England; and if it was a difficult matter to be well with Elizabeth at best, how much more so now when her suspicions were excited and her jealousy kept continually awake by the question of succession! The maiden Queen was not without that strange weakness of humanity, which so disquiets itself as to what shall become of its earthly possessions when it is gone—an anxiety no stronger in the monarch who has a kingdom to bequeath than in the old woman who has hoarded her forty shillings in a stocking. Will it affect them so much in that spirit-world, even if they learn it, to know that the dynasty has been changed, or the funded property squandered, or the entail cut off?

There is many a man now living who would rather lose an arm or a leg than think that the old avenue will be cut down when he is gone to a land where the trees of life and knowledge flourish in perennial verdure, and all the while young Graceless, his heir, is scanning their girth and substance with a wistful consciousness that the Jews *must* be paid at last. Horace has told us something about those 'dreaded cypresses,' which we would fain ignore. They will wave over our dwelling when the oaks in the park have been disposed of at so much per foot, and the family tree itself is withered and forgotten. Do you think it matters much to Smith deceased, the tenth of his illustrious line, that Brown should have succeeded to his place and property, or that B. should cede in turn to Jones and Robinson? 'A plague o' both your houses!' All this, however, has nothing to do with the house of Tudor.

Independent of the natural aversion entertained by every right-minded woman for another of her own sex who is sought after by a multitude of suitors, Elizabeth had a variety of excellent reasons for disliking the Queen of Scots. The latter was considerably her junior, unquestionably more beautiful and accomplished, gifted with that mysterious fascination which makes women angry and men foolish, and in addition, to these offences was indubitably the next heir to the English crown. Under such circumstances, it is not surprising that the maiden Queen should have delighted in heaping difficulties across the path of her widowed cousin, and this was done the more effectually by keeping well with her to all outward appearance, and interchanging a constant succession of rings, precious stones, letters of courtesy, and the like insidious compliments.

Nor was Mary deceived by these artifices. It is probable that she clearly perceived the hollow nature of her kinswoman's friendship, and returned it in kind, so far as her open generous character would permit. But it was not in this Queen's nature to cherish lasting feelings of ill-will, and she had also doubtless the good sense to see that in her precarious position Elizabeth's favour was essential to her security and support. So she corresponded with her regularly in a vein of cordial affection, amounting even to familiarity, and it is no wonder that Mary rose from the composition of one of these letters with an air of unusual exhaustion on her lovely face.

'Help me to seal these packets, my dear,' said she to the maid-of-honour, as the latter approached her table; 'my fingers are perfectly stiff with holding a pen. No wonder my forefathers esteemed the art of writing a disgrace, and swore that the grasp of a noble hand should never close on anything lighter than a lance. I often wish I was a man, to wear steel on my breast and at my side!' While she spoke she stretched her beautiful fingers, which did indeed look far too delicate to wield any weapon heavier than a needle, and pushing the state seal across to her maid-of-honour, threw herself back in her chair, as if thoroughly tired with her day's work.

Mary Hamilton occupied herself at once about her task, affixing the seal of Scotland, with its lion rampant and its crown-royal, to document after document, in a graceful, womanly way that attracted the Queen's notice, and caused her to regard her favourite maid-of-honour with more attention than common.

The latter was always pale, and unusually quiet in her demeanour, but of late she had become paler than ever, and her customary repose of manner had subsided into dejection. Without obvious ailment, she looked listless and out of spirits, languid in her movements, and far too grave for one so young.

Herself wearied and harassed, it struck the Queen particularly to-night, and she could not forbear noticing it.

'You are ill, Mary,' said she, 'and worse than that, you are unhappy. What is it? there is something the matter!'

'Nothing, madam,' answered the other, looking up with a transparent effort at cheerfulness. 'How can I be unhappy when I am at Holyrood, and near your Majesty?'

She did not say it in the complacent tone of a courtier, but with a warmth and sincerity that could not have been assumed, her large dark eyes moistening and shining in the lamplight. She thought she loved the Queen better than anything on earth, and so she did — save one.

'I know you are fond of me, child,' answered the Queen affectionately; 'that does not make me the less anxious about you. I think of all my Maries you are the most dependent upon me. Have a care, my dear! there seems to be a fatality about Mary Stuart. Those who love me best seem ever to be the most unfortunate.'

She spoke mournfully, and in an abstracted tone. Was she thinking of her dead bridegroom who had worshipped her? of the mother who had doated on her? of the loyal and brave and the true already proscribed, banished, or disgraced? was it memory or foreboding, the sorrows of the past or fears for the future, that thus so often cast a gloom over her spirit, and damped her royal courage at her need?

'Do you think that would not make me love you ten times more?' exclaimed the other with a flash from her glorious eyes that lighted up her whole face. 'Can there be love without sacrifice, madam? Nay,' she added in a sadder voice, 'can there even be love without suffering?'

'You are very young to say so,' answered the Queen, 'two years younger than I am; and I remember how I used to think that sorrow was the especial heritage of the old. I have learnt otherwise now; but you, Mary Hamilton, you whom I have always watched and sheltered as a bird shelters its nestling under its wing, what can *you* know of suffering?'

The maid-of-honour looked wistfully at her mistress while she replied—

'I never can know real sorrow, madam,' she said, 'nor real suffering; because I have a refuge more secure than even a queen's favours, and to that refuge I betake me whenever grief becomes too heavy to endure. Ah! madam, they may take everything from us here, but they cannot rob us of that; this world is sometimes very dark and sad, but the light is always shining just the same, far away at home.'

The Queen looked at her with concern and surprise. What could it be, this engrossing sorrow which cast its shadow over a young life that ought to have shone so hopeful and so bright? The girl must be very unhappy, she argued, to be so devout. Alas! that it should be so; that religion, instead of the pride of the strong, should so often prove but the refuge for the weak. And yet it is but one more instance of that mercy which knows no limit. The happy and the pious, too, enjoy indeed a favoured lot, but human nature is so warped, that in the majority continuous prosperity produces hardness of heart, and for these it 'is good to be in trouble.' When they have lost all (it matters not what constitutes it, fame, wealth, or affection) they run for consolation, like a child in distress to a parent, where it never is denied; and which of us is there who does not know how unspeakably precious is the balm of kindness to a bruised and empty heart? A few there are on whom adversity has a contrary effect—rebellious spirits, not without force of character and capacities for happiness, who become froward and desperate under the rod. Woe be to them! What shall bring such as these back to the fold? Human forbearance would say 'let them go in their wilfulness to destruction!' but it is well for us that it is not with human forbearance we have to do.

The Queen of Scots herself was of a gay and hopeful disposition, one which perhaps it required many reverses to steady and sober down. Plenty of them she sustained ere all was done! In the meantime her kind heart was moved to think that her maid-of-honour should have some secret grief she herself could not alleviate.

'Tell me, dear,' said she, 'what it is that thus weighs upon your spirits, and takes the colour out of your cheek. I have seen it for long. Confide in me, not as your Queen, Mary Hamilton, but as your mother or your elder sister. I too am a woman, a failing, weak-hearted woman like the rest. I can only imagine one cause for such deep-rooted sorrow, and yet I cannot think my beautiful Hamilton should be in such a plight. Is it,' and the Queen too looked confused while she asked the question, 'is it some unfortunate— some unrequited attachment?'

The maid-of-honour blushed to her very temples, and the lustrous eyes that had been gazing fondly into the Queen's face were lowered for an instant; but she raised them with an effort, and drawing herself up, with her colour deepening every moment, answered proudly—

'Nay, madam; we Hamiltons have your own princely blood in our veins, and do not give our love unasked or unreturned. The Maries, too, follow their Queen's example, and would deem it worse than unmaidenly to entertain a secret or unacknowledged preference. We hold our heads high, you know, madam, like our mistress.'

The Queen looked as if she did not quite agree with her, and was about to answer, when a soft strain of music rose from the Abbey garden, and arrested the attention of each lady as if by a charm. The casement was thrown open, and the night wind stole in, bearing with it the melodious tones of a lute struck by no unpractised hand, and the notes of a rich voice that each seemed to recognise simultaneously with mingled embarrassment and delight.

There was then a proverb current in Scotland, which the poet seemed to have embodied in the verses he now poured forth on a flood of harmony:—

'The brightest gems in heaven that glow
Shine out from the midmost sky;
The whitest pearls of the sea below
In its darkest caverns lie.
He must stretch afar, who would reach a star,
Dive deep for the pearl, I trow:

And the fairest rose that in Scotland blows
Hangs high on the topmost bough.

'The stream of the strath runs broad and strong,
But sweeter the mountain rill;
And those who would drink with the fairy throng,
Must climb to the crest of the hill.
For the moon-lit ring of the Elfin-king
Is danced on the steepest knowe,
And the bonniest rose that in Scotland blows
Hangs high on the topmost bough.

'The violet peeps from its sheltering brake,
The lily lies low on the lea,
While the bloom is on ye may touch and take,
For the humble are frank and free;
But the garden's pride wears a thorn at her side,
It has prick'd to the bone ere now,
And the noblest rose that in Scotland blows
Hangs high on the topmost bough.

''Twere a glorious gain to have barter'd all
For the bonniest branch in the bower,
And a man might well be content to fall
In a leap for its queenliest flower!
To win her, indeed, were too princely a meed,
To serve her is guerdon enow,
And the loveliest rose that in Scotland blows
Hangs high on the topmost bough.'

Mary Stuart and Mary Hamilton looked at each other in amazement.
The former laughed sweetly.

'It is our minstrel come back again,' said she, 'and as welcome as he is
unexpected. He has not forgotten the art in his absence from the inspiration.'

While she spoke she shifted the lamp from the writing table to the
window shelf, where its flame was sheltered from the breeze by the
unopened half of the casement.

The maid-of-honour answered nothing; but the Queen could not help remarking she became very restless and preoccupied, accepting her dismissal for the night in silence, but with more alacrity than usual.

Chastelâr in the garden saw the light shifted from its place in the Queen's apartment, and interpreted it into an encouragement of his own wild hopes. His heart leaped, his brain glowed, his blood ran fire. Long absence, rational considerations, obvious impossibility, had not quenched his folly. He had left d'Amville, had wandered to and fro, had returned to Scotland with no definite object but to look on the face that haunted him night and day. He was love-mad; it mattered not what became of him: to live or die he cared not; but it must be at the Queen of Scotland's feet.

And Mary Hamilton, in her solitary chamber, fell on her knees and thanked Heaven that she should see him once again.

CHAPTER XV

'Four-and-twenty nobles sit in the king's ha';
Bonnie Glenlogie is the flower amang them a';
In cam' Lady Jean, skipping on the floor,
And she has chosen Glenlogie 'mang a' that was there.

'Glenlogie! Glenlogie! an' you will prove kind,
My love is laid on you; I'm telling you my mind:
He turned about lightly, as the Gordons does a'—
I thank ye, Lady Jean, my love's promised awa'.'

Though it was mid-winter, the sun shone brightly as in June. The bold outline of Arthur's Seat cut against a cloudless sky; and a light air from the opposite coast of Fife cleared the Firth of its accustomed vapours, and brought out in fair relief the smiling bays and noble headlands of its romantic shores. Far to the eastward, where a white sail glistened in the sun, loomed the bluff island of the Bass, poised, as it seemed, in mid-air by the magician's art, so imperceptibly were sea and sky blended together in the distant horizon; while beyond it, North-Berwick Law reared its cone above the undulating line of coast that stretched away to the southward till it faded from the sight. To the west, the wooded shores, the jutting promontories, and the sparkling water, combined to form a scene such as men imagine in their dreams, shut in by the dark glades of Hopetoun and Dalmeny, dim, rich, and beautiful, like a glimpse of fairy-land. With the castle of her strength crowning her comely brow, the old town sunned her terraced streets and high fantastic buildings in the warmth of noon, looking down, as it were, with proud protection on the smooth lawns and dainty gardens that adorned the palace of her kings. Like some rare jewel, carved, rich, and massive, resting on a velvet cushion, lay the square edifice of Holyrood on its green and level site. Though the stately towers and delicate pinnacles of the Abbey were in deep shadow, the sun shone gaily on the Queen's Park beyond, crowded as it was with masses of spectators and glittering with the brightest and fairest of the Scottish nobility.

Barriers had been placed in this well-selected spot, lists for the exercise of chivalry carefully laid out, and galleries erected for the fairer portion of the assembly, whose applause was destined to encourage the competitors and reward the successful.

The Queen and her maidens occupied the most prominent of these stages; but Mary Stuart, true to the warlike predilections of her blood, descended from her position of advantage, and, followed by her train, proceeded in person to examine the arrangements for the pastimes, and the dress and horses of those engaged.

Loud acclamations greeted her as she passed through the crowd. Though habited in mourning, as was her custom, that bewitching face did not fail to produce its usual effect, even on the strictest of the Reformers. Here and there, indeed, some severer dame might shake her head and purse up her lips in obvious disapproval of her sovereign, but such demonstrations were confined to the female sex, and only to the oldest and ugliest of *them*.

The tournament of the Middle Ages had ere this period fallen into disuse. Gunpowder had already taught the warrior that his cumbersome array of mail and plate was no secure defence, and although he had not yet discarded corslet and head-piece, he was already beginning to learn the lesson of modern warfare—that sagacity is as important a gift as courage, and agility a more effective quality than strength. Perhaps also the untoward accident that, within a few years, had deprived France of her monarch, served to bring the tournament into disrepute; and the Scotch, who, beside their tendency to imitate French manners, were then, as now, somewhat of utilitarians, need not have been long in arriving at the conclusion that such conflicts were a waste of strength, courage, and mettle, both in man and horse.

Riding at the ring, however—an exercise requiring perfect horsemanship and great dexterity in the use of the lance—long remained a favourite amusement amongst the young Scotch lords. It was no easy task to carry off, on the point of a spear, a ring scarce two inches in diameter, suspended from a slackened cord, whilst moving at a gallop; and the cavalier whose hand, eye, and seat were alike perfect enough to accomplish this feat, would have been a formidable antagonist in the crash of a real encounter—man to man and horse to horse, armed *cap-à-pie* in steel.

On the present occasion the amusement partook somewhat of the character of a masque. The two Lords Stuart, in defiance of Mistress Alison Craig's prophecy, had not found themselves so tamed and spirit-broken by marriage as to give up their favourite occupations, and had been instrumental in setting on foot the pageant which had now collected so motley a concourse in the Queen's Park. Six gallants disguised as amazons, had resolved to hold the lists against other six disguised as savages, the victory to be decided by success in carrying off the ring. The Queen herself had given the prize to be contended for—a gold heart of exquisite workmanship, and a purse filled with broad pieces. To add to the interest, a dozen of ladies chosen by lot, amongst whom were the Queen and the Maries, had been entreated to select each one a champion, and it was partly for this purpose that the train of female beauty, with Mary Stuart at its head, now wound in and out amongst the barriers which enclosed the lists, together with the domestics and horses of those who were about to ride.

As she approached one of the savages, who was already in the saddle, and poising his lance in his hand, the Queen started and turned pale in obvious distress. She would have passed him without notice, but the rider, whose wandering eye and excited gestures denoted that he ought not to be at large, reined his horse across Her Majesty so as to oppose her progress, and casting his lance at her feet, demanded to be chosen her champion and her true knight.

The Queen drew herself up and looked really angry.

'This is too much!' said she. 'How far has the Earl of Arran's loyalty and good conduct been so pre-eminent that he can dare to claim this proud distinction? By the laws of chivalry every lady has the right to her own choice, and here is mine.'

The Queen pointed to the nearest horseman as she spoke. He was richly dressed as an amazon, and his glowing complexion and regular features would have done no discredit even to one of those female warriors. She had selected him at random as a proper rebuke to Arran's insane presumption, but, like many another act of her life, it was as untoward as it was hasty. Chastelâr, for it was none other, sprang from his horse, and knelt in acknowledgment at the Queen's feet, laying his lance down at the same time before her in an attitude expressive of humility and adoration.

'To the death!' exclaimed the poet, literally kissing the hem of the Queen's garment ere he sprang once more into the saddle and forced his horse in a series of managed bounds to the farther extremity of the enclosure.

One of the maids-of-honour looked disappointed and distressed. Mary Hamilton would fain have selected the Frenchman for her champion during the day, a distinction which would probably make him her partner also in the ball at night.

As the ladies passed on, the Queen's half-brothers, both habited as amazons, approached Her Majesty, dragging between them, with shouts and laughter, a lad of some sixteen summers, whose fair, beardless face was indeed blushing like a girl's.

'Choose him, madam!' exclaimed the merry lords, in a breath, while the younger, with a comical affectation of womanly reserve, spread his gilded buckler before the lad's crimson cheeks. 'George Douglas has never lifted spear before; he is indeed a redoubtable champion for a queen.'

Tears of shame and vexation started to the boy's eyes, yet he looked pleadingly at his sovereign, as if with a confused hope that the great ambition of his life might be realised.

Mary was always gentle and considerate. She smiled on him encouragingly.

'It is mettle that makes the man-at-arms,' said she. 'I would have chosen you, indeed, young sir, had these merry gossips of yours brought you to me sooner. Never mind, you shall ride to-day for Mary Hamilton.'

The young eyes glistened with pride and happiness; the young heart swelled. Those few kind words had riveted it for ever to the cause of Queen Mary.

The English Ambassador, who, in compliance with the directions of his Court, mingled in all the amusements at Holyrood, and who was as skilled in arms as in policy, now presented himself before the ladies. Mr Randolph's costume, as one of the six savages, was remarkably well-chosen and appropriate. A bear-skin hung from his shoulders, and he had decked himself and his horse with wreaths of holly, of which the red berries were strung and looped together as savages wear their beads. He dropped on one knee to Mistress Beton, craving permission to carry her good wishes with him in the ensuing courses; and Alexander Ogilvy, in the dress of the opposite party, looked on and wished he was an ambassador too, or at least might woo that haughty dame so frankly without fear of a rebuff.

The lace on Mary Beton's collar vibrated with pleasure as she bowed a gracious affirmative. In truth the stately lady was insensibly beginning to take no small pleasure in the attentions of her diplomatic admirer.

Mary Seton, in the meantime, had been inspecting with sarcastic scrutiny the persons and accoutrements of all the competitors. With a stinging jest or biting retort she had refused to accept the homage of one after another, and finally took as her knight one John Sempill, an Englishman, who had sought refuge at the Court of Holyrood, a plain, silent man, who appeared somewhat surprised to find himself in a scene of merry-making, and whose only recommendation in the eyes of the maid-of-honour must have been that he was the direct opposite of herself.

There was yet one of the Maries who had not chosen her champion. All unconscious that there could have been a witness to her *rendezvous* in the Abbey garden, Mary Carmichael rejected candidate after candidate, in hopes the right one would apply at last. With a brighter eye and a deeper colour than usual she followed in the train of her mistress, and more than one gallant observed that he had never seen Mistress Carmichael to such advantage, and were it not for the Queen, she would carry off the palm of beauty from all upon the ground.

But the eye grew dim by degrees and the colour faded, as Walter Maxwell, habited like a savage, remained aloof, standing apart, busy with the caparison of his horse, and obviously anxious to avoid notice and conversation. A sleepless night had somewhat paled his cheek, but otherwise his look was as composed and reserved as usual. A manly nature is as much ashamed of disclosing mental suffering as physical pain.

The girl was puzzled; she could not understand him: yesterday, so kind and loyal and frank; to-day, so distant and calm and cold. Had he been the most experienced carpet-knight that ever made war upon the sex, instead of an honest, true-hearted soldier, he could not have adopted a better method of aggression. She had never felt so much engrossed with him in her life. It is hardly fair to fight a woman with her own weapons; but we imagine it discomfits them exceedingly, the more so that they are well aware a man's coldness, unlike their own, is the result of real displeasure, and the forerunner of a rupture.

Eventually all the ladies had chosen but Mary Carmichael; all the horsemen were selected but Walter Maxwell. She detached herself from the rest, and walked to where he was standing apart, still fastening his bridle and caressing his good horse.

She tried to speak in an easy, off-hand manner; but a duller ear than his might have detected the forced tone of her voice.

'They are mounting,' said she; 'you will be left out. Will you not be my knight?'

'For to-day,' he answered, bowing low, and with a strained courtesy more galling than actual rudeness.

Then he too sprang into the saddle and galloped off to join his comrades. The girl bit her lip till the blood came; tears of shame and vexation rose to her eyes; and yet she had never liked him so well as at this moment.

The Queen with her ladies now returned to the gallery, from whence she could have a good view of the sports, dispensing once more amongst the crowd that good-humoured notice which is so fascinating from a sovereign. Many a reflective Scotch face smoothed its rugged brows as she passed; many a stern Protestant who followed weekly the vigorous discourses of John Knox with approval in proportion to the strength of their doctrine, and attention never diverted for a moment from the profound casuistry of their arguments, looked after her with a wistful, pitying admiration, as though loth to believe such a creature of light could be a chosen tool of the arch-enemy, and a vessel of wrath doomed to everlasting perdition. The younger members of the crowd blessed her audibly, while here and there some godless jackman, ruffling it in all the audacious freedom of inebriety, swore loudly that it was his profession and his pastime to die for the Queen.

The Earl of Moray and his bride occupied the next seats to the royal household. Matrimony had not altered the composure of the deep-scheming earl. His own attire and that of his lady were of the gravest and most sombre, rebuking by their austere simplicity the bravery of the Queen's immediate attendants.

Moray, while he kept well with the Court, was careful not to offend the prejudices of the strict Protestant party, in whose ranks he felt lay his chief strength, and while he smiled with a melancholy forbearance on the gaieties of his brothers and his royal half-sister, he never forgot for an instant the character he had assumed, of the rigid guardian and upholder of religion; the man in whom the 'country might have confidence,' the prop and stay of 'the godly' through the length and breadth of Scotland. His bride, a comely, laughing lass when she married him, was obviously taming down, day by day, to the required pattern of decorum. Like some flower denied the sunlight, she was fading from her youthful colour and brightness, into that premature old age which is so pitiful to witness—the waning of the heart and feelings before the face is wrinkled or the locks are gray.

And now the crowd are driven from the enclosure by a score of men-at-arms wearing the royal livery. As these push their well-trained horses amongst the foot-people, much elbowing and squeezing is the result. The *lads*, as Scotchmen are termed up to the most advanced period of life, bear the jostling good-humouredly enough; the lasses laugh and shriek, and display extraordinary unsteadiness, and an unusual craving for protection and support. But the lists are cleared at last, and the troop of mounted masquers come down like a whirlwind, in line, till they reach the Queen's gallery, when they wheel to right and left from their centre, and sweeping round at the same pace, take up their respective positions at either extremity of the lists.

In Her Majesty's gallery eager eyes are watching their movements. The Queen and her ladies criticise both steeds and horsemanship pretty freely, wagering gloves and trinkets on the result, but Mary Carmichael sits pale and silent, and sees everything in a mist, because she cannot keep back her tears.

The ring is up, and borne off fairly by several of the cavaliers. All acquit themselves with knightly prowess, but some of the horses are unsteady, and Lord John Stuart shooting at a gallop past the object, of which he has only struck the outer edge, encounters amongst the spectators the laughing face of Mistress Alison Craig.

'Fie on ye!' exclaims that unabashed dame, loud enough for the discomfited nobleman to hear; 'an' ye ride no better than that, ye'll never wear the orange and black in your bonnet again on Leith Sands!'

He cannot choose but laugh as he recalls his prowess the year before among the citizens while carrying the colours of the mercer's daughter, and Mistress Alison with becoming modesty puts down her wimple to hide the cheek that has long since forgotten how to blush.

At last Mr Randolph, young George Douglas, Walter Maxwell, and Chastelâr, alone remain to contest the prize. One failure withdraws the competitor, and but these four have borne away the little circlet at each attempt with graceful skill. The excitement amongst the ladies increases visibly, and there is an obvious feeling in favour of the handsome child, for he is scarcely more, who wears on his amazonian helmet the Bleeding Heart of the House of Douglas.

The crowd, too, cheer the boy lustily. The people have alternately loved and feared the Douglas since the days of 'Good Lord James,' but their Scottish hearts warm to that grand old line, and the lad's youth and beauty are sure to tell on such an assemblage as the present. He flushes to the eyes and casts a look at the Queen's gallery, then couches his lance and drives his horse furiously to his course.

Hand and seat and eye, all are true enough, but he is going a little too fast, and the glittering object is missed by a hair's-breadth. As he leaps from the saddle at the end of his career, the boy bursts into tears, and withdraws to hide his face amongst the crowd.

Mr Randolph also fails, but with a grace and dignity that in Mary Beton's opinion are more creditable than success itself.

Chastelâr, who, to the natural dexterity of a Frenchman, has added the skill acquired by constant practice, once more carries off the ring, and glances proudly at the Queen as he brandishes it aloft on the point of his lance.

Again it is Maxwell's turn to try his fortune. Mary Carmichael's heart beats painfully. If he wins the prize, how will he act? By all the laws of chivalry he must lay the ring at her feet, and she must deliver him the costly trophy. Already she anticipates the moment of triumph. Shall she enjoy it coldly and with dignified displeasure, making him as unhappy as she has been herself? No; she longs to forgive him, and be friends. All these disquietudes are wholly unnecessary; as he arrives within a stride of the object, his horse falls, rolls over him, and both disappear in a cloud of dust. Mary Carmichael utters a faint shriek, and then sits cold and rigid like a statue. At this moment the Queen discovers the secret of her maid-of-honour.

Chastelâr then turns his horse round, carries off the ring once more, and lays it at the Queen's feet, his dark eyes flashing with excitement.

With the graceful courtesy that becomes her so well, Mary presents the prize to the successful competitor.

'One more trophy,' says the Queen, 'to the Troubadour, who wins all hearts by the sweetness of his songs, and who wields the lance as successfully as the pen.'

Chastelâr strives to speak in reply, but his voice fails him and he turns ashy white. Mary Hamilton watching him from behind her mistress almost expects him to fall from his horse. He recovers himself after a short interval, and mutters a few unintelligible sentences; then opening the purse, scatters its contents amongst the multitude, and dismounting, falls upon his knees, and replaces the heart in the Queen's hands.

'Will you not keep it, madam,' says the poet, in a hoarse broken voice, 'a tribute from the humblest and most devoted of your worshippers; fitting emblem of all Chastelâr has to give? A pure heart of sterling gold is the most appropriate offering that can be presented to the Queen of Grace and Beauty.'

Somewhat unprepared for the compliment, Mary accepts it with a little confusion, and the crowd, shouting loudly, testify their approval of the generosity as well as the prowess displayed by the Frenchman.

Some discontent has indeed been manifested at the success of a foreigner, but the freedom with which the broad pieces have been scattered about has rapidly converted all invidious demonstrations into cordial applause. On such terms they would gladly see him win hearts and purses every day.

Though stunned and shaken for the moment, Maxwell was not seriously hurt. After changing his costume for his ordinary attire, he rejoined the party of gallants and ladies that had congregated round the Queen. A fall with a horse is no very serious affair to an accomplished cavalier in the pride of youth and strength; his bearing was as composed as usual, and save a mischievous glance from Mary Seton, and a little short speech of condolence in which good-nature and sarcasm were strangely mingled, little notice was taken of his mishap. While the Queen, however, whose French education had not destroyed her predilection for pedestrian exercise, made her way back to the palace on foot, followed by her train, Mistress Carmichael lingered behind the others till she found herself next to the fallen cavalier, and as he walked on for a time without speaking, she summoned up courage at last to take the initiative.

'I must condole with my knight,' said she; 'he did his part well, and had his horse not failed him I think we should have carried off the prize.'

She spoke with a constrained effort at playfulness, and was conscious that her heart beat very fast the while. Whence came this new feeling of subjection? She never used to be afraid of him like this.

'I should like to have won it for *your* sake,' he answered, but very coldly and gravely. 'You and I will have but little in common, Mistress Carmichael, after to-day.'

'What do you mean?' she gasped, thoroughly frightened now, and too anxious to be indignant; but ere he could reply the train of courtiers had already dropped back to them, and Mary Carmichael was compelled to join her companions with a weight of grievous apprehension at her heart.

Another sentence might perhaps have cleared up everything, or at least put an end to doubts and misgivings; but how could he speak it with a score of the sharpest ears at Court ready to catch every syllable as it fell? Perhaps an explanation might never arrive, or if it did would come too late; perhaps pride might rise up to prevent it, or the opportunity never occur at all. And thus originate half the misunderstandings and estrangements that embitter the whole existence of those who, could they but speak three words to each other alone, would never doubt or mistrust in their lives again.

CHAPTER XVI

'Knights were dancing by three and three,
There was revel, game, and play;
Lovely ladies, fair and free,
Dancing with them in rich array.'

Floods of light were again streaming through the lofty halls of Holyrood. Music was pealing loud and harmonious above the ringing of wine-cups, the clatter of a banquet and the merry din of voices. Massive plate, emblazoned with the royal arms of Scotland, glittered on the board; silks, satins, and jewels shone and sparkled around it. In goblets of gold the red wine bubbled to the brim, and stately heads were bent, and bright eyes glistened while gallants laughed and whispered, and ladies blushed and smiled. All that luxury could lavish, all that refinement could require, enhanced the splendour of the feast. Tall, elaborate devices of architecture, mythology, and fancy, peering from amongst winter plants and flowers, decked the tables; whilst the very claws of the pheasants and moor-fowl were gilt ere they were served; the peacock roasted, yet not despoiled of his sleek plumage, offered a lordly delicacy; and the boar's head, garnished with rosemary, grinned its fierce welcome with the customary apple in its mouth.

At a cross-table, behind a huge candelabra, shedding a refulgent light on her features, and in front of a sideboard piled with rich plate and burnished trenchers, till she seemed literally enshrined in gold, sat the Queen, with the most distinguished of her nobility on either hand. Her face was radiant with animation, for pomp and pleasure were not without their charms to her impressible nature; and her manner, as her guests could not but observe, combined inimitably the cordiality of the hostess with the dignity of the sovereign. Her Maries were placed at the adjoining tables, and more fortunate than their mistress, had at least the chance of sitting next those individuals in whose conversation they took especial pleasure. These lotteries, however, are very apt to turn up an unreasonable proportion of blanks, and while Mary Carmichael could not even see where Walter Maxwell was supping, and Mistress Beton, to her dismay, found herself placed three seats off from the English Ambassador, Mary Hamilton alone saw the seat next her occupied by the person whose society she liked best in the world, and none but herself knew how she trembled when her cup was filled by the poet Chastelâr.

Is it not always so? We take incalculable pains to prepare for our festivities; how anxious we are that they should *go off* well; how engrossed is the butler with his plate-basket and his ice-pail; how concerned the host that my lord's venison should not be overdone. Every plait must be laid to a hair's-breadth in the glistening tresses of the lady of the house. Two mirrors satisfy her, at last, that folds and flounces and flowers are still adjusted to a nicety, but still there weighs on her mind the list of precedence, and the probable contingency that the most important guest may not turn up at all. Perhaps it may come across even her conventional mind that there are games for which it is scarce worth while to purchase such expensive candles, and that a two o'clock dinner with the children is a more agreeable repast, after all. Ay! even at the best, there is a speck on the *épergne*, an earwig in the flower-basket, a flavour of wormwood in the liquid amber called champagne. *Surgit amari* over and over again! Perhaps it was not so in that banquet of which the halt and the maimed and the blind were invited to partake. Perhaps there are no insects in a dinner of herbs; no heart-burnings in the crust we share with hunger; no bitter drop in that cup, though it be but cold water, wherewith we pledge celestial charity, and 'entertain an angel unawares.'

Chastelâr was flushed and preoccupied; thus much was apparent to the eyes that watched him with such eager interest. Ever and anon he glanced uneasily towards the royal table, but ere long something he noticed there seemed to give him intense satisfaction, and filling his goblet to the brim, he devoted himself, like an accomplished gallant, to his fair neighbour. Such is the nature of his sex. A woman always feels a little humbled when she thinks she has been too gracious, even towards a favourite; a man, on the contrary, though his affections may be fixed elsewhere, considers it due to himself to be as captivating as he can. And then they talk of female vanity and female love of admiration.

'I was sorry for my young knight to-day,' said Mary Hamilton, not, it must be confessed, very truthfully, and without raising her eyes to her companion's face. 'Poor boy! he would have been so pleased to win. I wish he had carried off the prize.'

Chastelâr could not forbear giving her a meaning look.

'And yet you did not choose him,' he said. 'He was given you by the Queen. Did he really carry your good wishes with him, Mistress Hamilton? I marvel his lance could fail; if I had thought that, mine would hardly have been so steady.'

He scarce knew what he was saying. Flushed with success; intoxicated with his own wild happiness; excited as such imaginative natures are by music, lights, wine, and beauty, he was in that reckless mood which drains pleasure eagerly from every cup, and thinks not of to-morrow.

'You are jesting with me,' she answered, in a low, trembling voice.

Oh! had he known how these light words of his thrilled to that kind unsuspecting heart, he would have spared her for very pity's sake.

'Nay, fair mistress,' he replied, gaily, 'I do not jest with *you*; there are some with whom to break jests is like breaking lances, sharp-pointed ones, too, and ending in a combat à *l'outrance*. I am afraid of you, Mistress Hamilton.'

'Why so?' she asked, looking up at him with her clear, guileless eyes. 'Am I so very formidable? You do not seem much afraid of anything to-night.'

A gleam of triumph shot from his eyes, and once more he glanced towards the upper end of the hall, then lowering his voice, he whispered —

'There are contests in which to win is as perilous as to lose. There are lists in which the true knight fights unarmed whilst his adversary is clothed in steel. Give me my *coup-de-grâce*, Mistress Hamilton,' he added, with a bright smile, 'I must depart now to prepare for the masque. Before I go I yield me "rescue or no rescue."'

'You have a merciful jailer,' was all she could trust herself to reply; but as he rose from his seat and left the hall, Mary Hamilton's eyes followed him with a wistful, longing gaze, and Mary Hamilton's heart thrilled in her bosom, with a keen sense of pleasure that was not far removed from pain.

Meanwhile the banquet progressed merrily, not uncheered by those lively strains that have made Scotch music, from time immemorial, so appropriate to all scenes of merry-making or excitement. Wine, too, flowed freely, for the stalwart barons would, indeed, have deemed themselves wanting in respect to their sovereign had they stinted their accustomed measure because they sat at a queen's table. Thirsty souls they were, some of those iron old paladins, and quaffed such mighty draughts as their degenerate descendants would scarce believe; but it was observed that those among them who were most liberal in their potations, became also graver, more dignified and sententious, in proportion to the quantity they imbibed.

Here and there a vacant seat might be perceived, as several gallants quitted the feast by stealth to prepare for the coming pageant, which was tacitly conceded to be a surprise.

Ere long the lower tables, at the extremity of the hall, were drawn, and their occupants, gathering round the royal circle, began to display that flutter of expectation which pervades all assemblies when there is anything to be seen.

Presently two grave ushers with white wands threw open the folding-doors, and, amidst peals of laughter from the men, and exclamations of astonishment, not without a shriek or two, from the ladies, in rushed a troop of satyrs, and commenced clearing a space in the middle of the hall for the further exhibition of the performances.

These masquers were in uncouth and fantastic disguise: their flesh-coloured coverings were adorned with wreaths of oak-leaf and ivy; horns sprouted from their brows; goat-skins covered their nether limbs, which terminated in cloven feet; and long tails depended from their backs, which they brandished in their hands, and used as whips to clear a passage in the throng.

The Queen clapped her hands, and laughed aloud. 'None but Sebastian could have plotted this,' she exclaimed. 'Come hither, 'Bastian, that we may thank thee for thine ingenious device.'

The satyr thus summoned, who seemed indeed the leader of the rest, and no mean representative of the god Pan, approached the royal presence with quaint reverence, beating a measured dance with his cloven feet, and brandishing his tail the while.

James Geddes, the fool, in an irrepressible state of excitement, could not forbear imitating his gestures with a grotesque fidelity that provoked shouts of laughter.

Sebastian, somewhat irritated, and taking advantage of his position, struck at him viciously with his tail; but the fool, familiar with such salutes, dodged it adroitly, and the blow fell across the shapely leg of the English ambassador, who winced, and turned crimson with the pain.

Mr Randolph, however, had far too much self-command to betray his anger, which was little alleviated by the laughter that the Queen could not repress.

'How now?' quoth the statesman, trying hard to force a smile; 'is Pan like Atropos, that he spares neither Wisdom nor Folly, but smites down all alike?'

'It's the knave aye gets the fule's arles,'[7] remarked James; 'or he wadna be siccan a knave; an' it's the fule aye tynes[8] them, or he wadna be siccan a fule!'

[7] Wages.

[8] Losses.

And so speaking, he sat composedly down at the Queen's feet, pulling a grimace at the same time that was too much even for the Earl of Moray's gravity.

The satyrs then proceeded to enclose a space for the coming masque. So thorough was their disguise as to baffle even the keen eyes of those who were most interested in their identity; and as the sylvan monsters ranged themselves on each side the hall, soft voices behind them whispered—

'Are you Sholto?' or, 'It *must* be Archibald!' to receive no more satisfactory answer than a stifled laugh.

A flourish of music now announced the continuation of the pageant, and the three planets, Mercury, Mars, and Venus, made their appearance, habited in robes of silver gauze and spangles: the first, winged strictly according to mythology at head and heel; the God of War, armed with glittering helmet, flashing buckler, and greaves of burnished gold; and the Queen of Beauty, represented by young George Douglas, extremely embarrassed with her draperies, and blushing as Venus surely, save on one memorable occasion, never blushed in her life.

These representations of the starry host were then succeeded by the Nine Muses, all in different colours, and, notwithstanding their beardless faces and classical folds, displaying legs unusually muscular for Muses, and also a good deal more limb than is customary with that sex to which the 'tuneful Nine' are supposed to belong.

Melpomene, too, could not forbear laughing outright; Clio, albeit the daughter of memory, forgot whether she was herself or Urania; and Terpsichore, somewhat flushed with sack, caught her feet in her petticoats, and narrowly escaped the indignity of entering the royal presence on her head. They trooped off, however, after making their obeisance to the Queen, and ranged themselves in front of the satyrs on either side the hall.

After them a score of cavaliers, mounted on the well-known hobby-horse, of which the sweeping housings concealed its rider's real legs, whilst his false ones dangled outside in ludicrous union with its gambols, plunged and frolicked into the apartment. Half were represented as huntsmen, half as heathen Turks, and they blew their horns, or brandished their scimitars, with an energetic gravity edifying to behold. One truculent-looking Saracen earned immortal honour by the life like manner in which he backed his hobby-horse the whole length of the hall, and then caused it to rear straight on end ere he took up his position, counterfeiting inimitably the coquetry of the practised rider, and the repressed mettle of the unwilling yet obedient steed. Some of the courtiers whispered that it was Lord John Stuart; others, the Grand Falconer; not a few believed it to be the Warden of the Marches in disguise; but the better informed were all the time aware that it was no less a personage than Her Majesty's head cook.

Then came pilgrims decked with sandals and scalloped shell, leading with them bears, wolves, tigers, and an occasional unicorn; all these quadrupeds presenting alike the anomaly of a pair of hind legs jointed the wrong way, but performing their parts in other respects with decorous fidelity, and an obvious difficulty in keeping up with their leaders. These were succeeded by musicians bearing lutes, harps, wind instruments, and guitars, dumb indeed in reality, but going through all the motions of a lively measure, which the Queen's real musicians were playing for their encouragement.

Next came two little cupids armed with silver bows and baldricks, their rosy limbs uncovered, and their golden curls mingling with the wings of gauze that stood from their shoulders. Pretty urchins they were, but somewhat too young for their task, and already rubbing their sleepy eyes with dimpled little fists. Hand in hand, they trotted into the hall boldly enough, but ere half the distance was accomplished their hearts failed them; they stopped, looked about them, and one began to cry. This was too much for his little companion's philosophy, who incontinently followed his example, but both were immediately caught up by some of the ladies, and quickly caressed into composure. The Queen, too, had them brought to her forthwith, and soothing them with kind words and sweetmeats, sent them to bed happy and consoled.

During this unexpected interlude, the principal feature of the pageant, and one which had tasked to the utmost the ingenuity of its contrivers, now entered the hall. It consisted of a fleet of ships constructed of light wicker-work, and moved upon wheels, which were worked unseen from within.

The sides of these galleys were formed of cloth, coloured to represent beams of cedar, fastened and inlaid with gold; the masts and spars were gilt, the tackle of silver tissue, and the sails of gauze. A murmur of admiration greeted the pageant as it glided up the hall with the stately motion of ships sailing over a smooth sea.

On the deck of each bark stood an unknown lord, dressed with the utmost magnificence, and closely-masked. So resolved were these silken pirates not to be identified, that their doublets, their hose, and even their gloves, were padded so as to conceal the shape of their figures, their limbs, and their very hands. They were known to be gallants of the Court, but that was all. The nobles laughed and applauded, their dames whispered and speculated, when, with a burst of music rising into loud, triumphant tones, the ships increased their speed, and the leading galley, closely followed by the rest, bore swiftly down upon the circle which contained the Queen and her ladies, with obvious intention of a capture.

Each masquer took a partner by the hand, and courteously entreated her in dumb show to enter his gorgeous bark. The Queen first set the example of compliance, and amidst shouts of admiration the barks veered round, and, doubly freighted, floated once more proudly down the hall.

Then the squadron divided, the sails were furled, the voyagers disembarked, and each gallant kneeling low as he gave his hand to his companion and helped her to alight, unmasked at the same instant, while the music changing to a merry lilt, the couples found themselves arranged in due order to tread a well-known measure called 'the Purpose,' on the polished floor.

This 'Purpose,' as it was called—a word which signified confidential conversation—was a dance resembling the cotillon so popular with our grandmothers, and not entirely despised to-day when lights are waning after a night of festivity, and gloves are soiled, and flowers faded, and cheeks begin to pale before the coming dawn. Then is the moment to infuse fictitious vigour borrowed from excitement into the closing scene—then the careful mother at the emptying doorway, with shawl and wrapper on her braceleted arm, waves her unwelcome summons to the bounding damsel, warmed up into bloom once more, and every turn is precious now because every turn must be the last. Then shall the prey, which has been playing round it all night, gorge the glittering bait for good and all. Wind up the reel, in with the tackle, out with the landing-net—goldfish or gudgeon, he is gasping helpless on the bank; but had it not been for the cotillon, he might have been wriggling his tail even now in derision through the elusive waters, might have despised the fire and ignored the frying-pan to this day.

The 'Purpose' was so called because the figure exacted that at stated intervals the couples should dance together through the doorway into an adjoining room, and having made the circuit of that apartment, should return, unbosomed of any secrets they might have had to interchange, to the rest of the laughing company. It was a figure obviously adopted for the triumph of coquetry, and the discomfiture of mankind.

The leading pirate had dutifully borne off the Queen, and when he unmasked, Mary discovered that Chastelâr was to be her partner in the dance. The poet's manner was more full of deference than usual, but there was a light of unearthly happiness in his eye.

Randolph had secured Mary Beton, nothing loth. That very morning the ambassador had received instructions from his Government to leave no stone unturned till he had discovered the Queen's predilections amongst the numerous marriages that were proposed to her, all and each of which gave Elizabeth such disquiet. He proceeded now deliberately to sound her principal maid-of-honour, under cover of making fierce love to her himself.

With the loud music and the long intervals of inaction there was ample opportunity for the process.

'We shall soon have nobler doings even than these,' observed Mr Randolph, whispering confidentially to his partner, 'when another royal wedding gladdens the walls of Holyrood. Shall we dance the Spaniard's bolero, or the Austrian's gavolte, or our own old English brawl? Whatever be the measure, Mistress Beton, my only hope is that we may dance it together.'

Randolph looked very tenderly at her while he spoke, and his partner's ruff heaved visibly.

'Nay; you statesmen are too premature,' she replied. 'Ladies are not to be thus wooed and won in a day, much less queens. The Archduke, Don Carlos, Lord Robert—which of them can be called a fitting mate for our Sovereign? You must not hurry us thus, Mr Randolph; you are indiscreet.'

'And cannot you guess why I am so anxious for your mistress to marry?' whispered the insidious statesman, pressing nearer to his listener. 'Is it not that alone which will free her beautiful maidens from their self-imposed celibacy? Till that auspicious day even our thoughts are not our own, and a man of honour must be tongue-tied on the subject nearest his heart.'

Mary Beton blushed and trembled. It was almost a declaration, and from that impenetrable and capable man! The staid maid-of-honour was losing her head every moment.

'It may come sooner than any of us think,' she murmured, giving him her hand to lead her, as the dance demanded, on their tour through the rooms. 'Sooner than any of us desire,' she added, with a sudden resumption of her usual stateliness.

He pressed the hand affectionately, and his voice became exceedingly trusting and confidential. Mr Randolph was a man who never hesitated to waste a sprat for the purpose of catching a salmon.

'It will not be Lord Robert,' said he; 'I can tell you that, though it is as much as my life is worth. But I would trust you with my head, beautiful Mistress Beton—far rather than my heart,' he added, in a low fond voice; 'were it not indeed too late to make that reservation.'

The light seemed to swim in Mary Beton's eyes, and the music was like surging water in her ears. A true woman, despite her natural caution and her court education, she returned confidence for confidence.

'They do talk of a bridegroom,' she whispered. 'It is a secret, Mr Randolph; but I feel I am safe with you. The Countess of Lennox has already suggested her son, and I think the Queen is not averse to the idea. If it *should* ever be,' she added, with rising colour and some hesitation, 'we shall be differently circumstanced, of course; and, in short, the future must always be uncertain for us all.'

He replied with less warmth than she perhaps expected; but his commonplaces were extremely polite, nay complimentary, and when he led her back to the company, there was that complacent expression on his countenance, which is worn by a man who finds in the hand dealt him the leading card of the game.

Far different was the 'Purpose' entertained by Walter Maxwell and Mary Carmichael, in their interval of conversation. With the frank kindliness of his nature, that honest gentleman had determined at least to ask an explanation, ere he condemned at once and for ever the woman he felt he still loved only too well.

With this intention he had joined the merry band of masquers, though his heart was sadly out of tune for mirth, and had carried off his mistress without hesitation from the fair circle who were waiting to be abducted. Nay, when he unmasked, and Mistress Carmichael, who had recognised him from the first, stole a look at his face, it wore its usual grave but kindly expression, and the displeasure which had so discomfited her all day, and spoilt her gaiety all night, had entirely disappeared. He was determined to be just and kind and temperate in his dealing with her, though more than life depended on the result.

When he spoke it was in a low, soft voice, but every syllable was strangely emphatic and distinct.

'I behaved unkindly in the Queen's Park,' said he, 'but I was hurt and offended at your conduct. Had I not cause?'

She blushed, yet her eye was bright with repressed exultation.

'How have I offended you?' she asked, quickly. 'I would not do so willingly, you know.'

'I thought you different from the others,' he resumed, with more agitation. 'In common charity I ask to be undeceived. Did I not see you in the Abbey garden the night before last?'

She trembled all over, but looked him full in the face nevertheless, yet so scared, so startled.

'What then?' she murmured, in obvious agitation.

'You were not alone,' he continued, with a severe brow; 'who was your companion?'

She drew a long breath as if immensely relieved, nay, she almost smiled as she replied—

'Then, you do not know? you cannot even guess?'

'Had I known,' he answered, significantly, 'it would not have been the lady I should have questioned.'

She raised her head haughtily.

'And by what right do you question the lady now?' she exclaimed. 'Am I answerable to Walter Maxwell for my conduct? I take leave to think, sir, you might be better employed than in watching my movements.'

He was growing very angry and consequently calmer every second.

'You had rather give no explanation?' he said, with studied politeness.

She bowed her head in silence, but the colour was fading faster and faster from her cheek.

'You decline it,' he added, still very low, but through his set teeth.

'Distinctly!' answered the lady, adding, as only a woman would at such a moment, 'You are neglecting the figure, the dance is going on without you.'

After this the pair derived but small gratification, we imagine, from the amusements of the evening. Walter Maxwell took the earliest opportunity of departing to cool his irritation in the night air, whither, as we dislike seeing a strong man wrestling with pain, we will not follow him. Mary Carmichael, however, bore her part bravely to the end; and although her answers were at times a little absent, and her laughter somewhat misplaced, none could have guessed by her outward bearing that she had so recently seen the great stake of her life's happiness set, played for, and lost. She was not the only gambler in the hall. There was one heart amongst those dancers within a few yards of her that had resolved to-night to play the great game in which the odds were incalculably against it, and which to lose was ruin entire and irretrievable. There were a couple now gracefully moving through the figure of 'the Purpose,' as the music swelled and sank in triumphant harmony or pleading sweetness, of whom one was enjoying unconsciously the gratification of the moment, gay, kindly, generous, and impressionable, yet calm and dignified because thinking no evil, and the other with beating heart and swimming brain was steeped to the lips in the intoxication of that madness which comes but once in a lifetime, and seems to have but one fatal and invariable result.

Woe to the idolater! It is written on the tables of stone: Woe to the idolater! Be the image what it may, wood brass, or marble, or one 'a little lower than the angels,' whom the worshipper must needs exalt above the Being to whom the heavenly Host itself is but as dust in the hollow of a man's hand. The punishment shall not come from abroad; it shall not be wrought by foreign enmity, nor owe its keenest pang to foreign injustice. If so, the sting would be extracted; the vengeance incomplete. No; Dagon alone shall crush the deluded votary who grovelled at Dagon's pedestal. It is the hand he trusted that shall strike him to the heart, the feet he kissed that shall spurn him in the dust. When he shall have stripped himself of all to do his false god service; when he shall have lost his friends, his wealth, his fame, his self-respect, and forfeited his honour, and pawned his birthright, then, and not till then, shall the image of stone rock and totter and fall upon him and crush him to powder. Were there no world but this, it would indeed be better for that man that he had never been born.

The Dagon of to-night was fair to look on, queenly and graceful and gloriously beautiful. It seemed unnatural to refuse her homage; it seemed ecstasy to kneel and supplicate and adore. The worshipper was in the wildest stage of his idolatry. He looked for no greater glory than to lay down life and heart and soul at her feet.

What good results could come from such a link between the lovely Queen of Scotland and the infatuated minstrel of France?

CHAPTER XVII

'He either fears his fate too much,

Or his deserts are small,

Who dares not put it to the touch,

To win or lose it all.'

Mary Stuart still wore in her bosom the gold heart that had been won by Chastelâr in his victory of the day. This it was that had so elated him at the banquet; this it was that gave him courage in the dance to speak words of love to his Queen.

The distant music had subsided to a low, plaintive strain; the apartment into which, in their turn, the two had seemed to float upon those floods of melody was bathed in a subdued and softened light; the odour of perfumes loaded the atmosphere; and the sounds of far-off revelry did but add to the languor and seclusion of the scene. Mary's cheek was a shade paler and her step scarce so buoyant as usual. She seemed fatigued, and whilst awaiting the louder peal of music that should summon them back to the dance, the Queen seated herself on a low chair near the doorway, and fixed her eyes upon the floor with a dreamy, listless gaze. Chastelâr remained standing, bent over her chair as if fascinated, spell-bound. The music sank lower and lower, and they were alone!

At last the Queen raised her eyes to his, and what she saw there brought the blood reddening to her brow. It broke the charm, however, and the poet found his voice to speak, though his lips trembled so that he could scarcely form his words. He knelt before her as he would have knelt to a saint.

'Ah! madam,' he exclaimed in broken accents, 'accept my homage, my thanks, my everlasting gratitude. This is the day in Chastelâr's life that he had better lay him down and die in his great happiness, for the sun can never shine on such another for him again.'

She smiled on him, half-kindly and half-pitiful.

'Why should you thus thank me, Chastelâr?' she said. 'What have I granted to my Troubadour that is not richly merited by one so loyal, so devoted, and so true?'

She spoke lightly and playfully, yet was there a tone of repressed feeling in her voice. No woman alive could have looked unmoved on the depth of intense devotion that glowed in Chastelâr's face.

'Ay, madam,' he replied, 'you have ever been kind and condescending and gracious to your slave. You know not what your notice is to him: how he watches every turn of your face, and hangs on every word of your lips. What the blessed sunlight is to creation—its hope, its love, its pride, its whole existence—such is your presence, O Mary! O my Queen! to me.'

'Nay,' she replied, half-rising from her seat, and looking round as though not caring that their dialogue should be overheard; 'nay, Chastelâr, how you are trenching on your own prerogative, and wasting on my solitary ear the materials for a sonnet which should delight the whole Court. I cannot listen to such compliments from my Troubadour, save in verse.'

'You will listen to them thus,' he exclaimed, eagerly. 'You will allow me to lay at your feet a volume I have long wished, but not dared, to pray you to accept. May I experience this great happiness? Is it a promise?'

She bowed her fair head in acquiescence, and her colour went and came. Queen though she were, Mary Stuart was also a woman to the heart's core; and it was not in woman's nature but to experience a tinge of gratification and triumph in an authority so despotic, a dominion so complete as this.

Emboldened by the permission, he hurried on:—

'I would lay all I have—my fame, my happiness, my life, nay, my very soul—at your Majesty's feet, and thank and bless you, even did you trample them to dust. O madam! have you not read of such devotion? can you not believe in it? Do you not *know* that there may exist a love so pure, so holy, so self-denying, that its blessing and its privilege is to give all and ask for nothing in return?'

Again she looked around her, startled and confused, but there were no listeners near. Still the strain of 'the Purpose' stole soft and low and soothing on her ear. She resolved she must never hear him speak again like this; but the moments were all the more precious at the time. It would be too unkind to check him harshly now. He was madly in love with her, no doubt; and his punishment would come quite soon enough: meantime, she thought it better to treat the whole affair playfully.

'I too can write verses,' said she, with a bright smile. 'Shall I repeat you a couplet or two I composed to-day? They are not amiss, Chastelâr, at least for a queen! and considering they are in rhyme, they are tolerably true—too true, I fear; the more the pity. Listen, Troubadour, and take a lesson in your own trade; moreover, beseech you, mark the moral, for that is the whole merit of the stave:—

'Wild Folly, so the legends tell,
Was wedded to a maid,
A dusky maid that used to dwell
In drowsy summer-shade.

'Their offspring is a fairy elf,
A thing of tricks and wiles;
He plays with hearts to please himself,
And when they break he smiles.

'Unpitied pain and toil in vain
That little tyrant brings;
And those who fain would slip his chain,
Must cheat him of his wings.

'To Cupid's tortures, you may guess,
Each parent lends a part;
The chain, the toils, from Idleness,
While Folly adds the smart.'

'And yet, madam, there are chains that the slave hugs to his bosom,' answered Chastelâr, gazing on her with looks of imploring affection; 'there is a labour of love that is sweeter than the profoundest repose; there is a pain that we prize and cherish, clasping it tighter and tighter till it pierces to our hearts, and so we die.'

'Such chains I would not lay on *my* servants,' said the Queen: 'such labour I would never impose; such pain I could not bear to inflict.'

He looked up brightly.

'Say you so, madam?' he replied; 'then indeed do you give me new life, and something to live for. You graciously accepted that trinket from me to-day; and the proudest moment of my existence was when I saw it on your breast to-night; that gold heart is but an emblem of mine own; it is yours, my Queen, if you will deign to take it. Do with it what you will; keep it, or break it, or cast it scornfully away.'

He took the Queen's hand as he spoke, and pressed it fervently to his lips; but he had gone too far, and Mary, rising from her chair, snatched her hand from him, and drew herself to her full height.

'You forget,' she said; 'you must surely forget where we are, and to whom you speak! This is Holyrood, Monsieur Chastelâr, the royal palace of the kings of Scotland; and I am Mary Stuart, its mistress and its Queen. Lead me back, sir, to the dancers; the music warns us; and do not expect to be forgiven if you should so far presume again.'

She spoke angrily, yet some feeling of compunction smote her the while; and perhaps she was not quite so angry as she looked. She gave him her hand to lead her back to the dance with lofty condescension; and it was remarked on her return to the hall, by more than one acute observer, that the Queen seemed to have quite recovered her fatigue, and that her colour was deeper, her glance brighter, and her step firmer than during the earlier part of the evening. One pair of eyes, too, that never left him save when they met his own, that shone with liquid lustre when he was present, and filled many a time with unbidden tears when he was far away, gazed wistfully on Chastelâr to-night, and a fond heart wondered why his face was so pale, and his manner so dejected and wild and sad.

Mary Hamilton was one of those characters less rare in her own than in the stronger sex, with whom, to use the poet's expression, 'love is its own avenger.' For such, happiness, when it does come, should indeed be intense, for their sufferings are acute, their doubts harassing, their self-depreciation unsparing in proportion to the abandonment with which they merge their whole existence in that of another. It is good to love for those who can love wisely, but, alas! for the self-inflicted tortures of the heart that loves too well.

The revel was at its height; louder and louder pealed the music, faster and faster flew the dancers; all seemed bent on the enjoyment of the hour, and resolved that the concluding scene of the festival should be the wildest and merriest of the night. To look at those panting forms, flushed cheeks, bright eyes, and floating tresses, who would have believed but that here, if anywhere, was to be found the gaiety that flings itself without reservation into the pleasures of the moment? Who would have thought there could be room for care or sorrow in the fair bosoms heaving proudly under pearls and gold, or detect the ring of spurious metal in the joyous tones that told of gratified vanity and partial approbation, and careless, thoughtless mirth?

It is better to leave your partner when you have shawled her deftly at the door; there she bids you a cordial, perhaps even a tender 'good-night' with her mask on, the same mask you always see, that is painted in such a radiant smile. It comes off though in her dressing-room, when the aching temples are released from their garland, and the shining tresses are unbound, and the being that you have envied as a model of good sense, gaiety, and content, sits her down with a weary sign, and dismissing you and your platitudes, with which she seemed so highly delighted, from her thoughts, leans her head upon her hand, while the hot tears trickle through her fingers for the sake of somebody you never saw or heard of, who is far, far away.

Perhaps you are even with her; perhaps you, too, meeting her gloved hand in the dance, wince under the senseless exterior which you assume with your evening clothes, in painful consciousness that you cannot quite forget a Somebody of your own, the very rustle of whose dress was music to your ears in the olden golden days that are spent and vanished like a dream; ay, though you seemed so gay and caustic and *debonair* in the cloak-room a while since, when you walk out into the night, the stars you loved to watch for *her* sake long ago, look down upon you more in pity than reproach, and the sighing wind reminds you, as it never fails to do, of the gentle face that was all your trust and treasure once, that is lost to you now for evermore. There is no need for you to hum the refrain of that beautiful song, wailing for 'the tender grace of a day that is dead.' Are you likely to forget it, clinging as it does about your heart like ice, and chilling you to the marrow even now? Never mind! you have 'done your ball' handsomely and creditably, both to self and partner; it matters little that you are a couple of well-dressed hypocrites, covering your respective sores under broadcloth and Mechlin lace; you have offered your incense at the conventional altar; you have sacrificed religiously to society; you are at liberty to take off your trappings now, and wash the paint from your wan faces, and go both of you away by yourselves, to be as wretched as you please.

The Queen and her Maries danced on, fresh and gay to the very last. Even the musician's well-trained fingers seemed less untiring than the ladies' feet. But the revel came to an end soon after midnight, and the sentinels at the palace gates, relieved at that hour, glanced admiringly after the noble groups that departed in quick succession; some of the older and statelier forms, be it observed, walking with a more staid and solemn air than usual, attributable to the excess of the Queen's hospitality, and the excellence of the French wines that graced her table.

There were two individuals, however, now strolling away arm-in-arm with an appearance of great cordiality, who never suffered their brains to be heated beyond their self-control, and who, relying on their wits as the good swordsman on his blade, were careful to keep those weapons constantly bright and keen and tempered for immediate use. They were engaged, even in this friendly promenade, in a kind of moral fencing-bout, with muffled points indeed, and bloodless intentions, yet such as should prove to each his adversary's strength against the future possibility of a real encounter.

Said Mr Randolph to Secretary Maitland—

'The revel hath indeed sped gaily. I never witnessed a merrier even at the English court, where my royal mistress hath always given so hearty a welcome to the Lord of Lethington. The masques were quaint, the music exquisite, the supper beyond all praise. Holyrood was indeed to-night one blaze of splendour.'

'And our Scottish ladies?' asked the Secretary, who had not failed to observe his companion's attention to Mistress Beton, and, suspecting his design, glanced curiously at his face to gather what he could from that inscrutable volume.

The Firth down yonder sleeping in the moonlight, could not have been less unruffled than the Englishman's countenance; nevertheless, his language was too enthusiastic to be sincere.

'They are above all praise,' said he. 'Were I one of those soft-headed, iron-handed paladins of fifty years ago, I would break any number of lances in maintaining your Queen and her Maries to be the brightest bevy of beauty in Christendom! But those follies went out with the mass to make room for others! And, by the way, what thinks worthy Master Knox and his godly party of all this feasting and fiddling and mummery?'

'There is a strong feeling of religion amongst our townsfolk,' was the guarded answer, 'combined with loyalty to Her Majesty.'

'Then they desire to see her wedded,' resumed Randolph. 'It rejoices me to hear this, guessing, as I think I can, at the Queen of England's wishes. Frankly now, and between friends, hath your beautiful Mistress no predilection for any of her wooers?'

'I am only a statesman,' answered Maitland, laughing. 'I can fathom a plot or an intrigue; but a woman's schemes are far too deep for me. I believe, however, that on this subject ladies are not prone to speak their real minds.'

'Lord Robert Dudley is a stanch Protestant?' proceeded Randolph, interrogatively; 'and a comely, personable nobleman besides?'

'Would your mistress like to part with him to mine?' said the other, with increasing mirth. 'If Dudley aims at a crown-matrimonial, Mr Randolph, he need not cross the Tweed to fetch it, or we are strangely misinformed in the North.'

'Nay,' answered the Englishman, 'I will be frank with you. The Maiden Queen would be loathe to resign either title. But it is not on her marriage that the eyes of all Protestant Europe are fixed. The destiny of the Reformed Church will be strongly influenced by Mary Stuart's choice of a husband.'

'She will be guided doubtless in this, as in everything, by the wishes of her people and the advice of her royal cousin,' was the diplomatic reply. 'The Austrian and the Spanish match are alike distasteful. The Archduke is a greybeard, and Don Carlos a puling, sickly boy. You see, I can be candid with you. Our Queen will have none of these.'

Mr Randolph, in common with the general public, had known this important disclosure for weeks. It was his cue, however, to accept the communication for somewhat more than it was worth.

'As we are in confidence, then,' he continued, 'I will round in your ear an idea of mine own. What if the Scottish Queen should unite herself to one of her own blood, and of suitable years, thus avoiding all foreign influences, the while she does no violence to her natural inclinations? —a goodly young gentleman, of honest nurture, and of the Reformed religion. Surely such a mate could be found amongst the noble families in both kingdoms.'

It was a leading suggestion, from which Randolph hoped to gather a corroboration of Mary Beton's intelligence; but he had to do with one as skilled in state-craft as himself, and equally unhampered by compunctions as to truth or sincerity.

'There is none that I can think of,' replied Maitland, with an air of such exceeding candour that the other felt convinced he was telling him a lie—'unless it be young Lord Darnley; and there are so many objections to his claim, that although it has often been considered, it has never been entertained for a moment. Is it possible that it would meet with your Court's approval?'

'I cannot answer without instructions,' said Randolph, laughing: and wishing each other 'good night,' the well-matched pair separated, without either having gained a decided advantage in the encounter of their wits.

The Laird of Lethington, indeed, who had been acting on the defensive, was satisfied with his own reticence, although his suspicions were aroused, and the eternal question, 'What is he aiming at?' that haunts the diplomatist, followed him to his pillow; but Mr Randolph was puzzled and discomfited. He could not piece his information together as he liked into one of those perfect specimens of workmanship which he delighted to forward to Secretary Cecil for the inspection of his Queen. Nevertheless he sat up far into the night, writing a state-paper to the English grand vizier, and when it was finished, such is the inconsistency of man, dwelt with considerable complacency on the handsome stately image of the lady who had suggested it. The road to power is not often strewed with flowers. Mr Randolph had no objection to gather them when he could do so without going out of his way, though he was the last man to keep them when withered, or indeed care for them one jot after the first freshness was off their bloom.

But what were the musings of a weary courtier, or even the misgivings of a baffled diplomatist, to the tide of anxiety and anguish that surged through the overwrought brain of Chastelâr, till the poet felt as if he must go mad? Alas! for the gift, dangerous as it is brilliant, of a vivid imagination acting on a deep and tender heart. There are certain insects in the tropics, with which, unconscious of the cruelty, ladies are wont to trim their dresses, that sparkle like diamonds, when thus impaled in torture: while they suffer they glow, and when they cease to glow they die. So it is with certain temperaments, and those not the dullest nor the least amiable of their kind. Their very lustre arises from the pain that is goading them within. The flash that sets the table in a roar springs often from an aching heart: the glowing words that clothe immortal thoughts in godlike imagery rise to lips wet with the bitterest draught of all. Who can describe happiness so vividly as he who feels that it can never be his own? Who yearns for beauty with the thirst of him to whom all that is fairest in earth and heaven but mocks the impotence of his despair? If such temperaments enjoy keenly, and indeed it would be hard if they did not, they suffer with an intensity of pain that goads them nearly to madness, and causes them to rush into follies and extravagances such as less ardent natures are never tempted to commit.

Chastelâr left the hall tortured with shame and doubt and fear. Sometimes he wondered at his own recklessness, that could thus risk his very existence on a word; for he felt that if Mary were really offended, and he were banished from the Court, he had better die. Then he taxed the Queen with perfidy, injustice, hardness of heart. Anon, a softer feeling argued that his offence was not of so grievous a nature after all, that the Sovereign might pardon and look kindly on a confession of such devotion to the woman, nay, that it might have been welcome to her and expected long ago. But Mary's image, rising from her chair in offended majesty, dispelled this brighter vision; and though his very heart was flooded with the remembrance of her beauty, the sense of hopelessness that had chilled it so often, seemed to creep over him and paralyse him as of old. At least he felt he could not bear her displeasure. She had turned away from him when he had sought her eye after the dance. Perhaps she was mortally offended, and would never speak to him again. Like all others under the same spell, he was totally incapable of judging his own case, and saw everything in a false light. He was even himself aware that he could no longer rely upon his faculties, and yet he felt an irresistible impulse goading him to action, no matter what. There is method in every phase of madness save one, and that is the madness of a man in love.

He paced his room in an agony of irresolution. At last he made up his mind to ask the Queen's forgiveness. He could not sleep without it. He must have it this very night before she retired. He bethought him of the book that she had consented to accept. It was a happy idea: that unconscious little volume should befriend him. He would present it to her on his knees, and would read his sentence in the looks with which she received the token. He was more composed now, and felt as if he were about the most rational proceeding in the world.

Acting on this suggestion, Chastelâr, with his offering in his hand, stole softly through the gallery and up the staircase that led to the Queen's private apartments. The lights were already extinguished, and none were moving in the palace, save one or two tired domestics, loitering drowsily to bed. With a beating heart and noiseless tread he reached the door of an ante-room that led to the Queen's chamber, and paused for an instant to listen. The latch of the door clanked loudly as he opened it, but all was dark within.

Whilst deliberating whether to enter or not, a light shone along the passage, and a measured step, accompanied by the rustle of a lady's dress, made his heart leap to his mouth. At this juncture, his presence of mind, which had so strangely abandoned him all night, came back in a moment. Without looking to identify the intruder, he laid his book upon the door-sill, and stooping down imprinted a kiss on the threshold, as one who takes his last leave of the shrine that guards his idol ere he retires. In rising he encountered the Queen herself, still in her robes of ceremony and alone. She was proceeding from the Countess of Argyle's chamber to her own, and had dismissed all her attendants save the two that were even now waiting for her in her bedroom. She started when she saw Chastelâr, and the blood came to her cheek. Was it the light that shone round her like a glory in the poet's heated imagination that produced the semblance, or was it his own fancy, or could it be reality? He thought her eyes looked wet with tears.

This was too much for his overwrought feelings. He flung himself at Mary's feet, and taking the skirt of her robe in his hands, literally kissed the hem of her garment again and again.

'Forgive me, madam, forgive me!' he exclaimed, in broken accents, and weeping like a woman or a child. 'I could not bear it; I could not rest; I felt I had offended you—I who would die to give you a moment's pleasure. I was mad! I knew not what I did; but I crept here to lay my offering at your feet, and to pray for your forgiveness; although you would not know it, would never hear or heed me. Pardon! oh! pardon me, my Queen!'

She could not but pity him; she who was so good and tender-hearted and pitiful to all: his sorrow was so obvious, his misery so complete. She gave him her white hand and bade him rise to his feet; then she chid him gently, kindly, with a grave sorrow on her young face, like a mother who takes to task a dear but froward child.

'You would not grieve me, Chastelâr,' said she, 'I know. Not one of my Scottish subjects is more loyal and true than my French minstrel. Give me your book; I will accept it as a pledge of your service and fidelity to your sovereign. To your sovereign,' she added, with a significant look, before which his eyes were lowered, and his whole countenance fell. 'I am not only Mary Stuart,' she added—and perhaps it was but his fancy made him think there was a dash of sadness in her tone—'I am the Queen of Scotland as well. This country, too, is not like France; there are grave eyes watching here to which the lightest matters are a scandal and an offence. Enough of this. I have resolved to trust you, Chastelâr: I will employ you in my service. You will be far from Holyrood, but you will be fulfilling my wishes and furthering my interests. To-morrow you will receive your instructions. Chastelâr, I can count on obedience. Farewell!'

There was a tone of sorrow in her voice, and she looked on him very sadly as she passed on into her apartments out of his sight.

Though he heard her words, they were unable to rouse him; though he saw the glance he appeared to heed it not; his frame seemed crushed and powerless; his head was sunk on his breast; when he lifted it, she was gone. Then he drew himself up and looked around him like a man who wakes from some ghastly dream. His face was very white when he walked away, and there was a smile on it not pleasant to behold. You may see such on the face of one who is sentenced to death.

Why should he be pitied? If a man must needs sit down to play his all, whose fault is it that he gets up a beggar? If he grasps at the phial, though it be marked 'Poison,' and drains it to the dregs, what is he to expect? Experience will not warn the gambler, he must go to the workhouse at last; nor reason stay the hand of the suicide, he must die like a dog—in a ditch.

CHAPTER XVIII

'To seek hot water beneath cauld ice,
I trow it is a great folie;
I have asked grace at a graceless face,
But there is nane for my men and me.'

The Queen and her brother sat in grave deliberation in her Majesty's private apartment. Moray's face betrayed, under its usual composure, a sense of triumph and satisfaction. The scheming earl had succeeded in bringing about an interview, from which he expected great things, forgetting, as such intriguers often do, the frank nature of his sister, and the uncompromising character of the churchman whom he wished her to conciliate. He glanced anxiously now and then at the timepiece, for men of his stamp have scant leisure to spare, and something like a smile overspread his features as he detected a bustle in the ante-room which indicated an arrival.

Mary seemed absent and depressed. With her cheek leaning on her hand, she had listened to her brother's arguments like one whose thoughts are far away. She was already conscious that the burden of state-craft was too heavy for her to bear; her young head and heart, too, were aching under the weight and restrictions of a crown.

She looked up with a weary sigh when the door opened, and a staid usher, too long schooled at court to betray surprise, whatever he might feel, announced the entrance of Mr John Knox.

The Reformer advanced with the grave, dignified air that was habitual to him, and that sprang from no advantages of bodily presence, but from the consciousness of unshaken integrity within. His flowing beard and long black gown accorded well with the severe and thoughtful brow. For an instant, as he lifted his eyes to the beautiful face of his sovereign, they shone with an expression of pity and admiration, that softened his whole countenance; but the gleam was transient, soon to make way for an increased rigidity of demeanour, as the churchman recalled the sacred nature of his office, and the interests he felt commissioned to represent.

The Queen rose when he entered and greeted him courteously. They formed a strange contrast, that pair of disputants; icy winter and leafy June, the budding hawthorn and the gnarled oak-branch, the smiling sunbeam and the keen north blast, could not have been more different. For a moment they were silent, and scanned each other narrowly. Her Majesty, as became her rank, was the first to speak.

'I have summoned you, Master Knox,' said she, 'for that I would not willingly mistrust a friend without an explanation, or condemn a subject unheard. There is sedition abroad in Scotland, and those in whom a Queen should put her confidence conspire to bring her authority to nought. Master Knox, Master Knox! can you answer to your sovereign the heavy charges brought against you?'

'To *my* Sovereign, and to *hers*,' replied the Reformer, pointing upward. 'Confront me with mine accusers, madam, and I will put them to open shame.'

'Nay,' resumed the Queen, glancing at her brother as if for support, 'I can judge of your sedition for myself. Have you not written a book expressly to overthrow my just government, wherein the casuistry and lore for which you are celebrated have been employed for the worse purpose; but which, nevertheless, I will commission the most learned men in Europe to refute? Have you not stirred up rebellion, and even caused bloodshed, in England, to sap the very foundations of my throne? Have you not practised the black unhallowed art of magic, rather than leave a stone unturned to further your cruel and undutiful enmity against me, your Queen?'

'Madam,' replied the preacher, not without a certain sarcastic admiration in his tone, 'you are skilled in the knowledge of the schools, and for a gentlewoman tolerably familiar with the laws of logic and the rules of disputation. I will answer your charges categorically and in order. If to teach the word of truth to the discomfiture of idolatry; if to exhort the multitude to that worship of the Spirit which is alone acceptable in the sight of Heaven; if to fulfil the commission of *my* Master by waging war to death against the Roman Antichrist, to hew down root and branch, and cast into the fire the deadly upas-tree—its breviaries, its scapularies, its masses, its mummeries, its rank blasphemous ceremonials: if this be sedition and rebellion, I plead guilty. If princes are not better served by those who have cast off the yoke of the popish despot, and if subjects are not more loyal who fear God and honour the king, than those who flatter the crown and obey the crozier—if your Grace have not more cheerful homage from your free Scottish people than ever your fathers enjoyed from our priest-ridden forebears—I plead guilty. If mine enemies can prove that one drop of blood hath ever been shed by my influence or my consent, if they can deny that wherever I have lived, at Geneva, in England, at Berwick, and now in Edinburgh, it has been my constant endeavour to inculcate the doctrines of "peace and good-will," and God hath so blessed my labours that they have borne fruit an hundredfold—I plead guilty. With regard to the charge of magic, I can the more easily bear the brunt of that indictment when I mind me that my Master while on earth was taxed with the same accusation. What said the priests? the priests, madam, who like your own were fain to own all the wealth and power of earth at the loss of heaven—"He casteth out devils," said they, "by Beelzebub, the prince of the devils." So far as I have striven to walk in the footsteps of my Master—so far as my weak unworthy efforts have been directed to follow His example—to this also I plead guilty. But if these charges fail, as fail they must when your Grace brings your own clear-sighted reason to bear upon them, the verdict will be "not guilty," and the accusation of rebellion and sedition falls to the ground.'

Mary had been listening with obvious impatience and no very close attention. She had perhaps made up her mind beforehand. She had again seated herself, and tapped the floor fretfully with her foot, glancing occasionally at her brother as if to ascertain his opinion of the controversy. Moray looked on with the calm approval of a partisan, who thinks his own man is getting the best of it. When Knox paused, the Queen broke in with unusual vehemence.

'And the book? At least you cannot deny the book, nor its object, nor its reflections on my mother and myself. Even the nice casuistry of Master Knox cannot refine away his authorship of that "First Blast of the Trumpet against the Monstrous Regiment of Women." Oh! it is a worthy title for a worthy production! and, in any other country under heaven but this, it would have brought its writer to the block. By the crown I wear, in a parallel case, my cousin of England would have had it burnt by the common hangman!'

She breathed quick, and gesticulated more than was her wont. She was lashing herself into anger, the gentle Queen, as she thought of her own weakness and Elizabeth Tudor's strength. Knox met her glance unmoved. When thus embarked on the tide of argument, he was no more to be influenced by force than persuasion; the softest eyes that ever smiled, and the sternest brows that ever frowned, were alike to him. In the pride of his calling, and the fierce delight of disputation, a man of marble within and without.

'As to the book that so angers your Majesty,' said he, 'I own to it freely. Yes, I wrote it deliberately, and on reflection; nor is there a position laid down, nor an argument adduced in the whole of it, that I fear to establish and substantiate before any ten of the most learned men in Europe!'

'Then you maintain that I have no just authority even over my own subjects?' urged the Queen, with difficulty keeping back her tears.

'These are all fair matters for dispute, madam,' was his reply. 'The learned may surely be suffered to discuss such questions unmolested, when they refrain from putting their theories of good government into practice. Plato himself, as I need scarcely remind your Majesty, argued the necessity of many reforms fundamentally opposed to the very principles of the commonwealth in which he lived. The *litera scripta manet* indeed, madam; but it is for future generations; and no book written, if left unfortified by persecution, ever yet subverted the authority existent at the time it was composed, and against which it may seem to have been aimed. Besides, madam,' added the churchman, warming into good-humour as he got into the full swing of his oratory, 'my book was not directed so much against yourself as your namesake, the bloody Jezebel of England, with her wicked satellites, godless Gardiner and blaspheming Bonner, the one on her right hand, and the other on her left! Had I meant to have troubled *your* estate, madam, would I not have chosen a more fitting time, and a weaker breach in the defences, for my assault?'

'But at least,' resumed Mary, a little mollified by this admission, 'ye cannot deny that ye have taught the people to follow a religion different from that of their prince. How is this to be reconciled with the divine command that subjects should obey their rulers? I cannot wrestle with you in argument, Master Knox; I am but a foolish woman after all; yet here, methinks, I have you on the hip.'

He paused a moment, like a true rhetorician, gratified at an opposition he deemed worthy to be controverted.

'The objection, madam,' he answered, 'is a fair one; yet thus do I demolish it. True religion, it cannot be disputed, cometh from God, and not from the king, else why are we enjoined but to honour the latter, whilst we are to fear, and consequently obey, the former? This is the argument positive. Of the negative, I can produce instances in abundance. The following may be thought sufficient:—The Hebrews were not to conform to the idolatry of Pharaoh or the self-glorification of Nebuchadnezzar the King, nor were the primitive Christians to practise the degrading superstitions of the Roman Emperors.'

'Good,' replied Mary; 'yet we read not that Jew or Christian was justified in resisting with the sword.'

'The Almighty had not seen fit to give them the power,' answered Knox.

'Then you hold that subjects are entitled to take up arms against their sovereign,' proceeded Mary. 'In good faith, Master Knox, this is a dangerous doctrine even in these lawless times.'

'Extreme means are allowable in extreme cases,' was his reply; 'the father hath authority over his family, but if the father be seized with madness, it is lawful for the children to rise up against him, and, stripping him of his power, to place him under constraint, for his safety and their own. So is it with princes, madam; and that prince who goeth about in his frenzy to commit iniquity, must be disarmed, deposed, and cast into prison until he hath been brought to a more sober mind, and disciplined to submission under the will of Heaven.'

It was a bold argument to propound in a royal palace in the presence of majesty itself. The Queen looked at her brother, astonished and aghast. True to his part, Moray assumed an air of profound reflection and conviction after mature thought. Again Mary felt goaded to irritation as she wondered how Elizabeth would have brooked a similar discussion, but she commanded herself with a strong effort, and shifted her ground for a new attack.

'And where shall we find this will of Heaven declared,' argued the Queen, 'or who shall decide between you and me when each interprets differently the same command?'

'The words of Scripture and the ordinances of the Church are sufficient for our guidance,' replied the preacher.

'But *your* Church is not *mine*', retorted the Queen. 'I believe in my heart the Church of Rome to be the true Church of God.'

'Your *will*, madam,' said the other, 'cannot impose a *reason*, neither doth opinion constitute argument; I am fully prepared to bear witness against the Scarlet Woman whom ye would fain substitute for the pure Spouse: but I will employ the weapons of controversy, in which mine adversaries are so skilled, to do battle for the right. I will undertake to prove, against the strongest of your priestly disputants, that the Romish Church hath more degenerated from the truth and purity of apostolic teaching, than the Jews from the ordinances handed down to them by their first lawgivers—Moses and Aaron—when they shouted to the Roman governor that he should crucify the innocent, and let Barabbas go free.'

'My conscience tells me it is not so,' answered Mary. 'I cannot contend with you in argument, as it is neither my profession nor my pleasure; but I have read and studied and formed my own conclusions. Why should not my views be as clear as yours, or may we not both be right?'

'Impossible!' thundered Knox. 'Ye shall come out from the ungodly, and shall not be partakers with them—no, not of one single drop in the cup of their abominations. There is but one straight path for monarch and subject, the queen on her throne and the beggar at the gate. I tell you, madam, that if you deviate from it one hair's-breadth, you shall be lost in the howling wilderness, and become the prey of the raging lion. I will not concede to you one jot nor one tittle; I will prove to you that your tenets are false, your practice sinful, and your ceremonials blasphemous. Stone by stone will I destroy the edifice that priestly ambition hath raised on the foundations of corruption, and cemented with the blood of the prophets from time to time, even unto this day. First of all, I will demolish the very keystone on which the whole fabric rests; I will cast down the idol and trample it under my feet; I will testify in the face of all men against the gross and godless mummery of the mass.'

Mary looked shocked and a little scared at his vehemence; she was irritated, too, by this unscrupulous attack on all she held most sacred, but she controlled herself, and only replied, quietly—

'Abuse is not argument, Master Knox; neither are assertions of much weight until they are proved.'

He settled his gown on his shoulders, and spreading his hands before him, proceeded to demonstrate his propositions in the manner that had become habitual to him in the pulpit, checking off the main points of his argument on his fingers as he proceeded.

'Ye maintain the mass,' said he, 'to be a sacrifice, and, as such, to be holy in itself, for that things are sanctified which have been once placed upon the altar! Ye argue that in the Scriptures are to be found antitypes that shall support this doctrine, and that Melchizedek, when he brought out bread and wine before Abraham, prefigured the offering which ye now esteem to be the holiest of mysteries. I will not pause to discuss with one of your Majesty's learning the object with which Melchizedek brought forth these provisions, nor the arguments which may be produced for and against the probability that he simply offered them as refreshment to Abraham and his company. We will let this be for the present, and proceed at once to the very root and core of the matter. Ye shall observe, madam, that of sacrifices, there are two kinds—the sacrifices of propitiation, and the sacrifices of thanksgiving—the *propitiatoriæ* and the *eucharistiæ*. Now, with regard to the former,'——

'Hold, sir!' interrupted the Queen, much to the divine's disappointment. 'Now ye are launched on the depths of controversial divinity, which are too profound for me, and ye would fain confuse and overwhelm me with your learned Latin terms; I pray your mercy. Under favour, I shall find those who are better capable than I am of holding their ground in argument against Master Knox.'

'So be it, madam,' answered the Reformer, proudly; 'as in the dark ages our ancestors feared not to encounter the strongest champions armed with fleshly weapons in the lists, so shall I be found, I humbly trust, prompt at the hour of trial to do battle in the cause of truth.'

'Those champions, at least, turned not their weapons against a weak, helpless woman,' replied Mary, in a tone of considerable exasperation. 'When they opposed their sovereign, it was to resist tyranny and oppression: not to deprive him of his dignity, and even curtail him of his very amusements. They fronted him boldly in the field, but they would have scorned to wound him in his tenderest feelings, or to attack him in the privacy of his household.'

'Your Majesty's shaft is well aimed,' replied Knox; 'yet doth it rebound harmless from the armour of duty in which the minister of the Word is encased. It is my calling, madam, to reprove sin from the pulpit, whether it be found rearing its head on high in the palace, or crawling among the sewers of the street. I tell you, Mary Stuart, that the day will come when your masques and your music and your mummeries shall be recorded against you in such characters of fire as roused Belshazzar and his nobles from their last revelry on earth. In your feastings and fiddlings and dancings, do ye remember the dance of death, down which ye are footing it so thoughtlessly? When your ears are tickled by the foolish squeaking of your lutes, your rebecks, or your virginals, do ye reflect on the awful blast of the last trumpet, and the wail of perdition coming up from the lake of fire?'

'Then you esteem a simple, innocent measure to be an unpardonable sin?' retorted the Queen, in high scorn. 'Master Knox, Master Knox! is there not a certain virtue called Charity, without which all the others are of no avail?'

'The guilt of the action, madam,' answered he, argumentatively, 'depends on the motive of the dancer. David, indeed, leaped and danced before the ark; but it was in pious zeal and singleness of heart. Not so, that child of sin, the daughter of Herodias, graceful and fierce-hearted as the panther, when she danced off the head of John the Baptist. Think ye, madam, that the walls of Holyrood will shelter the guilty more securely than the roof of Antipas? Think ye that can be but a harmless folly in the Queen of Scotland, which entailed the curse of blood on that flaunting minion who so charmed and cozened the Tetrarch of Galilee?'

'And you dare compare me to her!' exclaimed Mary, rising from her chair with flashing eyes. 'This is too much! Moray! Brother! I appeal to you! This is too much!'

And turning away she covered her face with both hands and burst into tears.

Even Knox could not see her thus, unmoved. He hastened to explain away all that was most offensive in his allusions. As far as lay in his uncompromising nature, he strove to modify the virulence of his declamation.

'Nay, madam,' said he, 'to be effectual the remedies of the physician must be unpalatable; but I mean not to offend your Majesty, not to be guilty of any disrespect towards your person. I would that you could see many matters in another and a clearer light, for your own welfare and that of your people. It is my zeal for your Majesty's happiness here and hereafter that makes me so stern and so unpleasant a counsellor. I will fulfil my duty even at the risk of your Majesty's displeasure, and yet it grieves me in my human weakness to see your fair face sad. It is my daily prayer that Mary Stuart should be brought into the right path. I am an old man, madam, if not in years, in labour and bodily infirmities. I am no courtier, ye know right well. Believe me, I cherish no disloyalty towards your person. I would fain see you a happy triumphant monarch, the joy of your people, the hope and stay of the godly, a fruitful branch in the vineyard, and a second Deborah in Israel!'

The Queen was easily mollified. A bright smile dried the tears on her face, and she stretched her hand graciously to the zealous Reformer.

'Ye shall advise with me from time to time, Master Knox,' said she. 'If I cannot compete with you in argument, I can at least equal you in truth and sincerity, and a good-will to that which is right.'

The churchman's stern nature was moved. He bent over the hand she gave him, and made as though he would have touched it with his lips; then dropped it somewhat awkwardly, and resumed with a little embarrassment.

'I am at your Majesty's service always, second only to His whose minister I am. Yet I beseech you to dismiss me. I may tarry no longer; even now I shall be blamed that I am not at my book.'

'Ye cannot be always at your book,' replied the Queen, smiling. 'Doth not Solomon tell us, "there is a time for all things?"'

'Even so, madam,' answered Knox, moving respectfully towards the door; 'yet must Time himself be seized by the forelock, for his poll is bald behind. Master Buchanan would not fail to remind your Majesty —

"Fronte capillatâ post est occasio calva."'

The Queen either imperfectly heard or did not perfectly understand, for she bowed her farewell without replying; but Moray, pondering on the adage, shook his head as he murmured more to himself than to her—

'There is a time even for seizing the time; and it is but an indiscreet haste that would pluck the pear before it is ripe!'

As Knox traversed the ante-room in leaving the royal audience chamber, he found the Maries sitting at work in that apartment, and paused for an instant on his way through, to contemplate that which was in truth a sufficiently pleasing scene. The ladies were seated in different attitudes at their embroidery, and although, doubtless, they had been in the full tide of conversation previously, there was a profound silence at the moment of his entrance.

Wistfully, nay sadly, with the concerned air of one who looks on a bed of lilies that he foresees are to be withered at night by the early frost, the preacher gazed for an instant on this bevy of beauty ere he uncovered his head to salute them. In doing so, his cap slipped out of his hand to the ground, and it was curious to observe the behaviour of the Maries at this juncture. It is needless to state that Master Knox enjoyed but a small share of popularity amongst these ladies. As the official reprover of all their gaieties and amusements, it may easily be understood that they looked on him with no approving eye, and that if they had one favourite aversion at the court, next to a wet Valentine's Day, it was Master John Knox.

Though of active habits, the great Reformer was somewhat stiff and enfeebled with rheumatism; he stooped with difficulty, and for a while could not recover his lost head-gear.

Mistress Beton, sitting bolt upright, looked straight beyond him at the opposite wall with the air of being as unconscious of his presence as Mary Hamilton really was. The latter had indeed been all the morning immersed in a brown study from which it seemed impossible to extricate her. Mistress Carmichael was not in the best of humours, and it may be observed that her fair brow had of late been continually clouded, and her eyes full of tears, without apparent cause. She made not the slightest movement of assistance in the old man's favour, and even whispered something to Mary Seton with marked and offensive indifference; but the latter, springing gaily from her chair, picked up the fallen skull-cap and returned it to its owner with a pleasant smile, which, saucy as it was, brightened her whole face, like a sunbeam.

'I thank thee, fair mistress,' said Knox. 'These old limbs of mine are stiff now, and the time is not far off when they shall be motionless for evermore. Your knees are young and supple; the more cause have you to be thankful and to bend them while you can in prayer.'

'The neck may be stiff as well as the knees,' answered Mary Seton, glancing meaningly towards the Queen's chamber. 'I hope my loyalty may outlast my lissomeness, if I live to be as old as your reverence!'

He smiled on her sorrowfully yet kindly.

'The young,' said he, 'think that they are to live for ever, and the old hope still to live a few years longer. Fair mistress, fear God, do your duty, and snap your fingers at the chances of life.'

Mistress Beton here interposed with stately scorn.

'We shall scarce take lessons of Master Knox,' said she, 'in our duty towards the Queen. Under favour, sir, we need none of your reverence's teaching in loyalty and obedience.'

He turned good-humouredly towards her, still smiling.

'Ye are angry with me, fair ladies,' said he, 'and why? Because I am too old to learn your courtly graces, and too honest to use your courtly terms? Because I call a fig a fig, when I see one, and a spade a spade. Nay, ye should rather prize and cherish one who can look even on *your* beauty without his eyes being dazzled, and tell you the truth for your salvation, rather than a lie for your ruin.'

'Ye speak fairly,' answered Mary Seton, who in virtue of her previous civility seemed to have constituted herself in some sort his protectress. 'Yet I warrant me ye spake not so tenderly to her Majesty even now. I marvel that ye are not abashed to look thus boldly in the face of an anointed Queen!'

'Nay, young lady,' answered the preacher, in a tone of pleasant humour, 'why should the fair face of a gentlewoman frighten me, who have fronted many angry men? Think ye a bonny brow, unscored by guilt, can be an object of terror, whether it be crowned with a circle of gold like hers, or a wealth of bright hair like your own? No, no, the old man can neither be coaxed nor frightened from doing his duty.'

The Maries looked from one to the other in uncertainty. Knox had obviously gained their attention, and he added a few words with a good motive.

'I tell ye the truth, fair ladies,' said he, preparing to withdraw. 'Better take it from me than the truth-teller to whom ye must listen some day, whether ye will or no. Ay! what a goodly life were this if it could last for ever, or if we might but pass to heaven with all this gay gear; but out upon the knave death! that cometh whether we will or no, and strippeth us of all, and taketh us we know not where! Prepare yourselves for him now, fair ladies, while he is afar, so when he cometh ye shall be found watching, and may laugh in his face.'

His admonition was well meant and received with sufficient decorum, but the impression soon faded away, for he had not been gone five minutes ere they fell to discussing his outward appearance, the severity of his manners, the fashion of his garments, and the general unloveliness of his demeanour.

CHAPTER XIX

'I freighted my bark with the rich and rare,
Alice of Ormskirk, all for thee,
Little I reckoned of cost or care,
But I launched her out on a summer sea—

'A summer sea and a smiling sky,
Never a ripple and never a frown,
Never a token of shipwreck nigh:
What did it matter? The bark went down.'

John Knox went back to his studies and his labours. The Queen and her Maries betook themselves to the duties of adornment and the preparations for a journey. The court was about to move for a season to the pleasant seaside town of St Andrews, in Fife, a favourite resort with her Majesty, and much affected by the household, as their sojourn in the old episcopal city was marked by a gaiety and freedom from restraint exceedingly welcome both to the sovereign and her court. The cavalcade moved off in high spirits. It was but a small party, consisting at the most of not more than twenty equestrians, including the four maids-of-honour, and the more immediate attendants on the person of royalty. Horses stamped and snorted, and shook their bridles merrily, as they were mounted at the palace gates to move on in gay procession down the winding causeway that led towards the Firth. Feathers waved, spurs jingled, men's voices rose in merriment, and the soft laughter of women floated like music on the pure calm air. The dames of Queen Mary's household, like their mistress, were skilful horsewomen, yet it was wonderful how many of those little attentions, which are so delightful to render and so welcome to receive, they exacted from the cavaliers who accompanied them. Horses were insufficiently bitted, saddles insecurely girthed, housings unbecomingly disposed; it seemed as if each of the fair travellers had reason to complain of her groom's negligence or incapacity, yet they bore it with exemplary good humour notwithstanding. Even Mary Carmichael, after refusing assistance from every gentleman in turn, and bending her pretty fingers backward against an obstinate buckle, was fain to apply to Walter Maxwell for his help; and although it was rendered in the gravest and coldest manner possible, thanked him with a bright and kindly smile. It was, perhaps, the most provoking way to treat him. Had she quarrelled with him outright, he would have known how to act, for he was hurt and angered to the depths of his loyal and resolute heart, but this off-hand good humour was irritating in the extreme. It was treating him like a child, he thought, and he chafed under it inwardly, the while the girl herself was only striving to avoid a final rupture, and longing to be friends with him as before.

'Do you journey with us to St Andrews?' said she, glancing timidly at his immovable face; 'or do you return to Holyrood from the waterside?' and her heart beat faster while she waited for his answer.

'As the Queen shall direct,' he replied, it must be admitted, not with his natural sincerity. 'I confess I am profoundly indifferent myself.' He spoke in a hard, dry tone, and she made her horse bound forward from his side, and bent her head down to caress the animal, till her bright hair mingled with its mane.

The others rode gaily on, talking and laughing joyfully, all but the Queen. Mary Stuart was a thought paler than her wont, and unusually silent and preoccupied. Was it that her remonstrances of Master Knox had sunk into her heart? or was she overladen with the cares of her kingdom? or was there some feeling of pity and compunction gnawing her, foreign to the weightier considerations of religion and policy, yet, perhaps, keener and more engrossing than these? Whatever might be the reason, she, who was generally so eager, so buoyant, on an expedition like this, now rode listlessly and carelessly with her hand resting idly on her knee, and her rein lying loosely on her horse's neck. 'Black Agnes,' however, by no means shared the dejection of her mistress. That favourite palfrey, a gift from her brother Moray, and called after the famous Agnes of Dunbar, who was Countess of Moray in her own right, was in the highest spirits at her release from the stable, and, sharing the mettle of the tameless heroine whose name she bore, was no eligible conveyance for an inattentive horsewoman. Ere the gleaming waters of the Firth were in sight, the black mare shied at a beggar on the road-side, and swerved from him with such activity, that Mary, unprepared as she was, must have been unseated had a dexterous hand not seized her bridle-rein at the decisive moment, and a ready arm supported her till she regained her balance in the saddle.

'It is the last service I may render my Queen,' said Chastelâr's low, sad voice in her ear. 'O madam, send me not away from you, I beseech you!'

She knew he was in the cavalcade, indeed she had never retracted the permission originally given, that he should accompany the court to St Andrews, and perhaps something had told her he was not riding very far off, although she had resolved to treat him henceforth with enforced coldness and reserve. As she turned to thank him now, and marked his gallant bearing, the skill with which he rode his mettled chestnut horse, the bravery of his apparel, the respectful deference of his manner, and the pale worn face that told of so much sorrow and suffering, the Queen's heart swelled with that remorseful pity which is not many degrees removed from a softer feeling.

'You must leave me now,' she said, hurriedly. 'I will tell you more when we are embarked. You shall come to me then for your last directions, Chastelâr, and to bid me farewell!'

'Is there no hope?' he asked, in a low stifled whisper.

'None,' she answered, firmly, in the same guarded tone. 'O Chastelâr! I pity you,' she added, while the tears sprang to her eyes; 'from my heart I pity you; but it *must* be so.'

He fell back quietly and humbly. Mary put 'Black Agnes' into a gallop, and the cavalcade were soon engaged in all the bustle of embarkation at the waterside.

It was Valentine's Day, and the weather was indeed in unison with that mild and popular saint. It was one of those soft pleasant days, with a calm atmosphere and a serene though clouded sky, that come in the early spring to remind us of the principles of growth and fragrance still existing, though dormant, in the bosom of the teeming earth. The russet sward was saturated with moisture, and not a bud had yet started into life, not a snowdrop lifted its gentle head on the southern side of the sleeping braes and shaws, heavy with the promise of another year. Ashore, the rooks were flocking to the fresh-turned glebe, where the bright ploughshare, sticking in the furrow, marked that the half-day's work was done; while, on the broad Firth, soft and smooth and white as milk, the dark sea-bird rode calm and motionless, as if at anchor, poised on the surface of his home; the distant mountains loomed grand and dim and sullen, the nearer points and promontories shot sharply out into the water, clearly defined against the sheeted level of the Firth; the very tide seemed but to heave and sob at intervals, lapping drowsily against the dripping sea-weed on the rocks. It was a scene of beauty, but beauty of a softening, saddening tendency, and all on board were fain to acknowledge its melancholy influence and partake in the depression it produced.

The sturdy boatmen bent to their oars; the courtiers, disposed in different attitudes, appeared chiefly intent on arriving at the termination of their voyage; and Mary, sitting in the stern of the boat, dipped her hand idly in the water, silent and gazing downwards, in obvious disquietude of mind.

Chastelâr watched the Queen with eager eyes. After a while he struck a few notes on the lute, without which he seldom travelled; and observing that this, as usual, was the signal for general attention, and that Mary did not seem to disapprove, proceeded to play a mournful melody, which, as it rose and fell, he accompanied in apparent abstraction with his voice.

'Gone! wholly gone! How cold and dark;
A cheerless world, of hope bereft;
The beacon quench'd, and not a spark
In all the dull gray ashes left.

'No more, no more, a living part
In life's contending maze to own;
Dead to its kind, an empty heart
Feeds on itself alone! — alone!

'The present all a blank, and worse;
No ray along the future cast;
All blighted by the blighting curse,
Except the past! — except the past!

'Ay, if the cup be crush'd and spilt,
More than the sin the loss I rue,
And if the cloud was black with guilt,
The silver light of love shone through.

'And though the price be maddening pain;
One-half their rapture to restore,
And live those blissful hours again,
I'd pay the cruel price once more.

'Dreams! dreams! Not backward flows the tide
Of life and love — it cannot be:
Well — thine the triumph and the pride,
The suffering and the shame for me!'

As he concluded, even the rough boatmen looked from one to the other in undisguised approval. Never insensible to the charms of music have been these bold sons of the sea. To this day they are persuaded that the silver shoals of herring are attracted by harmonious sounds, and they dredge for oysters with a low monotonous chant, that they believe peculiarly grateful to that retiring zoophyte. Long after Chastelâr's last notes had died gradually out over the silent waters, they laid to their oars with a will, and seemed to pull their long sweeping strokes in measured cadence to the unforgotten strain. The Maries, too, applauded enthusiastically, all but one, and she was weeping in silence, because her heart was full.

In the stern of the boat, a wide roomy shallop, pulled by some six or eight oars, the Queen sat apart from the rest of the company. More than once she had glanced at Chastelâr while he sung, and varying expressions, none of them in keeping with the serene sky overhead, had crossed her brow. After he had finished, she remained silent for several minutes, absorbed in deep reflection. By degrees, as they approached the opposite shore of Burntisland, and the hills of Fife began to rise clear and brown above the black, jagged rocks and level strips of white sand that edged the water's margin, the attention of Her Majesty's train became diverted to the different objects around, and anon a shoal of porpoises, tumbling to windward in grotesque succession, drew them, with many exclamations of wonder and amusement, to the bows.

None were now left in the stern of the boat save the Queen and the steersman. That ancient Triton's whole attention was riveted, seaman-like, on the shallows they were nearing, where, for the first time during their passage, the rolling waves were breaking languidly into surf. Chastelâr remained in the place he had never quitted, his eyes fixed on the Queen's face. She beckoned him to approach, and in an instant he was at her side.

'We remain at Burntisland to-night,' said Mary, in a low measured voice that seemed the result either of extreme indifference or perfect self-command. 'In the morning we shall ride on to St Andrews. I have a packet that must be delivered without delay at Dunfermline. Can I depend upon you to undertake its safe arrival there before to-morrow's dawn?'

He assented eagerly. This was no such distant banishment! He should be under the same sky, within a day's journey! The light of hope shone over his face, but while the Queen proceeded in those dry, chilling tones, it faded as it came.

'You will ride thence to Stirling, where you will remain until you receive instructions from Maitland or Melvil. They will be accompanied by letters for the French Court, and on the instant of their receipt you will depart for Paris. Chastelâr, I depend upon your obedience—you will not fail me.'

The cold drops stood on his forehead. It was in a broken, hollow voice that he replied—

'My life is in your hands. Do with me what you will!'

Again her kindly heart smote her sore. It was a fearful gift this charm that she possessed. It was a dreadful responsibility thus to hold the happiness of a human being, so to speak, in her hand. Could she dash it to pieces without some tinge of pity and remorse? She resumed her task very sadly and unwillingly.

'It is better,' said she, 'that this should be done at once. Queen though she be, nay, *because* she is a Queen, Mary Stuart may not listen for a moment to the voice of her own feelings, nor the impulse of her own heart, pitying as it does those who are in trouble, though their sufferings and their sorrows spring from their own deed. Nay,' she added, seeing him about to speak, and deprecating his words, as it were, with a gentle, almost a caressing gesture of her white hand, 'there is nothing you can urge that shall induce me to alter my determination. A woman's heart is weak, but her *will* is iron as a man's. It *must* be so, Chastelâr, for your own sake—and—and for mine!'

'O God!' he exclaimed, in an agony like a man writhing under a death-blow. 'Have pity—have pity! Anything but this—any disgrace, any punishment, any ordeal. But oh! think of the forlorn, despairing prayer, "Entreat me not to leave thee!"'

The tears dropped fast from her eyes, and the beautiful face quivered in its struggle to be firm. What was that to him? He could only think her hard, unfeeling as the seaboard rock. She yielded not an inch.

'It *must* be so,' she repeated; 'loyal and true, you will not fail me at last!'

His eyes flashed with anger. Man's nature can scarce endure great sorrow without a tinge of resentment.

'Loyalty and truth are soon forgotten in the absent,' said he, bitterly. 'Lip-service and flattery are more welcome to princes. I cannot refuse to make room for a newer favourite!'

She smiled on him gentle and forgiving through her tears.

'You are unjust,' she said, 'and unkind; you know it is not so; and when you are far off it will be your punishment to think that you could have spoken such words to me to-day.'

The reaction of his feelings was frightful: he put his hand to his throat as if he was choking, and gasped out in broken syllables—

'Forgive me! only forgive me before I go out from the light into eternal darkness and despair!'

'Obedience?' she asked in her turn, looking wistfully at the shore, which they were now approaching; and on their arrival at which, something perhaps warned her that she must take her last leave of Chastelâr and his unselfish, unexacting devotion.

'To the death!' he replied; and even while he spoke the boatmen shipped their oars, and those who were forward leaped out waist-deep in water, to steady the shallop for the disembarkation of the ladies.

This was no such easy task. In these days people walk from a roomy steamer roofed in and glazed like a conservatory, across a platform securely railed on to a substantial stone-built quay that reaches a quarter of a mile out into the Firth, and renders them as independent of tide as the vessel herself does of weather; save for the slight oscillation caused by the motive power, a blind man, unless in a gale of wind, would never know that he had left *terra firma*. But even within the recollection of those now scarce past middle age, the crossing of the Firth was an affair of considerable discomfort, if not a little danger. The state of the tide was of paramount importance; the transit in an open boat, generally of the smallest and craziest description, to the steamer moored half-a-mile off, was in itself a voyage of no slight apprehension to the timid, especially if the wind had been blowing for two or three days steadily from the east: and the disembarkation on the northern side was, if possible, worse; the boat had to be beached with practised dexterity not to capsize altogether, and under the most favourable circumstances the pursuing waves were pretty sure to come dashing in over her stern, wetting to the skin those unwary passengers who had not taken refuge at the prow.

At low water also a considerable journey had to be made which partook of the discomforts both of land and sea, inasmuch as it was performed in the ungainly fashion termed by schoolboys 'pick-a-back,' on the shoulders of veteran boatmen wading knee-deep through the surf. To a heavy weight and a timid rider this mode of progression was also not without its terrors, for if the bearer, generally old and often infirm, made the slightest false step, a very complete ducking was the inevitable result.

In this hazardous mode it was necessary to land the Queen and her ladies on their arrival at Burntisland: the scene was one of bustle, dash, and excitement, none the less picturesque for the hard-weather appearance of the boatmen and the gaudy dresses of the fishermen's wives and daughters, who came down in numbers to welcome their Sovereign, and shrank not from criticising in loud ear-piercing tones the personal appearance of the party, and the whole details of the proceeding.

The horses that had been conveyed across in the boat accompanying the Queen's, splashed one after another into the water, amidst shouts of laughter, and half-swam, half-scrambled ashore as they might. The retainers and men-at-arms jeered each other merrily as they waded through the waves, or wrung the wet from their boots and clothing on the sand; the female spectators screamed out their advice and opinions, fluttering aloof shrill and pertinacious as the sea-mews themselves; whilst white-headed urchins ran hither and thither through the crowd, devising impossible jobs which they professed their readiness to perform for the smallest remuneration in copper. But the Queen's shallop excited the interest and attention of all.

One by one the ladies were received into the arms of their attending boatmen, to be conveyed tenderly and carefully ashore. In right of his years, his experience, his patriarchal dignity, and his solemn demeanour, the oldest of these boatmen was entrusted with the person of the Queen. He was a stalwart, fine old man, broad in the shoulders, deep in the chest, large of stature, and strong of limb. He took Mary in his arms as if she had been a baby, and waded with her deliberately through the surf; another score of yards, and she would have been safe on land; but whether the veteran had been celebrating his prospective distinction by deep potations of alcohol, or whether his toil-worn frame failed him at the pinch, or whether it was indeed by one of those fatalities for which it is impossible to account, he made a false step, a fruitless effort to recover it, and but for prompt assistance must have precipitated his royal burden before him into the water.

Need we say that it was Chastelâr who was at hand to save; that it was his grasp which plucked the Queen from her falling supporter at this critical juncture; and that for a few blissful moments, worth to his delirious fancy whole ages of torture, the love-stricken poet for the first and last time bore the precious form of Mary Stuart in his arms?

Slowly, carefully, gently, he waded with her to the land; not a word was spoken—not a look exchanged; the Queen's face was cold and impassive as marble, and Chastelâr, in the tumult of his love and his despair, was conscious but of one frantic wish, that the waves would rise over their heads and cover them, and they might be at rest fathom-deep down there together for evermore.

CHAPTER XX

'Night by night must I pace the shore,
Longing, lingering, to and fro,
Questioning, "May I not see her once more,
Alice of Ormskirk?" answering—"No!"

'And still the echoing sea-cave rings
With one unceasing pitiless strain;
And still the wild wave dashes and sings—
"Never again, love! never again."'

The episode of idolatry and madness was fast drawing to a close. When the Queen and her household went to establish themselves in the lodging where they designed to pass the night, Chastelâr remained on the beach, apparently unconscious of all about him, gazing out to seaward, as a man does who is utterly lost to the interests and occupations of the shore. Amongst the many mysterious sympathies that connect natural objects so inexplicably with the mind, there is a strange affinity between human sorrow and the watery element—be it the gentle ripple of a running stream, or the dash and recoil of the mounting wave breaking on the beach, or the dark-blue line of a sea-horizon clear against the sky.

There is some morbid attraction to mortal grief in the contemplation of each of these; there is something that takes man out of himself, and though it speaks not of hope or consolation, seems to promise oblivion and repose at last. Ay, we love to prate of the beauties of nature, to enlarge upon the pleasures of smiling skies and gorgeous landscapes and magnificent scenery. Are we quite honest about the effect produced by such objects? and can we declare that they create sensations of unmixed gratification? On the contrary, most of us, if sincere, will confess that when we were happy, we took very little notice of them; and it was but in some keen, hopeless sorrow we turned to nature for an anodyne, and found she added sharpness to our pangs and mocked us with a smile as she poured fresh venom into the wound. No; if we would be consoled, we must look to where the running stream loses itself in the ocean that we have never seen; we must carry our thoughts athwart the far horizon in search of the eternal shore; we must strain our eyes to pierce the smiling heaven, and catch if but a glimpse of the undying world beyond.

Chastelâr paced to and fro upon the sand with all the worst passions of our nature tearing at a heart that yet seemed formed for better things. Utterly undisciplined in his wild, imaginative character, he had never prepared himself for such complete desolation as this. For many years, more than he now dared count, the smiles of that beautiful Queen had been to him dearer than the very air he breathed. A less enthusiastic temperament would have asked itself long ago to what result this abject service, this blind adoration, could eventually lead, and would, at least, have prepared for the final shock, which it required little sagacity to foresee must sooner or later tumble the magic edifice to the ground; but Chastelâr's was a character that never stops to count the cost.

There was to him an unspeakable joy in the very abandonment of his attachment, in the lavish devotion which only asked to be received without return. Full of a generous fire kindled in his own ardent imagination, and nourished by those seductive follies which constituted the very essence of an age of chivalry, it seemed to him as rich a happiness to cherish his hopeless attachment for the Queen, as it would have seemed to a coarser and stronger mind to possess itself of Mary's heart and person. The poet never dreamed the time could come when he should be told that even this self-sacrifice was unwelcome; that for one unguarded word, wrung from him by the very depth and tenderness of his feelings, he should be banished from her presence, and that she who was the light of his eyes should herself determine that he must look upon her no more.

Presently the devil got into his heart; the rebellious spirit, that is never so strong as when men feel they have been virtuous and self-denying in vain, rose tumultuous now, all the fiercer for having been kept down so long, and urged the counsels of despair. Of what availed his old and faithful service, his constancy, his loyalty, his obedience, and truth? She flung them away as nothing, and less than nothing; she could take his warm fresh heart from him when it suited her, as a mere matter of pastime, and squeezing it, as one would squeeze an orange, give it him back again when she had no further use for it, all withered and empty, the very essence of its existence gone.

Queen though she were, she had no right to do this. She forbade him her presence! He would see her whether she would or no! He had done with obedience now, and discretion and consideration! He would speak to Mary Stuart once more, if all the devils in hell rose to prevent it!

Turning on his steps he strode fiercely along the now solitary shore in the direction of the hamlet of Burntisland, where the Queen was to pass the night. Already the day was waning, and the evening mist, gathering from the eastward, crept slowly up the margin of the Firth. A light drizzling rain had also begun to fall, and the sea-gulls, no longer floating in repose, were screaming and turning restlessly on the wing, as they flitted to and fro in search of shelter for the night. Boatmen and fishwives had betaken themselves to their homes, and none were left to witness the gestures of anger and despair with which the unhappy Chastelâr accompanied his racking, maddening thoughts. He wrapped his cloak round him, and walked faster and faster as he began to shape his resolve.

But within a short distance of the hamlet he met a figure approaching him through the increasing gloom: a female figure cloaked and hooded, walking swiftly, yet with smooth, majestic gait, and of a stature that seemed unusually lofty in that uncertain light. For an instant the blood gathered round his heart as a possibility flashed across him that even in his madness he could scarcely dare believe. In that space of time a thousand frantic surmises swept through his brain. Reaction, remorse, a woman's pity, and a woman's tenderness, overriding all, even the reserve and dignity of a Queen. But the foolish fancies died out rapidly as they arose, for the figure stopped, handed him in silence a small packet tied round with a morsel of silk (he could notice such a trifle even then), and while she threw back her hood with a gesture of relief, the clear, guileless eyes of Mary Hamilton looked him sadly and inquiringly in the face.

She spoke not for a while; she seemed to stop and take breath; then she said, very quietly and coldly—

'The Queen bade me bring you this. She says it must be forwarded without delay.'

He bowed courteously. He had recovered himself now, for he had a scheme in view, and shaping it out rapidly in his working brain, he bethought him that here was an unconscious instrument which he might turn to good account.

'How did you know where to find me?' he asked, forcing himself to smile.

A bright blush swept over the maid-of-honour's forehead, but she paled again almost immediately as she replied—

'I saw you from our window walking on the shore. I knew it was you, and I asked to bring the packet myself because they tell me you are going away to-night, and I was anxious to bid you farewell.'

This was a great deal for Mary Hamilton to say. No successful gallant could have wrung such an avowal from her lips; but the keen eye of affection had told her that Chastelâr was dejected and unhappy; so she longed to console him and speak kindly to him ere he went away.

Should he not have pitied her? He who knew what it was to love in vain? Of all women on earth he should have spared *her*; but the devil had entered into him and he saw in this pure, unselfish affection a way to his own object; so she, too, must be sacrificed without remorse. What did it matter? Was *he* alone to suffer and be trampled under foot?

'It was good of you, Mistress Hamilton,' he replied, with a soft glance from his dark eyes, that made her flush and tremble where she stood. 'Few but yourself would have been so considerate, and I should have valued the kindness as much from *none*. Shall I leave *one* person at Court to regret me when I am gone?'

'More than that,' she answered, hurriedly, and scarce knowing what she said, 'there will be no music for us now, at least none worth listening to. The Queen said so herself—and—and—are you not coming back again?'

'Never!' he replied, darkly; and then, seeing her scared and troubled face, adding, with a laugh, 'Never is a long word, is it not? and who can tell in such a country as this what a few months may bring? But I shall be absent a weary while, Mistress Hamilton, and I cannot bear unkindness from those I love. I would not willingly be forgotten and supplanted by newer faces.' ·

Her eloquent eyes told him *that* was impossible, but she dared not trust herself to speak.

'Will you think of me when I am gone?' he proceeded, in a lower tone, and pressing nearer his companion's side. 'When you are feasting merrily at Holyrood, and enjoying dance and song and revelry, will you not keep one little corner in your heart for the absent who used to do all in his poor power to make your time pass pleasantly, who will be thinking every hour so sadly and longingly of you?'

Even in the midst of her astonished happiness she experienced a shadowy misgiving that it was too good to be real; but she could only reply—

'You must think very poorly of us all, Chastelâr, if you imagine we could ever forget you.'

'It is not distance that can separate those who care for each other,' resumed the poet, dreamily; 'after all, it is thought that unites soul to soul;

that sea-bird's wing would droop ere he had traversed a thousand miles of ocean, and yet twice the distance separates the lover from his mistress no more than a score of yards and a brick wall. He can be with her in spirit, although his body may be at the uttermost end of the earth. Nevertheless, for all this, Mistress Hamilton, it grieves me sore to bid you farewell.'

She could have listened to him for an hour; she loved to hang on his musical accents, and drink in the tones of his rich, southern voice; above all, were such sentiments as these congenial to her own lofty conceptions of an ideal, and her trusting, clinging heart.

He was pitiless; he went on speaking low and hurriedly—

'We may not meet again for many, many months—perhaps never in this world. Do you think I am a man of marble that I cannot feel? Do you think *mine* is a happy lot, thus to leave all I value or esteem and take not even hope with me into exile? Mary Hamilton, you will not refuse me what I ask you on such a day as this?'

'I would give my life for yours,' she answered, scarce above her breath. 'What is it you would have me do?'

'Listen,' he replied. 'I must be in the saddle soon after nightfall. For reasons I cannot explain to you, it must be supposed by the household that I have departed at sun-down. My very life is in danger, if I am known to have remained. I cannot tell you why. Do you trust me?'

She bowed her head.

'I trust you,' she answered, very quietly, and he needed only to look in her face for confirmation of her words.

'Then grant me my request,' he resumed. 'It is a foolish fancy of mine, but *you* at least cannot blame, though you may scoff at it. There is one person whom I must see the very last before I depart. One face of which I must take the picture with me, into banishment, engraven on my heart, one hand of which the farewell pressure must remain on mine till we meet again. An hour after supper I will be at the door of the small garden into which your apartments open. You will meet me there for the last, *last* time?'

She looked a good deal frightened and discomposed.

'But I shall not be dismissed so soon,' she urged, 'and if I am absent they will come to look for me everywhere, and oh! I ought not! I ought not!'

He was prepared for her objection—he knew the Queen's habit so well—this was exactly what he wanted.

'Nay, then,' he resumed, 'I will ask you to risk nothing for my sake; and yet, see the last of the dear face, I must and will. The days are short now. It is already twilight, and it will be as dark as midnight in an hour. I will go make my preparations for departure. Do you, as you enter, unlock the garden-door and take the key with you; it cannot then be fastened from the inside. I will conceal myself amongst the shrubs and wait for you there. As soon as you are dismissed for the night you can come out and bid me farewell.'

'It is better not,' she murmured, in sad perturbation. She could not bear to refuse him, and yet all her womanly feelings revolted at the clandestine nature of such a proceeding. 'We are close at home now. All good attend you, Chastelâr. I will pray for you night and morning—farewell!'

She gave him her hand, as if to take her final leave, but she had not the heart to withdraw it at once. It lingered long and lovingly in his clasp.

'Mary!' said he, and the dear name came so tenderly off his lips. 'Mary! you will not let me part from you thus?'

'I will do as you wish,' was all she answered, once more dropping the hood over her face and hurrying away. They were within a stone's throw of the Queen's lodging, and it was already time for her to resume her duties. Her mind was in a sad tumult when she left him. She felt she was going to do wrong, deliberately wrong; yet how could she refuse him? She loved him so, and he was going away!

With a wicked smile, suggestive of anything but mirth or happiness, engraven, as it were, on his countenance, Chastelâr strode up the narrow street to the stable in which his trusty chestnut was disposed. This animal was a gift from the Queen, and valued accordingly. We would fain describe him from his velvet muzzle to his flinty hoofs, for where shall we find so seductive a theme as the beauty of a horse? but will only observe that he was in every respect a fitting present from royalty. The Frenchman ordered his favourite to be saddled with considerable parade, and spoke loudly of the journey before him. Then, ostentatiously assuming his arms and valise, mounted and rode away in the direction of Dunfermline, followed, as his figure disappeared in the gloom, by the admiring glances of such ostlers and retainers as his noisy departure had gathered to observe him.

For a mile or so he proceeded along the coast, and then, turning off the horse-track into the recess of an old quarry, dismounted and fastened his horse to the roots of a whin-bush, growing from the chinks in the cold blue stone. For all his feverish excitement, he disposed the animal in a nook sheltered from the chill east wind, and taking his own cloak from about him cast it over the flanks of his dumb friend. Then, with a farewell pat, he returned on foot the way he had come, rapidly and breathlessly, never stopping till he reached the hamlet of Burntisland, and saw the lights twinkling once more in the Queen's lodging.

He stole softly to the garden-gate, of which he had spoken to Mary Hamilton. It opened noiselessly to his push. By this time it was quite dark, and on entering the enclosure he found no necessity for concealment amongst the scanty shrubs it contained. Here he drew off his heavy horseman's boots with extreme caution, and thus, with his rapier at his side, and his pistols in his belt, took up his position close against the door of the house, which opened outwards.

Here he waited, watched, and listened. A drizzling rain was falling, and the wind was very keen, but, though stripped to his doublet and hose, Chastelâr was unconscious of the weather. Had he been immersed in snow, he could scarce have felt cold while that fever burned and raged so fiercely at his heart.

CHAPTER XXI

'For constancy hath her place above,
And life is thorny, and youth is vain,
And to be wroth with one we love,
Doth work like madness in the brain.'

The Queen's supper and the *couchée* which succeeded it seemed endless. Her Majesty, though by no means in her usual spirits, eating but little, and scarcely speaking at all, was yet none the more disposed to dismiss her ladies and betake herself to repose. Mary Hamilton, with flushed cheeks and unsettled gestures, busied herself about every arrangement she could think of that should further the process of retiring for the night, till even the Queen, rousing from her meditations, taxed her with being fatigued after her ride, and did not scruple to hint at the remarkable restlessness of her demeanour. After this she controlled herself, indeed, with an effort; but felt the while, that if the suspense continued much longer it would drive her mad.

It was Mary Seton's turn and hers to put the Queen to bed; and the gossiping propensities of the former, whose lively disposition never acknowledged fatigue or low spirits, did by no means conduce to the despatch of matters. For reasons of her own, too, this young lady chose to ask a series of questions concerning the Earl of Bothwell, and the probability of his returning to Court, interspersed with remarks on that nobleman and his borderers and his enemies—all delivered with considerable freedom and a flippancy peculiar to herself. The Queen, who seemed to-night more or less impatient of every subject broached, at length called her a 'saucy chatterbox,' and bade her good-humouredly 'hold her tongue.' As usual, the reproof only produced a merry smile and a provoking little grimace, at which Her Majesty could not forbear laughing, though she looked sadder than ever a moment afterwards.

Wearily the minutes passed on. Mary Hamilton had never before thought royalty so exacting, or an attendance on her own dear mistress so tiresome. One by one the Queen's garments had to be taken off, folded up and disposed, each in its proper place; then the loose flowing gown was brought her by the senior maid-of-honour, and the junior let down the long, rich hair that covered her more nobly than the mantle of royalty itself. While Mistress Seton combed and stroked those chestnut tresses carefully, Mistress Hamilton brought a basin and ewer, offering it on her knees; after which ceremony, it was her duty to place an ivory crucifix, and a small lamp, with the Queen's breviary, on the table by her bed-side; then she handed Her Majesty's beautiful rosary, consisting of beads of sandal-wood, inlaid with silver, and Mary Stuart betook her, after the manner of the ancient faith, to those devotions she never neglected in her chequered life, and that served her so nobly in the hour of trial with which it closed.

The maids-of-honour retired. Mary Seton would fain have prolonged the conversation, even on the threshold of their mutual chamber. She was never tired, not she! but her friend, vowing she had forgotten something in the supper-room, hurried away down-stairs, with a feeling of intense relief, and yet horribly frightened and uncomfortable, as she fled like a lapwing along the dark passages towards the garden.

The servants and retainers had all gone to their repose, wearied with the toils of the day, and anticipating an early start on the morrow. Even in that small house there was something gloomy and alarming in the profound silence. Mary Hamilton, while conscious of the purity of her motives, trembled, as innocence always does tremble, far more violently than guilt; and it was with a beating heart and quick-coming breath that she reached the door, and, unfastening it gently, peered out into the thick darkness beyond.

For a minute or two she waited, listening anxiously. Not a sound was to be heard but the dull beat of the tide upon the shore. Then she advanced a few paces into the garden, now that it seemed likely to elude her, more resolved upon the interview than she could have believed possible a short while ago. The small rain struck chill against her face, and she strained her eyes in vain to pierce the surrounding gloom.

Had she turned round at this moment, she might perhaps have faintly distinguished a dark shadow that passed swiftly from behind the door, and entered the house by the passage she had just quitted.

But she was intent only on Chastelâr. She stepped softly to the garden door, and peeped into the sandy lane on which it opened. Here there was a little more light, and she could see some ten or a dozen paces to right and left. No living object was discernible; the rain fell faster, and the tide moaned and gurgled in its ebb and flow against the shallow beach.

Mary Hamilton was puzzled and distressed. An hour ago she would have hailed as an unspeakable relief the news that Chastelâr had actually gone without further parley, but now that she had been schooling herself and stringing her nerves for an interview, it was provoking that so much agitation should be wasted for nothing; it seemed hard and cruel not to see him just once again.

She ventured on a gentle cough; a timid whisper, very soft and cautious; there was no result. At last she spoke his name out loud, and then, half-frightened and a good deal disappointed, made her way back into the house, barring the door after her with as little noise as her trembling hands would permit.

Poor Mary Hamilton! In that dark passage she paused to lay her head against the wall and weep. She dared not return at once to the chamber which she shared with her comrades, in case any one of them should be awake. She felt she could not brook observation or remark on her streaming eyes and agitated looks. As the tears flowed silently, they did her so much good! For weeks the girl had been living in a morbid state of overstrung excitement. Continually in the presence of the man she loved, and that man gifted with many brilliant qualities exceedingly attractive to the female heart; never convinced of his preference, yet suspecting it from a thousand trifles that she naturally interpreted in her own favour; living in an atmosphere of alternate hope and fear, exposed to the daily charm of his person, his conversation, his musical talents, and his warm foreign cordiality, it was no wonder that she hailed as a blissful relief the certainty which she was persuaded had burst upon her to-day, even though accompanied by the miserable conviction that she must bid him a long, perhaps a hopeless farewell. The sweet and the bitter were strangely mingled in the cup she had drained so eagerly—the cup that slakes, but never quenches thirst. She was so relieved, and yet so troubled; so proud, and yet so fearful; so happy, yet so sad.

What could a poor woman do but droop her head and weep her heart out, simply because she *was* a woman?

Suddenly she started as if she had been shot. A loud shriek, followed by a succession of outcries for assistance in the Queen's voice, rang through the small house, and were quickly followed by the scuffling of feet, the banging of doors, and the tumult of many tongues, in which the shrill tones of the maids-of-honour predominated. Lights were already glancing in the passages; women in white, with pale, scared faces, and half-dressed men but half-awake, snatching at whatever weapons came to hand, rushed to and fro tumultuously; everybody seemed exceedingly alarmed and excited, but none to know the least what was the matter. All this Mary Hamilton observed as we see things in a dream, while she rushed up-stairs, and dashed unhesitatingly into the Queen's chamber.

The sight that met her there arrested her as if by magic on the threshold. In the twinkling of an eye, the warm impulsive woman seemed frozen into a statue.

Pale as her night gear, breathless and trembling, while she clung to her brother's shoulder for support, yet with the 'Stuart frown' stamped sternly on her brow, the Queen was gazing in fear and anger on the dark figure of a man who stood with his arms folded, in the corner of the apartment. That man, calm, erect, defiant, almost sublime in the intrepidity with which he confronted threatening brows and levelled weapons (for already the royal retainers were filling the place), was Chastelâr. Mary Hamilton turned sick and giddy while she looked. The Queen raved and shook, and seemed half-mad with fear and shame; her ladies crowded about her in helpless astonishment and dismay, while the servants and men-at-arms glanced from one to another, utterly at their wit's end. Except the fatal cause himself of all this disturbance, Moray alone seemed to retain his presence of mind. Alternately, he soothed his frantic sister, and gave directions to the astonished bystanders.

'Stab him!' exclaimed the Queen, pointing with shaking hand at the unfortunate man who stood there, so pale, so calm, offering no attempt at escape or resistance. 'Brother, for the honour of our house, put your sword through him, an' ye be half a Stuart. Let him not live an hour to boast of this daring, this atrocious insult. Oh, it is too much—too much!'

The Queen covered her face with both hands, completely overcome; her beautiful hair, escaping from the ribbon which confined it, fell over her shoulders to her waist.

Chastelâr looked proudly and lovingly at her even then. Madman! even then!

'Nay, madam,' urged Moray, with soothing accents, 'bethink you, I beseech your Grace. In the name of prudence and discretion, bid me not dip my hands in the blood of this man. Remember, you have yourself treated him with over-courtesy and kindness, to the offence of your nobility, and, pardon me for saying it, to the scandal of the Court. Reflect, madam, what shall the world think of it when they hear that a queen's musician was found in a queen's bed-chamber, and put to death lest he should tell the tale.'

The Queen raised her head with flashing eyes.

'You *dare* to shield him, Moray! You! my own blood!' she vociferated. 'On your allegiance, I charge you. What! You will never let him speak! To the death with him on the spot!'

But Moray knew the pliant and forgiving nature of her with whom he had to deal.

'Nay, madam,' said the prudent earl, 'patience; I entreat you, patience; the unhappy man is clearly distraught; let us not shed his blood unwittingly. He shall be brought to justice, and punished according to his deserving; so shall his treason be sufficiently expiated by death. Remove him,' he added, speaking composedly to the men-at-arms, who crowded round the door. 'Bind him forthwith, and let him be placed securely in ward.'

Chastelâr still remained perfectly immovable; never once had he taken his eyes off the Queen's face; never once had the strange longing, loving gaze, with its dash of wild triumph and its depth of intense affection, faded or varied for an instant. While they bound him fast, drawing a girdle tight round his arms above the elbow, he neither seemed to feel the pressure, nor to be conscious of the indignity; while they pressed round him and hustled him from the room, his looks never strayed for an instant from the Queen.

All this Mary Hamilton saw as if in a trance. Though every stroke of her pulse beat with a loud stupefying clang upon her brain, she knew that this was reality, that this was truth, that there was no hope of awaking to find it all a dream; but when Chastelâr reached the door, and beholding the Queen no longer seemed roused to consciousness at last, she met his eye for the first time, and the whole hopeless misery of her situation rushed upon her at once.

He smiled on her very sadly and kindly; there was a pitying, remorseful expression in his face—a wistful, mournful tenderness in his glance: she could bear it no longer, and she fainted dead away upon the floor.

CHAPTER XXII

'"And grant me his life!" Lady Margaret cried;
"Oh! grant but his life to me!
And I'll give ye my gold and my lands so wide,
An' ye let my love go free.

'"And spare me his life!" Lady Margaret prest,
"As ye hope for a pardon above;
And I'll give ye the heart from out of my breast
For the life of my own true love!"'

Although the gayest of the gay, where revelry was in the ascendant, and gifted with that tameless courage and those qualities of endurance which were the characteristics of her family, alas! too often proved in the reverses of that ill-fated line, Mary Stuart was subject to constitutional fits of dejection, the more painful that she struggled bravely against the incubus; and, however much it may have darkened her spirits, never suffered it to affect her temper. The Queen was always kind, considerate, and smiling towards her household, even while her eyes were full of tears, and her heart was sore with undefined anxieties and anticipations of evil for which she saw no obvious cause. Her Majesty was generally more free from such depressing influences at St Andrews than elsewhere. The keen sea-breezes of that bracing locality seemed to have a favourable effect upon her health, and she enjoyed, above all things, the absence of state and ceremony, on which she specially insisted in the old cathedral town. Fond as she was of the saddle, it was a great pleasure to the beautiful Queen to gallop over the spacious sands that skirt St Andrews Bay, where she could enjoy a stretch of two miles and more, to the mouth of the river Eden, careering along on the firm hard surface, with the spray of the German Ocean wet on her cheek, and her horse's feet splashing amongst the spent waves of the receding tide. Then she delighted to fly her hawk at the wild fowl abounding a mile or so inland, returning by the well-known chain of grassy, sandy hillocks, that are there called links, and devoted in modern times by the Scottish gentry to their national recreation of golf. Sometimes crossing the Eden at the shallows near its mouth, she would roam over the waste of low grounds that stretch to the northward, perhaps as far as a small straggling hamlet, in days of old a Roman settlement, defended by one of their masterly encampments, and called by the legions, *Lochores*—a Latinism which the Scottish peasant of to-day reproduces in the name of Leuchars.

Then, on her return from these joyous expeditions to the small house in the South Street, selected for her own royal residence, she gathered her few intimates and friends around her, and passed the evenings in amusement and hilarity, from which the very name of business was rigidly excluded.

To one who was so staunch a supporter of the faith in which she had been brought up, not the least attractive feature in this picturesque town was its beautiful cathedral, that goodly edifice which the over-zealous followers of John Knox thought it no sacrilege to devastate, and of which a fine ruin alone remains to suggest to us what it must once have been.

The antiquary prowling about the moss-grown flag-stones that pave its aisles, or prying into nooks and corners of sinking buttress and mouldering walls, finds memory sharpened and curiosity stimulated at every turn. The philosopher, contemplating the length and breadth of that spacious area, heretofore rich with the decorations of architecture, and glowing in the pomp and pageantry of Romish piety, recalls the solemn music, the swinging censers, the carven images, the twinkling lights, the florid altar, the gilded crozier, and the mitred abbot, with his train of monks and choristers winding solemnly up the dusky nave. He speculates, half-pitying, half-sneering, on the various modes in which men offer their homage to the true God—the Mollah exhorting the faithful Moslem from a minaret, the priest pattering Latin in a corner before a crucifix, the precentor's nasal psalmody quivering within the unsightly walls of a Presbyterian meeting-house—and he reflects that the forms of religion change like the fashion of a garment, and that the offertory of yesterday becomes the superstition of to-day, and the mummery of to-morrow; but the Christian, looking upward to that ruined arch, through the stained glass of which, as through a prism, the light was wont to stream with rainbow colouring, sees the blue sky of heaven smiling changeless in its span, and rejoices to believe that clear as the blessed light of day is the light of piety, penetrating the disguises and the ceremonials and the ignorant prejudices of weak humanity, like the sunshine that vivifies as surely the dusky slab lurking in the gloomiest corner of the cathedral, as the fresh daisy raising its head on the free mountain side. What matters the fashion of the cup, chased in gold, or of broken pottery, so the parched lips can but drain their fill of the waters of life?

It was the Queen's habit to devote the early part of the day to such affairs of state as would not excuse neglect, even at St Andrews, and to the usual household duties, which every lady in the land, royalty included, then found to occupy a considerable portion of her time. At twelve, she dined temperately and hastily, after which she mounted her horse, and, accompanied by as small a retinue as possible, devoted the afternoon to exercise and amusement.

It was on the second day after her arrival at St Andrews that she agreed to Mary Hamilton's request, who begged that she might be allowed to accompany her mistress in the daily ride. The Queen had seen with concern the sad change that had come over her favourite's looks, and although surprised at this departure from her usual habits (for the maid-of-honour was a timid and unskilful horsewoman), willingly acceded to a proposal that promised to bring back the colour to her cheek and the light to her eye. With a couple of men-at-arms and a page, as their sole escort, they left the town by its southern gate, taking the horse track that led to the broad expanse of Magus-Muir, a locality destined in subsequent troubles to obtain an odious celebrity for the murder of Archbishop Sharpe at the hands of the Covenanters, but only interesting to Mary and her courtiers that it was rich in an abundance of wild fowl.

Chastelâr had been already tried on the charge of high treason, and sentenced to death; he was to be beheaded the following morning at daybreak. It was perhaps natural that neither Mary nor her maid-of-honour should have exchanged a syllable concerning his fate.

The Queen was riding 'Black Agnes.' As soon as they were clear of the town, she put her horse into a gallop, and never drew bridle for several miles. It did not, however, escape her Majesty's observation that the animal on which Mary Hamilton was mounted, a bay of great strength and spirit, usually uncontrollable by the gentle hand of a lady, was going in a perfectly docile and collected form; also, that the girl seemed to-day perfectly free from the timidity which commonly left her miles behind her mistress in these scampers across a country. They had already lost sight of the sea, and had gained a wild inland district of moss and moor, varied here and there with patches of cultivation, and interspersed with a few fir-trees of stunted growth, and an occasional cairn of stones breaking the level sky-line, when the Queen pulled up at the top of an acclivity, and pointing to a solitary horseman stationed, as if expecting them, at the foot of the slope, observed to her companion, with a wild attempt at cheerfulness obviously forced —

'You scarcely thought, Mary, I was entrapping you to witness a *rendezvous*. It is a romantic spot for the purpose, nevertheless, and yonder is the gallant who has kept tryst with me as he promised, faithfully enough.'

Mary Hamilton would have felt it an unspeakable relief to have burst into tears. The whole fabric of her morning's work was swept away by the sight of that plain dark figure, so stationary yonder on his horse. She would have given her life for half-an-hour's conversation with the Queen alone, although (strange inconsistency) she dared not ask her indulgent mistress point-blank to accord her that trifling favour, and now, this hateful stranger would probably hang about them all day, and to-morrow it would be too late. A thousand shadowy and incongruous impossibilities crossed her brain, too, at the same moment, all turning upon the one sickening certainty, that even while she grasped at their consolations, she felt too surely it would be out of mortal power to avert. She answered with a ghastly smile that startled the Queen, and totally unconscious of what she said the while—

'Let us go to meet him, madam; it may be that he can give us some hope.'

Mary stared at her attendant vaguely, and shook her head, then, putting her horse in motion, descended the slope towards the solitary traveller, flushing a brace of wary old moor-fowl and a curlew, while she plunged and scrambled with characteristic fearlessness through the broken ground that intervened.

The horseman dismounted as she approached, and did her homage with a grave dignified air, not without something of caustic humour that recognised the peculiarity of the situation.

'I might not fail to do your Grace's bidding,' said he, 'even in so light a matter, as to see you fly your hawk on Magus-Muir, but in good faith, madam, a younger cavalier could scarce have ridden harder than I have done since sunrise, and my old bones ache to some purpose for my punctuality.'

'Nay, Master Knox,' answered the Queen, with marked favour, 'those of your blood have been ever willing to set foot in stirrup at the bidding of the Stuart, and I have been taught to believe that a black cassock may cover as stout a heart and as loyal as a steel breastplate. Behold, I have here a fitting reward for your punctuality, to be given with the cordial good wishes of your Queen.'

Thus speaking, Mary drew from her bosom a crystal watch of curious and elaborate workmanship, large, substantial, and of considerable thickness, but esteemed a triumph of mechanical ingenuity, and presented it to the gratified Churchman, with a charm of manner that increased the value of the gift a thousand fold.

He bowed low over the royal hand that proffered so flattering a favour, and mounted his horse once more with an air of extreme satisfaction and the ready alacrity of a youth.

So far all was progressing smoothly, but Mary Stuart, judging of the human temperament by her own, was persuaded that the exhilarating influence of a gallop would produce the mollifying results she desired, and render even stern John Knox malleable to the purpose she had in view.

'Ye are not so strict,' said Mary, 'but that ye like well to see a fair flight, and I have a hawk here, Master Knox, that hath not her equal on the wing this side the sea; nay,' she added playfully, as he seemed about to excuse himself, and muttered something of 'business' and 'distance,' 'ye have thought fit to reprove all my other amusements, my feastings, and fiddlings, and masquings, and such-like, nor have I borne you any grudge, for that I believed you to be sincere, but ye love a good horse well I know, and can reclaim a hawk, for all your solemn bearing and grave studies, with the best of us. By these gloves, I will never forgive you, an' ye join not my pastime to-day.'

Thus speaking, the Queen signed to her page, who came up with a beautiful falcon on his wrist. The bird was transferred to Her Majesty, and seemed to shake its bells more gaily, and raise its hooded head more proudly, as though it knew and loved the hand that sleeked its neck-plumage with so gentle a caress.

The churchman was nothing loth. Despite a weak frame and failing health, his bold ardent nature, the same disposition that under different circumstances would have made him a soldier, a statesman, an explorer, or an adventurer, bade him take delight in the free air of the moorland and the stride of a good horse. He settled himself in the saddle, gathered his reins, and professed his readiness to attend Her Majesty.

'These creatures,' said he, arguing down some scruples of his own which much enhanced the promised gratification, 'are given for our lawful recreation. Man is doubtless lord over the beasts of the field. I will stay to witness one flight of that long-winged falcon; 'tis a goodly bird indeed if I know aught of the craft. One flight, and so crave your Majesty's licence to depart.'

The Queen smiled her assent, and galloped merrily on to a waste marshy surface, where the tramp of their horses ere long flushed a wisp of wild-fowl, and Mary, throwing her hawk in the air, was soon scouring over the moor at a break-neck pace, her eyes fixed on the sky, and her whole attention absorbed by the gyrations of her favourite.

John Knox, too, casting aside for the moment his cares and responsibilities, entered into the sport with the eagerness of a boy. It was seldom indeed that zealous man shared in any of the lighter amusements of the time; but in pleasure as in business, whatever he found to do Master

Knox went about with his whole heart and soul. The wrinkles seemed to smooth themselves on his brow as the wild wind swept back his thin gray locks, and he felt ten years younger, while the blood leapt warm in every pulse, and he urged his steed forward with leg and rein in the excitement of the flight.

Mary Hamilton rode like a woman in a dream. The bay horse, accustomed to fret and chafe under the restraining influence of the bit, seemed bewildered by his unusual freedom. He had plunged and bounded away with his head in the air, according to his wont, prepared for a contest in which he was sure to obtain the mastery, and he may or may not have been disappointed to find that his rider's carelessness of consequences exceeded his own, and that he was suffered to exhaust his mettle far more rapidly than he expected. With a stony white face, and her abundant hair streaming over her shoulders, the maid-of-honour sat back in the saddle, and flew along at a pace that even 'Black Agnes' could not surpass, unconscious apparently of amusement, or danger, or excitement, or anything but the relief afforded to her mental anguish by the physical sense of being carried with such velocity through the air. When the mallard was struck to earth at last, and the horses were pulled up, with panting sides and dilated nostrils, and wild eyes all a-glow with excitement, the Queen gazed on her reckless attendant in surprise, and even the severe Reformer remonstrated with her, Popish damsel though she were, for the utter disregard in which she seemed to hold that white neck of hers, and the probability of breaking it in such a headlong career.

'Fair mistress,' quoth Master Knox, 'there is reason in all things; over-caution supposes want of faith, but the contrary extreme, such as you have exhibited to-day, denotes presumption and fool-hardiness. You are young; humanly speaking you have many years before you. You would not willingly be cut off like a flower in its bloom. Why should you thus risk your life as if there was no to-morrow?'

She did not seem to hear him. She answered nothing, but the last word of his sentence seemed to strike some chord within her, for she turned away muttering below her breath, 'To-morrow. It will be too late to-morrow,' and clasped her hands upon her breast as if in pain. John Knox did not observe her, for his attention was now taken up by the Queen, who seeing in his face, which was bright with repressed excitement, that the propitious moment had arrived, motioned him to her side, and moving her palfrey out of ear-shot of the others, broached the subject that had led her to invite him thus to join in her favourite amusement.

'I have brought ye a long ride, Master Knox,' she said, 'and I would ye could return and taste a cup of sack at our poor lodging in St Andrews, but I know your busy avocations, and that ye will not willingly be absent from Edinburgh a day longer than is necessary. Ere you depart, I would fain ask your opinion on a subject of toleration.'

At the ominous word, the divine's whole countenance changed as the sky changes after a chance blink of sunshine in December. The clouds of controversy gathered on his brow, and suspicion gleamed in his cold piercing eyes. The Queen saw the storm brewing, and added, with a pleading sweetness few men would have been able to resist, 'The sun smiles on all alike; the blessed rain of heaven falls on the just and on the unjust. Which of us shall penetrate our neighbour's motives, or judge our neighbour's heart?'

'Ye shall have no dealings with the ungodly,' replied Knox, hastily, with an instinctive prescience of what was coming; 'the Amalekite is to be smitten root and branch till he be destroyed out of the land. But I anticipate your Grace, and have not yet been favoured with your commands.'

He took himself up shortly, as though aware and a little ashamed of his ill-manners. The Queen, reining in her horse, proceeded with great earnestness.

'The spring is now approaching, and you know with what devotion we, of the Catholic faith, look forward to the solemnities of Easter. I am not ashamed to solicit your interest that my fellow-religionists should be suffered to observe that festival with their accustomed ceremonies unmolested. I know too well the feelings of the party who call themselves the Reformed Church. I know (none better, and ye cannot deny that I have reason) Master Knox's influence with that powerful majority, and his sovereign entreats him thus in confidence to exert it in the cause of charity and peace and good-will amongst men.'

It was a powerful appeal from a monarch to a subject, especially under the peculiar circumstances of the moment. Riding alone over the breezy upland with that beautiful woman, under the exciting influence of wild scenery and an inspiriting gallop, the heart softened by the smile of nature, and the blood tingling with exercise, few men but would have found it impossible to resist a suppliant, who was at the same time a Queen, and *such* a Queen. Loyalty demanded obedience, self-interest whispered the advantages of royal favour, and the impolicy of refusing a sovereign, ambition drew a dazzling picture of the eventual triumph of the cause wrought out by the judicious concessions of one man alone, and that man venerated as the great pillar of Protestantism in Europe; but conscience thundered 'No;' and to do Knox justice, he never wavered nor hesitated for an instant. His lineaments looked more rugged, his brow more uncompromising than usual, when he rejoined—

'Your Grace has addressed me frankly, and as frankly I reply to you. If by holding up my finger I could retain for the Church of Rome any one of the privileges that are daily and hourly slipping from her grasp, if by so doing I could relieve her from one of the least of the indignities or calamities which are surely gathering round her head from the four quarters of heaven, see, madam, as I ride here a living man before you, I would keep it clenched down by force till the nail grew through the palm of my hand! I am a soldier, I will not desert my banner; I am an heir, I will not alienate my birthright; I am an honest man, I will do my duty at all hazards, in the face of every prince in Europe.'

He looked sublime while he spoke; the weak, ungainly figure reared itself in the saddle with all the pride of a Colossus, and never a belted earl could have borne a nobler front in coronet and ermine than did that minister of the Church in the fearless integrity of his purpose. Mary grew pale with anger and disappointment; nevertheless she had long since learned the painful lesson of self-control, and she forced herself to speak calmly, while her very blood was boiling within.

'Would ye refuse to others the liberty of worship ye exact for yourselves? Would ye persecute men who differ from you only in their mode of worship, more ruthlessly than the pagan emperors persecuted those early Christians who were our teachers as well as yours? Bethink ye, Master Knox, this is a world of change. The old faith hath many staunch supporters still. Men's minds may alter as they have altered ere now, and those who are all-powerful to-day may find themselves petitioners for mercy to-morrow. Is it well to exasperate beyond endurance those who may in their turn come to have the upper hand?'

The implied threat was injudicious and ill-timed; she would have done better, knowing with whom she had to deal, either to have given vent to her indignation and defied him outright, or to have repressed it altogether; but she was only a woman after all, and womanlike, could not entirely separate the two sensations of anger and fear, so she adopted those half-measures to which her sex is fain to have recourse in a difficulty, and roused his spirit while she tried to work upon his apprehensions.

'I defy the Romish Antichrist as I defy the principle of evil itself,' replied Knox, with kindling eyes and excited gestures. 'Am I watchman set upon a hill, and shall I leave my post because the enemy is at hand? Am I a shepherd in the wilderness, and shall I abandon my flock because the storm is gathering on the horizon? No, madam, once again I tell you that if you count on my allegiance in this matter, I renounce it; if you depend on my loyalty, I am a rebel!'

'It seems so,' she replied very coldly, and yet there was a tone of utter sadness and desolation in her voice that smote on the Churchman's heart. With looks of tender pity and concern, such as a father bends upon a favourite child, he would have argued with her once more, would fain have expounded to her the fallacies of her doctrines, and recalled her from the way which he conscientiously believed to be the very high road to destruction; but as is often the case in such disputes, the more one yielded the more the other encroached, and she cut him short with haughty impatience, reining in her horse, and pointing with outstretched arm towards the south.

'Yonder lies your homeward way, Master Knox,' said the Queen, 'and here is mine; I sent for you to listen to my proposals, not to hear your pulpit declamations at secondhand. When next we meet, others may have found means to tame that haughty spirit, and the avowed rebel may be glad to solicit pardon from his sovereign. I have no further need of you; you may depart!'

The dismissal was as peremptory as it was unceremonious; though burning to reply and charged with argument, he could not pretend to misunderstand it, and unwillingly withdrew. Ere the tramp of his horse had died out on the heathery sward, Mary burst into a passion of tears which she could no longer control; then bending her head low to her horse's neck, put 'Black Agnes' once more to her speed, and followed by her attendants, galloped off in the direction of St Andrews.

Independent of her own private sorrows and distresses, the Queen's political position was at this time one of peculiar difficulty and anxiety. A sincere Catholic, and consequently, from the very nature of her faith, an ardent upholder of its infallibility, and advocate for proselytism, she was compelled by the exigencies of her station to give countenance to its most determined foes. Not only did she see its tenets repudiated by the great majority of her people, but the very toleration they extorted for themselves, was denied to her, and it was a subject of open discontent that the Mass, which had been suppressed elsewhere, was suffered to be performed in the Queen's own chapel at Holyrood. The very adviser on whom she placed the utmost reliance, her half-brother, the Earl of Moray, was the chief support of the Protestant party in her kingdom. And although Seton and a few more of her nobility remained secretly attached to the old faith, their number was comparatively trifling, and their zeal scarcely proof against the temptations of ambition and self-interest.

Then, as if her difficulties were not sufficiently perplexing without foreign interference, her relatives, the Guises, lost no opportunity of reminding her that they looked to her alone for the restoration of the Religion in Scotland, and eventually over the whole of Britain; whilst a strong party in Spain furnishing her, for aid, with nothing but unasked advice, actually reproached her for lukewarmness in the cause to which she was sacrificing day by day her authority, her comfort, her very safety, and to which she was so sincerely attached, that, rather than resign it, she would have lost, as she afterwards did lose, her crown, ay, and the head that it encircled.

The insults levelled at her person, through her belief, constantly goaded her to anger, which prudential considerations urged her to suppress; and when pictures were paraded before her in the streets, ridiculing all that she held most sacred, and priests maltreated in her own chapel for the performance of their ritual and hers, it is painful to imagine the feelings of a sensitive woman and a Queen compelled to forego her revenge, and even to court the favour of those undutiful subjects who had originated such overt and outrageous scandal.

No wonder she galloped on with burning cheeks and swelling heart, reflecting only on the failure of her benevolent scheme so thwarted by the obstinate integrity of Knox, and insensible as the very horse that carried her to the beautiful scene opened out at her very feet.

Before her lay the noble sweep of St Andrew's Bay, framed, as it were, in its golden sands, that stretched far to the north along the coast of Forfarshire, till their tawny line was lost in the distant ocean at the jutting promontory of the Red-head. Clear against the blue expanse, clotted here and there with a white sail, rose the delicate pinnacles of the cathedral, supported on the right by the bluff square tower of St Regulus, firm and massive like some bold champion, proud yet careful of his charge. On the left, far out into the water, stood the sea-girt defences of the castle, while between these prominent objects many a graceful arch and pointed spire denoted the churches and colleges adorning that stronghold of learning and piety, refining the taste with their exalted beauty, whilst they carried the eye upwards towards heaven. Below these, the smiling town, with its white houses and gardens scattered more and more as they neared the water, straggled downwards to the beach; and, beyond all, the broad sea lay, calm and mighty in the serenity of its majestic repose.

On her bridle-hand, Mary might have scanned the wide champaign of two counties, through which two rivers ran in parallel lines to the ocean, the intermediate space dotted with woods and rich in cultivation, the river Eden gleaming like silver in the foreground, the smoke of Dundee floating white against the dark heights of Forfarshire, as it followed the downward current of the Tay, and in the far distance, the dim outline of the noble Grampians, losing their misty tops amongst the clouds that streaked the placid sky.

Yet Mary marked nothing of this. With a flushed cheek, with a drooping head, and, oh! with a cruel sorrow at her heart, she galloped on, and never checked her pace, nor addressed her attendants, till she reached the gate of the ecclesiastical city once more.

Then she drew rein, and as they rode together up the South Street, she blamed herself that she had not sooner observed and taken pity on Mary Hamilton's obvious exhaustion both of mind and body.

The bay-horse was, ere this, reduced to a state of abject submission and docility; the bridle, on which he was wont to strain so eagerly, lay loose upon his neck, and he seemed to be looking about for his stable with a very wistful expression of fatigue and discomfiture; but his rider's face was pale and rigid, while her eye was wide open, and her mouth firmly set; she seemed unconscious of all that was passing around her, and disclosed that vacant, yet pitiful expression of face which is only to be seen in those who walk in their sleep, or who are undergoing some racking torture of mind by which their outer faculties are benumbed.

'You are weary, child,' said the Queen, kindly. 'I should have remembered you are not so indefatigable a rider as myself. Well, we are at home now, and I shall not require you again this evening.'

So speaking, the Queen leapt lightly from her palfrey, and flung the rein to the attending page, but as she did so she looked once more in the face of Mary Hamilton, who was dismounting, and something she saw there made her start back, and exclaim in an agitated whisper—

'What is it, child? You frighten me! What is it?'

The other found her voice at last, but it came husky and broken to her lips.

'For mercy sake, madam!' said she, 'let me unrobe you, my kind mistress, do not deny me this one favour! Let me unrobe you, and alone.'

The Queen, though still startled, blushed vividly as something crossed her mind, that yet seemed partly to reassure her, and she beckoned her maid-of-honour to follow as she entered her private apartments, then dismissing her other attendants, threw herself into a chair, and with the colour not yet faded from her brow, bade Mary Hamilton unburthen herself of this dreadful grief that was weighing on her mind.

A burst of hysterical weeping was the result, but it calmed and relieved the sufferer, until she could find words in which to offer her petition and tell her pitiful tale. Women are wonderfully patient of such affections in their own sex, and the harshest of them will be gentle and considerate with one of these outbreaks that they have agreed to call 'nervous attacks.' Much more so, kindly Mary Stuart; soothing her attendant like a child, she soon restored her to sufficient composure to make intelligible the boon she had all day been striving to entreat. What this was an hour or two would disclose. In the meantime, the Queen and her maiden sat whispering in the darkening twilight, till the shafts and pinnacles of the neighbouring cathedral loomed grim and fantastic in the shadows of nightfall, and the light in the sacristan's window told that the time of vespers was already past.

At the same hour, John Knox, riding steadily along the road to Edinburgh, was beguiling the gloomy journey with a proud recollection of his resistance to the Queen's advances, sternly reminding his conscience that animosity to the Papists was a Christian's duty, and that forgiveness was no Christian virtue to one of another faith.

And Chastelâr in his dungeon was preparing for death by reflection on the pitiless beauty of her in whose face he would never look again.

CHAPTER XXIII

'While hate itself is fain to shrink,
Love freely ventures—lose or win—
And friendship shivers on the brink,
Where love leaps boldly in.'

The wind was rising out at sea with fitful sullen moans; the town of St Andrews was wrapped in thick darkness, save that at long intervals a light glimmered from some lofty window, showing where the pale student bent over his weary labour; the gathering waves rolled in with increasing volume, breaking heavily against the rocky base of the old castle; but the sentinel at its eastern angle, though he felt the spray wet on his face, could not distinguish the white surf leaping and boiling down yonder in the dark gulf at his feet; the vaulted chambers, the winding stairs and gloomy corridors of that stronghold were cold and dismal enough; but what of the dungeons down below the water-line, where the light of day had never penetrated yet, where the salt froth oozed and trickled from the bare rock, and the clammy slime stood on its chill surface, like the death-drops on the brow of a corpse? Ay, what of the dungeons? Ask those who were forced down the narrow stair with pinioned arms and muffled faces, knowing that their feet would never ascend the slippery steps again! Ask those who were immured in narrow cells, hollowed like living sepulchres from the rock, and so built in that the soul, indeed, might, but the body never could, escape from its imprisonment! Ask those who were let down by a cord into the black, loathsome pit from which they never came out alive! The answer may, perhaps, some day be spoken in tones of thunder before earth and heaven.

Even now they tell you how the marks of blood remain in evidence on that accursed keep; how the very stones bear witness to a foul and murderous deed, none the less guilty that victim and perpetrators were equally steeped to the lips in homicide and crime; that it was the accomplishment of Divine vengeance and the fulfilment of a martyr's prophecy.

When the proud cardinal, leaning over his window to behold the frightful holocaust at his ease, smiled bitterly on George Wishart at the stake, did not his heart sink within him to hear the martyr's solemn denunciation?

'David Beatoun, though the flames shall lick up my blood, yet shall thine remain to stain the very wall on which thou leanest, as a witness against thee till the day of judgment!'

When the Laird of Grange and the two Leslies dragged their enemy from his bed and slew him at that very window, must not remorse have whispered in the moment of despair that there is a retribution even here on earth? and when we learn that the fierce murderers did actually hang his body over the wall as a butcher hangs a carcase in the shambles, till the blood soaked and sank into the very stone-work, and that centuries have not washed out its stains, what can we say but that the Divine will doth not always postpone justice to a future world, and that Divine vengeance seldom fails to work out its own precept, 'whoso sheddeth man's blood by man shall his blood be shed.'

The only cheerful apartment in the castle was the guard-room; although the night was dark and stormy, the wind sighing, and the waves beating without, a huge wood-fire blazed and crackled in the ample chimney, reddening the weather-beaten faces of the men-at-arms, and glancing fitfully from their shining head-pieces and bright steel corslets. Small care had these rude hearts for the weather without or the woe within; the spray might dash against their casement, and the weary prisoner moan his wrongs in the neighbouring cell.

'What would you have? 'tis but the fortune of war,' quoth the soldier; 'my luck to-day, yours to-morrow; a bed of heather for this one, a lair of straw for that; a free discharge and a fresh enlistment at last. Put another log on the fire; I wish we had got something more to drink.'

Their captain sat somewhat apart, his head resting on his hand, and his sheathed broadsword lying idle on the floor. As the flame flickered on his forehead a frown seemed to pass and repass across its surface, but his eyes were intently fixed on the red glow of the embers, and perhaps he was drawing pictures that had no semblance of reality in their glare.

A moody man of late was Alexander Ogilvy; once the best of comrades, and the blithest of merry-makers, he was becoming captious, contradictory, and quarrelsome. The hand stole to the sword-hilt now on the lightest word of provocation, and although he was still ready to pledge his brethren-in-arms with the wine cup, it seemed to be no longer the desire of good fellowship that stimulated him, but a fierce morose thirst that he was resolved to slake in gloomy defiance.

Perhaps some of the phantoms he was watching in the fire might have accounted for this untoward change in the young soldier; perhaps it was not pleasant to picture to himself in those glowing depths the stately figure of Mary Beton, with her flowing skirts and quivering ruff, bending her lofty head so graciously towards a sharp spare man, in gorgeous apparel, with a clever face and a sneer, that if Ogilvy had ever formed any idea of Mephistopheles, would have presented to his mind's eye the very expression of that sarcastic personage; perhaps it did not enhance the harmony of the group to recognise in the hottest corner a figure bearing a grotesque resemblance to himself, watching the pair with jealous supervision, and presenting the undignified, if not ridiculous exterior, of one who runs second in the race of love.

With a movement of impatience he drove his heavy heel against the logs, dispelling the whole representation at a blow, and causing the fire to burn out fiercely, and the sparks to fly in thousands up the chimney.

At this moment a man-at-arms entered the guard-room, and approaching his captain informed him that two persons at the gate demanded admittance.

'Impossible,' said Ogilvy; 'the wicket is locked, and the watch set; bid them go to the devil.'

'One of them bears the Queen's signet,' answered the man, 'though she winna let it out of her hand. I doubt it's one of the leddies,' he added, 'an' I ken the tither yane fine; it's daft James Geddes, the fule.'

This altered matters considerably. The royal signet-ring was esteemed a voucher for any one who bore it, and all guards, warders, and such officers of the sovereign, had strict orders to consider it in the light of a direct communication from Majesty itself. So Ogilvy, taking down a torch from the wall, proceeded to the wicket in person.

On arriving there, he encountered a female figure, cloaked and hooded, that after a moment's hesitation he recognised as Mary Hamilton, and half-watching over her, half-sheltering himself behind her, much after the manner of a faithful dog, but with less expression of countenance than that sagacious animal, the ungainly figure and broad unmeaning face of James Geddes, the fool.

Ogilvy knew the maid-of-honour personally well enough; also, on the universal principle (for though she was not the rose to him, she had been *near* the rose), he was disposed to oblige her for the sake of Mary Beton, and bowing courteously, begged to know if she had any authority, at that late hour, to enter the castle.

'I have come to visit a prisoner,' replied she in a hard-set voice, showing him at the same time the Queen's signet-ring, which James Geddes watched as if he expected the captain of the guard would swallow it at a gulp.

Ogilvy bowed and withdrew the many bolts and bars that secured the wicket, then calling a soldier to fasten them again, preceded his visitors along the vaulted passage that led from the entrance to the guard-room. Mary Hamilton shuddered as she heard the gate clang to behind her; and the fool looked more than half-inclined to draw back and abandon his adventure at the outset, but a glance at his protectress reassured the latter, and the former, seeming, as it were, by a violent effort to adopt a fresh part, assumed an air of gaiety and carelessness strangely at variance with her bloodless face and horror-stricken eyes.

Arrived in the light of the guard-room, she produced an ample stone-bottle from beneath her cloak, and placed it on the rude oak table.

'The Queen has not sent me to visit her brave soldiers empty-handed,' said she, with a wild, dreary smile. 'While I am about Her Majesty's business, I hope they will drink Her Majesty's health.'

The fool's eyes glistened at the sight of the liquor, but once more he glanced at Mary Hamilton, as the well-trained dog looks at its owner ere he ventures to touch the tempting morsel placed before him. The soldiers gathered round with well-pleased faces; the bonds of discipline were not at that period drawn so tightly as at present, and a carouse was a sufficiently acceptable variety to the monotony of a night on guard. Ogilvy, too, who might, under other circumstances, have objected to such an employment of those he commanded, for the reason we have before hinted at, was unwilling to disoblige one of the maids-of-honour, and set the example himself by filling a cup to the brim with the strong fiery liquor, and emptying it to the Queen's health. James Geddes prepared to make sport for the rude soldiery, and one and all disposed themselves around the table for an hour or two of conviviality.

The fool, although habitually not averse to imbibing as much drink as he could honestly come by, seemed, on the present occasion, unusually cautious in his potations, and whilst he encouraged the laughing soldiers to drink deep from the stone jar, only put his own lips to the cup that was freely offered him, and for once appeared resolved to keep his poor faculties as keenly as possible on the alert. He glanced, too, ever and anon, at the door by which Mary Hamilton had left the guard-room, and seemed to watch and listen attentively for the slightest noise.

It was painful to see the gleams of anxiety that broke at intervals through the dense stupidity of his broad flat face. At such times his countenance again assumed the wistful sagacity of a dumb animal, and instinct seemed to warn him that he must summon all his faculties to meet some vague catastrophe for which his reason was unable to prepare.

The soldiers jested with the poor half-witted creature according to their wont, and as their draughts began to ascend into the brain, proceeded to coarse practical jokes, and much boisterous mirth, of which his infirmities were made the butt. James Geddes, however, never relaxed from his vigilance. Sometimes a lurid gleam shone for an instant in his eyes as a grossly offensive insult penetrated even his obtuse nature, and occasionally he gave vent to his feelings by a low moaning noise, and the rocking of his body to and fro, as was his custom when more than commonly irritated or distressed; but he was always careful to fill the soldiers' cups for them to the brim—was always watchful of the demeanour and presence of their commander; and whilst his glance wandered furtively to the door, his whole attention seemed painfully on the stretch to catch the sounds of that voice which it was his nature to obey with the attachment and fidelity of a dog.

Mary Hamilton, after exchanging a few words, in a low tone, with the captain of the guard, in which an acute observer might have detected successively the accents of remonstrance, entreaty, and command, had produced a small lamp from beneath her cloak, and lit it at Ogilvy's torch; then taking a key from his hand, which he seemed to deliver very unwillingly, proceeded alone towards the dungeon, casting over her shoulder one glance at the fool, in which caution was speakingly impressed as she departed. The soldiers were already launched on their carouse, and Ogilvy, though he seemed watchful and restless, often starting from his seat, and taking short turns up and down the guard-room, joined at intervals in their revelry.

The maid-of-honour stepped cautiously down the winding-stair that led to the dungeon. Mary Hamilton had nerved herself for the undertaking on which she had embarked, and now that she was fairly within the dreaded Castle of St Andrews, the agitation which had rendered her so helpless all day, had given place to the calm, resolute bearing of one who is prepared to succeed in a hazardous enterprise, or die in the attempt. It was, indeed, a trying situation for a young tender-hearted woman. The man she loved lay in that loathsome dungeon, condemned to die; she believed that she alone could save him. She had the means and the opportunity; all must depend on her courage and presence of mind. Yes, she would save him, and her reward would be to see him prostrate himself at the feet of another! It was a bitter thought, and yet she never wavered for an instant.

As she reached the door of his cell, she thought she heard his voice, the well-known voice, rich and melodious even here, and the sound of her own name made her pause and listen. He was consoling himself in his prison, this man who was to die on the morrow, with the illusions of his art. He had composed a ballad, of which her name was the refrain, and was singing it himself in his cell.

'There's a bonny wild rose on the mountain side,
Mary Hamilton.
In the glare of noon she hath droop'd and died,
Mary Hamilton.
Soft and still is the evening shower,
Pattering kindly on brake and bower;
But it falls too late for the perish'd flower,
Mary Hamilton.

'There's a lamb lies lost at the head of the glen,
Mary Hamilton.
Lost and miss'd from shieling and pen,
Mary Hamilton.
The shepherd has sought it in toil and heat,
And sore he strove when he heard it bleat,
Ere he wins to the lamb it lies dead at his feet,
Mary Hamilton.

'The mist is gathering ghostly and chill,
Mary Hamilton.
And the weary maid cometh down from the hill,
Mary Hamilton.
The weary maid but she's home at last,
And she trieth the door, but the door is fast,
For the sun is down and the curfew past,
Mary Hamilton.

'Too late for the rose the evening rain,
Mary Hamilton.
Too late for the lamb the shepherd's pain,
Mary Hamilton.
Too late at the door the maiden's stroke,
Too late for the plea when the doom hath been spoke,
Too late the balm when the heart is broke,
Mary Hamilton.'

She heard it every word, and for a time her composure gave way. A burst of passionate weeping relieved her, and, drying her eyes, she unlocked the door and entered the dungeon.

The light she carried streamed on Chastelâr's figure, dressed in the very clothes in which she had seen him taken. He was half-sitting, half-lying, in the extreme corner where the stone was dryest, and took no notice of her entrance, thinking it was the jailer, but continued to hum the air he had just been singing. When he lifted his eyes, however, and recognised his visitor, he rose at once, with his habitual courtesy, and bade her welcome to his habitation, laughing pleasantly the while.

'You find me poorly lodged, Mistress Hamilton,' said the poet; 'and although I live in a castle I am but scantily provided with room. It is not for long, however, as to-morrow morning, I am informed, they mean to remove me to a narrower chamber still.'

She could not bear to see him thus; again the warm tears filled her eyes as she gasped—

'The doom has gone forth; I heard of it to-day; there is but one chance left.'

He smiled a sweet sad smile.

'I have done with chances now,' said he; 'I set my all on one cast, and I do not complain that the luck has gone against me. It was kind of you to come and visit me, Mary'—he dwelt fondly on the name and repeated it more than once—'I was thinking of you even when you appeared. I was wishing I could see you once more. What of the Queen?' he added, with an eager glance. 'Is she here at St Andrews?'

'She sent me to you this very night,' replied the other. 'What I do is by her command, and according to her directions. You shall not die, Chastelâr; she bade me save you, and we have the means; only be obedient, and, above all, keep silent.'

His whole face lighted up as he seized her hand and covered it with kisses. Life was sweet to the poet, with his warm impulsive nature and his glowing hopes; all the more so when he learned that he would owe that life to the favour of the Queen. He listened eagerly while the maid-of-honour detailed to him the proposed manner of his escape, which, indeed, seemed feasible enough. She hoped, through the potency of the brandy which she had left behind her in the guard-room, and with the assistance of her half-witted confederate, to bring the soldiers to a state of hilarity at which the eye is not very keen, nor the suspicions very easily aroused; while in her whispered conversation with Ogilvy she had already, with the unscrupulous shrewdness of a woman, made use of his attachment to Mary Beton to win him half over to her enterprise. She calculated, at least, on his ignoring her proceedings; she then proposed to dress Chastelâr in her own hood and mantle, which, as their statures were not very dissimilar, would form a thorough disguise, and she had sedulously tutored James Geddes, who took an unaccountable delight in the whole proceeding, to conduct the captive to the gate with the same deference and care as if it were herself. It was difficult to make the faithful fool understand this part of the plan, but she had instilled it into him at last. He was to encourage the inebriety of the men-at-arms to the utmost of his power, and directly Ogilvy's back was turned to go his rounds, which something she had told him would induce the captain to do at an earlier hour than usual, James Geddes was to return to the dungeon and summon the visitor to depart. Chastelâr, in Mary Hamilton's clothes, would then accompany him to the gate, and she herself would remain a prisoner in his place.

'And when they find you here,' exclaimed the poet, all his generous impulses protesting against such an arrangement, 'think of Ogilvy's rage! think of the rude drunken soldiers! It cannot, it shall not be! Your life would have to pay the penalty.'

'And I would give my life freely for yours,' she replied, a bright smile breaking over her face, causing her to look for the first time to-night like the Mary Hamilton he remembered in the Queen's chamber, when all was so different and so happy.

'For mine!' he repeated, with a sadly troubled face. 'Oh, too late! too late!'

'Do not say so,' she continued, speaking very rapidly and eagerly, with her slender fingers grasping the prisoner's arm like a vice. 'I would not have told you this but that we shall never meet again. The very terms on which the Queen yielded to my entreaties were these: That you leave Scotland within twenty-four hours, and pledge your honour never to enter Mary Stuart's dominions more. Oh, if you knew how I knelt and prayed and pleaded ere I could wring from her the token that gave me access here; if you could have seen her angry frown while I implored, or heard the cold resolute voice in which she said at last, "I consent, but only on these terms, that I never behold him more," you would have pitied me, Chastelâr; you should pity me now, for though I have saved your life, oh, I am very, very miserable.'

Again she burst into a fit of weeping, the hot tears fell upon his hand, but he heeded them not; he scarce seemed conscious of the devoted broken-hearted woman trembling there before him; the Queen's words struck like a poniard to his heart, and he was mad! love-mad once more!

He broke rudely from his companion; he flung her hand from his arm, as if the touch were a viper's; his eye glared, and he ground his teeth together in the agony of a wounded spirit, and a pride humbled to the dust.

'I scorn her mercy!' he shouted, in wild frantic tones; 'I renounce her pardon, and I refuse her terms! Tell Mary Stuart, from me, from Chastelâr, who will be led out to die at sunrise to-morrow, that the last words he said were these: "If every one of these hairs were a life"'—he passed his fingers while he spoke through the abundance of his dark clustering locks—'"I would lose them all ere I would accept the smallest, lightest token of the Queen's favour. Because I have dared to love her more dearly than man ever loved woman here on earth; because I love her wildly, fondly, madly still." Ha, ha! she cannot rob me of that! Queen though she be, she cannot recall the past! Mary, Mary! ere to-morrow's sun be set, that cold heart shall ache, as it hath never ached yet, and Chastelâr will have had his revenge!'

And now the pure unselfish nature of Mary Hamilton's character rose superior to the crisis. Another who had loved him less would have turned away in wrathful scorn, and left him to his fate: not so that gentle, faithful heart; on her knees she besought him to listen to reason, to yield himself to her guidance, to accept of life for her sake.

The moments were very precious. Already James Geddes was beating impatiently at the door, warning them that he had fulfilled his ministering in the guard-room, and that Ogilvy was absent for the nonce. She clung to him—she urged him—she implored him, and the man was obdurate, pitiless of himself as of her, hardened in his despair, reckless, miserable, and resolved to die.

How many before and since have been like him! How many have turned obstinately from the pleasant easy path of safety and contentment, to reach wildly at the impossible, scaling the slippery crag just so high as shall dash them to pieces in their fall! There are spirits that seem ever destined to be striving after the unattainable, doomed in a punishment more cruel than that of Tantalus to thirst for a *mirage* that is never even within the bounds of hope. Be it love, wealth, ambition, their craving seems to be in its very nature insatiable, and, perhaps, even were the wildest and most extravagant of their desires to be granted, they would but turn aside indifferently, as if success must needs be loathsome, and long incontinently for something else that could never be their own.

It is well for the philosopher who has learned to create for himself his life's essentials. Blessed is the barmecide who can make believe that the tasteless water from his earthen pitcher is a draught of nectar from a cup of gold. But woe to the sanguine enthusiast who cannot be convinced that 'half a loaf is better than no bread;' the fool who shouts—'all or none,' for his war-cry, while he runs a tilt against the invincible windmill of conventionalism, and getting, as he deserves, none instead of all, has every bone in his body broken into the bargain for his pains.

Mary Hamilton pleaded for dear life; far dearer, indeed, was that life to her than her own. James Geddes, hearing her sobs and broken accents, became so importunate at the door of the cell, that one or two drunken soldiers from the guard-room, aroused by the noise, came loitering down the dungeon stair; and, at the same moment, Ogilvy, not in the best of humours, returned from his rounds, and the last chance was gone for evermore.

Whether the captain had met with any disappointment in visiting the different posts under his charge, or whether he had reason to suppose that his midnight walk was to be more agreeable than usual, and felt aggrieved to find its dulness unrelieved by any variety, it is not our province to inquire; but he certainly showed more zeal for discipline than on his departure, and entering Chastelâr's cell in person, after kicking poor Geddes away with a bitter curse, ordered the maid-of-honour imperatively to be gone, and summoned two of the soberest men-at-arms to mount sentry for the rest of the night at the head of the stair.

Mary Hamilton neither screamed, nor fainted, nor wept. She knew that all was over now, and accepted the inevitable catastrophe with that resignation which Providence seems to bestow in mercy on those who are destined to endure great suffering. She bent over Chastelâr's hand as she bade him a silent farewell, and though her lips moved as if in prayer, not a sound escaped them. Then she raised her head proudly, and walked rigidly and slowly out of the cell, less like a living being than a figure set in motion by mechanical means. The boisterous men-at-arms, in the guard-room, stood aside, respectfully, to let her pass; and James Geddes, as he followed her, cowered and shook with a mysterious fear.

But Chastelâr, in the selfishness of his great love, so strong even at the threshold of the grave, scarcely noticed her; nay, he even called out to her as she departed with a message for the Queen. The ruling passion was, indeed, strong in death. As his short and brilliant life had been valued only for her sake, so she was his last thought now that he stood on the brink of eternity.

'Tell her,' he said, 'that I commend me to her with my last breath. Thank her for all her kindness and the mercy she would have shown me even to-night, but say that I choose to die rather than be banished from her presence, and so Chastelâr bids her farewell,—the fairest, the proudest, and the best beloved princess under heaven!'

He seemed composed, even cheerful. To all appearance, the man was in possession of his faculties and in his right mind, yet these were the last words Chastelâr ever spoke on earth.

CHAPTER XXIV

'They led him forth to the silent square,
In the gray of the morning sky,
And they brought him a cup of red wine there,
To drink, and then to die.

'Without the gate, Lady Margaret stood,
And she watch'd for the rising sun,
Till it blush'd on the stone-work, and gleam'd on the wood,
And the headsman's work was done.

'Not a limb she stirr'd; but when noon-day's glow
Smote fierce on her temples bare,
A brighter sun had not melted the snow
That streak'd Lady Margaret's hair.'

The morning broke dull and gloomy; the wind that had been blowing steadily all night had subsided towards dawn, but a chill easterly breeze was still creeping in from seaward, and a light vapour rested on the surface of the ocean, beneath which the lead-coloured waves rose and sank in the sullen monotony of a ground swell. Little by little the cheerless dawn stole imperceptibly over the rugged bluffs and scaurs that to the northward formed a bulwark for the town, and disclosed at every minute new rents and fissures in their sea-worn sides—new wisps of dripping sea-weed trailing in ungainly streaks across their slippery surface; the ebbing tide, too, receding as though unwillingly, with many a landward leap and backward whirl, disclosed here and there round black rocks, peering like the heads of sea-monsters above the restless waters, while a solitary sea-mew, turning on its white wing downward from the cliff, screamed, as it were, in disappointment of its fishing after the storm.

The castle walls rose sullenly against the misty sky; black, massive, and impenetrable, they suggested no feelings but those of inhospitable and uncompromising grandeur. Their battlements, weather-stained with the gales of centuries, frowned dark defiance down on the ruffled ocean, and the royal flag, with the golden lion of Scotland ramping in its folds, half-unfurled and dripping with last night's brine, flapped drearily and heavily in the fitful breeze.

To and fro for a space of some twenty yards under the wall, a female figure was pacing with swift irregular steps, and her fingers twining convulsively as she held her hands clasped together before her. Mantle and dress were wet and disordered from the inclemency of the past night, but the hood of the former covered her to the brows, and it was only by the lower part of her white, rigid face, that a passer-by, had there been one at that early hour, could have recognised Mary Hamilton.

In a sheltered corner, screened from the wind by a massive buttress, cowered the ungainly figure of James Geddes; rocking himself backwards and forwards, he moaned as if in pain, and blew upon his cold fingers, huddling himself together for warmth the while, but his eyes travelled wistfully after Mary Hamilton as she walked, and though she seemed unconscious of his presence, they never quitted her figure for a moment.

Once, when close to him, she paused in a listening attitude, and he took courage to address her, whining like a troubled child —

'Will ye no gang hame? will ye no gang hame? 'Tis cauld and dreary biding here for sunrise. I'm wantin' hame; I'm wantin' hame!'

She started violently when he spoke; but, turning from him in impatience, only walked backwards and forwards faster than before.

And now a dull knocking might be heard in the square of the castle, and the noise, as of heavy beams put in motion, broke the stillness of the early morning. At each fresh sound, Mary Hamilton stopped in her walk, and started on again as if goaded to exertion by internal agony; the fool shivering and moaning in his corner, yet still watching her intently, at length rocked himself off into a fitful half-slumber, waking up at intervals to implore his unheeding companion to go home.

Within the castle preparations were already making for some grave and unusual event. The soldiers, though flushed and fevered after their debauch, yet preserved an ominous silence, and betrayed on their coarse faces an expression of pity and dismay. Ogilvy himself looked pale and sorrowful. Once when he caught sight of a sharp, polished instrument, propped carefully that its edge should not be frayed against a corner, a tear might have been seen to steal down the captain's cheek till it hung in his heavy moustache; but his voice was gruffer than usual, as he gave some necessary order a minute afterwards, ashamed, doubtless, as men commonly are, of those emotions which betray that they have a heart.

Two or three workmen had been already admitted at the wicket, and were taking advantage of the increasing light to erect an ominous fabric of boards and scaffolding in the centre of the Castle square. They went about their job in a prompt business-like manner enough, but they spoke in whispers, and when a basket of sawdust was brought out, it was disposed almost reverently in its place. After this a taint of death seemed to pervade the atmosphere, and one of the artificers, a strapping young fellow, six feet high, had recourse to a dram of strong waters on the spot.

Down below in his dungeon, Chastelâr was asleep. Strange as it may appear, men always *do* sleep before execution. Be it that the faculties are so completely worn out by the wear and tear of anxiety that usually precedes condemnation, or be it another instance of the Divine mercy which would fain shorten that time of agony to the sufferer, such is the fact; and, in the last moments of criminals, it is almost invariably the case that body and soul both taste their last repose on earth, ere the one sleeps and the other wakes for all eternity.

What were the poet's dreams in that short welcome rest? Did he anticipate the great change, and fancy his spirit already free from its prison, wandering through those unknown regions which good Eneas, and rich Tullus and Ancus, and your grandfather and mine, and a host of those we both knew and valued, and would have followed into any danger, or on any expedition, have ere this thoroughly explored—to which you and I, though we think so little about it, are bound just as surely and inevitably, and with which to-morrow, or the day after, or this time next year, we may be familiarly acquainted? Or did he retrograde to the past, and revel and ruffle it at Holyrood once more, riding the sorrel horse alongside of 'Black Agnes,' and sunning himself in the bright eyes of the Maries, and above all the smiles of her their peerless Queen? Perhaps a vision of that face he had worshipped so fondly shone on him for the last time kindlier and lovelier than it had ever appeared in reality, and to wake from such a dream as that was so bitter that even death became welcome as promising sleep again.

The knocking on the scaffolding failed to arouse him, and when Ogilvy went gently into his cell with a torch, the soldier passed the light half-pitifully, half-admiringly, over the manly face that could look so calm and peaceful at such a time.

And in the royal house in the south street, within a culverin's distance of the castle, were all the inmates sleeping soundly at the dawn of that gloomy morning? Was that a bed of rest, on each post of which was carved a crown, and at the head of which the arms of Scotland were emblazoned so richly in embroidery and cloth of gold? Was the lovely face, so flushed and troubled, thus buried in the pillows to exclude the light of day; were the white hands pressed against the throbbing temples and covering the beautiful little ears, in dread of the morning gun which would be fired at sunrise, and tell that all was over?

It was no fault of Mary Stuart's that Chastelâr was doomed. All that lay in her power had been done to save him; all that royal dignity and womanly shame would permit. Perhaps she believed him to have escaped even at the last; she would hardly guess at such infatuation as he had shown even in *him*, and yet the victim's sleep had probably been far sounder than hers for whom he was about to die.

Lights were burning in the Queen's chamber, heavy curtains at the window excluded the faintest glimpse of dawn, yet she was turning and tossing restlessly on her couch, while Chastelâr was pacing in grave composure up the dungeon-stair that led into the gray morning, the last he would see on earth.

But one bed, at least, in the royal house remained cold and unoccupied — Mary Hamilton had never returned home all night. Under the castle wall she kept her weary watch; and, as the dawn widened into day, she was still pacing hurriedly up and down, up and down, and at every fresh turn casting a horror-stricken look towards the sky.

Presently the mist rolled slowly away, curling downwards from the heights of Craigton and the bleak outline of Drum-Carro Hill, disclosing the bare and cheerless table-land that forms the eastern boundary of Fife. The changing wind cleared the loaded atmosphere, and glimpses of blue became apparent through the fleecy vapours dispersing rapidly as they were driven out to sea; already the beams of morning were gilding the sands of the bay, and two or three fishing-boats, hoisting their white sails, were putting out hopefully from the shore; the cheery voices of the sailors came pleasantly over the water, and reached the ears of the watcher under the castle wall. Still the hood was drawn over her face; still she paced with that monotonous tread up and down, up and down; still the poor fool, crouching under his buttress, moaned and rocked and shivered, urging pitifully that he was 'wantin' hame—wantin' hame.'

Then, though the castle yet remained a huge black mass in deep shadow, spire and pinnacle on the cathedral began to blush and glow in the morning sun; presently, when Mary Hamilton turned in her walk, her eye was dazzled by his horizontal beams streaming along a pathway of molten gold as he rose cloudless from the sea. Retracing her steps, she saw the whole massive building before her shine out at once in a flood of warm yellow light; then she stopped short, bending forward with her hand outstretched, and listening eagerly.

Comforted by the warmth, the fool rose from his lair and rubbed his hands together, with an attempt at cheerfulness, shifting alternately from one foot to the other in a kind of measured dance, and striving in his vacant, half-witted manner to attract the attention of his companion.

She neither moved nor noticed him; still in the same attitude, with her neck bent forward, her hand stretched out, and the lower part of her face visible beneath her hood, white and rigid as if cut from marble.

He pulled her cloak impatiently—'Come awa' hame,' he whimpered like a child left alone in the dark. 'I'm feared here—I'm feared here; it's no sae canny sin' the dawn.

> Wi' a rising wind,
>
> And a tide comin' in,
>
> There's a death to be;
>
> When the wind's gaed back,
>
> An' the tide's at the slack,
>
> There's a spirit free.'

He crooned this doggerel over twice or thrice, pointing at the same time to the wet sand below them, and the black shining rocks left bare by the ebb; but she never answered him, for ere he was silent the heavy boom of a culverin broke on the morning's stillness, and a wreath of white smoke, rising above the walls of the castle, floated calmly and peacefully out to sea. The fool cowered down and hid his face in his hands. She did not start— she did not shriek, nor faint, nor quiver; but she threw her hood back and looked wildly upwards, gasping for air; then, as the rising sun shone on her bare head, Mary Hamilton's raven hair was all streaked and patched with gray.

CHAPTER XXV

'"How should I your true love know

From another one?"

"By his cockle hat and staff,

And his sandal-shoon."'

While the grass was growing tall and rank on Chastelâr's grave, the beauty that had bewildered and destroyed him was unconsciously sowing dissensions and intrigues in half the courts of Europe.

Not only on the southern side of the Tweed did every turbulent noble and ambitious statesman look to Mary Stuart's marriage as, in one way or other, a stepping-stone to his own aggrandisement, but each of the numerous parties in the state was prepared to put forward and support its candidate for her hand, totally irrespective of the lovely Queen's personal feelings and predilections. Austria, Savoy, Spain, had also their claimants for the desired alliance; and it would be difficult to calculate the multiplicity of schemes and combinations originating in the desire of possessing the heiress to two kingdoms, and the most fascinating woman of the age.

Perhaps the proposed union with the Crown-Prince of Spain was, of all matrimonial overtures, the most unpopular in Great Britain; and the Protestant party, now completely in the ascendant both in England and Scotland, would have resorted to the strongest measures rather than submit to such an arrangement.

All the engines of an unscrupulous diplomacy were ready to be put in motion for the purpose of thwarting Don Carlos, and over-reaching his emissaries. Nor were Elizabeth and her agents likely to be restrained by any over-refinement of delicacy in a matter which concerned the stability of the English Queen's power, and the very existence of her government.

In the meantime, Mary and her maidens floated, so to speak, on the surface of all this turbulence and vexation, as the sea-bird floats with unruffled plumage on the restless waves. Their life was indeed one of constant variety and adventure, for their royal Mistress was too thorough a Stuart not to identify herself with all the difficulties and troubles of her kingdom, whilst the bonds of affection which riveted her attendants to her service were but drawn closer every day, by the dangers and hardships they shared in their huntings and progresses and judicial proceedings, through the length and breadth of Scotland.

Nevertheless, winter after winter found them established once more, over their peaceful embroidery, at Holyrood; beautiful and merry and unchanged as ever—all but one.

Mary Hamilton, though she still showed the same unbounded devotion to her mistress, the same sweetness of disposition towards her companions was cruelly altered now.

It is very sad to read in any human face the unerring symptoms of a broken heart; to watch the eye sinking, the cheek falling, and the lines about the mouth deepening day by day; to note the listless step, the morbid craving for solitude, the painful shrinking from all that is bright and beautiful—from a strain of sweet music, a gleam of spring sunshine, or the laugh of a happy child, as the aching eye shrinks from light, and, above all, the dreary smile that seems to protest patiently against the torture, while the sufferer is kind and forgiving still. We are almost tempted to ask, why should there be such sorrow here on earth? But we are satisfied and reassured, recalling a certain pledge that cannot deceive, remembering who it was that declared in mercy and sympathy—'Blessed are they that mourn; for they shall be comforted.'

Her companions could not fail to notice the change that was thus wasting the very existence of their favourite, and each, in her own way, strove to show her fellow-feeling and her concern. Mary Carmichael was, perhaps, the least demonstrative of the three; but this young lady had of late been extremely engrossed with her own affairs, and seemed to acquire additional hardness of character and reserve of demeanour day by day. Her interviews with the stranger in the Abbey-garden, always clandestine, and always affectionate, took place at regular intervals; and she seldom saw Walter Maxwell now, avoiding, indeed, every occasion of meeting him, and treating him, when they did happen to be together, with a coldness and displeasure, which he was the last man on earth to accept with resignation, and which was gradually, but surely, estranging his affection from her altogether. He did not see the longing looks that followed him when his back was turned; he did not hear the sigh that rose so wearily to her lips when she was alone; he only thought her fickle, heartless, ungenerous, and unjust, determined to have nothing more to do with her, felt hurt and angry, yet very much ashamed of himself for entertaining either of these sentiments on her account.

All this time Mr Randolph had not been idle at the Court of Holyrood, fulfilling his ministering with a tact and energy peculiarly his own, and valued as they deserved by his bustling mistress and her astute adviser, the celebrated Cecil. Wherever there was an intrigue brewing, the English ambassador was not to be satisfied until he was at the bottom of it; wherever there was a mystery he sifted it thoroughly; analysing with diplomatic chemistry its component parts, and amalgamating the whole into a confusion worse confounded when he had done with it.

The many marriage proposals to the Queen kept his hands full, and the contradictory orders he received from his sovereign, who, with all her great qualities, was sufficiently a woman never to be quite sure of her own mind for two consecutive days, by no means tended to simplify or facilitate the duties of his office. Nevertheless he found time to press his suit ardently with Mary Beton, insinuating himself sufficiently into her affections to worm out of her all the intelligence he could possibly obtain, yet with characteristic caution never failing to stop short of the boundary beyond which he must compromise or embarrass himself. And yet Mr Randolph, with his clever scheming, well-balanced mind, and his thoroughly disciplined heart, was but human after all: none other was so pleasant to him as this daily duty of making love to Mary Beton; her dignity and her beauty gratified his fastidious taste, and her obvious admiration of himself could not but make an impression on his callous heart.

Sometimes, even over him, the hardened man of the world, stole a soft vision of something better than ciphers, and protocols, and despatches—of pleasant words and loving looks, and little children and a home; but a moment of reflection brushed all such weaknesses from his path, and the perusal of a state-paper from Cecil soon restored him to his philosophy. Then he remembered that in a career like his every stepping-stone to greatness must be prized and used only as such; however fair its polish, however valuable its quality, it must be crushed under his heel to gain a firmer foot-hold, and spurned in turn when done with, for his upward spring to the next. Randolph sought out tools for his own purpose in all directions; when he failed to find an appropriate instrument, he shaped one to his hand for himself.

Now it had not escaped the watchful eyes of Mistress Beton that a certain stranger, with whom Mary Carmichael seemed extremely intimate, came and went at stated intervals to and from the Court. With all her vigilance, however, she had never been able to discover the exact object of these frequent visits. Had she been satisfied that it was a simple love affair, she might, indeed, on her own responsibility, have stifled the whole proceeding by authority; but a hint to that effect hazarded to the Queen had been so coldly received as to convince her that the intrigue, whatever might be its object, was carried on with Mary's cognisance and approval.

More than any of the other maids-of-honour, Mistress Carmichael had free liberty to come and go as she chose. On occasion she was closeted secretly with her mistress; and more than once these private consultations were known to have been preceded or followed by an assignation with the mysterious stranger. Mary Beton could not make it out; she was satisfied that her junior had a lover who was deeply engaged in a political intrigue. She must have been more or less than woman had her curiosity not been aroused and her disapprobation excited. It was a relief to tell Randolph of her suspicions, and a pleasure to listen to the eloquence of his gratitude for the confidence thus reposed in him. In consequence of these disclosures the diplomatist resolved to cultivate a greater familiarity with Maxwell, of whom he had never entirely lost sight, and whose honest nature he doubted not he could mould to his own purposes; the more so that, in common with the rest of the Court, he was aware of Walter's feelings towards Mary Carmichael, which the lover believed to be inscrutably hidden in his own heart.

To a cynical disposition it is no small amusement to watch the demeanour of an offended swain. Women, who are hypocrites from the cradle, manage to conceal their feelings creditably enough, and we may take leave to doubt whether these feelings themselves are so engrossing as they would have the other sex believe; but a man, one of the Lords of the Creation, who 'dotes yet doubts, suspects yet strongly loves,' is an object that may at least be termed deplorable, if not ridiculous. He always over-acts his part so completely, his affection of indifference is so transparent, his bearing of scrupulous courtesy and offended dignity so ludicrous, and his sudden fits of remorse so unaccountable, that the world in general contemplates him with comical surprise, and the object herself regards him with secret triumph and outward contempt.

'Treat a woman frankly,' quoth Lovelace, in his treatise on this difficult topic, 'and, strange as it may at first sight appear, like a rational creature. This course is sure to produce a misunderstanding; but remember the sooner there is a trial of strength the better. Afterwards, if you cannot preserve a *bonâ fide* and complete indifference, take care to absent yourself from the subject under treatment. It is indispensable never to appear at a disadvantage. If elsewhere, the subject, whose imagination is vivid, will picture you as more pleasingly employed than in its society. This rouses emulation and stimulates self-esteem, of both which qualities it possesses a large share. When it is satisfied you can do perfectly well without it; if it has the slightest inclination to be tamed, it will come to the hand of its own accord; if it has not, all your pains are but labour thrown away, and only render you less fitted to cope with such other subjects of the species as it may seem desirable to reduce to obedience. Always remember this, that the men whom women love best are those over whom they have the least influence, and of whom they stand somewhat in awe.'

Is Lovelace right? We have quoted from memory, but such is the gist of his theory, the truth of which our own observations of such matters would lead us to concede; the difficulty seems to be in reducing it to practice. The generous nature is more willing to give than to receive, and takes all the shame and all the suffering ungrudgingly on its own shoulders.

'Malo cum Platone errare.'

It may be better to fail thus, than to triumph with Lovelace.

Walter Maxwell was proud, lonely, and unhappy. It was under these circumstances that Master Randolph bade him to dinner in his lodging at twelve o'clock noon, and studiously avoided asking any other guest to meet him.

The refined taste of the Englishman had gathered about him even in the northern capital every luxury of which the age admitted. Good living and diplomacy have ever gone together, from the roast mutton consumed in council before Troy to the Nesselrode puddings of to-day.

Honest Jenkin, an invaluable domestic, received his master's guest with a grin of recognition. He had not forgotten their night skirmish on the Border some two years ago, and after the manner of his kind had assumed a vested interest in Maxwell for the rest of his life.

'Master Randolph was in his closet concluding a despatch,' he said, placing a seat for the visitor in the chimney-corner. 'The soup would be on the table in five minutes; would Master Maxwell divert himself in the meantime with examining these silver-mounted dags? They were pretty pistolets enough. We would have been none the worse of them that moonlight night in the "Debatable Land."'

Maxwell smiled, and whilst Jenkin bustled to and fro about his hospitable labours, warmed himself at the wood fire and took a survey of the ambassador's apartment.

It presented the same medley of refinement and simplicity, of comfort and contrivance, which may be observed in an officer's barrack-room of the present day. Sundry mails and leather trunks, all adapted for carriage on horseback, were converted into cases for books and writings, and otherwise served temporary purposes for which they were not intended. The massive oaken chairs and tables, rough primitive furniture belonging to the mansion, were covered by skins and shawls of considerable value, Randolph's own property, and presented to him at different times by the great personages with whom he came in contact. Costly arms of beautiful workmanship, richly-chased drinking vessels, and elaborate ornaments of great value in small compass, that had come into his possession in the same manner, were scattered about the apartment. A sword of the finest temper Italian forges could produce, inlaid with gold and ornamented with precious stones, the gift of the Duke of Savoy, lay carelessly on a writing-table across a Bible printed at Geneva, as the inscription on its leather cover attested, for Mr Randolph's especial acceptance; and propped against the hilt of this beautiful weapon smiled a miniature portrait of Elizabeth, with tightly curling yellow hair, set profusely in diamonds. Quantities of papers and memoranda, none, we may be sure, of the slightest importance, littered the floor; a pair of spurs, a hawking glove with a set of jesses and a lure, were on the high chimney-piece, grouped about the beautiful cup that the Queen of Scotland had herself bestowed on the Minister; whilst ranged in a semicircle before the fire, ripening and mellowing in its comfortable glow, stood a row of tapering flasks, blushing with the goodly vintage of Bordeaux. As Jenkin appeared with the dinner at one door, Randolph came forward with his open pleasant manner to meet his guest through another.

'Work is done for to-day!' exclaimed the diplomatist, with the bright air of a boy released from school. 'Master Maxwell, you are heartily welcome, once for all. Be seated, I pray you. Were a despatch to arrive post from my gracious mistress herself, I should thrust it aside like the noble Roman, fill me a cup of wine, as I do now, to your health, and say, "Business to-morrow!"'

'No man has so good a right to leisure as yourself,' replied his guest, doing as he was bid, and returning the pledge in a hearty draught, 'for no man gets through so much work in so short a time. Even Maitland, who is our most accomplished penman here in the North, vows that he cannot but marvel at the despatch with which the English affairs are conducted.'

'It is all plain sailing,' replied Randolph, with an appearance of the most engaging candour. 'My instructions are usually so intelligible and above-board that I have but to act on them without delay. Frankly, my friend, between you and me, the only complications I have are owing to the mystery that is kept up about your Queen's marriage. But this is no time for business. Fill your cup once more. Honest Jenkin's catering requires to be washed down with good wine. The fare is moderate enough, but at least I can answer for the liquor.'

Both by precept and example Randolph encouraged his guest to do justice to his hospitality, and led the conversation as he well knew how, to such topics as he thought would most interest a man of his companion's age and habits. Horses, hawks, and hounds, wine, women, the latest gossip at Holyrood, the newest jest from the French Court, and the recent improvements in warlike arms and tactics, such were the subjects lightly touched upon in turn, and each was made the reason or the excuse for a fresh bumper; but all the while the diplomatist's attention was never taken off the object he had in view. Like some skilful chemist, he watched the gradual fusion of his materials, and waited patiently for the moment of projection. It did not escape him, however, that Maxwell was preoccupied and out of spirits; that though he bore his share in the dialogue courteously enough, it was with an obvious effort, and that every fresh cup he emptied seemed rather to drown than to cherish the few sparks of hilarity which he had shown at the commencement of the entertainment.

At a sign from his master, Jenkin set a flask of rich Cyprus wine on the table, and Randolph, dismissing the domestic, heaped fresh logs upon the fire, and drew his chair towards his guest, as if he were growing exceedingly confidential and communicative.

'Are you for the revels at the Palace to-night?' said he, with a meaning look at the bravery of Walter's attire. 'We may as well go together. In the meantime (we are old friends, good Master Maxwell), I have something to say to you,—of course, in the strictest confidence.'

'Of course,' replied Maxwell, with rather a disturbed expression of countenance, which subsided, however, almost immediately into his usual steady composure.

The ambassador filled his guest's cup and his own.

'You and I are interested in the same matter,' said he, not entirely repressing his habitual cynicism, 'and such a community forms the strongest bond of friendship. If I can prove to you that by helping me you benefit yourself, can I count upon your assistance?'

'You must explain your meaning more clearly,' replied the other, with something of contempt in his tone. 'Remember, I am a soldier, and no diplomatist.'

'You are a soldier, I know,' rejoined Randolph, 'and a brave one. You are loyal and generous and true. Mr Maxwell, I will be frank with you. There is an evil influence at work here, which I think you have the power to crush. Listen. Would you stand by and see your Queen deceived and trifled with by a political cabal, of which the principal emissary is blackening and destroying a reputation that I believe is dearer to you than your own?'

'What mean you?' exclaimed Maxwell, with forced composure, but putting so strong a constraint upon himself that the silver goblet he grasped was dinted by the pressure of his fingers.

'It is no secret now,' answered the other gravely. 'Courtiers' tongues wag freely enough on such subjects, and you must not be wroth with me for repeating in your own behalf simply what I hear. It is well known that Mistress Carmichael, beautiful Mistress Carmichael, cold Mistress Carmichael, proud Mistress Carmichael' (he watched the effect of each epithet in succession on his irritated listener), 'has taken to herself a friend, an admirer, a lover, call it what you will, with whom she holds clandestine interviews in the Abbey garden at night. As I live, 'tis the common talk of the palace; and people laugh and whisper and sneer about the spotless Maries, and wonder why the Queen takes no notice of it. Nay, chafe not with *me*. In good faith, man, I do but tell you this as a friend. I have little enough to do with ladies, you know.'

'And what is all this to me?' asked Maxwell, with such admirable self-command that Randolph could not help thinking what a pity it was he did not follow out the profession of state-craft. Nevertheless, every word had struck home, and although his voice was so steady and his face so calm, the perspiration stood on his brow, and there was a dangerous glitter in his deep-set eyes.

'Why thus much,' returned Randolph—'that had this intriguer, whoever he may be, no claims but his own merit to the notice of Mary Carmichael, I believe, and those who know her best affirm, that she would never have condescended to notice him. But these interviews, granted for some hidden purpose unconnected with gallantry, are compromising her till she is gradually falling into his power, and the poor girl will find herself at last compelled to accept as a lover the man for whom she does *not* care, unless she be extricated from her false position by the man for whom she *does*.'

'Meaning me,' said Maxwell, looking steadily in the minister's face.

'Meaning you,' replied the latter, continuing in the most friendly tone; 'you have the right, it seems to me, and you ought to have the will, to unmask this intruder. It is your own fault, Maxwell, with good friends at your back, if you have not the power. Come, you may count upon me for one in this matter. To-night I have reason to believe Mistress Carmichael will again meet this mysterious personage in the Abbey garden, whilst the revel is at high tide in the palace. Follow her to the tryst, confront your rival and compel him to declare himself, or to do you reason with his sword. If needed I will be at your back, and should all other means fail, six inches of cold steel can easily square accounts between you.'

'And your reason for thus interesting yourself in my concerns?' demanded Maxwell, with a dry laugh. 'Is it purely out of friendship for me, Master Randolph?'

'Now you speak like a sensible man,' replied the diplomatist, 'and I answer you with the frankness you deserve. No! with all my regard for you, this interest, on my part, is *not* entirely for your sake. I have reason to mistrust this stranger; I have my suspicions of some dark plot, against which it is my bounden duty to be on my guard. If he be a friend, my plan will at once set matters on a proper footing, both as regards yourself and the lady of whom we speak. If an enemy, the sooner he is removed from our path the better. Have I not convinced you that our interests are identical? The day wanes; one more cup of the Cyprus, Master Maxwell, and then, first to the Palace, afterwards to the garden.'

Maxwell filled and emptied the cup of Cyprus as he was bidden: but his was a temperament on which wine took but little effect, or rather, in which it stimulated the faculties without upsetting the judgment. Even Randolph's brain, powerful as that organ undoubtedly was, could not have been less affected by his potations than was the soldier's.

As the pair, ostensibly dismissing the subject from their minds, talked gaily on about other matters, it would have been amusing to note the dexterity with which the diplomatist adapted his conversation to the purpose he had in view. How with a casual remark here, a covert sarcasm there, he endeavoured to stimulate the other's jealousy and to arouse his alarm, whilst, at the same time, with many a plausible argument and choice anecdote, introduced as it were by chance, he endeavoured to establish the expediency of prompt and desperate measures on all occasions where a man had to deal with cases of mystery and intrigue.

Maxwell listened attentively, but the inscrutable repose of his countenance baffled even Randolph's penetration, and he contented himself with vague and general replies, of which the other could make nothing. Nevertheless, he was resolved in his own mind what to do. With all his exterior of adamant, he was sufficiently vulnerable within. Bitterly hurt and offended at Mary Carmichael's conduct, he had determined to forget her; but the old wound was only superficially healed over, and it would not bear being touched or tampered with yet. Also his attachment to that young lady had been of the purest and most unselfish order, and such an affection never fails to evoke all the latent generosity of a noble heart. His own impulse, as a gentleman, was to give his rival every fair advantage; to treat him, at least, as an open and honourable foe; to warn him that his movements were watched and his personal safety endangered; and to tell him, point blank, that he had done this for the sake of her whom they both loved. Surely such frankness would meet with the return it deserved; and then, if Mary really preferred this stranger, why, the dream was over, that was all. Any privation was better than this continual uncertainty; it was but giving her up, and the world would be before him again—something whispered that it would be a very different world, nevertheless. However, he made up his mind, and was more than usually merry with Randolph as they proceeded together towards Holyrood.

CHAPTER XXVI

'I leant my back into an aik,
I thought it was a trusty tree;
But first it bowed and syne it brak,
Sae my true love did lightly me.

'Oh, waly, waly—gin love be bonny
A little time while it is new;
But when it's auld, it waxeth cauld,
And fades away like morning dew.'

It was the anniversary of Twelfth-night, and the feast of the Bean was in act of celebration with great glee and splendour when the English Minister and his companion entered the reception-rooms of the Palace. This favourite pastime, borrowed from the Court of France, has come down to us in modern days under the form of 'drawing for king and queen;' the bean was concealed in the twelfth cake, and the dame to whose share it fell was chosen with much mock solemnity as queen of the night. On the present occasion the lot had fallen to Mary Beton, and her indulgent mistress, with that playful good-humour which so endeared her to her attendants, had insisted on decking the leader of the revels with the most splendid attire her own royal wardrobe contained.

In case that any lady should condescend to look into the dry pages of a historical novel, we will endeavour to the extent of our poor abilities to present the details of a 'grande toilette,' of the fifteenth century.

A sweeping robe of cloth of silver, heavy with embroidery and ornamented with medallions of pearls down the front of the dress, which was looped backwards at the knee and fastened with bunches of red and white roses, disclosing a petticoat of white silk damask, long and ample so as to cover the feet encased in their satin shoes; at the waist a girdle of precious stones arched over the hips, and coming downwards to a point in front, marked the outline of the figure; while a collar of sapphires and rubies, close round the neck, lurked and sparkled under the clouds of scalloped lace that composed the ruff; the sleeves of the gown, open at the elbow, terminated in ruffles of the lightest gauze, and thick gold bracelets on the wrists; the hair, gathered into heavy masses at the back of the head, was dragged somewhat off the temples, so as to show the delicate ears with their glittering ear-rings; whilst over the whole figure, relieving its dazzling whiteness, was thrown a satin mantle or scarf of *cramoisie*, the well-known deep rich hue, something between crimson and plum-colour, which was such a favourite with the elaborate *coquettes* of that sumptuous period.

Thus attired, majestic Mary Beton looked every inch a queen, and had it not been for the presence of her mistress, simply dressed in her usual morning garb, yet 'beautiful exceedingly' where all were beautiful, the maid-of-honour would have riveted every eye on her magnificent exterior. Randolph felt a thrill of triumph and gratification when she caught his attention, something akin, perhaps, to that which is experienced by the wary deer-stalker while he contemplates the royal stag with his branching antlers, the pride of the forest, within point-blank range of his rifle. The Ambassador, however, had but little time to admire, for the Queen called him to her with such marked favour immediately on his entrance, that he felt convinced something of more importance than usual was in the wind, and resolved, from whatever quarter it blew, that at least it should not throw any dust in *his* eyes.

After receiving very graciously the compliments which Mr Randolph proffered on the splendour of the entertainment, Mary darted at him a keen glance of mingled watchfulness and amusement, then observed carelessly—

'What think ye of this chamber for a real King and Queen to hold their state in, Master Randolph? Since it hath been newly decorated, methinks a King-Consort might be satisfied with his lodging. Ere another Twelfth-night comes round, the lot may have fallen, who knows? and these faithful damsels of mine may have been released from their vow.'

He stole a look at Mary Beton, surrounded by her mock courtiers, and immersed in the game of forfeits which they were all playing with the eagerness of children, and wondered whether he would like to marry her or not; but he answered the Queen as if the subject she had broached, so far from being unexpected, had occupied his attention for days.

'Your Majesty anticipates the congratulations I am but waiting an opportunity to offer. May I give my own mistress joy on your acceding so cordially to her views for your welfare?'

'You may do what you have authority for, and no more,' replied the Queen severely. 'My cousin can scarce spare me that master of the horse of hers, whom she so much regardeth herself, nor am I so scantily supplied with suitors that I need trespass on her generosity for so precious a bridegroom. Come, Mr Randolph,' she added gaily, 'this is Twelfth-night, and we read riddles and play at forfeits. Can you not read me mine?'

'Your Grace must condescend to instruct me,' replied he, running over his information and calculating probabilities with inconceivable rapidity in his own mind; also studiously abstaining from the guess he thought most likely to hit the mark. 'Where the prize is of such value, all are so unworthy that it reduces the competitors to a level. I can aim no nearer the white than my first shaft, your Grace. A suitor for such a hand as yours should have some weighty influence to back him, in addition to unbounded merits of his own.'

'You seem to have considered the subject deeply,' said the Queen, laughing. 'Come, Mr Randolph, for very pastime let us hear the qualifications you deem indispensable to an admirer of Mary Stuart.'

He paused for an instant, enumerating in his own mind the different qualities of the nobleman whom he was instructed, at least ostensibly, to put forward, and then proceeded with an air of the utmost deference and humility—

'He should be a gentleman of admirable presence; of skill in courtly exercises; of varied accomplishments; familiar with the customs of palaces; brave, noble, and learned; he should be of no foreign extraction, neither Frenchman, Spaniard, nor Italian; suitable in point of years, of language, and of country.'

She nodded archly every time he paused in his catalogue; then added with an inquiring look—

'And of royal lineage as well? Surely like pairs with like, and a Stuart should only mate with a Stuart.'

It was a home thrust. It corroborated much that he had already suspected, and explained a good deal that had sufficiently puzzled even Randolph, but he never winced or started; to judge by his face it was the communication, of all others, for which he was best prepared, and whilst he ran over, as quick as thought, the different combinations to which such a projected alliance might give rise, and already, in his mind's eye, saw the young Lord Darnley, the suitor to whom Mary alluded, helpless in his toils, he bowed humbly to the Queen, and begged her to accept his heartfelt congratulations that she had made her choice at last.

Mary laughed more than ever.

'Not so fast,' said she, 'not so fast. I am discussing possibilities, Master Randolph, and you are accepting them for certainties; but enough of this—amusement is our chief business to-night. See, the queen of the revels is looking anxiously this way, and you have not been to pay her your homage yet. Delay no longer, her displeasure to-night is far weightier and more implacable than mine.'

As she spoke she dismissed him with a courteous gesture, and Randolph, nothing loth, commenced paying his court most assiduously to Mary Beton, with the double object of spending his time agreeably and worming out of her, ere the night was past, some corroboration of the Queen's vague hints as to her approaching marriage.

It was with secret pride and exultation the Twelfth-night queen, in all her assumed splendour, beheld the ambassador approach the circle that formed her sham Court. It would be too much to say that Mary Beton was deeply in love with Randolph, but she experienced from his attentions certain agreeable feelings, that originated in gratified vanity and a sense of her own superiority to her companions. It was indeed no petty triumph to have secured the homage of the fastidious and cynical Thomas Randolph: the man who was the type of refinement and the incarnation of selfishness, avowedly a despiser of women and a free-thinker in love. The pleasure, too, was doubtless in no small degree enhanced by the care-worn face of Alexander Ogilvy, who continued to haunt the Court, with a hopeless perseverance truly edifying, and made himself miserable with the self-immolating regularity peculiar to a lover, and totally inexplicable on any grounds of reason or expediency.

Mary Beton had no objection in the world; she liked to have two strings to her bow. Two! Where is the woman who would refuse half-a-dozen? With all their vanity and all their libertinism, thus much we may safely say in favour of the ruder sex—a man is usually indisposed to have more than one attachment on his hands at a time. He may behave ungratefully, unfeelingly, brutally, to Dora, but it is for the sake of Flora. For however short a period it may be, yet, *while* he wears those colours, Nora looking out for prey in every direction, shall strive to fascinate him in vain. But how different is the conduct of the last-named personage: brilliant and seductive, it is no reason, because she is herself in love with Tom, that she should refrain from the massacre of Jack, Dick, and Harry; nay, if Bill be fortunate enough to spend an hour or two in her company, away with him to the shambles too! Shall we pity Nora so very much when she wears the willow for the faithless Tom, and finds out too late that she never really cared a pin for the other victims who, more or less damaged, have made their escape from the toils?

The wrongs of the sexes towards each other are of the crudest, and it is generous and manly that our sympathy should be given to the weaker portion, but the injuries are not all one way. Many a rugged face is only so grave and stern because it *dare* not, quivering there behind its iron mask, lose for one instant its self-command; many a kindly heart has turned to gall, many an honest nature been warped irrevocably to evil, because the pride of manhood forbids it to ask for that relief which never comes unsought; of course it serves them right: of course we do not pity them; but are they the less lost on that account?

It would have moved even a courtier to witness the expression of sharp pain that swept over Ogilvy's face when Randolph led Mary Beton out to dance, but it was gone in a moment, and nobody detected it save the fair cause herself, who moved, we may be sure, all the more proudly through the measure in consequence, and listened, well-pleased as ever, to the mingled honey and vinegar of the ambassador's flatteries and sarcasms.

Meanwhile the Queen, followed by her other maidens, glided through the throng, dispensing her notice graciously to all her guests, and more especially those whom she had reason to consider somewhat wavering in their loyalty—a distinction not lost upon Mary Seton, who whispered to her companion—

'This would be a fine time for poor Bothwell now to come back again; see, my dear, even Lord Ruthven has had soft words and kind looks to-night.'

To which the lady addressed, no other than Mary Carmichael, only answered by a smothered sigh, for that nobleman was popularly believed to tamper with the Black Art, and to be an especial adept in the compounding of charms and potions both for friend and foe. She was thinking how delightful it would be to have one of his specific love-philters to do what she liked with, and to whom she would give it. Certainly not to the stranger in the Abbey garden; he loved her quite well enough already.

Somehow at this moment her eye sought out the figure of Walter Maxwell, who was standing apart in the recess of one of the windows, and looking at her with a kind of pitying sadness, as men do on an object once dearly prized which they will never see again. It was so unusual now for them to exchange glances, much less words, that the sight troubled her; she turned red first and then very pale. He stirred and made a step forward, as if to advance and speak to her, but seemed to think better of it, crossed his arms upon his breast, and resumed his former position. Following the Queen, she was obliged to pass very near him, and lowering her eyes to avoid meeting his glance, she was distressed and ashamed to find that they were full of tears.

There is a mysterious kind of sympathy often existing between those who have some common cause of suffering. Two gouty old gentlemen are never tired of detailing to each other their respective symptoms of *podagra*; and weak-minded ladies subject to 'nervous attacks' have been overheard to interchange the most surprising confidences regarding that remarkable ailment; in the same manner a couple of lovers, not a *pair*, are drawn towards each other by a community of sorrow.

Alexander Ogilvy took his place by Mary Carmichael's side, and sought in that lady's blue eyes, at least commiseration for his sorrows. Placing a chair for her a little out of the crowd, he conversed with her on the heat of the room, the beauty of the dresses, her own successful toilet, and such like topics, gradually lowering his voice and bringing the conversation round to the subject nearest his heart.

'A bird hath whispered in my ear,' said he, 'that we must look ere long to have a king-consort at Holyrood. The Maries are more interested in the matter than the whole of Scotland besides. You will be freed from your vow: choose each of you a mate, and pair off, like the fowls of the air, ere another St Valentine be past. What say you, Mistress Carmichael? sings my little bird true or false? I am no courtier, you know.'

'And yet you are much at Court,' she answered, absently, 'particularly of late, Master Ogilvy; it was but yesterday the Queen, pointing you out to Mary Beton, commended the bravery of your attire.'

Ogilvy coloured, looking very much alarmed, yet not altogether displeased.

'And what said Mistress Beton?' he asked anxiously.

His discomposure was so obvious, that it was well for him he had not to do with mischievous Mary Seton, or even with his present companion, had she been in other than a subdued and melancholy frame of mind. In most women the temptation to mockery would have been irresistible, but Mistress Carmichael only replied carelessly—

'That you were the properest man at Holyrood, and that she thought our gallants of the Court wore the French air more naturally than did the Southrons.'

'Did she *really* say so?' he exclaimed eagerly; 'and do you believe she meant it? You know her well, Mistress Carmichael; is it not true that she is herself too irresistibly attracted towards the Southron? Do you not think that when hood and jesses are fairly doffed once for all, she will fly her pitch toward the border, aye, and strike her quarry far on the southern side?'

Mary Carmichael followed the direction of his glance to where Mistress Beton stood radiant in her Twelfth-night bravery, and listening with a heightened colour and a well-pleased air to Randolph's flatteries; but she pitied whilst she marked the suffering that was too apparent in her questioner's gaze, and replied gently to his thoughts rather than his words—

'Gratified vanity is one thing, and real preference another. A women oft-times likes that suitor best whom most she seems to avoid. Perhaps for that very reason, perhaps because she is weak at heart and cannot help herself.'

She spoke the last sentence low, and more to herself than to him. She was willing to console him, for the deeper a kind nature is wounded, the more it feels for the sorrows of others. Also, it may be that she found a certain relief in repeating the lesson it had cost her so much pains to learn.

He drew closer to her.

'Thank you,' said he, with a beaming look of gratitude. 'You are a true friend! Believe me, Mistress Carmichael, I am not ungrateful. Can I serve you in any way in return?'

'It is no question of that,' she replied. 'Our positions are so different. I only say to you, remember your own motto—"To the End." If I were a man I think I could trust and hope for ever. I think I could be staunch and unselfish and true, in defiance of sorrow, suffering, opposition, nay, even of ingratitude and neglect I would prove to the woman whom I had chosen that at least she must be proud of my choice, that a man's honest affection was no vacillating fancy, but an eternal truth; and even if she did not love me, I would force her to confess that it was her own inferiority of nature that could not mate with mine. But why should I talk thus to you?' she added, breaking off with rather a bitter laugh. 'You are a *man*: you cannot understand me; you will not believe in anything unless you can see it with your two eyes, and grasp it in your two hands, and be told by all your friends besides that it is there. If you had but one gold piece in the world, you must beat it out thin, and lacker it over your spurs, and your housings, and the hilt of your sword; you could not hide it away in your bosom, and keep it unspent and unsuspected next your heart!'

'I know not,' he said with a brightening face; 'your words give me hope. I seem to see things differently since you have been speaking to me. You are my good angel. Help me; advise me; tell me what I had better do.'

'In the first place, go and talk to somebody else,' she replied, laughing. 'You will scarcely advance the cause you have at heart by whispering with me in a corner. Looks of inquiry, if not displeasure, have been already shot this way; and although, perhaps, we are the only two people in this room who never could be more than friends, courtiers' eyes are so sharp and their inferences so good-natured, that they have probably ere this made their usual grand discovery of that which does not exist. And so, good Master Ogilvy, my last word is, think of your motto and speed you well!'

Thus speaking, she made him a stately curtsey and withdrew towards the Queen; but Mary Carmichael was right, and their interview, short as it was, had been remarked by more than one interested observer.

Though it costs the animal many stripes and much vexation doubtless to acquire the accomplishment, we have seen a dog so well broke as to forego at his owner's word a tempting morsel placed within his reach, licking his lips indeed and looking longingly after it, yet exhibiting, nevertheless, a noble mastery over his inclinations. But let another dog come by and snatch the bone thus ceded to a sense of duty, and all his self-restraint vanishes on the instant. Open-mouthed he rushes to wrest it from the intruder, and that which but a moment ago was an advantage he could philosophically resign, becomes immediately a necessity that he will break through all bounds to attain. So is it with mankind. We can give up, or rather we fancy we have given up, the one bright hope that gilded our existence. We see the dear face that used to make the very sunshine of our heart altered and estranged, perhaps cold and distant, perhaps turned scornfully away. We think we can bear our burden resignedly enough. There is a great blank in our lives, felt less in the time of sorrow than at those seasons when, were it not for our loss, we think we should be so contented, so happy. There is a sense of desolation, a consciousness of old age coming on and being welcome—a morbid inclination to receive adversity with open arms; but yet we man ourselves against the calamity, strong to oppose and constant to endure. We have not felt the sting yet. Whilst we are in the cold shade let the dear face beam upon another; let the tones, so cruel now and hard to *us*, fall with the well-remembered cadence on *his* ear; let him be the recipient of the thousand tender cares and winning ways that used to bring tears of affection into our eyes; then, and not till then, have we sustained the sharpest pain that life has to inflict; then, and not till then, do we feel that there is no sorrow like to our sorrow, and that it is well for us it is transient from its very nature, or heart and brain would give way under the stroke.

Mary Beton was well satisfied to receive the homage of her English admirer, and, in order to ensure it, was perfectly willing to discard her sincerer suitor. Poor Ogilvy might pine and sigh as he pleased, without gaining so much as a kind word or an approving glance; but this rigorous treatment was only to endure so long as she felt he was her property; the dog's wages were to be given to the dog's honest obedience and fidelity.

It was quite a different matter when he appeared to have transferred his allegiance to another. Though she did not like him well enough to give up Randolph for his sake, she had no idea of losing him altogether. Even if she had no use for him, he had no right to belong to any one else, and it was with far more of anxiety and concern than usually overspread those calm features that Mistress Beton glanced continually towards the corner where he was whispering with Mary Carmichael, while she listened to the smooth phrase of the English ambassador with an absent air and a forced smile.

Nor was the stately maid-of-honour the only person in that noble assemblage who felt acutely the difference between the active and passive moods of the verb 'to give up.' Walter Maxwell, hurt, jealous, and indignant, had for long accustomed himself to look upon Mary Carmichael as one who was dead to him for evermore; had trained himself to meet her coldly and calmly when their respective duties brought them unavoidably together, and to shun her on all other occasions with scrupulous self-denial; nay, was beginning to find a certain gloomy satisfaction in the violence he was capable of doing to his own feelings, and a certain savage triumph in the reflection that he, too, could be as unkind and heartless and indifferent as a woman! But when he saw her thus engrossed with Ogilvy's conversation, evidently of a mysterious and interesting nature; when he marked, as he did at a glance, the softened expression of her face and the wistful tenderness in her blue eyes, he experienced a sensation of pain once more, to which he had thought he was henceforth to be a stranger, and felt again for an instant as he had felt that well-remembered night when he came upon her so unexpectedly at her tryst in the Abbey garden.

The same cause produces strangely different effects upon different individuals. Whilst Mary Beton, under the influence of jealousy, was becoming restless, captious, and even irritable (much, it must be confessed, to the secret amusement of Mr Thomas Randolph), Walter Maxwell felt a fresh impulse given to that generosity, which prompted him to put an end to-night to his anxieties and misgivings once for all.

The Queen, in the meantime, seeking, in her innocence and gaiety of heart, to keep up the characteristic merriment of the feast, was unconsciously exciting the displeasure of her nobility, and unwittingly preparing the downfall of her versatile little favourite—the Italian Riccio.

Disregarding the coarser witticisms and grotesque antics of James Geddes, who indeed had become a duller fool day by day, since the shock his feeble intellect sustained on the morning of Chastelâr's death, Mary had summoned her private secretary into the centre of the illustrious circle which surrounded her, and, with a familiarity exceedingly displeasing to the haughty Scottish barons, bade him *improvise,* after the manner of his country, for their amusement. Nothing daunted by bent brows and scornful looks, the glib foreigner, placing himself on a cushion at the Queen's feet, commenced a lively tale, of which the incidents and the language, for it was related in French, were most displeasing to his audience. It turned upon one of those fables so popular at the time in Italy, and was, indeed, both in its details and its catastrophe, especially unsuitable to the practical nature and affected asceticism of the Scottish character at that period.

'There was a beautiful flower,' said he, his little black eyes twinkling at the Queen while he spoke, 'growing in a fair garden, through which ran a mountain stream, and the birds of the air and the insects of the noontide came to pay their court to this flower and to win a breath of her fragrance, for she was the pride of all earthly plants and the queen of the garden. So the humming-bird flitted by in his bravery, and she marked not his liveries of blue and gold, nor bent her head towards him, but let him pass on to court the flowers of his own tropical land, gorgeous without perfume, dazzling but loveless, like a fair woman without a heart. And the nightingale sang his life away to please her, and, wooing her with his last notes, died hungering when the evening star shone out above the trees. Then the butterfly brought his painted coat and his gay manners and fluttered about her, making sure that a courtier like himself must prevail; but she bent not her head nor moved one of her leaves towards him, though the breeze was sighing softly around her and shaking the dewdrops from her stem.

'None of the gay and gaudy seemed to win the favour of that queenly flower. At length a bee came buzzing home from his labours, laden with the honey-dew that he had been gathering far and wide. He thought to rest on her petals and distil fresh treasures from her chalice, but she shook her beautiful blossoms merrily in the breeze and waved him scornfully away.

'All the birds of the air and the noontide insects marvelled that she would have none of them, for they deemed her haughty and unsociable, whispering to one another of the pride that goeth before a fall.

'Now, even as she shook her petals in disdain, she opened her heart to the daylight, and at its very core lay concealed a lazy useless drone. Then the humming-bird and the butterfly and the bee laughed together, for they said—

'"Of what avail are beauty and bravery and worth, against possession? And if she have taken the dullest of all insects to her heart, we have but lost our time in suing her, and the nightingale, on the cold earth yonder, hath given his life in vain."

'There is a moral in my fable, ladies!' added Riccio, with a smile and a shrug of his crooked shoulders—'a moral that you will all of you acknowledge if you tell truth.—Who shall dictate to a woman's fancy, or reduce to rule the wandering inclinations of a woman's heart?'

The ladies laughed and whispered, some protesting against the conclusion, others pitying the poor nightingale, but all uniting in condemnation of the useless drone.

Lord Ruthven, who had been eyeing the narrator with looks of fierce scorn, strode up to where he was sitting at the Queen's feet, and asked him, in a loud, contemptuous voice,—

'Were there no Wasps in yonder garden of which you spake, Master Tale-teller,—wasps that might give the drone a lesson, and teach him his place was somewhat lower than the bosom of its choicest flower?'

The Italian looked up somewhat scared in his grim questioner's face.

'Nay, signior,' he replied humbly, 'in courtly gardens the wasps must leave their stings behind.'

'Aye! sticking in the carcase of the drone!' returned Ruthven, with a brutal laugh, which was echoed by Morton, and one or two other savage-looking noblemen who stood near.

The Queen seemed highly displeased, but, true to her conciliatory principle, hastened to change the subject ere these turbulent spirits should further forget their own dignity and the respect due to her presence. Calling her maidens around her, she bade them bring her harp, a beautiful instrument, highly ornamented, and proposed it should be the prize of any lady in the company who could sing to it an impromptu measure on a subject she would herself propose.

'I shall play on it no more,' said Mary, with a half-melancholy smile. 'It is only maiden-queens who have time for such follies. A busier day, for aught I know, may be about to dawn, ere long, on Mary Stuart' (here she cast a sly glance at Randolph, who, without seeming to heed her, was listening, all attention), 'and I cannot leave my favourite instrument in better hands than hers who wins it fairly by her skill. Behold! which of you, ladies, will undertake to strike these strings and improvise a song, as deftly as our little secretary here has told us a story?'

It was an attempt requiring considerable confidence in such a presence. The ladies gazed on one another in obvious hesitation. Presently a handsome, intellectual-looking woman stepped forward, and curtseying to Her Majesty, bent gracefully, without speaking, over the instrument.

'Beatrix Gardyn!' exclaimed the Queen, with a bright smile, 'the Sappho of the North! I know of none better qualified to do justice to my poor harp; will you begin, Beatrix, at once? Are you waiting for inspiration?'

'The theme, an't please your Majesty?' said Beatrix, bowing her classic head with the utmost composure, and sweeping a masterly prelude over the strings.

The Queen gave another meaning glance at Randolph, and laughed again.

'What say you to my marriage, my *possible* marriage, and the consequent release of my four bonny maidens from their celibacy? The subject, methinks, is a noble one; and see, the Maries are listening all attention for your strains.'

Beatrix Gardyn struck a few wandering chords, then with bent brows and kindling eyes fixed on vacancy, broke into a melody to which, with but little hesitation, and now and then a meaning smile, she adapted the following words:—

THE MAIDENS' VOW.

'A woman may better her word, I trow,
Now lithe and listen, my lords, to me;
And I'll tell ye the tale of the "Maidens' Vow,"
And the roses that bloom'd on the bonnie rose-tree.

'The Queen of the cluster, beyond compare,
Aloft in the pride of her majesty hung,
Bright and beautiful, fresh and fair;
The bevy of blossoms around her clung.

'So the winds came wooing from east and west,
Wooing and whispering frank and free;
But she folded her petals; quoth she, "I am best
On a stalk of my own at the top of the tree."

'And they folded their petals, the rose-buds too,
And closer they clung as the wind swept by,
For they'd vow'd a vow, that sisterhood true,
Together to fade, and together to die.

'"Never a wind shall a rose-bud wrest,
Never a gallant shall wile us away,
To wear in his bonnet, to wear on his breast,
Rose and rose-buds answering, Nay."

'So staunch were the five to their word of mouth,
That they baffled all suitors who throng'd to the bower,
Till a breeze that came murmuring out of the south
Stole home to the heart of the queenliest flower.

'She droop'd in her beauty to hear him sigh,
And ever the brighter and fairer she grew;
What wonder, then, that each rose-bud nigh
Should open its leaves to the breezes too?

'Oh! gather the dew while the freshness is on;
Roses and maidens they fade in a day;
Ere you've tasted its sweetness the morning is gone;
Love at your leisure, but wed while you may.

'Winter is coming, and time shall not spare ye,
Beautiful blossoms so fragrant and sheen;
Joy to the gallants that win ye and wear ye,
Joy to the roses, and joy to their queen.'

Rounds of applause followed the conclusion of the song. The approval with which Mary received it was tantamount to an acknowledgment of its truth; and the courtiers scarce refrained from cheers and such noisy demonstrations of their acquiescence in its purport.

Congratulations were freely tendered to the Maries on their coming release from the vows by which it had been long understood they were bound; and many facetious remarks were directed at those young ladies on a topic, which although next to death the most serious and important in the human destiny, has been considered, from time immemorial, as a fitting subject for stale witticisms and far-fetched jokes.

In the midst of all this clamour and merriment, Walter Maxwell slipped quietly out of the presence; and when Mary Carmichael, wondering how he would be affected by the news that thus seemed to stir the whole Court, stole a wistful look towards the corner he had lately occupied, behold, he was gone!

After this the buzz of conversation, the rustle of ladies' dresses, the strains of the Queen's musicians, seemed to strike wearily on her ear; how pointless seemed the jests that yet provoked bursts of laughter from the bystanders; how uninteresting the vapid compliments that were yet paid with such an air, and received so graciously; how dull and uninteresting the whole routine of a courtier's life, and the individual items that composed a courtly assemblage! As we must all do sooner or later, for the moment the girl saw life without the varnish, and wondered it had ever looked so bright; she longed for the hour of dismissal, when she, too, had a tryst to keep, a duty to perform. In the meantime we must follow Maxwell into the Abbey garden.

CHAPTER XXVII

'The foremost was an aged knight,
He wore the gray hair on his chin,
Says, "Yield to me thy lady bright
An' thou shalt walk the woods within."

'"For me to yield my lady bright
To such an aged knight as thee,
People wad think I war gane mad,
Or all the courage flown frae me."'

He paused as he emerged from the palace, to let the cool air fan his brow, and to give his thoughts and energies time to collect themselves for the great effort he felt he had to make. Then he walked steadily on to the well-known spot under the apple-tree, where he remembered to have witnessed the interview between Mary Carmichael and her mysterious admirer. Once he had loved that spot so dearly; once he used to linger there for hours together at night, and watch the lights in the apartment inhabited by the Maries; once he was fool enough to feel his heart thrill when *her* shadow crossed the casement. Well! that was all past and gone. It seemed strange the place could be so changed, and yet the same.

There is no feeling so sad as that with which we revisit our earthly paradise, whatever it may be, after our return has been forbidden, and the angel placed at the gate to warn us off with his flaming sword. Adam and Eve plodded away indeed contentedly into the wilderness, but we, their children, cannot always resign ourselves so philosophically to the inevitable. We plead and pray to be allowed to re-enter, and, perhaps to enhance our punishment, the angel is suffered to give way to our entreaties. Ah! it is the same garden still. Although the trees are lying prostrate, dank, and rotting, on the tufted sward; although the flowers are broken and withered and trampled into the earth; although there are dust and ashes now, and the darkness of desolation, where once the ripe fruit glowed, and the green leaves flickered in the golden floods of noon; yet it is here we first knew paradise; it is from this spot we first caught a glimpse of the dazzling depths of heaven; it was from that spring, choked and tangled and dried up now, we first drank the waters of life. All is ruined and defiled and destroyed, but it is our Garden of Eden still. We had rather sit here with bowed head and rent garments, than walk the fairest realms of earth, in purple and fine linen, lord and ruler of the whole.

Poor ghosts we are indeed, some of us, even while clothed in our fleshly coverings, and prone to wander to and fro about the spot where we buried our treasures, though they have been dug up and taken away long ago. If we could but sever that cord which links us with the past and cut out the moral gangrene, as we amputate the physical limb when mortification has set in, how healthy would be our spiritual being, how cheerfully we could limp, mutilated but painless, to the grave!

Alas! to some natures it is impossible. To such the punishment of Prometheus is no fiction. The chain and the vulture and the rock must be their portion. Nevertheless they are not eternal, and the Garden of Eden itself, glowing in the summer noon, was but a dreary waste compared with that garden which men enter by a strait way and through a narrow gate.

Maxwell looked about him with a heavy heart. He was young yet, and the lesson of life, which all must learn, came painfully to him in the freshness of his youthful hopes.

It takes a long time and a good many reverses to acquire the unenviable stoicism which always *expects* the worst and is seldom disappointed. He was, however, consoled and supported by the consciousness that he had come to a final determination, unselfish and sincere, which would put an end to his doubts once for all. Whilst the dice are yet unthrown, it is a wondrous moral sedative, that resolution to set our whole future on the cast. When they have come up against us, we are by no means satisfied to abide by the issue, but this is an after consideration, and affects not a whit the vigour of our purpose in the meanwhile.

The watcher had not long to wait. A tall dark figure, cloaked as before, was soon seen gliding to the accustomed spot. Ere he had well reached the apple-tree, Maxwell was already by his side, and had laid his hand upon his shoulder.

The stranger started. Under his cloak a few inches of steel showed themselves out of the scabbard, as his grasp closed upon his sword; but he drove the blade home with a clash, thoroughly reassured at Maxwell's first sentence.

'I am your friend,' exclaimed the latter, hastily but in a cautious voice, 'at least for the present. You are in danger, and I have come here to warn you.'

There was something so frank in his tones that the other responded immediately. He even lowered the cloak in which his face was muffled and smiled gaily as he replied—

'I am used to it, my good friend, but equally beholden to you, nevertheless. I would fain know, all the same, who you are that take such interest in my welfare, and wherefore. Nay,' he added, more abruptly, 'this is scarcely candid. I know *you*, Master Maxwell, and I believe you to be a man of honour and a gentleman; but what you can have to communicate to me is indeed a mystery.'

There was light enough to distinguish the speaker's features. They were those of a singularly handsome man in the prime of life, as his rival did not fail to remark, with a certain defiance and reckless good-humour in their expression. His hair and beard were somewhat gray, but not sufficiently so to destroy the general comeliness of his appearance, and his eyes would have been beautiful even in a woman.

'This is no time to bandy compliments,' answered Maxwell, still in the same low tone. 'You are engaged here in some intrigue; it may or it may not amount to treason. You have been coming and going secretly for months. If you are discovered and arrested, your very life is in danger. Is it not so?'

'Granted,' replied the other, smoothing his gray moustache with a provoking air of calmness. 'There is no game without a hazard. And what then?'

'You have been watched!' urged Maxwell, impatiently. 'You have probably been recognised by those who know you better than I do. Perhaps a few more hours may see you arrested. I tell you, Randolph is on your track, that Southron bloodhound who never over-ran a scent nor opened on a false trail. You had better have the devil for your enemy than the English Ambassador!'

'I trust devoutly I may prevail against both,' answered the stranger; then added musingly, 'You say true about Randolph; his schemes are both wide and deep, whilst his hand is as prompt to execute as his brain is subtle to devise. I pray ye, my friend, when did ye learn I was to be here to-night?'

'This day at dinner, and from Randolph himself,' replied Maxwell. 'The Minister spared not the wine-flask, I promise you; and had it been any other man I might have believed that he told me more than he intended, but not all the vineyards of the Rhine or the Garonne would influence Randolph's tongue to play false for a syllable to Randolph's brain. Nay, I will deal frankly with you, fair sir. I offered myself to be the means of unmasking you, in order that I might warn you in time and save you from your fate!'

'It was most friendly and considerate,' observed the other, with a laugh not far removed from a sneer. 'I would fain know, nevertheless, to what happy chance I am indebted for the interest Master Walter Maxwell takes in my preservation. Nay,' he again broke off abruptly, and added with complete sincerity, 'this is unworthy of both of us. You are an honest fellow, Master Maxwell, and a loyal gentleman. Roundly now, what is your hidden motive for this proceeding? Come out with it!'

'My motives are honourable enough,' replied the other, with some difficulty retaining his composure. 'I pray you attribute no hidden meaning to what I have to say. Be frank and open with me, whether friend or foe, as I swear I am frank and open with you.'

'I believe it!' exclaimed the other, extending him his hand; but Maxwell, without taking it, folded his arms across his heart, and proceeded in the low quiet tones of repressed excitement—

'I have no right to assume that your presence here in silence and secrecy is for any other than a political object, and yet from my own knowledge I am satisfied that there are further motives of a private nature. If you feel that what I have done for you to-night deserves any return, I claim your confidence in a matter that is to me one of life and death.'

He wiped the drops from his pale face as he spoke, and the stranger, pitying his obvious agitation, motioned to him courteously to proceed.

'There is a lady of the Court,' resumed Maxwell, still in the same concentrated voice, 'who has allowed herself to hold clandestine interviews with you in this spot by night. No man alive shall make me believe that anything but an ardent and sincere affection would tempt that lady so far to commit herself. Mistress Carmichael is above the weaknesses and petty vanities of her sex. I demand of you, on your honour as a gentleman, to clear her conduct in my eyes by avowing that you are her lover.'

The stranger had started violently when he heard mentioned the proper name of the adventurous damsel, whom in truth he was momentarily expecting, but the lower part of his face was again concealed in his cloak, and his whole frame was shaking from some strongly-curbed emotion, while he demanded—

'By what right do you ask so unwarrantable a question?'

'By the right of a pure and holy affection,' answered Maxwell, gravely; 'by the right of an unselfish love that would even give her up ungrudgingly to a worthy rival!'

'Hoity-toity, young gentleman!' exclaimed the stranger, breaking forth into an uncontrollable fit of laughter, all the more violent that he dared not indulge in it above his breath. 'Thou art not likely to lose aught for lack of asking; thou art one of these wild Iceland falcons, I warrant me, that will fly their pitch, hooded and jessed and all, to strike at every quarry alike. I ought to be angry with thee, man; but I cannot for the life of me. In faith I forgive thee; I forgive thee were it but for the jest's sake.'

He wiped his eyes while he spoke, and, turning away, stamped upon the ground, as he held his sides once more in a convulsion of mirth.

To Maxwell, with his feelings wrought up to a pitch of Quixotic generosity, all the more exalted that it was an unusual effort of his practical nature, such a display was irritating in the extreme. It is bad enough to hand over the last stiver you have in your pocket, but when the tears in the recipient's eyes are those of mockery rather than gratitude, it is sufficient to cause an outbreak in the most stoical temperament. The younger man's brow grew dark with passion, and he laid his hand upon his sword.

'At least,' he exclaimed, 'I will force a confession from you; I came here prepared for either alternative. Had you met me frankly and vowed your devotion to her, I would have been your friend for life; if you mean treacherously, I am your rival to the death.'

The other was still laughing.

'Pooh! pooh!' said he, carelessly, 'you are meddling with what concerns you not. I thank you for your warning, young sir; and, in return, I advise you to give up the championship of every dame who comes but with a muffler into the moonlight; I wish you good night, Master Maxwell; I would be alone.'

He waved his hand rather contemptuously and turned upon his heel; but Maxwell, now boiling with passion, placed himself in front of him, and drew his sword.

'You part not thus,' said he; 'by Saint Andrew, I am henceforth your sworn foe. Draw and take your ground if you be a man!'

The other put aside the weapon with his naked hand, and laughed once more. Maxwell's face was white with anger, and his eyes flashed fire. Quick as thought he struck his enemy a smart blow across the shoulder with the flat of his sword.

The smile on the stranger's countenance deepened into a very dangerous expression.

'Nay,' said he, in a hissing whisper between his teeth, 'a wilful man never yet wanted woe; ye have forced me to lug out, youngster, and it shall be to some purpose, I promise ye.'

With that he placed himself on guard with an ominously steady eye, and a hand that, as he bore against his blade, Maxwell quickly discovered to be as skilful as his own.

The wicked steel twined and glittered in the moonlight. As they warmed to their work each man grew more eager and more deadly in the murderous game; thrust and parry, give and take, delicate feint and desperate return, were rapidly and breathlessly exchanged, but at the end of a few passes, though neither had gained any advantage, Maxwell's youth and activity began to tell upon his elder antagonist. Already the stranger's brow was covered with sweat, and his breath came quick and short as he traversed here and there, and began perceptibly to give ground. With the true instinct of a swordsman, Maxwell pressed him vigorously when he began to fail, and was in the act of delivering a long-meditated and particularly fatal thrust, when he suddenly found his own blade encumbered with a woollen plaid that had been thrown over it, and himself at the mercy of his antagonist. Looking wildly up, he could scarcely believe his eyes when he saw Mary Carmichael's pale face frowning angrily upon him, while she clung fondly and imploringly on the stranger's sword-arm, effectually preventing the latter from availing himself, even were he so minded, of the diversion she had so made.

Stunned and stupefied, with his mouth open and his sword point resting on the ground, Maxwell stood like a man in a dream. Presently his face contracted with an expression of intense pain as he saw Mary once more enveloped in his rival's embrace, and heard her incoherent expressions of tenderness and alarm.

The stranger was soothing her gently and lovingly as a burst of weeping succeeded the effort she had made for his preservation. After a while he turned to his late antagonist, and said —

'You are satisfied now, sir, I presume, and have no wish to renew this foolish and untimely brawl.'

But Maxwell never heard him; with pale face and parted lips, his eyes were still riveted on Mary Carmichael. He advanced a step towards her, trembling in every limb.

'You love him, then?' said he, quite gently; but his voice was so changed that the stranger started and turned round, thinking some intruder had disturbed them.

'I do! I do!' replied the girl hysterically, still hiding her face on the breast to which she clung.

Maxwell smiled—such a dreary, hopeless smile! then sheathing his sword, turned and walked slowly towards the Palace without another word.

CHAPTER XXVIII

'I send him the rings from my white fingers;
The garlands aff my hair;
I send him the heart that's in my breast;
What would my love hae mair?
And at the fourth kirk in fair Scotland,
Ye'll bid him meet me there.'

The little crooked secretary had been educated in an atmosphere of political agitation and intrigue. To his native Italian shrewdness David Riccio added that quickness of perception, that power of reading men's characters at a glance, which can only be acquired by those who are compelled, amidst the storms through which they guide their bark, to watch every aspect of the horizon, to press every instrument into their service, and take every advantage that shall enable them to weather the gale.

During the Feast of the Bean, whilst the majority of the courtiers were but intent on the merriment of the moment, whilst ladies sipped flattery and lords quaffed wine, it had not escaped the notice of a pair of black southern eyes that Maxwell seemed unusually restless and unhappy; that, in spite of his outward composure, there was something wild and defiant in his glance: nay, that he wore the look of a man in the right mood for a desperate undertaking—one to whom a dangerous enterprise would appear in the light of a relief.

Either purposely, or by chance, Maxwell, returning giddy and half-stupefied from the Abbey-garden, found himself confronted in one of the galleries of the Palace by Her Majesty's private secretary. The revel was dying gradually out; most of the ladies, following the example of their Sovereign, had retired, and but a few staunch wassailers were left, collected round the buffets and tables, at which wine was still flowing with a lavish hospitality more regal, perhaps, than judicious.

The secretary (though he had to rise on tiptoe to do it) clapped the soldier familiarly on the back.

'Not to bed, Master Maxwell,' he exclaimed in jovial tones, 'not yet to bed, without one cup of sack to wash the night air out of thy throat and wet the wings of sleep, as we say in Italy, so that she cannot choose but fold them around thine head!'

While he spoke he desired one of the Queen's cellarers, who was passing at the moment, to pour him out a measure of the generous liquid, and the man, more than half-drunk, gladly filled his goblet to the brim.

Maxwell, though in no mood for revelry, was still less disposed for solitude. Half-stunned by the blow he had received, he yet dreaded the moment at which he must stand face to face, as it were, with his great sorrow, and caught eagerly at any interval of delay as a respite from his sufferings. A draught of the rich, generous wine seemed to restore him somewhat to himself. Riccio, meanwhile, trolled off, in his mellow southern voice, a few notes of an Italian drinking song.

He was no mean physiologist, the little secretary, and he saw that his man was weary and saddened, and both morally and physically overpowered. So he gave the charm time to work, and when his companion had emptied the cup, poured him out another forthwith.

'Master Maxwell,' observed Riccio, as he marked the eye of the former brightening and the colour returning to his cheek, 'the ladies of the Court vow you are a true knight. Like our chevaliers of Italy, sworn before the Peacock to do them service, you are bound to refuse no adventure in their behalf. Is it not so?'

Maxwell winced a little. The subject was no pleasant one, and he was at this moment particularly sore on that point; so he answered in a cold, hard voice—

'I have little respect for the mummeries of chivalry, Signior Riccio. A man should do his duty, whatever it be, for its own sake. And as for the ladies,' he added, with a sad smile, 'I leave it to younger and happier men to fulfil their wishes; if indeed they are fortunate enough to be able to find them out.'

The secretary laughed gaily.

'Is it so?' he said; 'must all men alike discover that the little finger of a white hand is heavier than the arm of a Douglas sheathed in steel? I thought it was a lesson only learned by the dwarfed, the misshapen, the unsightly, like me. But you, Master Maxwell, the handsome, the straight, and the tall; can it be that a woman listens unmoved to such men as you?'

There was no covert sarcasm, no leavening of ill-nature in his voice— nothing but the good-humoured banter of a laughing boon companion. And yet it may be, that even under his jest, David Riccio was glad to learn that the prizes of life did not fall so readily to those personal advantages which he coveted with the longing of deformity.

'Enough of this!' replied Maxwell, interrupting him rudely, and holding out his cup to be filled yet once more. 'Months of Holyrood have not succeeded in making me a courtier. I love the free open sky better than these tapestried walls. I love the sound of a trumpet better than a woman's false whisper, and the shaft of a Jedwood-axe better than an ivory fan. I can hearken to a plain tale, and accept a defiance given in my teeth, but I have no skill in reading the thoughts of others by the rule of contrary, and I never could understand our Scottish proverb that averreth how "Nineteen nay-says make half a grant."'

He was still chafing under his ill-usage, and talking more to himself than his companion.

The latter looked at him long and eagerly. Apparently satisfied with his scrutiny, he patted him on the shoulder once more.

'You are young,' he said; 'you have life before you; you are quick-witted, brave, and adventurous. What, man, there are more prizes than one in the lottery! If love be a false jade, ambition is a glorious mistress. Is it not better to sit at the back of the stage and pull the strings than to be one of the puppets and dance because another moves you; perhaps a fool's dance, with a fool's guerdon, for your pains at the end?'

Maxwell shook him off impatiently.

'You speak in riddles,' said he, 'and I have no skill in expounding such parables. If you have aught to say, out with it, like a man. Midnight is already past.'

'And a fresh day begun,' added Riccio,—'a fresh day, a fresh scheme, a fresh triumph. What say you, Master Maxwell, have you stomach for an adventure? Have you a mind to draw your riding-boots on for those silken hose, and don corslet and head-piece on a Queen's errand? Or are *you*, too, under the spell that paralyses youth and strength and manhood? Are *you*, too, bound to some slender wrist by the jesses you dare not break, and a prisoner here at Holyrood because the rosy-lipped jailer will not let you go?'

Maxwell laughed a fierce, wild laugh, and dashed his goblet down upon the board with an emphasis most unusual to him. Though habitually possessed of much self-command, for an instant the tide of his feelings surged up beyond control.

'Holyrood!' he exclaimed, mockingly; 'what is Holyrood to me? One place is like another, and all are barren! Talk not to me of jesses. Your wild-hawk soars her pitch, and strikes her quarry, and buries beak and singles in the dripping flesh; but, bird of the air though she be, she knows the false from the true, and will not stoop to the lure. There is no spell can fetter the limbs of a brave man who is determined to be free; and be the jailer never so fair, I would not waste a look over my shoulder at my prison-house for the sake of the rosiest pair of lips that ever were kissed on the dawn of St Valentine! Again, what is it you would with me, Signior Riccio? Were it an errand to the gates of hell, I think I have spurs that would serve me to ride there; and in good faith,' he added in a lower tone, 'a man need hardly wish to come back even thence to such a dreary world as this.'

Not a whisper of his voice, not a shade on his countenance, escaped his sharp little companion. What cared *he* how hot the furnace were, so that it tempered the tool aright? Nay, he was even willing to burn his own fingers a little, rather than fail in perfecting his instrument. At heart he thought how lucky it was that there should be men who allowed themselves to be influenced by less rational feelings than those of self-interest and ambition. Perhaps he felt something between pity and ridicule for that morbid state of mind which could forget its own advantage in anger, or pique, or sorrow. His swarthy face, however, wore nothing more than its usual expression of comical good-humour, as he linked his arm in Maxwell's, and fixing his twinkling eyes upon him, said—

'You are more trusted than half the peers in Scotland—ay, and more trustworthy too. Come with me to the Queen's chamber.'

Thus speaking, he led Walter out of the banqueting room and along the dim passages, in which the lamps were now expiring, to the foot of a winding stair, the same up which 'Dick-o'-the-Cleugh' had twisted his great body under the guidance of Mary Seton. Here the secretary paused for an instant and listened cautiously. It was pitch-dark, and he gave his companion a hand to guide him through the obscurity, then opening a narrow door, and pushing aside a heavy curtain of tapestry, ushered him into a blaze of light and the presence of four ladies, crowded together in so small an apartment that Maxwell actually touched the robe of one of them while he entered, and was somewhat abashed to discover that its wearer was no other than the Queen.

It was Mary's custom, when the pageantry or duty of the day was over, to retire to this narrow retreat and sup in the strictest privacy, with two or three of her ladies at most. The proportions, indeed, of the apartment would admit of no larger party, as its area was little more than twelve feet by eight, and of this circumscribed space, a wide chimney and a window occupied a large share. It was here that, at a latter period, the shrieking Riccio clung to his Queen for the protection she strove to extend to him with all a woman's pity, and more than a woman's courage; it was here that, in brutal disregard of her majesty, her beauty, and her situation, the high-born ruffians of the Scottish peerage butchered their victim before her eyes, nay, clinging to the skirts of her garment, and laid the weltering body down, within a few feet of her, to soak with its blood the very planks of their Sovereign's bed-chamber.

But to-night all was a blaze of light and warmth and comfort. The table, with its snowy cloth, was drawn close to the crackling wood-fire, which sparkled and glowed again in the cut crystals and rich plate that adorned the choice little repast; an odour of some rich incense, such as is burnt in Roman Catholic churches, pervaded the apartment; and the strings of a lute that had just been laid aside were still vibrating from the touch of a fair and skilful hand.

The Queen herself, all the more lovely from the slight languor of fatigue, sat at the supper-table with her relative the Countess of Argyle, a lady whose flaxen locks and ruddy, laughing face formed no bad foil to the delicate colouring and deep, thoughtful beauty of her mistress. Mary Seton, all coquetry, animation, and vivacity, as usual, busied herself in arranging and disarranging everything on the table; whilst another lady, turning away from the rest, with her head bent low over her task, was disposing some winter flowers in a vase with peculiar care and attention. It needed not the turn of her full white arm and dimpled elbow, nor the curl of rich brown hair that had escaped over her shoulder, to tell Walter this last was his *hated* love, Mary Carmichael.

The Queen gave him her hand to kiss as he entered the room.

'Welcome, Master Maxwell,' said she, 'rather to the simple dame who has bid you visit her here, in private life, than to the Scottish Queen at Holyrood. We have put off our royalty with our robes. To-night we shall charge you with an errand that affects the woman far more than the Queen; to-night you must be less than ever our subject, more than ever our friend. You are faithful and trustworthy, we know; and, indeed, there are few men on whose truth a lady would offer to stake her life,' she added, smiling, 'as one of mine did, not five minutes ago, on yours.'

Mary Seton laughed and pretended to hide her face in her hands.

Walter looked wistfully in the Queen's face; he did not turn his eyes towards Mary Carmichael, or see how the white neck had turned crimson while Her Majesty spoke.

'I can trust you, Maxwell?' added the latter after a pause, in her frankest and most engaging manner.

'To the death, Madam!' answered he, in a tone of suppressed emotion; 'I have but little merit, I know, but I am as true as the steel I wear; I would give my life for your Grace willingly, now, this very minute!'

'I believe thee,' said the Queen, exchanging at the same time a rapid glance with Mary Seton; 'I trust, however, mine errand may be done without shedding of blood. Nevertheless, Maxwell, it requires courage, discretion, above all, a silent tongue and a faithful heart. Listen! My good sister entertaineth causeless grudges against me; she will endeavour to thwart my aim and cover the mark I shoot at; she liketh not of marrying or giving in marriage. It may be that she mistrusteth her own power to rule in that state,' added Mary, while a gleam of feminine vanity crossed her brow. 'It may be that Elizabeth hath more dominion over men's heads than their hearts; nevertheless, if she and her agents were to suspect thee of bearing such a secret of Mary Stuart's about thee, they would probe for it with their daggers but they would find it ere thou wert a dozen leagues across the Border. Bethink thee, man, 'tis a dangerous burden; art not afraid to carry it?'

'Your Majesty is jesting with me,' replied Maxwell, raising his head proudly, almost angrily, 'and I can but answer with a jest; yes, I fear to do your bidding as I fear a good horse when I am in haste, a cup of wine when I am thirsty, or a down pillow when I am weary and would fain lay my head down to rest.'

Mary Carmichael shot at him one glance of ineffable pride and tenderness, then busied herself amongst the flowers deeper than before. He could not see it; his head was turned towards the Queen; he had not forgotten, no, he never would forget, the embrace of that stranger in the Abbey-garden.

'I knew it,' exclaimed Her Majesty, triumphantly, 'believe me, I was indeed only jesting with my brave and well-tried servant. Listen then, Walter! To-morrow you must be in the saddle at daybreak; I reckon on your arriving at Hermitage before nightfall.'

At the name of Hermitage the Queen lowered her eyes for an instant, and looked somewhat confused ere she continued—

'In that stronghold you will find the Earl of Bothwell, who has returned with no leave of mine from his well-merited banishment in France; nevertheless, "a Queen's face should show grace," and we women forgive more readily than you of the sterner sex. You will summon him to appear before his Sovereign in Holyrood, so shall he receive pardon for his errors. Or stay! this were an ungracious behest to so tried a servant for one venial offence; you shall bear him Mary Stuart's full and free forgiveness, and bid him, as he loves his Queen, bid him on his loyalty and allegiance, that he speed with all his heart and all his strength the object of your journey.'

'And that object, madam?' inquired Maxwell, observing that Mary paused, blushing rosy red and averting her eyes from his face.

'Is my coming marriage,' proceeded the Queen, hastily, whilst Lady Argyle and Mistress Seton interchanged an arch glance and smile. 'An alliance that I take heaven to witness, I contemplate more for the welfare of my people than for any foolish longings of my own weak heart. Henry Stuart is of royal blood, no unworthy mate for the proudest princess in Europe. Lord Darnley is a comely, gentle, and well-nurtured youth, of whose affection any lady in the land might well be proud. You will explain this to Bothwell; you will teach him that Mary has made no unworthy choice; you will tell him that she has confided in him, her old and tried servant, because she can depend upon him more securely than on any other lord in Scotland.'

'Would it not be well, madam, to write the earl a few lines with your own hand apprising him of your intentions?' hazarded Maxwell, who was sufficiently a man of the world to appreciate the delicacy of his mission; and who, in good truth, was sufficiently familiar with the temper of his powerful kinsman to relish not the least the delivery of the message with which he was charged.

Mary, however, would not entertain such a proposition for a moment, and hurried on with far more of agitation than the occasion seemed to warrant.

'Letters may be intercepted, changed, forged, misunderstood. Master Maxwell, you will fulfil my bidding as I charge you, or leave it alone. I can trust you, I feel. I know you will do justice to the fair intentions of your mistress. I know you will not allow Bothwell to misunderstand my motives, or my feelings—Bothwell, who has always believed so implicitly in his Queen! Nay, for letters,' added Mary, with her own sweet smile softening and brightening her whole countenance, 'I will charge you, indeed, with this one for my Lady of Lennox, and with this token, always subject to his mother's approval, to be given as an earnest of my good-will to her son. Take them carefully, Master Maxwell. Our warden's strong hand will pass you safely through the thieves that infest the Border, and when you get among the southrons, I know you will guard them with your life. I pledge you, my trusty messenger, to the success of your mission!'

While she spoke, the Queen filled out a cup of wine and put her lips to the brim, handing him, at the same time, a packet carefully sealed and secured with a silken thread, which wound in and out through the folds of the missive, so that the silk must be cut before the letter could be opened. Also a small casket, containing a beautiful antique ring, representing a cupid burning himself with his own torch, as a keepsake for her future husband. The messenger received them on his knees in token of his fidelity and obedience, and the Queen, according to the custom of the age, bade him finish the cup of wine in which she had recently pledged him, and refresh himself ere he departed.

'It must be a stirrup-cup, your Grace,' said Maxwell, with a smile; 'I shall hope to be out of sight of Holyrood ere the sun rises. Have I received all your Majesty's directions?' he added, preparing to take his leave.

'There is no such hurry for a few minutes,' replied Mary, graciously. 'Do you sup with royalty every night, Master Maxwell, that you are in such haste to be gone?'

But Maxwell was enduring an amount of pain to which he would willingly put a period. To be in the same room with Mary Carmichael, nay, so close that her very dress touched him when she moved, and yet to feel, by her averted face, by his own offended and aching heart, that they were completely and irrevocably estranged, was a trial to which he had no wish to subject himself for a longer time than he could help.

'I must crave your Grace's license to depart,' said he; and added, looking round with a forlorn hope that just this once he might meet the eyes that he had resolved should never gladden him again, 'Have none of your ladies any commands for merrie England or the Border?'

Mistress Carmichael stirred uneasily, and grew very pale, but she neither looked at the speaker nor answered him. Mary Seton, however, with rather a noisier laugh than common, charged him with a message on her own part, of which, as she said merrily, he was not to purloin nor spill any portion by the way.

'If you should chance to see that rude giant who calls himself Lord Bothwell's henchman,' said that young lady, 'tell him from me, that I hope he has not forgotten, in his wild glens, all the polish we had such difficulty in imparting to him at Holyrood. Commend me to him, in sober earnest,' added she, demurely; 'I would send him my love had I not the fear of Mistress Beton before my eyes, for, in good truth, he is the only honest man I know in Scotland, except yourself, Master Maxwell, and you are so stern and unforgiving, that I am quite afraid of you. If a woman loved you ever so dearly, I think you would give her up for the slightest misunderstanding.'

The shaft might have been shot at random, but it pierced home to at least two hearts in that little supper-room. For an instant *his* eyes met *hers*, and that sad, reproachful imploring glance haunted him afterwards for months. Then Mary Carmichael, pale, proud, and sorrowful, turned away from him once more to her former occupation, and Walter Maxwell, taking a respectful leave of the Queen, was ushered by Riccio from the presence.

As he sped southward through the chill air of morning, after the few hasty preparations had been completed for his departure, he could not but acknowledge that the world had never seemed so dreary, that he had never felt so sick at heart before. Perhaps it would have cheered him though, to know that another's sufferings were even keener than his own, lying broad awake behind him there at Holyrood, pressing a pale cheek against a pillow wet with tears.

CHAPTER XXIX

'But had I kenn'd or I cam' frae hame,
How thou unkind wad'st been to me,
I would have kept my Border-side,
In spite of all thy peers and thee.'

'Hood her up, Dick! The worthless haggard! Like all her sex, I would not trust her a bow-shot out of hearing of the whistle, out of sight of the lure. Curse her! I should have known she was but a kestrel. By the bones of Earl Patrick, she shall never strike quarry in Liddesdale again!'

The warden was in a towering passion. His favourite hawk, a bird that he had chosen to name 'The Queen,' had not only missed the wild-fowl at which he had flown her, but spreading her broad pinions to the wind, had sailed recklessly away for several miles ere he could recover her, a salvage that had only been made at considerable expenditure of patience and horseflesh.

He was now standing by the side of his panting steed at the head of one of those deep, grassy glens which give such a pastoral character to the wilds of the Scottish Border. A severe and exhausting gallop the warden must have had, to judge by the condition of the bonny bay, whose heaving sides were reeking and lathered with sweat; yet the good horse pawed, snorted, shook himself, and got back his wind, ere the rider recovered his temper.

'Dick-o-the-Cleugh,' too, had mercifully taken his long body out of the saddle, and was now busy replacing hood and jesses on the recent captive.

'There's no siccan a falcon 'twixt here and Carlisle,' said Dick, smoothing with no ungentle hand the neck plumage of the refractory wild bird. 'Whiles she'll gang her ain gate when she misses her stoop, and what for no? A falcon's but a birdie when a's said and done, and she's just the queen of falcons; bonny and wilful, as a queen behoves to be!'

Bothwell turned angrily upon his follower. The warden's temper had become more violent and uncertain than ever.

'Hood her up, man, I tell thee!' said he, with an oath or two, 'and fasten up my girths; it is time we were back at Hermitage.'

Thus speaking, he threw himself into the saddle, and, followed by his henchman, proceeded down the glen at a gallop.

The earl was at this period of his reckless and chequered life, perhaps more than at any other, a dissatisfied and miserable man. After his imprisonment in Edinburgh Castle subsequent to his brawl with the Hamiltons, an imprisonment he felt he did not deserve, at least at the hands of the Queen, he had returned to his fastness in Liddesdale, where he had been obliged to remain in a state of seclusion and inaction, extremely galling to one of his adventurous nature and ardent temperament. Here he received no direct communication from Mary herself, a neglect which irritated whilst it distressed him; and he only heard of her continued displeasure through others in whom he could place no reliance, and whose interest he more than half suspected it was to create dissension and mistrust between him and his Sovereign. He then went for a short period into France, hoping, perhaps, that this self-imposed exile might elicit a recall to Holyrood; but finding no notice taken of his movements, and assured on all sides of the Queen's continued coldness, he returned to his strong Castle of Hermitage in a maddening state of uncertainty as to the future position he should assume. The wild borderers were all as devoted as ever to their chief. He had at no time been actually deprived of his office as Warden of the Marches and Lieutenant of the Southern Border, nor had he been superseded, was it probable that a successor could be found bold enough to take upon him the duties of the office. Accordingly the earl remained at Hermitage in the anomalous position of a sovereign's representative whilst held to be an avowed rebel to that sovereign's authority; in the agitating dilemma of one who is at variance with the person to whom he is most devoted on earth, and whom self-love forbids to offer that reparation which pride whispers may be contemptuously refused.

The warden galloped on in silence for several minutes, till the nature of the ground and the jaded condition of his good horse brought him perforce to a more sedate pace. With an impatient jerk at the bridle and a curse on the stumble that provoked it, he relapsed into a walk, and summoning 'Dick-o'-the-Cleugh' to his side, proceeded to vent the remainder of his petulance on his companion. That worthy's good-humour, however, was proof against all such attacks, and Bothwell, calming down after a time, took back the favourite falcon to his own wrist, and began to caress the bird whose wild flight had so much aroused his wrath.

"'Tis a royal pastime, in good truth, Dick,' said he, as they emerged from a deep, narrow glen, and beheld spread out before them a broad expanse of moorland, patched and brown and sombre, yet suggestive of sport and freedom, a sound sward whereon to breathe a horse, and a soft gray winter's sky in which to watch the flight of a hawk. 'I would rather be here in the saddle than mewed up in the old keep over yonder,' pointing while he spoke to the square towers of Hermitage, looming dim and grand in the distance; 'would rather handle any weapon than a pen, and track any slot rather than unravel a cipher. I marvel that the Earl of Moray can keep his chamber, as he doth, the live-long day, writing, plotting, calculating; never a stoup of wine to cheer his heart, never a breath of the free air of heaven to cool his brow. I'll wager you a hundred merks, Dick, that how long soever he remains in my poor castle he never sets foot beyond the moat till the stirrup cup is in his hand.'

'The brock[9] likes fine to lie at earth,' answered Dick, with a loud laugh, 'and I doubt there's no a brock in Liddesdale that's a match for the Earl of Moray in takin' his ain part. But hegh! Warden, there's a sight for sair een!' exclaimed the henchman, interrupting himself suddenly. 'See to yon canny lad ridin' down the glen; if yon's no Maister Maxwell, may I never lift cattle nor plenishing more! I wad ken the back o' him 'mang a thousand. 'Odd, man! but ye're welcome to Liddesdale again.'

[9] The badger.

In truth, while the borderer spoke, Maxwell made his appearance on the track that led to Hermitage, exchanging, as soon as he spied the earl and his henchman, for a brisk hand-gallop the more steady pace at which he had been prosecuting his journey. The greeting between the kinsmen was sufficiently cordial, between 'Dick-o'-the-Cleugh' and the new arrival, of the most boisterous and demonstrative nature. The rough borderer would have been at a loss to explain to himself why he entertained so warm a regard for Walter Maxwell. As the three rode slowly on together towards Hermitage, the emissary thought it a good time to broach the business which had been entrusted to him by his sovereign.

Slowly pacing over the open moor, where everything breathed peace and repose, where not a tuft of heather stirred in the soft still air, and the call of a moor-fowl or the dull flap of a heron's wing alone broke the surrounding silence; where the softened gleams of a winter sun came down in sheets of mellowed light, and heaven above and earth below seemed wrapped in security and content, Maxwell poured into no inattentive ears the tale that was rousing all the fiercest passions of our nature in the heart of one of his listeners.

Bothwell, after bidding him a hearty welcome to the border, heard him patiently and in silence, with an enforced composure that was more ominous of subsequent evil than would have been the wildest outbreak of that wrath which he suppressed with such an effort. His jaded horse, indeed, felt his rider's thighs tightening on him like a vice as the tale proceeded, and exerted himself gallantly to meet the unusual pressure; but only a very close observer could have marked, by the clenched jaw, the widened nostril, and dilated eye, that every word was driving its sting deeper and deeper, poisoned and festering, into the warden's heart.

Once indeed when a brighter gleam of sunshine than ordinary lighted up the moor, and the old towers of Hermitage coming into view imparted a picturesque and even beautiful aspect to the scene, Bothwell looked up to heaven as if in helpless expostulation with the mocking sky, and then in one bitter and defiant smile, took leave for ever of those nobler and better feelings which had hitherto redeemed his character from utter reprobation.

It was at this moment that Maxwell urged his kinsman to forward him at once upon his journey.

'I will but break bread with you, my lord,' said he, 'and so with a fresh horse speed my way to the southward once more; mine errand brooks no delay, and he that goes wooing for a queen must not let the grass grow under his feet while he is about it.'

'Is her Grace indeed so hurried?' answered Bothwell with an evil sneer. 'Can she not wait a matter of twenty-four hours, more or less, for this long smooth-faced lad on whom she has set her princely heart so wilfully? God speed the royal wedding, say I, and good luck to the bold suitor who would lie in a queen's bed! Here, Dick, your horse is fresher than mine; gallop on to the Castle and bid them prepare for Master Maxwell's refection; see, too, that the Lord Rothes' men and horses be well looked to if they be come. I have guests to-night with me at Hermitage, Walter; I pray you be not so niggardly as to depart without a supper and a night's rest. It is ill travelling on the Border after nightfall, and I will speed you on by sunrise to-morrow with the best horse in my stable and a guard of my own men. And now that long knave is out of ear-shot, tell me, Master Maxwell, is this marriage but an affair of state and policy? or doth the Queen seem to affect it for herself? Is her heart in it, think you?'

While he asked the question Bothwell busied himself about the hawk on his wrist, it may be to conceal the trembling of his lip, which extended itself even to his hands, for his strong fingers seemed unable to take off her hood or loose the fastenings that secured her jesses.

'In faith,' answered Maxwell honestly, 'her Grace bade me make no secrets with your lordship. When she spoke of marriage her colour went and came like a village maid's going a-maying; I reck but little of such follies,' he added with a sigh, 'but if you ask me the truth, I think, Queen though she be, she loves him as a woman should love the man whom she bids to share a throne.'

Bothwell swore such a fearful blasphemy that his companion, whose attention had been somewhat engrossed by the irregularities of the track, looked up astonished in his face. The earl excused himself by vowing that his falcon had struck her talons into his arm.

'The foul-hearted haggard!' he exclaimed, flinging the bird violently from him into the air; 'let her fly down the wind to the Solway an' she will! She may stoop on the southern side ere I whistle for her; no such false kestrel shall ever perch on wrist of mine again.'

The hawk soared freely up into the soft calm sky, then spreading her wings to the breeze, sailed gallantly away to the westward, and was soon out of sight.

Maxwell was too good a sportsman not to be surprised at such an action on the part of his host, but attributed it to one of those outbreaks of temper in which he had heard the earl was prone to indulge; and as they now proceeded to the Castle at a gallop by the warden's desire, who spurred his tired horse with savage energy, he had no opportunity of pursuing the subject on which they had been engaged.

That evening, however, there was much consternation amongst the retainers on discovering that 'the Queen' was missing from her mews; much discussion as to who should take upon himself the perilous task of informing the chief of his loss; much astonishment at Bothwell's unexpected answer to the stammering varlet who apprised him of it—

'May the foul fiend fly away with every feather of her! Never speak of her again! Go fetch me a stoup of wine.'

In the meantime the earl and his guest sprang from their reeking horses at a postern-door, which admitted them privately into the Castle of Hermitage. Already its courtyard was filled with the retinue of the Lord Rothes, a powerful Fifeshire baron, who had even now arrived with no inconsiderable following, on a visit to the disgraced warden. His men were well-armed and determined-looking, their horses strong, swift, and of considerable value. It argued little for the repose of the country, when lord met lord upon a peaceful visit, with fifty or a hundred spears at his back.

Extorting an unwilling promise from Maxwell that he would partake of his hospitality for one night, a concession only made by the latter on the express agreement that relays of horses should be sent forward immediately to enable him to prosecute his journey with extraordinary speed on the morrow, Bothwell placed his guest in the hands of an elderly person, whose black velvet dress, white wand, and grave manners, could only belong to the *major-domo*.

'See my cousin well bestowed in the eastern turret,' said the warden, 'and bid them serve supper without delay. Tell Lord Rothes I will give him a welcome to my poor house the instant I have doffed my soiled riding-gear. Bring me the key of the wicket in the winding-stair, and tell "Dick-o'-the-Cleugh" to have six picked men and horses ready to-morrow at daybreak.'

With many grave deliberate bows the old man received the orders of his chief, and then preceded Maxwell solemnly to his chamber, while Bothwell, with swift irregular strides, betook himself up a winding staircase to a chamber in a remote tower of the Castle.

Knocking, but not waiting for permission to enter the apartment, he walked hastily to a table at which a man sat writing, who looked up on his approach. Then, with an expression of irritation and impatience at the calm face that met his own, Bothwell flung himself into a chair, and commenced pulling and twisting the long moustaches that overhung his mouth.

Moray, for it was the Queen's illegitimate brother, whose occupation the warden had interrupted, looked at his host with his usual wary scrutinising expression, that seemed to extract the thoughts of others, but afforded no clue to his own. It was a handsome face, too, this mask so well adapted to conceal the workings of a mind in which diplomacy stifled every instinct of manhood, every chivalrous spark of honour, loyalty, and good faith. The bright fair complexion, the regular features, the keen gray eyes, deep-set, and glittering with scornful humour, forcibly repressed, the thin closed lips, shutting in, as it were, upon an ill-omened smile, and the broad square chin, denoted rather the daring schemer than the dashing soldier, the wary politician to whom, so as it led at last to his object, the path was none the less welcome for being devious, rather than the stout-hearted champion who would break his own way for himself through every obstacle, with his own right hand.

Gravely and plainly dressed, though in a rich suit of sad-coloured velvet, adorned with costly pearls, the figure that supported this inscrutable face was formed in fair and graceful proportions. The manners of the man were those of an accomplished courtier, dashed with something of that stealthy gravity which marks the Romish priest; yet Moray was now of the strictest amongst the Reformers.

'A shining light,' so said the followers of John Knox, 'an advanced disciple and assured professor of the true faith!'

'Mine host appears disturbed,' said Moray, in the low impressive tone which acted as a sedative on all who came within its influence. 'What ails ye, my Lord Earl? Hath your falcon flown so high a pitch she will perch on your wrist no more? or have our friends on the southern side so far forgotten themselves as to drive a raid across the Border? I think we have influence with the English Queen for "heading and hanging" at Carlisle as promptly as at Jedburgh!'

Bothwell winced. Hating the intrigues in which he found himself involved; balancing, as it were, on the verge of a precipice to which his passions hurried him, and from which his better nature held him back, he loathed in his heart the master-spirit that he was yet fain to obey. The demon was under the spell of the magician, but his submission was as unwilling as it was complete. He burst out angrily—

'See to what your schemes and your intrigues have led at last! Is this the upshot of my Lord of Moray's plotting and counter-plotting, and Randolph's promises, and Maitland's crabbed ciphers? Faith! a couple of hundred spears and a closed horse-litter would have done the work long ago far better than all your bonds and all your treaties. And now it is too late. The noblest Queen in Europe, the fairest woman on earth, is to be wasted on a half-witted boy, a beardless minion of the English Court. Out upon you, Earl Moray! I have worn steel since I was twelve years old, and man hath never so deceived me yet. Again I cry shame on you! Answer me how you will!'

If Moray was startled at the intelligence or angered at the manner in which it was conveyed, neither sensation was suffered to betray itself for an instant. He smiled pleasantly on his chafing companion, and answered composedly—

'All's not lost that's in hazard. Surely no lord in Scotland knows this better than the warden of the marshes. Tell me the worst intelligence you have gained, and how you learned it.'

Moray's brow grew darker and darker as his host detailed to him, not without violent gestures and many a wrathful expletive, all he had gathered from Maxwell concerning the Queen's proposed marriage. Whether new to him or not, the intelligence seemed to give him great concern, and once, although it was now twilight, he turned his face from the window so as to conceal its expression from his dupe. When Bothwell had finished his story there was a dead silence for a few minutes. He had lashed himself into a violent passion; he was now calming down into a sullen despair. Moray's face, on the contrary, wore a brighter look after he had ruminated a while, but his voice was as cold and distinct as ever when he spoke again.

'And the messenger is here, you say—here, in this very castle. Lord Bothwell, if we gain time, we can place the pieces on the chess-board for ourselves. Your borders here are not without their disadvantages. 'Tis bad travelling for single horsemen; they may be robbed of letters and even jewels. Nay, if they make much resistance they are sometimes heard of no more. 'Tis a numerous family, the Maxwells, and a loyal. One more or less makes no such great odds.'

'Nay, nay, he is my kinsman,' urged Bothwell, who perfectly understood the dark suggestion of his guest, but to whose frank and ardent nature such counsels were most distasteful. 'Besides, she trusted me; she trusted me. My Queen's own words were, that "she could depend upon me more securely than on any lord in Scotland."'

'You best know the value of the stake you play for,' answered Moray, with a very sinister smile, 'and the amount you are willing to set against it. Master Maxwell is a trusty messenger, no doubt, and will do his part faithfully, an' he get not his throat cut ere he reach Carlisle. Should this marriage ever take place, it will be prudent, Lord Bothwell, for you to make early court to young Henry Stuart. He has a noble future before him in truth. The crown-matrimonial of one kingdom; the crown in reversion of another; a Catholic alliance, or I am much deceived, with France, Spain, and Austria; lastly, no small temptation, Lord Earl, to young blood, Her Grace, my sister, the fairest woman in Europe, for a bed-fellow. In good faith the prize is worth struggling for!'

The arm of the chair which Bothwell held broke short off in his hand.

'Enough!' he exclaimed, 'it shall never be. What! am I not warden here? Have I not power of life and death on the marches? But no blood shall be shed; no blood, Moray. Can we not bestow him in safe keeping? Counsel me, my lord, for I am at my wits' end.'

Moray laughed outright.

'I will tell you a story,' said he, whilst he shuffled his papers together and tied them up, preparatory to changing his dress for supper. 'When we were studying at college in France, my brothers and I had great dread that the prize would be carried off by one of our companions who had more book-learning than all the rest of us put together; well, we invited the clever youth to an entertainment, and we drenched his brains with wine—just such a red generous Bordeaux as I saw a runlet of pierced only yester even here in the buttery—then we tied him on a horse, a sorry French nag enough, but able to carry him some ten leagues away into the country, where we left him to sleep off his carouse. When he returned next day the examinations were over, and I myself, for as dull as you may think me, had taken the first prize. All is fair in love and war, my lord. The curfew is already ringing; it is time for both of us to meet Rothes at the supper-table.'

The hint was not thrown away upon Bothwell.

'I will bestow him securely,' said he, as a bright idea seemed to flash across him; and he too departed hastily to make preparations for meeting his guests at supper.

Contrary to the usual custom of Hermitage, this meal, instead of being served in the great hall and shared with Bothwell's jackmen and retainers, was brought into a smaller apartment furnished with extreme splendour, and as near an approach to luxury as the times and locality permitted. This was perhaps done as a compliment to the presence of Moray, who was already beginning to accustom the nobility to his assumptions, and while he treated them with the outward cordiality of an equal, to cozen them insensibly of the attentions due to a superior.

The dishes were served with great pomp by the grave *major-domo* and two staid attendants splendidly dressed; the Lord Rothes, a dark handsome man, with a sinister expression of countenance, sat on the left hand of his host, Maxwell faced the latter, and the Queen's half-brother was in the place of honour on his right; also Moray's chair was somewhat higher than those of his companions, and of a different form.

When the meal was over, the wine, according to custom, circulated freely; whatever designs might be lurking in the breasts of the four men, the conversation was merry and jovial enough, embracing the usual topics of hawk and hound and horseflesh, with a good-humoured gibe or two at the opposite sex, and a free criticism of their charms.

Maxwell might be pondering on the difficulties of his task; Moray weaving additional meshes in that web which entangled himself at last; Rothes reflecting on his frailties or his debts his past follies or his coming embarrassments; and Bothwell eating his own heart in combined pique, disappointment, and vexation; but each man filled his cup, and pushed round the flask, and passed his frank opinion or his loud jest, with a merry voice, an open brow, and a cordial smile upon his face.

When the wine began to take effect, Maxwell excused himself from further participation in the carouse, and asked permission to retire on the plea of his early departure in the morning. After a faint resistance exacted by the laws of hospitality, Bothwell acceded freely to his request; meditating, as he did, a foul treachery against him, the earl felt his cousin's absence would be a relief. Moray, indeed, would have had small hesitation in so spicing his wine that he would need a sleeping-draught no more, and few scruples would have deterred Rothes from ridding himself of a troublesome guest with six inches of cold steel; but the lord warden had still some rough soldier-like notions of fair play about him, and had not lost all at once every trace of the chivalry and manhood that had made him heretofore the stoutest champion of his Queen.

When Maxwell had retired, his host sat moodily for a while, wrapped in meditation, drinking cup after cup in gloomy silence, and playing ominously with the haft of his dudgeon-dagger, a weapon that was never for an instant laid aside.

Moray seemed to divine his thoughts. After a few whispered words to Rothes, who treated the whole affair as an excellent jest, he observed in a cold measured voice, and as if continuing the thread of a conversation in which they had already been engaged.

'You cannot so prudently bestow him here, my lord, though it were a good jest to keep a queen's ambassador mewed up in a queen's fortress, and the prisoner would be well lodged with his affectionate kinsman.'

'Why not?' demanded Bothwell, rather fiercely. 'The walls of Hermitage are pretty strong, my lord, and these riders of mine are held to have a somewhat close grip when once they lay hold.'

'Nevertheless,' argued the other, 'this would be the first place suspected. Nay, it might be well that you should even deliver up the Castle to Her Majesty with a clean breast. I have thought more than once of urging you to demand an audience at Holyrood, to resign your lieutenancy or obtain a just acknowledgment of your loyalty from my royal sister.'

Bothwell's face brightened.

'True!' he exclaimed, dashing his heavy hand on the board. 'We must have no stolen horse in the stall when the ransom is told down! A clean breast and a "toom-byre,"[10] as we say here on the Border. I must send him elsewhere.'

[10] An empty cow-house.

Rothes filled his cup, with a laugh.

'I can lodge him at Leslie,' said he; 'any kinsman of Lord Bothwell's is welcome in my poor house. "Food and wine he shall not lack," as the old song says; ay, and a bed too, my lord, if so you will it, that shall serve him till doomsday.'

Bothwell flushed dark red with wrath and shame.

'Not a hair of his head must be jeopardied!' he exclaimed passionately; then controlling himself, added in a more friendly tone, 'I am beholden to you, Leslie, nor will I forget your courtesy. I shall, indeed, commit my kinsman to your care for a brief space. Four of my knaves, commanded by one whom I can trust, shall convoy him to-morrow into Fifeshire; though its lord is here with so gallant a following, Leslie House is, doubtless, not left ungarrisoned.'

'Trust me for that!' answered Rothes, an evil sneer again marring the beauty of his countenance. 'They are peaceful knaves enough, the men of Fife, yet they would like well to harry the old corbie's nest up yonder, and clear off scores for a few of Norman's doings, to say nothing of my own. It will be long, though, ere they crack the stones of my poor fortalice with their teeth, and I care not to ride in Fife without some fifty spears at my back; there are more than as many there even now. Hark ye, Bothwell, take my signet-ring here; give it to your lieutenant, and he will find himself at Leslie House "master and more."'

Moray, pretending not to listen, now asked for more wine with a great assumption of joviality and recklessness. A close observer, though, might have remarked that he scarce touched his own cup with his lips, whilst he encouraged his companions, who indeed were nothing loth, to empty theirs again and again. Artfully leading the conversation to the Queen's possible marriage, to her different suitors, and other topics connected with Mary, he watched Bothwell writhing under the torture, and drowning his sufferings in revelry, with covert interest tinged by a sardonic amusement.

It was midnight ere the reckless orgie broke up, when Moray, calm, cool, and smiling, bade his companions a placid 'good night;' while Rothes, flushed and boisterous, trolled off a ribald drinking-song; and Bothwell, in whom wine had been powerless to drown the stings of conscience, sought his solitary chamber with keen remorse and torturing self-reproach gnawing at his heart.

CHAPTER XXX

'In solitude the sparks are struck that bid the world admire,
Though heart and brain must scorch the while in self-
consuming fire. In solitude the sufferer smiles, defiant of
his doom, And Madness sits aloof and waits, and gibbers
in the gloom. 'Tis dazzling work to weave a web from
Fancy's brightest dyes, And speed the task ungrudging all
we have, and hope, and prize. But it must make the devils
laugh, to mark how, day by day, The plague-spot widens
out, and spreads, and eats it all away. In vain the unwilling
rebel writhes, so loth defeat to own, And strives to pray, and
turns away, and lays him down alone. Oh! better far to moan
aloud, on earth and heaven to cry, Than like the panther in
its lair, to grind his teeth and die. Then help me, brother!
Help me! for thy heart is made like mine; The shaft that
drains my life away is haply wing'd for thine. It is not good
to stand alone, to scorn the rest, and dare; But two or three,
like one must be, and God shall hear their prayer.'

Heated with wine, stung with jealousy, torn by conflicting feelings, Earl
Bothwell paced the stone-floor of his bed-chamber, as a wild beast traverses
to and fro between the sides of his cage. His step had the same noiseless
elasticity, his air the same subdued ferocity, his eye the same lurid sparkle
that seems struck from some quenchless fire within. If there are indeed
hours at which the master-fiend is permitted to vex those human souls,
who, for some wise purpose, are delivered like Job into his hand, the Lord
Warden must have been that night a prey to the arch-enemy of our race.
It needed but little addition to the frenzy of his mood to imagine a dusky
shape, defining itself more and more distinctly in the gloom, stepping as
he stepped, turning as he turned, whispering in his ear suggestions that
curdled his very blood, while he pondered them, and yet were tinged with
the strange fascination which all frantic expedients possess for despair.
It takes a long apprenticeship to sorrow ere a man can bow his head in
resignation and cease to struggle, nay, even to quiver under the lash: but
he who has gained this faculty at the cost of anguished moments, none but
himself and one besides can count, is indeed master of his fate.

Such, however, was far from the condition of the tameless border-lord. He could have fought, struggled, died with the fiercest champion that ever set his teeth in the grim smile of a death-grapple; but the Hepburn blood was not the stuff of which martyrs are made, and the fiercest scion of all the bold, bad men that constituted the pride of his line, was now, so to speak, like some demoniac of antiquity, wrestling and striving against himself, torn, and rent, and infuriated by the possessing spirit, which refused to be exorcised and come out of him. That night in his lonely room at Hermitage, Bothwell learnt many new and strange things, never to be forgotten whilst he had life. Depths of guilt, into which, heretofore, he would not have dared to look, were now opened up to him, and there was seduction in the very immensity of the abyss. Crimes, dazzling from their boldness, now seemed feasible, nay, almost justifiable, and entranced him by the reckless daring with which they must be carried out. He had been dreaming hitherto a soft sweet dream for years. He was awake now, broad awake, and the vision should become reality, or he would never dream again. He had been cozened long enough! What? The game was not yet played out. Turn and turn about, fair dame! And it was Bothwell's turn now! He laughed a low hissing laugh within his beard, and then stopped, startling in his walk, for it seemed to him that the laugh was echoed by something in the room, and that the shape was close to his ear now, whispering, whispering, one continuous stream of upbraiding, and persuasion, and reproach, with maddening promise and stinging sarcasm, and here and there a devilish scoff.

But these paroxysms wear themselves out. By degrees the earl became calmer; by degrees he recalled the past and reviewed the present, and looked steadily on the future. The whirl of contending passions passed away to make room for a stern and gloomy resolve far more dangerous, and the molten stream of thought that had seared his brain, cooled down into the settled determination of the man.

There are seasons when the whole of our past lives seems presented to us as on a stage, each scene distinct and vivid as when it actually took place. Men are taught to believe that this occurs at the supreme moment ere the spirit leaves its dwelling, and when the heart clings so instinctively and so pitifully to its treasure *here*. Be this how it may, there can be no doubt that at periods of strong excitement, this *clairvoyance*, if we may so call it, acquires extraordinary power. For a moment it seemed to Bothwell that the gloomy walls of his chamber had disappeared, and he stood again beneath the sunny skies of France. Again the towers of Joinville started from the smiling plain, and he knelt once more to tender his homage to the fair widowed bride, who looked so sweetly down upon him, with her pleading womanly beauty, softening and enhancing the majesty of a Queen. It was the first time he had ever looked on that face, which, despite of all his madness, all his crimes, was imprinted thenceforth on his rebellious heart. He had seen it since in sorrow, in triumph, in levity, nay, in bitter anger and unjust displeasure against himself, but it was still the same face to him, the type of all that was pure and good and lovely upon earth, the charm that had wound itself into his whole being, that shed its magic glow over every scene and action of his life; whether he laid spear in rest, or flung his hawk aloft in air, or watched the last rays of sunset gilding the broad brown moor on a peaceful summer's evening, still that face was ever present to him, with its quiet thoughtful beauty, and the kind look in its deep winning eyes; then he thought of the many, many times when he had vowed in his heart to cherish undying love and loyalty for her alone, to ask no happier fate than to suffer shame and sorrow for his Queen. Would he not have given his life-blood for her, oh! so gladly that morning at Holyrood, when he alone of all her nobles had grieved with her on her day of grief, when, overcome by his faithful sympathy, and stung by the cold ingratitude of the rest, she had turned her face away and wept? And was he so changed now that he could be plotting treason against his sovereign and violence towards his love? For a moment his better nature mastered him; the fierce set features writhed, the strong frame shook, and though he was alone in the room, in the hush of midnight, the proud noble bowed his head and turned his face aside, ere he dashed away the drops that had stolen unawares to his shaggy eyelashes.

But the devil was watching his opportunity, and what a picture did he now conjure up! The beautiful Queen in her robes of ceremony, with the crown upon her head and the orb and sceptre in her hands; ambassadors from England, France, Spain, Austria, thronging with their sovereigns' congratulations; the nobility of Scotland proffering homage before the throne; and these regal honours shared by a tall handsome stripling, who would lift his lady-face scornfully, and stretch a weak girlish hand for *him*, Bothwell, to kiss! Worse than all, amongst the courtiers' jeering faces, Moray's cool sardonic smile, as of one who had foreseen the degradation from which, had his advice been taken, it would have been so easy to escape. And then the banquet and the wedded pair, sitting side by side, and the subsequent revel and the customary ceremonies, and the laughing guests departing one by one,—and then, and then,—the stillness of night brooding over the old pile of Holyrood, and Mary once more a bride, another's bride, and Bothwell a laughing-stock!

'Perdition! it shall never be!' exclaimed the earl, dashing down, while he spoke, with the violence of his involuntary gesture, the lamp that stood on the table by his side. The few moments consumed in rekindling it gave him time to compose himself, and to determine on his future conduct. It was but a brief period, yet was it long enough for Bothwell to bid farewell, at once and for ever, to all the higher and purer feelings of his nature; to change him from a man who, with many faults and with ungovernable passions, yet possessed a certain frank uprightness, a certain chivalrous devotion to the one idol of his life, into an unscrupulous ruffian, prepared to commit any crimes, to go any lengths in the prosecution of his schemes, and willing in brutal selfishness to drag his idol down to the dust, rather than see it enshrined upon the pedestal of another. One moment cannot indeed change the whole character of a human being, though it may influence his whole conduct; but as it is the last ounce that breaks the patient camel's back, so is it the one additional atom of sorrow, or unkindness, or disappointment, added to the mass, that overwhelms the poor sufferer's powers of endurance, and drives him into the frenzy of despair, or leaves him stunned and sick at heart, in the helpless apathy of a ruined man. It would be well to think of this sometimes when we see the bruised reed so nearly broken, the kind generous nature so wearied and suffering and overladen. It is but an ignoble triumph to lend the tottering mass that slight push which sends it crashing to destruction. It is cowardly and un-English to 'strike a man when he is down.'

Bothwell lit his lamp, and wrapping a furred bed-gown around him whilst he thrust his feet into the *mules* or slippers which would best muffle their tread, proceeded with swift and stealthy strides along the passages of his Castle, towards the eastern turret in which his kinsman was disposed. All was hushed and silent within the walls of Hermitage. The drowsy sentinels might have been sleeping on their posts, for neither stir of arms nor measured tread of steel-shod foot denoted their vigilance, yet, strange to say, the warden failed to observe this unusual silence. Nevertheless, preoccupied as he was, he marked a light still burning in Moray's chamber, and instinctively he shaded the lamp he carried with his hand when he passed the narrow casements on the opposite side of the Castle-yard. Arrived at Maxwell's door, he listened for a while, and satisfied himself by the deep breathing within that his kinsman was asleep; then shading his light once more, he entered the room softly, and made at once for the small travelling valise, in which he hoped to find the messenger had secured his despatches. But Maxwell had travelled the Borders ere this, and had profited by his experience. Ready dressed, booted and spurred, with his sword by his side, he lay prepared for a start, sleeping indeed, yet not so sound but that a sudden noise might waken him. Whatever he had about him of value was concealed in his breast, and could not be taken from him without disturbing his repose. Bothwell felt once for the haft of his dagger, and smiled grimly to himself, as he thought how easily he might possess himself of his guest's despatches, and how lightly he would think *now* of such a crime as murder under his own roof. There was even a wild devilish triumph in the reflection that he could have so changed within an hour!

After a moment's thought, however, he again passed unobserved from the room, and returned to his own as stealthily as he had come. There he spent the remainder of the night, still pacing up and down, up and down, and an hour before dawn summoned 'Dick-o'-the-Cleugh,' already astir thus early, to a long and mysterious consultation, in which, though he yielded eventually, for the first time in his life the retainer presumed to remonstrate with his lord.

CHAPTER XXXI

'Oh, they rade on, and farther on,
And they waded through rivers above the knee,
And they saw neither the sun nor the moon,
But they heard the roaring of the sea.'

The morning broke gloomily. A thick and heavy mist clung around the towers of Hermitage, dimming the arms and saturating the cloaks of the escort already mounted and waiting in the Castle-yard. The moisture dripped from the ears and nostrils of the horses, and stood upon the beards of their riders, while the former stamped and shook their bits impatiently, and the latter muttered a coarse jest or two, not without fervent aspirations after a tass of brandy to keep the raw air from their throats.

Presently 'Dick-o'-the-Cleugh' emerged from the turret containing the warden's private apartments, wearing an unusually gloomy expression on his face, and proceeded to examine the arms and appointments of his comrades, with a disposition to find fault, that elicited sundry growls, murmurs, and a round oath or two from the impatient jackmen.

There was, however, but little delay, in starting the cavalcade. Maxwell, who had been anxiously awaiting the spare horse prepared for him, was soon in the saddle exchanging a cheerful greeting with the troopers, to which Dick alone made no reply; and while it was yet scarcely light, the portcullis was raised, and the party filed out, intently watched from one of the narrow windows by a haggard eager face, that still looked and lingered after the croup of the last horseman had disappeared. Bothwell even made one hasty gesture, as if to recall his mandate, and order the party back, but changing his mind again on the instant, with a bitter laugh, he took a long draught from a wine-flagon that stood by his bed-side, and then flinging himself on the couch, turned doggedly to the wall and tried to force his senses into sleep.

Maxwell felt his sovereign's letter lying safe within his doublet. He examined, too, the priming of his pistols, and turned his sword-belt a little more to the front. Then he proved the mouth and mettle of his charger with rein and spur, deriving from the experiment all the confidence felt by a good horseman on a well-bitted steed. Satisfied at length on these important points, his spirits rose with the morning air and the excitement of his mission. Even Mary Carmichael's falsehood seemed less black in hue than it appeared yesterday. The future once more showed promise of something beside a dull apathetic response to the call of duty alone. He looked along its dim vistas, and saw the light shining, though faintly, at a distance. The mission was already in imagination half-fulfilled. He had made his journey prosperously through the rich districts of middle England, and gained the capital with unprecedented rapidity, thanks to good luck in procuring horses, and his own untiring powers in the saddle. He had delivered his credentials to Lady Lennox, and presented himself at Greenwich Palace to the Maiden Queen. He could even conjure up a picture in his mind of that redoubtable lady; could imagine the flaxen curls, the stately figure, the harsh yet not uncomely features, and the dignified gestures that veiled a woman's vanity beneath the majestic bearing of a British sovereign. He became a courtier for the occasion, and thought how he could serve his own dear mistress with a well-timed compliment, and a little apt flattery to her rival 'Good Sister.' He saw himself dismissed with honour, and speeding back to the North, triumphant at the safe accomplishment of his mission. Then he fell to thinking of Mary's kindly thanks, delivered with all that charm of manner which made a word from her better than a jewel from another, and his welcome reception at Holyrood by all the loyal and well-disposed party to whom it was of no small moment to see their Queen happily married.

Perhaps *others*, thought Maxwell, might not have served her so well. Perhaps *one* of her maidens, with whom, as with the rest, loyalty was still the master passion, might be inclined to give him a welcome far warmer and kinder than her proud and distant farewell: might think she had judged him harshly, prematurely: might wish when it was too late that she had not so scornfully rejected his devotion, nay, might long to possess now what she had valued so lightly when it was her own. Then he would teach her a lesson that it would do her good to learn; then how delicious would be the triumph of meeting her coldly, politely, with calm friendship and quiet good-will, far more cutting than any amount of assumed indifference and unconcern; then she would know that she had altered her mind too late, that a man of energy and action was not to be pulled hither and thither like a puppet by the weak hand of a woman holding the string; that she had flung the falcon from her wrist once, jesses and all, and he would soar his wing now, and never stoop to lure of hers again.

Oh! it would be a happy moment; and yet how much happier to forgive her freely, and without reproach to take her hand in his, look frankly in her face, and tell her he had loved her all along, even when she was most wilful and most unkind! Was he not a man—a bold strong man? What had he to do with pride as regarded her? Nay, was it not his pride to think that whilst he yielded an inch to no one else on earth, he would always be content to accept suffering, sorrow, even humiliation, for her dear sake?

Such is the usual conclusion of one of those love reveries in which men indulge whilst under the influence of the malady; such is the climax of an infinity of stem resolution and haughty self-reproach and bitter self-examination; we make ourselves very unkind and very uncomfortable, and after all leave off very much at the point from which we started, if anything, in a less rational frame of mind than at first.

Maxwell could not but compare himself at the moment to the horse of one of the leading files of his escort, which had got bogged up to the girths in a *well-head*, as those particularly soft pieces of morass are called, which abound on the Scottish moorland. The poor animal made two or three gallant efforts to extricate itself, stimulated not only by the great terror a horse entertains of such a catastrophe, but by a fierce application of its long-legged rider's spurs; each plunge only hampered it more irrevocably, and at last amidst the loud jeers of his comrades and a volley of oaths from himself, the trooper abandoned the saddle and wisely allowed the beast to be still for a few moments and recover its wind.

Maxwell's attention, which had hitherto been somewhat taken up with his own thoughts, was now directed towards the locality in which he found himself, and the mist clearing away as the day drew on, enabled him to recognise one or two of those acclivities and breaks of the sky-line which constitute the landmarks of an open moorland district, such as he was at present traversing.

Though he had been but once before at Hermitage, his soldier's eye had not failed to acquaint itself with the general outline of the surrounding country. He now recognised a conical-shaped hill on his left hand, that he distinctly remembered to have passed yesterday in riding from Edinburgh on his right; the wind, too, which from the appearance of the weather he judged to be easterly, struck cold upon his right cheek; he was convinced they must be going north. His first impression was that the party had lost its way in the mist; his first impulse to jeer its leader, his old friend Dick, on such a want of moss-trooping sagacity.

'How now, master Dick?' said Maxwell, cheerily, looking round for his friend, who rode silent and sullen in the rear; 'I should have thought you knew your way to the southern side better than this! If you wanted to drive Lord Scrope's horses, or empty a byre or two in Cumberland, you wouldn't take the road to Holyrood, as I am much mistaken if we are not doing, this morning. Why, man, I came by that very cairn on the green hill yesterday. Thou must be asleep, Dick, for I know the ale is not yet brewed that will make thee drunk!'

Dick shook himself sulkily in reply, and moving his horse alongside his questioner, laid his hand on the other's bridle-rein as if to guide him into a sounder path.

'I'm thinkin', Maister Maxwell,' said Dick, with an assumption of extreme friendliness and great caution, 'that it wud be mair wise-like just to whig cannily back to Holyrood, and leave a fule to gang a fule's errand for himself.'

Maxwell laughed good-humouredly. Even now he was persuaded the borderer had missed the southern tract, and was annoyed at his own stupidity, perhaps inclined to veil it from his men by affecting ignorance of his charge's destination.

'Holyrood is a fair palace, Dick,' said he, 'and I left it but yesterday at daybreak. Do you think I came all the way to Hermitage only to push the wine-cup round with wild Lord Rothes, and so back again, with red eyes and a singing brain, to my duties in the Queen's ante-room? Nay, nay, the sooner we strike the right track and cross the Border the better. Why, man, I should be half-way to York before sun-down!'

Dick seemed sadly disturbed. He fidgeted with his bridle, he loosened his sword in its sheath, he looked up and down and on all sides of him in obvious vexation. Once when a jackman rode nearer Maxwell than was convenient, he bade the man keep his distance with a hearty curse. He seemed hurried, and yet anxious to put off time, and talked at random as one does who has some engrossing subject of no pleasant nature to occupy his thoughts.

'Ye wad be better at Holyrood, Maister Maxwell,' said he, still harping on the old subject. 'An' ye were at the palace yesterday, nae doot, wi' the Queen an' her leddies, an' who but you? I wish ye were there at this moment, Maister Maxwell, an' that's the dooms truth o' it!'

'Orders must be obeyed, Dick,' answered the other, vainly trying to induce the whole cavalcade to increase their pace, which had now dwindled down to a very funeral walk. 'That reminds me, I have a message for you from one of the Queen's maids-of-honour.'

All the blood in the borderer's great body seemed to rush into as much of his face as was visible beneath his morion, then the colour faded visibly, and for the first time in his life 'Dick-o'-the-Cleugh' turned as white as a sheet.

'It wad no be from Mistress Seton!' said he, almost unconsciously, and with the true Scottish negative that affirms so much. 'Man! I wad like fine to hear it,' and he bent over his horse's neck and looked Walter in the face with something of the wistful eager expression that the Newfoundland dog, to whom he has already been compared, assumes when his master is going to throw a stick for him to retrieve out of the water. In the animal goes! A plumper off the pier, be it never so high, and the waves breaking never so angrily below, and you may be sure that in his noble instinct of fidelity he would drown ten times over before he would let go.

Walter freed his rein from the other's grasp, and struck into a trot.

'It was but to hope you had not forgotten all she taught you, Dick, good manners and such like. I may tell her when I see her again that you are such a courteous squire now, you guide the bridle-rein of a mounted man-at-arms as carefully as a lady's palfrey. Tush, man! we are wasting time; let us strike into the right path and get on. I tell thee mine errand admits of no delay!'

He spoke impatiently, but yet in perfect good-humour, and looking on his companion's face, was startled at the expression of intense pain that was apparent in its features. 'Dick-o'-the-Cleugh' looked like a man who had been shot through the body, and was endeavouring to hide his internal agony under an appearance of outward composure.

Inside that stalwart frame of his a terrible conflict was going on. Good feeling, manhood, a certain reflective sense of the duties of hospitality, above all, loyalty to the Queen, represented by an intense devotion to one of her maids-of-honour; all these sentiments were at war with the habits of a lifetime and the first feudal instinct of the henchman—implicit obedience to his chief. It is needless to say that the latter obtained the mastery.

Maxwell was a friend, and he had come from the immediate presence of her who was the one bright image that gladdened the man's honest unsophisticated heart, that elevated his rude nature and gave him a glimpse of something better than clash of steel and clang of drinking cups, the excitement of a foray, and the pleasures of a debauch; but, on the other hand, Bothwell was the master whom he had venerated and obeyed from childhood; whose mandate it never occurred to him to dispute; whose will was law. The Rutherfords had served the Hepburns by flood and field as long as either family could count their line. It was not for Dick, so he thought, to be the first traitor of his race; yet he loathed his task, too, this frank-hearted borderer, and his face was very stern and his voice rung hoarse and harsh when he spoke again.

'Ye say true, Maister Maxwell. Orders *must* be obeyed, Gude forgi'e us! and *the Laird's bidding must be done!'*

Startled by the altered tone, Maxwell turned in his saddle, and at the same instant a thick woollen plaid, thrown over him from behind, was drawn tight across his head and face, a sword-belt was as quickly strapped round his arms above the elbows, a stout moss-trooper pinioned him on either side, two more were at his horse's head, his weapons were secured, and he found himself, in the space of about half a minute, helpless, blindfold, half-stifled, and a prisoner!

Accustomed as he had been in his adventurous life to every sort of catastrophe, the present seemed to him the most unaccountable and startling of all. He had not witnessed the chafing warden's interview yesterday with calm, impassible, unscrupulous Moray, nor guessed how much he had to thank his host, that imprisonment rather than death was his present fate. He knew nothing of the conclave held over their wine after he had retired last night by the three nobles, when Rothes had suggested so jovially that he might be blinded or left in a dungeon for life, or hidden out of the way altogether, in any manner that was most agreeable to his boon companions.

'For,' as the peer politely put it, while he filled his cup to the brim, 'you need have no fear of inconveniencing *me*. We have a saying in Fife of which I have always endeavoured to uphold the truth—"Ask no questions of the Leslies, for their answers are sharp, silent, and to the point." If he goes down a certain winding-stair in my poor house you might never hear of him again till you wanted him; and if need be, I could produce you his bones, at any rate, twenty years hence. Do not hesitate, I pray you; I am only happy to accommodate the warden. Bothwell, your good health!'

Nor had he overheard the orders accepted so unwillingly by poor 'Dick-o'-the-Cleugh' an hour or two before dawn, nor that worthy's eager remonstrance and extreme unwillingness to fulfil his chief's behests. Perhaps the henchman never felt so keenly that he was a vassal as when he told off six stout jackmen for the unwelcome duty, and informed them of the catchword, '*the Laird's bidding,*' at which they were to muffle and pinion their prisoner.

Maxwell knew it was useless to complain. A request for a little air was so far complied with that the plaid, while it still blinded him, was enough loosened to admit of his breathing more freely; but no answer was vouchsafed to the few indignant questions that, in his first surprise, he had put to his captors. The pace, too, at which they were now going, forbade conversation, and in the few words exchanged at intervals between the jackman, their prisoner failed to distinguish the tones of 'Dick-o'-the-Cleugh.' Notwithstanding the henchman's treachery, Maxwell's heart sank a little within him to think that he was deserted by his last friend.

After many hours of hard riding, and when he could not but feel that his horse was becoming completely exhausted, the fresh sea-breeze made him aware that he was approaching the Firth. With no unnecessary violence, though with much rapidity, he was, ere long, lifted from the saddle and placed in a boat, but the plaid was still kept round his head, and an unbroken silence preserved even by the men who handled the oars. It must have been long after nightfall when they made the opposite shore, and Maxwell, despite his hardy frame, was becoming faint and exhausted from fatigue, vexation, and want of food.

As he was again forced into the saddle, however, a flask of brandy was applied to his mouth, and at the same time a strong bony hand grasped his own warmly, and 'Dick-o'-the-Cleugh's' welcome voice whispered in his ear—

'Tak' anither sup, lad, and keep your heart up. Ye've gotten a friend to your back for a' that's come and gone yet.'

CHAPTER XXXII

'Good morrow, 'tis St Valentine's day,
All in the morning betime;
And I a maid at your window,
To be your Valentine.'

There is one saint in the calendar, who at least has never lacked worshippers; at whose shrine the strictest sectarians, the bitterest Reformers, have never failed to lay their votive offerings, and in whose train shine myriads of the brightest and fairest beings we can picture to ourselves, the only angels that gladden the sight of us adoring mortals here below. Yes, blooming maidens, buxom widows, constituting a phalanx beautiful to look upon, as it is dangerous to deal with, have for centuries conspired to do honour to sweet St Valentine, and we can only regret that the anniversary of his martyrdom (kissed to death, we have always been taught to believe, and buried by turtle-doves, under a shower of orange-blossoms) should occur at a season of the year when in our own climate the usual concomitants of frost and snow seem so inappropriate to the indolent and relaxing amusement of love-making. We have no reason to believe that the 14th of February 1564, afforded any contrast to the usual boisterous inclemency of a Scottish spring, or that Queen Mary and her maidens, looking from the battlements of Wemyss Castle on the leaden waves of the stormy Firth, had any sunshine to gladden them save that which originated in their own breasts.

But the Queen at least was in the height of good-humour and good spirits; though subject to occasional fits of depression, Mary's usual state of mind was kindly and cheerful; nay, when in some rare interval of peace she was relieved from the pressure of actual distress, or the anticipation of impending calamity, her gay and cordial manner shed an influence of happiness over all who came within its range; and even Randolph—busy, intriguing, heartless, cynical Randolph—could not but admit that 'this Queen,' as he calls her, 'is a divine thing, far excelling any (our own most worthy only excepted) that ever was made since the first framing of mankind.'

Behold, then, Mary Stuart, and her maidens sitting at work in a chamber overlooking the stormy Firth from the seaward turret of Wemyss Castle. Without, the leaden hues of sea and sky form a grand though savage contrast to the white snow-mantle which wraps the undulating shores of Fife, while the opposite Lothian coast stands out, as it were, into the water with the distinct outline and startling appearance of proximity peculiar to an atmosphere charged with coming snow, and a wind from the north-east.

Within, an old oak-panelled chamber, hung here and there with faded tapestry, once of priceless value, but now frayed and worn and coming rapidly into rags; grotesque, gaunt ornaments are strewed about the room, the spoils of predatory warfare on the Danish coast, brought hither generations back by stern Sir Michael, the first Lord Admiral of Scotland. Strange-looking arms and a ponderous axe or two are not in character with the interior of a lady's bower, nor do the grim figures carved in wood that support the chimney on either side of the high wide fireplace, the least resemble such cupids and other gentle symbols as would be appropriate to the company and the occasion.

Bending over her work, the Queen's blushes come and go with a degree of graceful embarrassment that is not unmarked by her attendants. These are around her as usual, and, like their mistress, occupy their fingers with considerable energy, and doubtless allow their thoughts to stray far and wide during the task. We of the sterner sex have probably not the faintest idea of the comfort derived by woman from her natural weapon, the needle.

It is well known, we are told, to physiologists, and the fact is not lost sight of in our treatment of the insane, that manual labour requiring a moderate amount of attention, such as the prosecution of a handicraft, has a remarkably composing tendency on the mind; but carpentering is perhaps the only male pursuit which combines the exact proportions of physical and mental exertion supposed to produce such beneficial results. Few men, however, are carpenters, whereas, speaking in general times, all women can sew, and the very act of stitching we believe to be a complete and unfailing anodyne. The delicate fingers bend unconsciously to their task; the white hand flies to and fro as the dove flew round the Ark seeking the olive-branch on which it should find rest at last; the gentle head bends lower and lower, while thoughts, humbled by sorrow and chastened by resignation, wander further and further away. Presently the tears are dropping fast upon the pattern, be it the beads of a queen's embroidery or the hem of a peasant's smock; but like summer showers they do but clear the sky when they are over, and ere the hair is shook back, and the loving face looks up to thread the needle afresh, all is sunshine and peace once more.

Perhaps no woman of any degree had oftener occasion to practise this healing occupation than ill-fated Mary Stuart, destined to a pre-eminence in suffering as in beauty.

The only male attendant on the Queen was David Riccio. Splendidly dressed in the thickest velvet that could be procured, that poor little Italian shivered in a corner of the ample fireplace, preserving, to his credit be it said, his southern good-humour even in the rigours of a cold, raw climate, which, to use an expression from his own land, seemed 'to loosen every tooth in his head.'

Three of the maids-of-honour were unusually silent and depressed, Mary Seton alone incorrigible as usual.

A portentous shiver from Riccio, which he tried in vain to repress, made the Queen look up from her embroidery. She could not but smile at the chattering teeth and pinched features of her ungainly secretary, yet there was a slight tone of irritation in her voice as she said—

'Heap more wood on the fire, if you are so cold, Signior David; yet methinks the weather hath moderated since morning. It cannot be so bad even now on the landward side; but the wind whistles round this old keep of my brother's till we might fancy ourselves a plump of wild-fowl cowering together for shelter on the Bass.'

Her eye happening to rest on Mistress Beton while she spoke, that demure lady, who was plunged in a profound fit of abstraction, felt herself called upon to reply, and could find nothing more apposite to say than—

'Bitter weather indeed, your Grace, and threatening worse than ever over the Firth. Heaven help all poor travellers by land and sea!' she added piously, drawing at the same time her mantle closer round her shoulders, to the utter destruction of her stupendous ruff, a neglect of which ornamental structure always denoted in Mary Beton extreme discomposure of mind.

'Psha! child!' said the Queen, impatiently. 'Travellers are not so faint-hearted. What say you, Signior David? We wot of some that would ride through fire and water at our behest. Is not that the gallop of a horse I hear even now along the causeway?'

'I pray you patience, madam!' answered the cautious Italian, seeing that the Queen had risen from her chair, and was pacing up and down in obvious expectation. 'No traveller that your Grace wotteth of can be on this side the Firth to-day. Spurs are but steel; horses are but bone and sinew; riders but flesh and blood. There can be no arrival at the earliest for twenty hours. I have myself wagered a collar of pearls and rubies with Mistress Seton.'

'And lost! and lost! and lost!' exclaimed that voluble young lady, dancing rather than walking into the room from which she had not been five minutes absent. 'Even now the portcullis is up, and I saw him myself ride into the courtyard from the passage-window. Good lack, madam, such a tall cavalier! and his poor horse looked so tired! Not a living creature with him neither, and he called for a cup of wine before ever his spurs had touched the pavement.'

Mary Stuart's cheek turned very red, and her breath came quick and short! the woman could not but appreciate the compliment, however much the Queen must study to conceal her feelings. This looked like an earnest wooer in good truth; no laggard could thus have distanced his followers and arrived in such an incredibly short space of time from the southern shore. Aye! there was more lost and won on that ride of young Lord Darnley's than the collar of pearls and rubies which David Riccio delivered the same evening with such a good grace to saucy Mistress Seton. But the Queen's innate dignity soon reasserted itself. Signing to her ladies to attend on her, she paced majestically from the room.

'It would ill become us,' said she, 'to keep one waiting for an audience who hath shown such loyal diligence in obeying our summons; we will receive our guest in the great hall of the castle. Do you, Signior Riccio, apprise him that we are ready to accept his homage. Mary Carmichael and Mary Hamilton attend us for a few minutes to our tiring-room; we will all meet again here, and proceed at once to the hall.'

Mary seldom spoke in such a measured dignified tone. It may be that this stately manner covered some little trepidation and heart-beating; it may be that the Queen felt timid and bashful as the meekest village maiden. At least it was remarkable that the most beautiful woman in Europe should have thought it necessary to revise her toilet, and add to her attractions before receiving the homage of her vassal and kinsman.

It was no ordinary phalanx of beauty that Darnley had to confront when the venerable seneschal of Wemyss Castle ushered him into the lofty hall, at the end of which, on a portion raised by one step above the level of the floor, was placed the royal lady to whom he had dared to aspire as his bride; her exquisite loveliness only enhanced by the presence of the four prettiest women in Scotland who stood behind her. But 'faint heart never won fair lady,' and Darnley's was by no means one of those dispositions which are prone to fail from a retiring modesty and too low an estimate of their own advantages. Besides, he was playing a great stake, and playing it with all the reckless audacity of a gambler.

Young as he was, he well knew that the prize now before him represented not only the Majesty of Scotland, but possibly, nay, in all human probability, the eventual succession to the English throne. It was this contingency which made Elizabeth so jealous of all matrimonial overtures to her beautiful cousin; it was this which caused Cecil and Throckmorton, and their agent Randolph, to lay their cunning heads together and devise means for amusing the Scottish Queen with a procession of suitors, none of whom were ever intended to be more than the puppets of the moment, each to prevent the attainment of his object by the other.

The accomplished Warwick, the manly-looking, weak-hearted Norfolk, nay, the prime favourite of the English Queen herself, the selfish, handsome, and utterly unscrupulous Leicester, were successively put forward as appropriate sharers of Mary Stuart's throne and masters of her hand. But no sooner did the hapless object of all this intrigue and duplicity show the slightest preference for one over the other, the faintest inclination to accede to wishes which seemed so candidly expressed, than instantly, like some scene in a masquerade, the performers all changed characters at once. Elizabeth became the stern monitress, Randolph the delicate adviser, and the belted Earls and noble Dukes, no longer humble suitors and devoted champions of their idol, cooled at a breath into very coy and somewhat unwilling parties to an engagement of political expediency, only binding so long as it received encouragement at Greenwich or Whitehall. Thus was a woman's heart made an object of cruel traffic and shameful double-dealing, none the less disgraceful because its possession implied the occupancy of a throne. Some day, perhaps, the world may be brought to see that even in the highest places expediency can never justify heartlessness or crime, that not only is 'honesty the best policy,' but that chivalrous unselfishness and frank defiance of evil are the surest beacons to success.

In the meantime, it is sad to think, that the life's happiness and the life itself of Mary Stuart were pitilessly sacrificed by one of her own blood and her own sex. Surely, since the serpent, woman has had no such bitter enemy as woman.

Darnley, put forward at eighteen as the rival of so many distinguished nobles, entered on the contest with all the wilfulness of a Stuart, and all the joyous temerity of a boy. Though a tool in the hands of his seniors, it must doubtless have seemed to the adventurous young nobleman no unwelcome task to woo his beautiful sovereign—the kinswoman whom he had already once seen when they were both mere children, but whose charms even at that early age he had not yet forgotten. Few men would refuse the hand of a queen, even if she were an ugly one; what shall we say of a proposal to try his fortune with such a paragon as Mary Stuart? It was no wonder the lightsome young wooer rode horse after horse to death as he posted northward in the direction to which his star beckoned him; no wonder that he should arrive at Wemyss Castle all alone, far ahead of his scattered escort; no wonder that he should advance into Mary's presence, under all the disadvantages of haste, fatigue, and travel-stained riding-gear, with the gallant air of a gay young knight who goes forth to conquer, rather than that of a slave who comes to wear a chain. As he walked up the hall, his step was firm, his head erect, and his eye bright and open as that of a man who sees his destiny beckoning him forward fairer and fairer, more and more promising as he approaches.

The colour was very deep in Mary's cheek, and her eyes were fastened to the ground while he drew near, yet she stole a good look at him somehow, too, or she would not have been a woman. What she saw might have satisfied even her fastidious taste.

Darnley was very tall and slim, but his limbs were so well-proportioned, his hands and feet so small and beautifully shaped, that his excessive height only gave him an air of peculiar grace and distinction above ordinary men. Even in the riding-dress of the period, though we may be sure that the handsome young noble wore one of the richest material, and of the most tasteful fashion such a costume allowed, he betrayed those habits of refinement almost bordering on coxcombry, which, when they accompany a fine manly person, have such an attraction for the other sex. All the details of his toilet had been carefully attended to before he started, and disordered as he now was, at least on his exterior, nature had written *gentleman* in characters that could not be mistaken. Alas! that her pen can sometimes only trace skin deep.

His face, too, was in accordance with the high-bred beauty of his form. The line of features was soft and delicate as a woman's, the dark eyes shone out soft and tender from beneath a pair of pencilled eyebrows, the dark hair clustered in silken curls round a fair and open brow, pure and unruffled in the calm spring-time of youth, and though the mouth was that of a voluptuary rather than a hero, the small teeth were so white and regular, the lips so full and red, that, had it not been for the down beginning to shade its contour, it might have belonged to a girl. The whole countenance would indeed have been too effeminate, but for a bold sparkle in the eye, which corresponded well with the manly proportions of the frame.

The subject was not half so much abashed as the sovereign. Darnley advanced confidently up the hall, then kneeling before the Queen and kissing the hand she tendered him, he looked boldly in her face and asked leave to deliver certain packets with which he was charged from his mother and kinsfolk.

'But your mails have not yet arrived, my lord,' said Mary. 'You have outridden your retainers; you are the only one of your party who hath yet reached us here in our hiding-place beyond the Firth.'

She stopped in some embarrassment, unwilling that Darnley should learn how much his coming had been looked for and his arrival watched.

'I have them with me here, your Grace,' answered he, producing at the same time a packet from his bosom. 'I would trust my Queen's letters to no hands but my own, although to remind me of her I do not need to carry them next my heart.'

He dropped his voice at the latter part of his sentence, but looked her boldly in the face while he spoke, as if to mark the effect of his words. Boy as he was, he knew well how to woo a woman already, and had not been slow to learn that the reticence of true affection is the worst auxiliary in the world. He had studied his own motto to some advantage this adventurous young suitor, and now or never was the time to say—

'Avant, Darnlé,
D'arrière jamais.'

So he kissed the fair hand once more that took the packet from his own, and added—

'None of my servants can be here for hours, madam, and I have dared to appear before your Majesty all disordered and travel-stained. May my rudeness stand excused in the ardour of my desire to see the beauty which now dazzles me so that I can hardly look upon it, and my loyal anxiety to obey the commands of my mistress and my Queen? Am I forgiven, madam? 'Tis said that "a lady's face should show grace".'

'And well it might, to such a face as yours,' *thought* the Queen; but she only answered a few words of commonplace courtesy; bidding her cousin rise from his knees, and affected to busy herself in the packet of letters she had just received,—for Mary was again blushing deeply, and not unwilling to hide her confusion, in the task she had thus set herself. Truth to tell, though she had hitherto been so impervious to flattery, the words she had just heard were stealing their way very softly and pleasantly to her heart.

Seeing her thus occupied, Darnley proceeded to pay his compliments with graceful ease to the attendant ladies, finding time to note in his own mind their respective attractions, and to discover that Mary Seton was the most to his taste of all the four.

After a while, and it may be, somewhat disturbed in her studies by the merry voice of her gay suitor, who came (such is the advantage of being young) as fresh from his ride of so many hundred miles, as if he were lately out of bed, the Queen looked up, and with kindly courtesy bade him join them at the noon-day meal, then about to be served. The young courtier had the good taste to excuse himself, pleading the want of proper attire in which to meet Her Majesty at table, and reflecting in his own mind that he could satisfy the hunger which he now began to feel so keenly more comfortably alone. He saw too that he had made an agreeable impression, and wisely determined to give it time to work. So he asked permission to wait on his sovereign at supper instead, and retired to refresh himself in private, and curse the delay of his servants, whom he expected hour by hour, with some portion of his baggage.

It may easily be imagined that in the seclusion of Wemyss Castle, such an event as the arrival of a guest like Darnley created no small amount of excitement and conversation. Doubtless every point in his doublet, every hair of his head, was thoroughly discussed and criticised, in kitchen, buttery, and hall. The rumour spread like wild-fire through the Castle that this dashing springald was a suitor for the hand of the bonny Queen.

'Set him up!' as the Scottish lower orders say when they opine that the aspirant is hardly worthy of the prize. Nevertheless the young lord's height, appearance, and easy manners had already won him golden opinions of those who judge chiefly by the eye, and when he had finished the best part of a capon, and a goodly stoup of Bordeaux for his breakfast, the old seneschal delivered himself of the opinion that 'the youth was a bonny lad, an' a fair-spoken—forbye bein' a Stuart himsel', an' no that far off frae him that lies out bye yonder at Flodden!'

Had there been any dissentients, an allusion to their favourite hero, James IV., would at once have brought them over to an agreement with the majority.

But in Mary Stuart's bower the engrossing theme was canvassed with considerably less freedom. The Queen herself was restless and ill at ease, constrained in manner and reserved in conversation. Mary Carmichael was absent on certain household duties; Mary Hamilton seldom opened her pale lips now, save at matins or vespers, when she poured from them such floods of melody as if she were indeed an angel from that heaven to which she was so obviously hastening; Mistress Beton had been too long a courtier ever to broach a fresh topic of conversation, or indeed to give an opinion frankly upon any subject whatsoever—moreover, she had no means of learning what Randolph said to all this, and she felt somewhat at a loss to form her own ideas without the assistance of her false English lover; Mary Seton alone led the charge bravely, by asking the Queen point-blank what she thought of her young kinsman.

'Nay,' replied Her Majesty, with a smile, 'you would not have me give an opinion after a five minutes' interview. The *outside* methinks is of fair promise; at least, if "all be good that be upcome."'[11]

[11] A Scotch saying, equivalent to the converse of our 'Ill weeds grow apace.'

'Aye, he's well enough to look at,' answered the young lady, with the air of a consummate judge. 'Long and small, even and straight; a proper partner for a galliard, and, I should say, would grace velvet doublet and silken hose better than steel corslet and plumed head-piece. But *my* choice, now, would be something sterner, stronger, rougher altogether; something more of a *man*; like stout Earl Bothwell, for instance!'

The Queen started as if she had been stung, and answered angrily—

'How mean ye? The one is a loyal and accomplished gentleman, the other a brawling swordsman and a traitorous rebel.'

'A woman might have worse help at her need than the Lord Warden in jack and morion, with a score of those daring borderers at his back,' retorted the staunch little partisan, following out, it may be, some wandering fancy of her own.

The Queen did not seem loth to pursue the subject.

'You were talking of looks,' said she, 'not sword-strokes; and Bothwell, at his best, was bronzed and marred and weather-beaten, and built more like a tower than a man.'

'That was exactly what I admired in him,' interposed the damsel; 'I even thought that scar over his eye became his face as it would have become none other.'

The Queen smiled once more, and resumed, in the tone of one who is looking far back into the past—

'He certainly had more of the warrior than the courtier in him, and doubtless he hath always done his part well and knightly in the field; I will do him that justice. Poor Bothwell! he must have been ill-advised indeed when he could refuse to obey *me*. I thought I could have trusted him if all Scotland besides had failed me. Well, well! all must be forgiven now—and forgotten.'

She spoke the last words in a melancholy tone, and each relapsed into silence, for both the Queen and her damsels seemed to have ample food for thought; so their fingers flew over the tapestry more nimbly than ever, and the work proceeded with extraordinary perseverance till supper-time.

But if Darnley had been pleasant to look at in his travel-stained riding-gear, the most fastidious eye must have admitted that he was indeed splendidly handsome when he appeared, prepared to perform the menial offices of the Queen's supper-table, clad in a suit of gorgeous apparel, cut in the newest fashion of the English Court. Refreshed with food and repose, sleek from the bath and perfumes of his toilet, radiant with hope and excitement, the young courtier stood before his sovereign probably the best dressed and the best looking man that day in her dominions.

After he had gone through the form of presenting Mary with the basin and ewer, which she declined, she bade him sit down at the same table with herself and her ladies, for the Queen disliked ceremony, and always dispensed with it in private to the utmost. Then did Lord Darnley strain every nerve to be agreeable, and with so partial an audience, it is needless to say, succeeded beyond his highest expectations. Skilled in those outward graces which make so good a show and are so effective in society, it was an easy task to him, even in the presence of royalty, to lead the conversation round to those topics on which he was best qualified to shine.

His descriptions of his journey, his humorous account of the difficulties he experienced in procuring horses at the different posts, with a covert allusion here and there to his impatience to get on, were listened to with laughter and interest by all—with rising colour and heaving breast by *one*; while in no circle probably of either kingdom could his graphic sketch of the English Court, with its petty intrigues and latest scandal, have been appreciated with such thorough zest and good-will.

It does not follow that Mary Stuart was displeased because she checked him when he mimicked her 'good sister' to the life, hitting, with a happy mixture of fun and malice, on some of the most prominent foibles and grotesque points in the character of 'good Queen Bess.'

Ere the ladies rose from table they had made up their minds that this new acquisition to their society was of unspeakable merit; and later in the evening, when they discovered that he could play and sing as well as he could talk, and that his leg and foot were as beautiful as his face and hand, Mary Seton had almost decided that such courtly graces as these were worth all the ruder virtues of a less accomplished gallant; and judging from her subsequent conduct, we may fairly conclude that Mary Stuart's opinion followed on the same side.

A few more days of the seclusion of Wemyss Castle, lightened by the lively talk and winning manners of the guest, served but to establish Darnley more securely in the good graces of his sovereign. The weather was of unexampled severity, and a deep snow prevented all attempts at out-door amusements, and especially forbade those field-sports in which Mary took such delight. The society of a handsome young gallant, fluent and accomplished, was not likely to be rated below its real value, when it represented the only amusement available to five such ladies as the Queen and her Maries, shut up in an old house during a snowstorm; and Darnley found he had free access at all hours of the day to their agreeable presence; but he had as yet enjoyed no opportunity of seeing Her Majesty alone. Mary, with her own good sense and womanly reserve, had resolved to judge for herself more at leisure ere she committed her happiness to the keeping of her possible husband, or encouraged him avowedly in his suit.

The young lord, however, impatient by disposition, and now reckless on principle, had resolved that this brief visit to the old seaside tower should determine his fate; he would never have such a chance again; and on the last day of Mary's sojourn at Wemyss Castle he made up his mind to hazard all upon the cast.

Darnley entertained few scruples of delicacy when he had an object in view. He chose the hour when Mary Hamilton was sure to be in an oratory which the Queen had temporarily fitted up, to get the three other ladies out of his way; a few gold pieces judiciously administered induced the venerable dame who charged herself with the domestic details of the Castle, to request the presence of Mistresses Beton and Carmichael on a visit of inspection to vast hoards of linen hid away in an old walnut-wood press; then seducing Mary Seton into the long gallery under pretence of a match at billiards, or *bilies*, as it was called, he coolly left the game unfinished and turned the key upon that young lady, who found herself, somewhat to her dismay, a prisoner in a remote apartment of the Castle without the slightest prospect of escape. Chance, too, further favoured his designs, for a blink of sunshine had tempted the Queen out upon the battlements, and he found her there alone looking wistfully across the Firth towards the southern shore.

We are no eavesdroppers on the courtships of royalty. Turn after turn Mary Stuart paced up and down those leads, and still Darnley urged and argued and gesticulated, and still his fair companion blushed and listened and shook her head. That the interview was not entirely without results, Mary Seton gathered from what she witnessed at its conclusion. She had been released from durance by a domestic who happened to be passing the door of the gallery, and hastened immediately to excuse her absence to her Mistress. As she approached the battlements, Darnley was offering the Queen a ring, with every appearance of eagerness and agitation; and although the latter obviously declined the gift, it was with a kindliness and an embarrassment that made the refusal tantamount to an acceptance.

'For *my* sake,' said Darnley, imploringly, 'your subject, your vassal, your slave for ever!'

'Not yet,' murmured the Queen, in answer; and although she spoke very low, her whisper reached the keen ears of the attentive maid-of-honour.

As Darnley left the presence he did not stop to apologise to Mary Seton for their unfinished match. His colour was high, his eye was very bright, there was an air of joyous triumph in his whole aspect and bearing; perhaps he was quite satisfied in his own mind that he had won the game.

CHAPTER XXXIII

'We'll hear nae mair lilting at the ewe-milking,

Women and lasses are heartless and wae,

Sighing and moaning on ilka green loaning

The flowers of the forest are all wede away.'

The Court was now established at Stirling, and a very dull and melancholy Court it was. The visit at Wemyss Castle had indeed borne ample fruit; but as if there was some fatality hanging over Mary Stuart's head, the days of courtship which, with most women, form such a happy era in life, were fraught for her with much annoyance, vexation, and distress. Though she had listened coyly at first to her handsome young suitor, she had not prohibited him from broaching the agreeable subject again; and by the beginning of April Lord Darnley was known to the whole of Scotland as the accepted lover of the Queen. It is needless to dwell upon the confusion created by such an announcement at the different Courts of Europe, where her marriage had been made the subject of endless intrigue and diplomacy, nor the access of ill-humour which it produced in Elizabeth, who could never make up her mind as to the exact manner in which she should treat her cousin. Cecil was sharply reproved for not having earlier foreseen so probable a contingency; Randolph received a rap over the knuckles for his tardiness in forwarding the disagreeable intelligence; and Lady Lennox, for no graver offence than that of being Darnley's mother, was committed to the Tower.

In Scotland, the popular opinion was in favour of the match, although the vulgar, with their usual love for the marvellous, affirmed that their Queen's affections had been gained by magic arts; the favourite rumour being that Darnley had presented Her Majesty with an enchanted bracelet, made by the famous sorcerer Lord Ruthven, who had shut himself up fasting for nine days and nights for the purpose, and finished it off in so short a space of time with no assistance but that of the arch-fiend, his fellow-workman.

The spell, however, which the lover had cast upon his mistress was probably stronger than anything likely to result from the black art, originating as it did in beauty of person, charm of manner, and above all, the sympathetic attraction of young blood. That they had plighted their troth to one another was only to be presumed from the intimacy the Queen permitted him, and the obvious delight she experienced in his society.

Randolph was puzzled. He was fain to have some certain intelligence to convey to Cecil; and, although he had thoroughly sounded Mary Beton, who was beginning to get tired of attentions which never became more definite, he suffered no opportunity to escape him of watching the affianced pair.

The Court, we have said, was dull and melancholy. Darnley, stretched on a sick bed with an attack of measles, was sedulously attended by the Queen. His illness shed a gloom over the royal household, and Randolph was nearly satisfied in his own mind that the marriage was as good as concluded. He resolved, nevertheless, to place his suspicions beyond a doubt.

It was a sunshiny day in April, and the diplomatist knew that he was likely to see Mistress Beton on the southern terrace of the Castle about noon. He awaited her there accordingly, with a great affectation of anxiety and agitation. The lady, on the contrary, looked three inches taller than usual, and was as cold as ice.

'I have longed to see you, fair madam,' said the courtly gentleman; 'there is no sunshine for me where Mistress Beton is not, and I pine like some tropical bird for the reviving warmth of her smiles.'

The comparison seemed a little ridiculous, as she contemplated 'the bird,' dressed with scrupulous attention, in the extremity of the mode, and wearing an enormous ruff. She smiled somewhat scornfully, as she replied —

'You seem to keep your plumage marvellously sleek in the shade.'

'The bird seeks its mate,' answered he, laughing good-humouredly; 'and the two-legged creatures here below, like the fowls of heaven, always wear their gaudiest feathers in the pairing season. Mistress Beton, the cage-door is open at last, and you are now free. Is it not so?'

He took her hand while he spoke, and pressed it warmly, but she released it with an impatient gesture, and answered angrily —

'What mean you, Master Randolph? My freedom is not dependent upon *you*, I trow; nor do I see in what manner it concerneth you. I pray you, sir, let go my hand!'

'Nay, but is it not true that the Queen-bird hath chosen her mate?' he proceeded affectionately, and determined not to be affronted, at least not yet. 'In plain English, or rather in your pretty Scotch, tell me truth, fair Mistress Beton: this Queen of yours hath given her consent to her kinsman, and the maidens are released from their vow?'

'I am not here to tell my mistress's secrets,' answered the lady, none the less severely that her conscience reminded her she had not always been so discreet. 'Surely Master Randolph can get information more reliable than mine, or he hath indeed lived in ignorance for long!'

She was thinking that he had of late neglected her shamefully; but although his quick ear detected much of pique in her tone, there was so little affection in it, that he determined to alter his tactics, but warily, of course, and by degrees.

'You are offended with me, Mistress Beton,' said he, in a quiet, mournful voice, 'and therefore you are pitiless. Well, you will know better hereafter, perhaps when it is too late. I have but remained at this Court for the sake of others, and now it is time that I was gone. You must yourself know that my position here has been a false and delicate one: I am looked on coldly by your Queen; I am an object of jealousy and distrust to this new favourite of hers; I am continually reproached by my own employers for betraying too strong a bias towards the Scottish interest; and, worse than all, those whose good opinion I most value, and for whose sake I have lost so much, turn upon me at the last, and seem determined to fall out with me, whether I will or no. But it takes two to make a quarrel, Mistress Beton, and I am resolved not to be one. Farewell! we part friends. Is it not so?'

A woman could hardly resist such an appeal from a man whom she had once cared for, if ever so little. She gave him her hand frankly, of her own accord this time, and murmured a few commonplace expressions of leave-taking and good-will.

Randolph bowed over the hand he held, and drew a rare jewel from his doublet.

'You will accept this from me as a keepsake,' said he, coldly and courteously; 'perhaps you will look on it sometimes, and think of me more kindly when I am gone.'

It was a large gold locket, in the form of a heart, suspended from two clasped hands, richly ornamented with precious stones, and of a peculiar and fanciful device. Mary Beton started when she set eyes on it.

'Where did you get that?' she exclaimed, completely thrown off her guard. 'It belongs to the Queen!'

Randolph owned one peculiarity: he never smiled when he was really pleased, but had a trick of half shutting his eyes when he considered he had the best of the game; he looked as if he held a trump card now, while he answered quietly—

'That is surely mine own which I have fairly won. Lord Darnley paid me with that trinket in lieu of the fifty gold pieces he lost, when you and I beat Her Majesty and himself so handsomely at billiards the day before he was taken ill. I never thought the house of Lennox was overburdened with money, yet I can hardly believe its fortunes are at so low an ebb, that its heir must pay his debts with his love tokens.'

'It *is* so, nevertheless,' said Mary Beton, indignantly. 'It was the Queen's locket, and I saw her give it him with loving words, a thousand times more precious than the gift. Out upon him! a false knight! a recreant! I would have pawned my doublet first!'

Randolph had learned all he wanted to know. With a few kind phrases he soon took his leave of his companion, hurrying off, we may be sure, to convey the result of his inquiries without delay to his Court. It was not till he had been gone several minutes that Mary Beton cooled down sufficiently to reflect how indiscreetly she had suffered herself to be surprised, and how very unsatisfactory had been hitherto her dealings and relations with the English Ambassador.

The Maries were indeed all in trouble now, more or less. Here was their leader, the lady who expected them to look up to her for counsel and example, awaking to a sensation the most galling perhaps that can be experienced by the female heart—that of having been cozened out of its affections by one who has given nothing in return. In one way or another we all of us go on playing silver against gold all our lives through, but it is not in human nature to have this humiliating truth thrust upon its notice without vexation. Mary Beton fairly ground her white teeth together when she thought how near she had been to loving Mr Randolph very devotedly, and how that astute gentleman had been making a cat's-paw of her all through, never so much as burning the tips of his own fingers the while. It was an aggravation to reflect on Ogilvy's honest nature, and the sincere homage she had spurned for the sake of one so much inferior in every manly quality to the frank-hearted soldier. And now Ogilvy was absent from the Court, and perhaps consoling himself for her unkindness in the smiles of another. Well, he would come back again; and it would go hard but she would resume her sway, if once she turned her mind to it, and was really determined to try.

A woman's spirit is tolerably elastic. We may say of it, as Horace says of the shipwrecked merchant, 'mox reficit rates;'—the bark may have had awful weather to encounter, have lost spars, and masts, and tackle by the fathom, perhaps damaged her screw, and sustained one or two very awkward bumps against a shoal—never say die! she puts in hopefully to refit, jury-masts are rigged, fresh canvas bent, leaks carefully stopped, and damages repaired; the first fine day she launches forth to sea again, almost as good as new.

But there are some exceptions that cannot thus recover, some natures to whom one keen disappointment of the affections is a moral death-blow; nay, there are rare cases in which such a wound is physically fatal. Mary Hamilton had never been like the same woman since Chastelâr's death. With a pale cheek and a languid step she went about her duties indeed as usual, but the light of her life seemed to be gone, and the only time a smile ever crossed that beautiful sad face was when, in the exercise of her devotions, the soul seemed to assert its superiority over the body, and to lift itself out of this earthly darkness into the 'everlasting day' beyond. Everyone who came about Mary Hamilton seemed to acknowledge the refining influence of a spirit thus purified by suffering. The fiercest barons, the rudest men-at-arms felt softened and humanised while in her presence, and James Geddes the fool, after sitting gazing into her face for hours together, would break into a succession of such unearthly moans as subjected him to the discipline of the porter's lodge forthwith.

Lively Mistress Seton was losing somewhat of her spirits and her elasticity. The laugh was no longer so frequent, though it might ring out at times as saucily as ever, and the step, though light and buoyant still, had acquired a more sober and regular tread as she went upon Her Majesty's errands through the gloomy passages of Stirling Castle. The young lady was learning to think. In her heart she did not thoroughly approve of this proposed match on which the Queen was now so bent, and considered Lord Darnley, with all his outward advantages and accomplishments, by no means good enough for her dear mistress. Mary Seton had seen through him at once, as a woman often does, and detected under that fair outside the frivolous disposition, the reckless passions, and the utter want of heart beneath. If she had given her honest opinion, she would have said Bothwell was worth a dozen of him, and his big henchman, a hundred.

And what of Mary Carmichael? Proud, self-reliant, and undemonstrative, she was the last person on earth to have admitted that any anxiety or disappointment of her own could have deprived her cheek of one shade of colour, or dimmed her eye of one ray of brightness, and yet beautiful Mary Carmichael was losing day by day much of that brilliant freshness which had constituted no small portion of her beauty, and went about mournfully and in heaviness, as one who suffered keenly from some secret sorrow; yet the stranger who used to meet her in the garden at Holyrood had been seen at Stirling, and his clandestine interviews with the fair maid-of-honour had been of late more frequent than usual. If she was the happier for them, her appearance strangely belied her.

Yes, the Court was very dull now. Darnley was on a sick bed, and Mary and her maidens were in trouble, one and all.

CHAPTER XXXIV

'"Fear ye nae that," quo' the laird's Jock,
"A faint heart ne'er won a fair ladie;
Work thou within, we'll work without,
And I'll be sworn we'll set thee free."'

Our worthy friend, 'Dick-o'-the-Cleugh,' seemed strangely altered as he rode back into Liddesdale. A moody man was Dick, and a silent; no longer the jovial comrade and 'devil-may-care' trooper that the other jackmen had heretofore known him, but a sulky and captious fellow-traveller, an abrupt and peremptory martinet. The borderer was beginning to find that he had a conscience, and to discover how unpleasant are the remonstrances of that monitor when displeased. His heart smote him sorely while he reflected on the part he had been compelled to play with regard to Maxwell, a man whose whole character had inspired him with admiration and respect, in whom also, as a constant frequenter of the Court, he took an affectionate interest that he did not care to analyse. And now he had lured this frank and friendly soldier into a trap from which it was doubtful if he would escape with life. The towers of Leslie were thick and lofty, and well-guarded; the retainers of Rothes noted, like their chief, for an unscrupulous recklessness and defiance of all consequences. What chance for the naked prisoner in such a stronghold? Those damp and gloomy vaults could keep a secret well. It needed no outrage, neither steel nor poison, to silence an inmate for ever. The jailer had but to forget a small black loaf, neglect to fill a shallow cruse of water, and who would ever chronicle the prisoner's agonies in a torturing, lingering death? 'Dick-o'-the-Cleugh' turned sick and faint at the thought.

He had ample leisure to indulge these painful fancies, for the rapidity with which Maxwell had been conveyed into Fife necessitated a slow return, even on the same powerful horses that carried the men-at-arms of Earl Bothwell. Ere the weary animals pricked their ears to welcome the towers of Hermitage, Dick had come to a resolution which neither discipline nor loyalty would have tempted him to abandon. His comrades, more astonished than irritated at the change in one whom they had been accustomed to consider the very pattern of a moss-trooper, shook their heads, and whispered one another that 'muckle Dick was *fey*,' signifying *doomed,*—it being an old Scottish superstition that any sudden and complete change in the disposition of an individual denotes an early death. When Dick sat silent among the wassailers below the salt, and passed the black flagon untasted by, many a roistering associate looked a thought graver for the moment, as he pictured his old comrade stretched upon the heather, with the pale gleam of death upon his face, and a 'false Southron's' lance through his body, a thought graver perhaps, for an instant, till a coarse jest or a fresh draught of ale brought him back to the gross and the material once more.

Hermitage Castle was no lightsome residence now. But for the return of military duties and the clang of arms at stated intervals in the court, it might have been a college or a monastery, so rarely was the voice of merriment heard within its walls. No more hawking and hunting now. The drawbridge had not been lowered, nor the portcullis raised, since Moray took his departure with his solemn smile, following wild Rothes and his spearmen at half-a-day's interval, and leaving the lord of the castle in a mood of such stern and sullen defiance as caused the boldest of his retainers to shrink instinctively from his path. It seemed like another life, that they used to lead long ago,—dashing out in the dewy mornings with hawk on hand and hound at heel, or winding warily away in warlike order at set of sun for a moonlight foray on the Southern side. The rude spearmen consoled themselves with great meals of beef and floods of ale, but the henchman's platter often remained untouched, his cup unfilled, whilst the lord of the castle himself spent whole days of solitude in his own chamber, walking out at sunset to the northern rampart, where he would pace up and down for hours, far into the night.

His good angel had abandoned Bothwell at last, yet the spirit had left a gleam of his presence, a fragrance from its wings, about him still. Fast in the toils of unscrupulous Moray, the earl could yet look back with a painful longing to the days when he was a loyal subject and a devoted knight to his beautiful Queen. At times he would be tempted to forego ambition, pride, revenge, consistency, everything but his wild unreasoning affection, and, galloping to Holyrood or Stirling, fling himself at Mary's feet, entreat her to forgive him, and pledge himself, if it would make her happier, that he would never see her face again. Yes, there were moments when the proud, strong man felt he would ask no more welcome relief than to bow his head and pour his heart out like a woman in tears before his Queen; but then he thought of Darnley's youthful beauty, and Darnley's mocking smile—of the path that was still open to himself if he would crush all such foolish weaknesses, all such exaggerated notions of chivalry and forbearance. The fiend, who is always at hand with his temptations, if a man gives him the least encouragement, whispered in his ear that *nothing* is impossible to one who has no scruples, and who will ungrudgingly risk all; that when honour, honesty, faith, and humanity are but rated as flimsy superstitions to bind weak intellects, and crime itself is considered simply as an untoward necessity or a decisive manœuvre, the will becomes all-in-all, and the master-spirit, that can *dare* boundlessly and unflinchingly, may aspire to the fulfilment of its boldest wishes and its wildest dreams. Bothwell, too, had been brought up in no precise or scrupulous school. In his adventurous career on the North Sea, many a scene of bloodshed and rapine had come under his notice, and one who had accustomed himself to direct those predatory descents on the Danish coast, which were but authorised acts of piracy after all, was not likely to entertain much compassion for a woman's shriek or a man's death-groan. It would have been no shrinking from bloodshed that could have deterred Bothwell from any scheme on which he had once thought well to enter.

Moray, too, had got the Earl completely in his hands. That wary statesman, in whom the *suaviter in modo* seems to have been admirably combined with the *fortiter in re*, had the peculiar faculty of acquiring unbounded influence over his associates, a power sometimes observable in the calm impassive nature which never betrays its own feelings. Whatever might be the plot on which he was engaged, how high soever ran the waves through which the base-born Stuart steered his bark, not a shade of trepidation was to be detected on his quiet brow during its voyage, not a gleam of satisfaction when he had landed his cargo safely in port. It may be that men felt, so long as their interests were identical, they could *trust* Moray not to betray himself or them. It may be that, though sadly warped to evil, his was a superior nature, born to command. Whatever was the cause, no intriguer could be more plausible, no party-leader more successful.

And Bothwell, eager, hot-headed, vain, perhaps even romantic, was a mere child in the hands of such a man as this. What could avail the bluff straightforward courage of the swordsman against the diplomatic *finesse* of the equally bold but far more subtle statesman? It was the old story of the long sweeping sabre against the delicate rapier skilfully handled. The broad blade whistles through the air with mighty strokes that would serve to cleave a head-piece or to lop a limb, but ere it can descend amain, the thin line of quivering steel has wound its sinuous way under the guard and through the joints of the harness, and is drinking the streams of life-blood from the heart. Earl Bothwell was bound hand and foot to the half-brother of his Queen.

All these intrigues and vexations goaded the warden to the verge of madness. He could scarce bear to be noticed, much less addressed, by his retainers; and it was with a fierce oath and a savage glare that he accosted his henchman when the latter ventured to interrupt his solitary walk, one summer's evening, on the northern rampart.

The stars were coming out one by one in the soft twilight sky, and the warden paced moodily to and fro, looking ever and anon wistfully towards the north.

'What lack ye, man, in the fiend's name?' exclaimed the earl, angrily. 'Must every knave that clears a trencher come into my presence unbidden? Silence, varlet, and begone!'

But Dick, too, had a sore heart and a perplexed brain, a combination which renders a man somewhat careless of outward observances. He was not to be daunted, even by the displeasure of his chief, and he answered doggedly in return—

'I'll no be silent when it's for the laird's honour that I suld speak! Oh! Bothwell, man, me an' mine has served you an' yours ever sin' Scotland was a kingdom, I'm thinkin'. Will ye no hear me speak the day?'

Dick's voice shook when he alluded to his feudal services. Stern as the giant looked, he was hoarse and trembling with emotion. Something in the warden's breast responded to the appeal of his retainer, and he answered with assumed impatience—

'Say your say, man, in the devil's name, who seems to be commanding officer here; out with your report, if report it be, and have done with it.'

'I wad wage my life for you, Bothwell, and that ye ken fine,' replied Dick, with something almost like tears shining in his eyes. 'I wadna grudge to shed every drop of bluid I hae, just to keep ye frae watting your foot. It's no danger, an' it's no disgrace, an' it's no death that wad daunton *me* frae doing the laird's bidding. No, no, "Dick-o'-the-Cleugh" and Dick's forbears ha' eaten the Hepburn's bread and drunk frae the Hepburn's cup ower lang for the like o' that. But it's just rackin' my heart to think o' yon lad in the donjon-keep at Leslie, and him breaking bread in the Hepburn's hall, and setting his trust on the Hepburn's honour. And to think o' the like o' me pittin' his feet in the fetters and his craig in a tow; I wish my hands had rotted off at the elbows first!'

'What would you have, man?' said his chief, somewhat less impatiently than the henchman had expected. ''Tis a mettled gallant, I grant ye, and a far-off kinsman of my own. What, then? A soldier must take his chance; 'tis but the fortune of war.'

'An' whan the leddies speir for their messenger at Holyrood, an' the bonny Queen hersel cries, "Ou, he's safe enough, I trusted him to Bothwell;" how will we look if ever we come lilting into the Abbey-yard, and can give no tidings of our guest?'

The warden's brow softened, although he seemed considerably perplexed.

'I would he were safe back again, Dick,' replied he, 'I care not who knows it; but Rothes has a firm grip, and he would like well to make favour with Moray, even though he should disoblige *me*. I wish poor Walter may not be in a prison from which there is no breaking, at this present speaking. Aye, Dick! times are changed since my father's day. Earl Patrick, now, if he had wanted anything from the proudest baron in Scotland, would have gone and taken it with a hundred riders at his back.'

Dick snapped his fingers in great glee. He was reading his chieftain's thoughts as he would have read the track of a herd of cattle driven but yesterday into Cumberland.

'It wadna tak' a hundred men,' said he, exultingly, 'to lift the plenishing of Leslie Hoos itsel', though it were garrisoned with a' the loons in Fife. I wad but ask for Ralph Armstrong and "Lang Willie," an' maybe Little "Jock-o'-the-Hope," to bring awa' Maister Maxwell in a whole skin, gin he lay in the heart o' Carlisle jail!'

'It might not be a bad ploy for some of our lads,' answered Bothwell, with rather a fierce smile. 'Horses get fat and men lazy cooped up here within four gray walls, and I might require man and horse in proper trim before long. Hark ye, Dick! if ye want to go northward for some ten days or so, I shall not ask ye where ye have been at your return. No thanks! leave me, man! If it come to blows, that long body o' yours can take care of itself.'

For the next hour or two 'Dick-o'-the-Cleugh' looked like a different person as he busied himself preparing man and horse for a march that he determined should commence at nightfall. When the sun had set, and the earl, after deeper potations than ordinary, had retired from his habitual walk on the rampart, his henchman and three companions rode steadily out of the castle-yard, followed by many inquiring looks from their comrades, who, heartily wearied of their forced inaction, beheld with strong feelings of envy the departure of the little cavalcade. It consisted but of four individuals, nevertheless it would have been difficult among all Lord Bothwell's retainers to have selected a more efficient-looking *quartette*. With the exception of 'Dick-o'-the-Cleugh' himself, Ralph Armstrong was esteemed the most powerful man in Liddesdale; he was a stolid-looking fellow, too, with considerable mother-wit concealed under a composure that nothing could ruffle, and a courage that nothing could daunt. 'Lang Willie,' again, was an exceedingly voluble and amusing companion, chiefly distinguished for his extraordinary skill as a swordsman, and the readiness and coarseness of his repartees. Little 'Jock-o'-the-Hope,' so called simply because he was the youngest of the party, was an active, limber, powerful fellow, with all the mettle of his twenty summers and the sagacity of twice his age.

With such a following, and a moonless night in his favour, Dick would have been nothing loth to lay a wager that he would cross the Southern Border, and take Lord Scrope by the beard.

They rode all night merrily enough; steadily though, and careful not to distress their horses. As they neared the capital, Dick's spirits rose visibly, and his comrades could not but remark on his resumption of his old habits of good-fellowship; but at daybreak an incident occurred which cast a gloom over the henchman's superstitious nature, and plunged him once more into that gloomy taciturnity which was so foreign to his real disposition.

It was in the gray of the dawn. Dick was riding at the head of the party, who followed in single file, for the tract lay through some boggy and broken ground in which two horses could not go abreast. Suddenly a hare that had been cropping the dank herbage thus early, stole into the path in front of them, and leaped slowly along under the very nose of the henchman's charger. This, although an untoward omen, was too common an occurrence to create alarm. There was an established *formula* for all such cases made and provided. Though too good a Protestant to cross himself, Dick repeated the customary charm with edifying gravity; but, as though in defiance, the hare still kept on in front of them. At three different angles in the path she hesitated, seeming about to turn off to right or left, and then hopped slowly on in the direction they were travelling. The stout borderers grew pale. It was even proposed that they should retrace their steps and abandon the enterprise; but Dick suggested that as he was the person immediately in front, his must be the entire risk, and the warning must be especially intended for him. The others were well satisfied to take this view of the matter, and presently they were discoursing as blithely as before; but their leader felt a depression of spirits creeping over him, which he strove in vain to overcome, and as the gloom gathered darker and darker about him, he felt in the depths of his rude nature that presentiment of coming death, which, let philosophers say what they will, is no unusual precursor of the final catastrophe.

His past life comes back to him with strange vividness as he rides silently on. His father's rude gray tower at the head of the glen; the sunny, grassy nook, where he used to play, by the shallow burn, with five sturdy urchins like himself, and one golden-haired brother, whom they missed at last from amongst them, and told each other in awed whispers, looking up at the sky the while, how 'Willie was gone to heaven.' Till to-day he had almost forgotten the gleam of his father's broadsword, and the caresses of a gentle, care-worn woman who used to hush him to sleep with low plaintive songs. He remembers, too, with peculiar distinctness, that first ride on the tall bay gelding, and the mimic lance with which he drove his imaginary foray.

These early memories are clearer to him now than many a real scene of plunder and bloodshed in which he knows he has since taken too much delight, but his devotion to his chief is as intense as ever, albeit dashed with something of a melancholy tenderness that seems unnatural, and derogatory to both.

Another figure, too, comes flitting across the borderer's mental sight—a figure that is seldom long absent from his dreams either by day or night—a figure that he dares to dwell on now for the first time these long weeks past without shame, because he feels that he is about to vindicate his loyalty to all belonging to her, or to her Queen.

He can almost hear the ringing tones of her voice, can almost catch the flutter of her dress. Surely he is bewitched! Bewitched, or else irrevocably doomed to death. As he gathers a sprig of witch-elm and fastens it in his morion, he says to himself that if he is really to die, he should like to see Mary Seton just once again.

CHAPTER XXXV

'For this is love, and this alone,
Not counting cost, nor grudging gain,
That builds its life into a throne,
And bids the idol reign;

'That hopes and fears, yet seldom pleads,
And for a sorrow weakly borne
(Because it yields not words but deeds),
Can hide a gentle scorn;

'In pride and pique that takes no part,
Of self and sin that bears no taint,
The homage of a knightly heart
For a woman and a saint.'

The four borderers rode up the High Street of Edinburgh in the warm afternoon sun, and their leader, fortified doubtless by the sprig of witch-elm in his head-piece, and inspirited by his arrival at the Scotch capital, looked about him with the gleeful curiosity of a schoolboy on a holiday.

On any other occasion, though troops of armed horsemen were by no means a rare sight on the causeway, so well-mounted and stalwart a little party would have received their share of admiration; but to-day no man had eyes to spare for any other object than a brilliant group of foot-passengers surrounding two commanding figures, which neither their own nor any other country in Europe could have matched.

No more in widow's weeds, but bright and beautiful in all the freshness of her own charms, set off by the splendour of her dress, Mary Stuart walked by her young husband, the *beau ideal* of a monarch's bride: her husband *de facto* if not *de jure*, for a private marriage some weeks since in Riccio's apartments had united the destinies of the lovers, and paved the way for that public ceremony which should confer on the fortunate young noble the crown-matrimonial of Scotland.

Alas for Mary Stuart! even in those happy days of courtship, which for most women glow so brightly; immediately before and after the nuptial tie she was doomed to many anxieties and misgivings, originating in the ungovernable temper of the very man for whose sake she had braved Elizabeth of England's displeasure, affronted a large and powerful party of her subjects, perhaps even stifled and eradicated certain deep though unacknowledged memories in her own heart. Although with the utmost haste Darnley had been created Earl of Ross, he was dissatisfied that he had not been immediately raised to the Dukedom of Albany, and vented his displeasure in no measured language even on her from whose open hand he received all the benefits he enjoyed, and whose beauty alone, bending so tenderly over himself, should have commanded his entire allegiance.

Perhaps the Queen loved him none the worse for his petulance at first; perhaps it was not till long afterwards, when unlimited indulgence and increasing depravity had fostered the spoiled and wayward youth into a reckless and unfeeling profligate, that she may have contrasted Darnley's open insults and avowed indifference with the devotion of other worshippers, who, however faulty in many respects, had never failed in faith and loyalty towards *her*.

Darnley's exterior was indeed beautiful exceedingly, but it covered a disposition in which there were no brilliant qualities of the head to counterbalance the evil of the heart. The Earl of Ross was unfortunate in the possession of dishonesty without craft, indecision without foresight, and obstinacy without energy. Like a woman, he could not restrain his tongue; unlike a woman, he never knew the exact range and precision with which that organ is able to direct its shafts.

Even on his sick-bed at Stirling, when it was first obvious to him that he had won his way into his Sovereign's good graces, and that a little time and care could not but make the game his own,—even then, when it was essentially important to cement friendships and conciliate differences in every direction, he contrived to affront the two most formidable men in Scotland and purchase their enmity for life. To the Duke of Chatelhêrault, simply because he heard that nobleman was opposed to Her Majesty's immediate marriage, he sent his defiance from his sick-bed, not couched in the language of knightly courtesy, which shows a gracious respect even for a mortal foe, but threatening to 'knock his old pate as soon as he should be well enough.'

We may imagine how such a message would be received by one who boasted he was the proudest peer in Europe. But an observation he made concerning the Earl Moray, and which did not fail to reach the latter's ears, was even more ill-advised in its tendency and unfortunate in its results.

Scanning a map of Scotland, some one pointed out to him the vast estates of the Queen's half-brother, and the inconsiderate youth exclaimed hastily—

'This is too much by half!'

So untoward a remark was of course repeated to Moray, who received the information with his usual grave smile, and never made further allusion to it. So much the worse. He had forgotten it none the less for that, and it may be those half-dozen words one day cost Mary Stuart a husband and Scotland a king.

Meantime, who so brave in apparel or so *débonnaire* in demeanour as the young Lord Darnley? The eyes of all Edinburgh are upon him as he paces along so proudly by the side of their 'bonny Queen.' His dress, as it is fit, is one blaze of splendour; the materials indeed are unpaid for, and the jewels are mostly love-gifts from his Sovereign, yet they set off none the worse his lofty stature and his graceful form. The women look after him admiringly; the men's gaze is as usual riveted on the beautiful being who walks by his side. Mary Stuart has never shown to more advantage than to-day. It is not the stately folds of the damask dress, nor the delicate edging of scalloped lace, nor the rich mantle of glowing *cramoisie* that enthral the eyes in an irresistible spell; nor needs it that massive bracelet hanging from her shapely arm, which men say dark Lord Ruthven fabricated for a love-charm, with Satan standing over him while he worked, to account for Mary's influence; they need but to look on the bright smile and the deep, loving eyes turned in pride and tenderness upon her husband, and they feel in their inmost hearts that there is no witchery in all the lore of gramarye to equal the resistless power that lurks in a fond and trusting woman's face.

Darnley has turned back for an instant to exchange some light jest with one of the maids-of-honour; it must be of a strangely confusing nature to account for the vivid blush that has come over Mary Seton, dyeing her fair skin perfectly crimson from the roots of her hair to the hem of her bodice. 'Dick-o'-the-Cleugh,' riding up the street and watching intently the motions of the royal party, does not perceive it for the simple and somewhat paradoxical reason that, although he has been hoping to see her the whole way from Hermitage, no sooner has he caught her eye than his own glance is immediately withdrawn. He turns deadly pale, too, and the hand which guides his charger's rein trembles in every fibre; the good horse bends his neck and collects himself, expectant of some further indication after this unusual touch.

Perhaps, poor Dick, with all his courage, might have ridden on into Fife without more parley, so helpless and abashed had he suddenly become, but that the Queen's quick glance observed the cognisance of the Hepburn as he rode by, even recognised the tall retainer's face, and could have accosted him by name. There was a faint flush on Mary's brow as she stopped her company and bade the borderer approach. Dick was off his horse in an instant, and the courtiers could not but admire his magnificent form as he strode up to them in his clanging armour, manning himself for the effort, now he was in for it, with his natural audacity. Mary Seton did not fail to remark, with no displeased eye, that even Darnley, tall as he was, stood half a hand's-breadth lower than the henchman.

'What news from Hermitage, good fellow?' said the Queen, accepting Dick's awkward homage with gracious courtesy. 'How fares it with our Lord Warden yonder on the Marches? Mayhap he is coming northward with the main body, of which you are but the vanguard?'

She spoke with something of flutter and hurry that was scarce natural to her. Perhaps she wished the retainer to know that she bore his sullen lord no ill-will; perhaps she even expected her vassal to return to her feet in penitence and contrition; perhaps in her woman's heart, even now she could not but revert to the old times, when Bothwell's haste regarded neither pace nor horseflesh to gallop on far ahead of his following, only to be the first to kneel at his Queen's feet and touch the hem of her garment.

Dick answered stoutly, though in some confusion—

'The Laird's no ailing in body, Your Grace, though he wad be nane the waur to be whiles in the saddle a wee thing. The Hepburns' feet aye become steel stirrups better than velvet mules.[12] He's less wise-like than ordinar',' added Dick, with a shrewd glance in Her Majesty's face; 'but I'm thinkin' he'll bide in Liddesdale a whiley yet.'

[12] Slippers.

Mary laughed good-humouredly. It did not seem to displease her that Bothwell should be sullen and dispirited. Yet she bore him no grudge for it, obviously; rather the contrary.

'The Liddesdale lads are aye welcome at Holyrood,' said she frankly, and with the Scottish accent she knew how to assume so gracefully. 'Take a Stuart's word for it,' she added, giving him at the same time her hand to kiss, 'both for yourself and your chief.'

'Dick-o'-the-Cleugh' kissed the beautiful hand with the devotion of a worshipper to a saint; but his eyes wandered beyond the royal form and sought that of a lady in her train.

At this moment Darnley came up from behind and accosted the henchman with his usual overbearing assumption of manner.

'How now, whom have we here, my fair cousin?' said the young noble, flinging a contemptuous glance at the borderer. 'An ambassador from Limbo Castle, sometimes called Hermitage, by his crest! Accredited messenger from all the thieves and sorners in the Debateable Land. How ranges the price of good nags on the Border, knave? The nights are moonless just now, though they be something short; the droves should be coming in pretty fast from Cumberland.'

The moss-trooper's eye brightened.

'If it was Her Grace's wish,' said he, looking respectfully towards the Queen, 'we could bring the wale[13] o' the countryside up to Holyrood in a fortnight from this day. Lord Scrope rides a soar gelding,' he added, warming with the congenial subject, 'that steps as daintily as a bird lights on a bough. Forbye the colour would become rarely Her Grace's housings and foot-mantle. If I might make so bold, I wad engage he should be in Her Majesty's stable or he was weel missed at Warkworth. I wad send ain o' my lads back for him this very night!'

[13] Pick.

Darnley burst into a loud mocking laugh.

'A thorough moss-trooper,' he exclaimed, 'rider, jackman, plunderer, thief; call them what you will, they are all alike; fit followers of such a chief. Were I king of Scotland I would have the halters off the horses and put them on the men, and string them up in rows with this tall knave at their head, not forgetting his worthy master, the leader of the gang.'

The young man spoke in laughing boisterous accents that might be taken either for jest or earnest, but the borderer's face flushed dark-red, and the fingers of his left hand closed like a vice upon his sheathed sword.

'If ever you *are* king of Scotland,' said he, 'may ye die no less noble a death than him who lay by the Till, yon summer's evening, with the proudest an' the bauldest an' the best down about him like trees felled in a rank; and wha but the borderers sleepin', man by man, at gentle King James's feet! It sets a Scottish lord ill to speak again' them that keeps the Scottish line, an' warst of all a limber lad like your honour (no offence to ye), that's got soldier written on his brow, and swordsman marked on every yane o' his lang limbs.'

The compliment to his personal appearance, always an acceptable offering to Darnley, modified whatever he might have considered offensive in the henchman's plain-speaking. The Queen, too, who had listened to the colloquy with obvious displeasure and some uneasiness, now laid her hand on the arm of her consort and motioned him to proceed with their walk. The latter felt in his girdle for a couple of gold pieces, which were not, however, forthcoming, then with a careless laugh and a whisper in Riccio's ear, nodded insolently to the borderer, and passed on with Mary and her train.

One of these, however, lingered a few paces in the rear. Dick's face grew very pale once more when Mistress Seton turned back and accosted him with her own bright glance and her own merry smile.

'You are slow of speech,' said she, 'I know of old, though prompt in deed, and as true as the steel in your belt. Is it not so?'

His lips were white and dry. He could not answer in words, but his affirmative gesture was more convincing than a hundred oaths.

She laid her hand on his. Through the steel gauntlet that light touch thrilled in every vein and fibre of the giant.

'You will tell me the truth,' she proceeded. 'What of Walter Maxwell? We have had no tidings of him since the morning he rode away from Holyrood, weeks and months ago!'

It speaks well for Mary Seton's good nature that the subject uppermost in her mind was one which she believed so vitally affected the welfare of her friend. It was as much kindliness of disposition as female curiosity that riveted her attention on the borderer's reply.

Dick's face became a study of self-reproach and embarrassment while he related the treachery of which Walter had been the victim; neither concealing nor palliating his own share in the business, which seemed to himself the less black that it was taken in compliance with his chief's orders, and for which his listener either forgot or neglected to reprove him. It is impossible to take the same interest in other people's matters that we do in our own, and what a world of confusion we should have if the confidants and go-betweens in a love-affair were as much agitated as the principals.

Mary Seton heard him calmly enough, and then proceeded to interrogate him about Bothwell. The henchman's answers concerning his chief seemed to afford her matter both of surprise and gratification. The earl was evidently in a state of discomfort and restlessness that must be reported at once to the Queen, who had always betrayed extraordinary interest in everything connected with Hermitage or the Borders, and his rude follower seemed to have observed and analysed his feelings with a sagacity that must have been strangely sharpened by some influence from without.

If there was a more triumphant sparkle in Mary Seton's eye, a tinge of deeper colour on her cheek, as she reflected on the nature of that influence, who shall blame her? Was she not a woman; and is it not a woman's instinct, like a cat's, to tease and tantalise her prey to the utmost? Though the mouse be as big as an elephant, it is such fun to tempt him with the prospect of indulgence, or even liberty, and then sweep him irresistibly back again with one stroke of the cruel velvet paw.

Mary Seton smiled within herself, and felt twice as big as the great borderer trembling there before her. With a whole budget of news gained for her Sovereign, she reverted to the topic most interesting to her comrade.

'You think, then, that he is alive, though in close ward?' she asked. 'They are cruel folk, I have heard say, the "lightsome Leslies." I would poor Walter were safe out of their hands!'

Dick had found his voice at last:

'And safe he shall be!' was his reply, 'before another week has passed over his head. It may tak' time, an' it may tak' skill, an' it may tak' twa or three men's lives, but we'll ha' Maister Maxwell oot 'gin we ding doon Lesly itsel', an' mak' a low[14] that'll light up the twa Lommonds and the tae half o' the kingdom of Fife! That's what I'm here for now.'

[14] Flame.

She looked at him archly:

'Was that all that brought you to Edinburgh?' said she.

Again something seemed to choke the man-at-arms and prevent his reply. At last he spoke in a hoarse whisper—

'I was fain to see the Court once more—and the Queen-and—and—yersel', Mistress Seton! I'll no win back to Liddesdale, I'm thinkin'; but I'll tak' the brunt o' it bra' an' easy the noo, sin I've seen ye to wish ye farewell.'

Something in his tone so tender, so hopeless, and so respectful, touched the girl to the heart. She laid her hand once more in his, and he wrung it hard in his own strong fingers, but did not even presume to put it to his lips. Only as she turned away to join the Queen, a low stifled sob smote upon her ear, and looking back she beheld the borderer standing as if spell-bound on the spot where she had left him. The next moment he was in the saddle, and as he passed her moving up the street after the others, he detached the sprig of witch-elm from his morion and cast it at her feet ere he galloped off.

Mary Seton's eyes filled with tears while she picked it up, and Dick's honest heart would have leapt with joy, notwithstanding his forebodings, could he have seen her hide it away carefully and tenderly in her bosom. When she rejoined the royal party, Riccio's sharp countenance wore a look of curiosity, for his quick eye detected that she had been weeping; but the Queen called her to her side, and soothed and caressed her, speaking in gentle, loving tones, like a mother to a child.

CHAPTER XXXVI

'Oh! Espérance! Hope on! The fight
Is never lost while fight we may;
At home the hearth is shining bright,
Though yet unseen along the way:
And the darkest hour of all the night
Is that which brings us day.'

Long weeks of solitary confinement in a dungeon, dark and damp and dismal, nourished on bread and water, and cheered only by the periodical visits of an asthmatic jailer, appointed to that post because fit for nothing else, would destroy the courage of most men, as it would sap their bodily health and vigour. Walter Maxwell had need of all his strength of mind, all his natural qualities of bravery and endurance, to resist the influence of his imprisonment, ere he had spent many weeks in the strong room of Leslie House. This place of confinement, paved and walled with stone, lighted by but one window, narrow and iron-barred, communicated with a winding staircase, and a long gloomy subterranean passage terminating in a wicket, which opened on a pleasaunce and flower-garden. Prisoners might thus be smuggled in or out of the Leslies' stronghold without exciting observation; and unless the Lord of Rothes was much belied, this facility of ingress was used for a variety of purposes, foreign to its original object. On summer evenings, 'tis said, the flutter of a farthingale might sometimes be seen emerging from its dark recesses, while lighter steps and merrier voices than were likely to belong to a permanent prisoner echoed in the damp underground passage leading in and out of Leslie House. Under these circumstances, bars were sometimes left undrawn and locks unturned, nor was Walter ignorant of the occasional negligence in which lay his only chance of escape.

The old jailer, too, albeit short in temper as in wind, was not entirely destitute of compassion for a hungry and thirsty man. After the first fortnight, and when he found that his lord gave no orders for Maxwell to be starved to death, he brought him on rare occasions a morsel of venison, or even a flask of wine, mollified as it would seem by the courage and good-humour with which his charge bore the rigours of captivity.

Then old Ralph, as he was called, would sometimes put down his pitcher and his keys to remain for a few minutes' conversation, or what he considered such, being indeed a monologue on his own grievances, his own infirmities, and, when in high good-humour, his youthful prowess and general accomplishments. These occasional visits were as beneficial to Maxwell's moral condition as the meat and wine were to his physical man.

After a week or two without exchanging a word with a fellow-creature, the stupidest of companions is welcomed like an angel from heaven, the dreariest platitudes fall like spring showers upon a desert soil. Maxwell *really* rejoiced in the visits of his jailer, looking forward to them as the sole events of his long, uninteresting day, and old Ralph began to take a great pride and pleasure in the prisoner who greeted him so warmly, and showed himself such an accomplished listener. By degrees the warder became confidential, not to say indiscreet, though the last idea in his mind was to favour his prisoner's escape. Indeed he could not afford to part with him, and, little by little, Maxwell, with his energies aroused, and his intellects sharpened by the emergency of his case, made himself familiar with the arrangements of the castle, and the details, of which he hoped to take advantage at some future time.

The sensations of a prisoner enduring solitary confinement have been so often analysed and described, that it is needless to enlarge upon them here. Without some distant hope of escape, without some definite point for the mind to rest on, the infliction would become unbearable, and end probably in insanity. Maxwell, however, possessed one of those dogged, resolute dispositions, not uncommon amongst his countrymen, which, like iron at the forge, become only harder and harder the more heavily they are struck. From the first moment of his entrance, bound and blindfolded into the Leslies' stronghold, he had determined to escape. That he was not to be put to death he argued from the pains that had been taken to kidnap him; and the knowledge that 'Dick-o'-the-Cleugh,' notwithstanding his apparent treachery, was still his friend at heart, was a vague source of comfort and re-assurance. The hours, marked only by the shadows on the blank and dreary wall, were indeed long—oh! so long!—but the continued effort to keep mind and body in a condition to take advantage of any chance that might offer, served almost in lieu of an occupation and a pursuit.

The prisoner would force himself to pace the narrow limits of his cell for hours at a time, that he might not lose the wind and strength so necessary to that problematical flight which was the one fixed idea of his brain.

By degrees Walter observed that the precautions taken for his security became more and more relaxed. With all his senses sharpened by constant watching, he could hear the door, at the foot of the winding-stair which led to the subterranean passage, although carefully locked at sun-down, grating ajar on its hinges during the day, could detect the summer air stealing even to his remote dungeon, denoting that the door into the garden was also unfastened. By dint of constant attention he became satisfied at last that if he could but break out to the top of the stairs any time before nightfall during the summer afternoon, he might, at least, reach the garden without hindrance. Once there, though ignorant of the locality, he trusted to the chapter of accidents to make his escape into the open country beyond.

The first object was as far as possible to hoodwink Ralph, and that worthy's implicit confidence in the quiet demeanour of his charge would go far towards assisting him in his scheme; then, when the jailer was thrown completely off his guard, a bold stroke would effect at least the first stage of the project. We do not affirm that the idea of springing on his keeper, who, although armed, might have been overpowered by a younger and a stronger man, and beating out his brains with his own keys, did not present itself to Walter's mind, but such a measure was wholly repugnant to his character, and he resolved to attain freedom without shedding the blood of the old man who had mitigated, as far as he could, the rigour of his captivity.

By little and little the prisoner had discovered that no amount of outcry or disturbance in the dungeon could be heard without; of this he had satisfied himself by a series of experiments. This was always a step gained in the furtherance of his plan.

Fortunately for himself, also, Maxwell was a large-boned man, especially in the wrists. Every set of fetters in the castle had been successively tried on him and found too tight; so for a time he had been bound hand and foot with ropes; but on his complaining that these cut him, they had been withdrawn, and his limbs suffered to remain at liberty.

So all the fine summer days, when the June roses were blooming without, and the June grass growing, and the June birds singing on the tree, while within the rat and the spider were the only living creatures, and a green slime on the wall the only vegetable production, Maxwell was preparing his escape, and biding his time patiently for a favourable opportunity to put it in execution.

When Ralph used to bring his prisoner a draught of wine, he would sometimes, if in a particularly good humour, condescend to stay for a few minutes and help him to partake of it. On these occasions Maxwell, by a studiously quiet and even languid demeanour, contrived to throw his jailer completely off his guard.

One day he requested the wine might be left with him to cheer his solitude when his agreeable friend was gone; another time he complained of indisposition, but thought he might relish a cup towards nightfall. By degrees he collected a Scottish pint or so of strong red wine in a stone jar that he had begged might be applied to the purpose.

The weather was very hot; even in a dungeon its inmate could tell that the summer sun was glowing bright and fierce without. Old Ralph arrived, according to custom, with his prisoner's afternoon meal, and sat himself down on the stone floor like a man thoroughly overcome with his exertions.

'Take a draught of wine, man,' said Maxwell, pointing to the jar; ''t the coolest place in the castle here, and by St Andrew the prisoner hath the best of it to-day.'

The old man smiled grimly; then he took a hearty pull, as desired, and set the vessel down with a sigh of great satisfaction.

'An old man's bluid aye wants warmin',' said he, looking pensively into the vessel the while; 'but I've kent it far hotter ower sea. When I was in Flanders wi' Norman Leslie, ye ken;—aye! he was a wild lad, Norman, but a bra' soldier, fair sir, a bra' soldier as ever belted on a brand!—aweel, whan I was in Flanders wi' Norman——;' and forthwith the old man embarked upon a long story of which gallant Norman Leslie was the hero, moistening his narrative at frequent intervals with draughts of the strong red wine, and Maxwell watched with strung nerves and beating heart, how his eye grew dimmer and his speech more laboured as the tale progressed and the contents of the vessel waned.

Nevertheless the door was locked on the inside, and the jailer's fingers kept an instinctive grasp upon his keys. Once, catching Maxwell's eye fixed on these implements, he shifted them suddenly into the hand farthest from his prisoner, although in the act he interrupted himself in an elaborate description of a certain blue velvet surcoat, by which Norman Leslie set much store, and did not again recover the thread of his recollections until he had discovered that the wine was done, and it was time for him to be gone.

But it was obviously necessary to lull his suspicions and induce him to remain a few minutes longer.

'I should like to hear how that surcoat was finished and embroidered,' said Maxwell, with an affectation of interest. 'The time of my release is drawing near,' he added, 'and when I go out I should wish to have one of the same colour and conceit.'

He spoke in so matter-of-fact a tone that old Ralph was thrown completely off his guard.

'Oot!' said he, 'it's the first time ever I heard it, lad. I'll no say but I'll miss ye! Oot! Gude presairve us! Was there ever the like o' that?'

'I told you when I came in,' replied his prisoner, yawning and stretching himself lazily the while, 'the full turn will be out the day after to-morrow at noon.'

Old Ralph laid down his keys and scratched his head.

That instant Maxwell pounced upon them like a tiger. Almost with the same motion he seized the old man round the body, completely pinioning him, heavy and powerful as he was, till he had sent him staggering to the farthest extremity of the cell. Then, with one rapid turn of the key, that key at which he had often looked so longingly, and of which he knew every ward, he was through the door, as rapidly he locked and bolted it on the outside. His hand never trembled; his nerves were as true to him now in the moment of success as they had been through all the dangers and disasters he had overcome.

'Ah!' thought Maxwell, as he sped down the winding-stair like a lapwing, 'you may holloa your heart out, as many a poor prisoner has done before, but nobody will come near you till supper-time. If you get not free for a week you'll have had a lighter captivity than mine. And now for liberty and life, and—Mary Carmichael!'

He believed he had schooled himself to think of her no more, but she came back to him with the first gleam of the summer sun, the first breath of the summer air.

There is no catastrophe of grief or discomfiture so staggering to the nervous system as the shock of a great relief or a great joy. You shall attend the sick-bed of one nearest and dearest to you for days together, and see the life that is more precious than your very heart's blood ebbing away, as it were, inch by inch, and drop by drop, yet your eyes are dry; though your brain feels strangely hot and seared, your hand is steady, your tread firm, and your pulse regular. The moment on which hang the issues of life and eternity comes at last. The silent strife is waged between sleep and death, and the gentle conqueror triumphs by a hair's breadth. Never prone to give his opinion rashly, the doctor tells you that the dear one has escaped 'out of danger, he is happy to inform you,' and you wring his hand fiercely, but something gripping at your throat forbids you to speak your thanks. Then the tears gush freely to your eyes; then the strong frame shakes and quivers in every fibre, and down upon your knees you kneel before your God, even if you never knelt before. So in all the relations of life; the moment of success is the touchstone to the human character. It is far more rare to find men bear prosperity with equanimity than adversity. We have all heard of people going mad for joy.

For an instant, Walter Maxwell had to pause and collect his energies, manning himself as though about to undergo some formidable trial, when he found he was at least on the *outside* of that door which he had contemplated such a weary while as the bar between himself and freedom. Stealthily, and with a keen sense of delight, so overpowering as to be almost painful, he pushed open the iron wicket at the foot of the staircase and emerged into the garden beyond.

It was intoxicating to drink in the warm fragrance of the summer air at every pore. It was bewildering, from sheer delight, to feel the eyes ache in that dazzling sunshine, glowing on leaf and flower, whitening the gravel walk and the castle wall in its blinding glare. The prisoner paused in a corner of the passage ere he came forth, accustoming sight and faculties by degrees to the rapturous change.

Then he stole out and looked about him, taking in, with keen and wary eye, the features of the surrounding scene. Well he knew that in such a stronghold as that of the powerful Rothes his escape had only just begun.

He found himself in a beautiful little garden, neatly kept and tastefully laid out. Casting a hasty glance upward, he ascertained that he was overlooked by no windows from the castle; three sides of this parterre were bounded by the great blank walls of the house, the fourth was shut in by a dark impervious hedge of yews. With stealthy, hasty steps he was soon on the farther side of this leafy screen and traversing a bowling-green on which the bowls dotted the level surface at irregular intervals—denoting that a game had been recently interrupted—he emerged upon a beautiful little wilderness of shrubs and flowers beyond.

Three or four vases and a fountain adorned this exterior pleasure-ground, and the gigantic beeches of Leslie, perhaps the finest trees of Scotland, shaded it with their dark gleaming foliage. It looked like a paradise to the emancipated prisoner; but, alas, a paradise from which there was no escape! Surrounded by the outer wall of the castle, any biped, unprovided with wings, seemed as much a captive in those sunny glades as in the darkest recesses of the dungeon. How Maxwell envied the butterfly soaring into the air so freely over that smooth and cruel wall! It would be hard to turn back now after tasting even for five minutes the delights of liberty.

Casting about with anxious eyes and a fast-beating heart for some means, however desperate, of egress, he espied a portion of the masonry in which certain irregularities would admit of his climbing to within a few feet of the coping. At this very place, too, a friendly beech somewhat overhung the garden so that one of its branches drooped downwards inside the wall.

With a run and a bound, like that of a wild cat, he swarmed up its slippery surface and succeeded in reaching the pendant branch. It was a desperate exertion of strength, and the pain that shot across his chest warned Maxwell how an ounce more of weight would have turned the scale in the effort by which he swung himself into the tree. Once there, he paused to take breath, and looked back into the garden from which he had so happily escaped. What was his dismay to observe, for the first time, a tall stalwart man in the guise of a labourer, shuffling into his jerkin, and making for the house!

'Of course,' thought Maxwell, with a curse on his own stupidity that he had not perceived the man sooner, 'to give the alarm and turn out the retainers for pursuit!'

In truth there was nothing for it now but to slip down from the tree and trust to a light pair of heels and the chapter of accidents.

Already his legs were clear of the branches, and he was meditating a drop of some four or five yards upon the sward, when he drew them up again with wondrous precipitation, for the tread of feet through the grass, and the sound of voices in earnest conclave, warned him that he was hemmed in and beset on this side as well as the other.

Close under the tree, in which he couched like some hunted animal, three gallants halted and carried on their conversation in the deep, low, earnest tones of men who discuss those matters on which they have bound themselves to secrecy, and which the bird of the air itself is not to overhear.

Splendidly dressed, although half-armed—for a Scottish noble loved not to be utterly defenceless, even in the heart of his own residence, and the company of his staunchest friends—Maxwell recognised them at once, for three of the most powerful men in the kingdom—the wariest of statesmen, the darkest of intriguers, the most reckless of conspirators.

Not one of the three would have scrupled to cut the throat of an unwelcome eavesdropper on the spot, whether or not he thought a word of their conversation was overheard or understood. That 'makin' sicker' has been a favourite expedient in the annals of our northern politicians ever since Kirkpatrick left the Red Comyn weltering in his blood on the steps of the altar.

It was an unpleasant predicament for poor Walter. What could he do but hide himself up among the branches, keep quiet and listen, expecting besides every moment that the alarm of his escape would be given from the castle?

The little conclave continued their conversation eagerly, and as they stood beneath his hiding-place, Maxwell had ample leisure to observe the faces and bearing of his Queen's three worst and most pitiless enemies.

Rothes was, as usual, gay and careless in demeanour; his handsome face flushed with wine, was not out of keeping with the disordered bravery of his apparel. He could break his jest on treason as on any other crime; could pass through life and its most important avocations as though it were but one long feverish debauch in which the merriest and wildest roisterer bore his part the best.

Argyle, who repressed his host's ill-timed mirth whenever opportunity offered, and listened attentively to the calm, measured accents of the third person present, seemed thoughtful and ill-at-ease. Though of a courageous character, his was a nature that weighs well every scheme on which it enters, and loves not to put forth its full powers unless it sees its way clearly to success. He could not go hand over head into a plot like Rothes, simply for the excitement and amusement of the turmoil.

Grave in demeanour as the man to whom he was now listening so attentively, and not unlike him in character, he was yet far inferior in foresight and acuteness, above all in that mysterious force of will which bends and warps more pliant natures to its own ends. Maxwell, watching him intently from the tree, could not but mark how scruple after scruple disappeared, how gradually and completely conviction seemed to steal over his countenance, as he followed, step by step, and argument by argument, the bent of that master-mind which formed the third and dominant element in the conclave.

And who was this third conspirator, this evil spirit so much mightier and so much more daring than the two it controlled? Who, but Moray, the Queen's half-brother? Staid, quiet, composed as usual; less splendidly dressed, less energetic in gesture, less striking in appearance than either of his companions, yet obviously the leader whom they trusted implicitly and obeyed without remorse.

One more faithful adherent to the House of Leslie completed the party. His honest face and loyal courage seemed strangely out of place where treason was brewing; a large handsome bloodhound kept close at the heel of Rothes, poking his wet nose at intervals into his master's hand.

Even in the extremity at which he found himself, Maxwell could not forbear contrasting the surrounding scene with the principal actors. The white stems of the beeches shone like silver in the glowing afternoon sun, while thrush and blackbird carolled gaily from the deep rich screen of their heavy foliage. Life and light, beauty and fragrance filled the atmosphere, peace and prosperity smiled around; white sheep were feeding on a grassy slope over against him between the trees; red roses blooming and clustering around steeped his senses in their perfumes; the bee hummed drowsily by in the warm still air; overhead the swallows flitted to and fro against the blue laughing sky; and there, at his feet, within a spear's length of him, frowned the three dark pitiless faces, while Moray's measured voice unfolded the plot that chilled his very blood, though it roused his vindictive hatred, as he listened.

Not one of the others drank in every syllable as did that eager fugitive, crouching like a wild cat along the arm of the old beech tree.

'I tell ye, gentlemen, it cannot fail,' said the degenerate Stuart, with more earnestness than usual; 'the net is so spread that fly which way she will, the bird cannot but find herself within its meshes. I can tell ye for as certain as if I heard her say so now, that she leaves Perth after dinner to-morrow and rides to Callander, for the young Livingstone's baptism, direct; she will have no following beyond her personal attendants, and some twenty or thirty spears. Your Leslies, my lord, may surely make account of these.'

He turned to Rothes while he spoke; the latter answered with a savage laugh, and the bloodhound murmured simultaneously a deep angry growl.

'Why, "Hubert" seems to be of the same opinion,' pursued Moray, carelessly patting the dog's wide forehead, a liberty 'Hubert' seemed hugely inclined to resent. 'But I always counsel force enough in these little matters of necessity. "Never stretch your hand out farther than you can draw it back again," says our Scottish proverb; and "Never strike at your foe if your arm be not long enough to reach him," say those who know how to make war with prudence and moderation. Nay, I would have no risk run of failure or miscarriage for want of an odd score or two of horsemen. What say you, my lord of Argyle?'

That nobleman pondered a few moments ere he replied.

'My following moves forward to-night. I shall find four hundred spears at the Paren-Well to-morrow ere the sun has gone down two hours from the meridian.'

'Good!' answered Moray, nodding his head. 'And you, Rothes? The Leslies are sure to be swarming when there is aught stirring that promises a fight or a capture.'

'You shall count them yourself to-morrow, at sunrise, before we march,' answered the other, gaily. 'If you drink a cup to-night, at supper, for every hundred men, your brain, my good Lord James, will hardly be so clear in the morning as you like to keep it when there is business to be done. Be quiet, "Hubert!" the fiend's in the dog! What? down, man! art thou bewitched?'

The bloodhound's bristles were rising fiercer and fiercer, and he growled ominously as he snuffed the air with his broad black nostrils.

'Then this is the plan of the campaign,' resumed Moray. 'Argyle's forces and your own join at the Paren-Well, and in that lone district ye may dispose them to advantage, and keep the greater part out of sight from the Perth road. To avoid suspicion, I would counsel that ye do not anticipate the hour of rendezvous. My imprudent sister might be informed even when some miles upon her journey, and turn back. When Her Grace's palfrey enters the pass at the Paren-Well, fourscore men-at-arms can do the business readily enough. If there is any attempt at resistance, another troop or two may strike in. Be careful to keep a large force fresh to protect Her Grace's sacred person when taken. I have arranged for her lodging to-morrow night with her kinswoman at Loch-Leven Castle. For the lady-faced lord, if not knocked o' the head in the skirmish, he must be disposed elsewhere. You shall have him at Leslie, Rothes, an' ye will, though I doubt you and Darnley are but unfriends at heart. We will meet in Edinburgh next week to consult on state affairs; but to-morrow, being Sabbath, I have thought well to explain my views to you both to-day. Gentlemen, I think we understand each other?'

Argyle murmured an assent. Rothes laughed again somewhat dangerously.

'If there is any resistance?' said he.

'I will not have a hair of Her Grace's head ruffled, or a fold of her dress,' replied Moray, firmly. 'For the escort, they must be overpowered, of course; but Her Grace's person *shall* be respected, and her immediate attendants.'

'You promised me the Maries!' urged Rothes, reproachfully; 'come, man, you shall not go back from your word; you promised me the whole four, or at least my pick of them. I would not have gone into it, but for the saucy Seton; and that sunny, silent lass—how call you her?—Carmichael! I have ordered all sorts of toys to be here, expressly for them, to-morrow. Down, "Hubert!" be quiet, man!'

Maxwell's blood boiled within him, and he griped the branch of the beech as if it had been the last speaker's throat. Meantime 'Hubert' had been baying furiously, glaring upwards into the tree with flaming eyes, and springing furiously against the trunk.

'The Maries must take their chance,' replied Moray, in the same quiet tones. 'If Her Grace be safe, I shall ask no questions. That dog hath cause for his uneasiness, my lord; take my word for it, we have been overheard. He scents a fresh foot in our neighbourhood.'

With a great oath Rothes drew his sword, and Argyle followed his example.

CHAPTER XXXVII

'So soon. But now among all the rest
The champion of a hero-band,
With a gleaming blade and a flashing crest,
And a haughty front and a ready hand.

'There cometh a crash, and a cry of need,
A puff of smoke—and no more to tell,
But a dangling rein and a plunging steed,
And a rider lying where he fell.

'Ere the smoke hath melted in air above.
Or the blood soaked in where the hoof hath trod,
The true heart beateth its last for its love,
And the soul is gone home to God.'

The moment was one of intense anxiety and terror. Concealed by the leaves of the old beech, every leap of the frantic bloodhound threatened to disclose the listener's hiding-place. The Earls of Rothes and Argyle, with drawn swords and bent brows, looked high and low for the cause of the dog's fury. Besides the dread of a violent death, all the more terrible at this his first hour of escape from captivity, Maxwell now felt that on him depended the liberty of his Queen; more than this, the life and honour of the woman he still so dearly loved. To do him justice he would willingly have died on the spot to be able to advertise his Sovereign of her danger.

For an instant the desperate expedient darted through his mind of leaping down on Argyle's upturned face, wresting the sword from his grasp, and thus armed doing battle with Moray and Rothes; but, even then, he reflected, how surely the former, who was never surprised or at a loss, would run to the castle for assistance. If retaken, Walter shuddered to think, not of his own fate, but of Mary Carmichael's capture on the morrow.

Nevertheless there seemed nothing else for it; he had even collected his breath, and nerved his muscles for the spring, when a trumpet sounded in the castle, and a puff of lurid smoke swept across the faces of the three noblemen, who were searching about with eager looks and bare blades, encouraging 'Hubert' the while with voice and gesture.

Again the smoke came rolling in a dun-coloured volume against the clear sky, and the bloodhound, his attention distracted by the new catastrophe, or his powers of scent dulled by the smell of fire, ceased to leap at the old tree, and lowering his stern, began to howl in abject terror and dismay.

Rothes could not forbear laughing, though he coughed and swore at the same time.

"'Tis the alarm!' said he, as the trumpet again rang out in the castle-yard. 'Faith, Moray, I cannot but think they are burning the old house about our heads. Gentlemen both, I counted not to give ye so warm a reception as this!'

Nothing escaped Moray's quick eye. While they hurried back towards the building, he observed the smoke and flames issuing from the turret Maxwell had so recently quitted.

'The wind is favourable,' said the earl, as another cloud rolled over them, 'and you need not fear for more than the prison tower; for the sake of humanity, I trust, my lord, that it may be empty!'

Rothes did not answer; truth to say, he had quite forgotten Walter Maxwell, and even had he remembered him, would have thought the life of one poor prisoner mattered but little at such a time. The three noblemen addressed themselves to the task of quenching the fire with characteristic energy. Backed by the exertions of Rothes' disciplined followers, they soon succeeded in subduing the flames, and, ere nightfall, Leslie House had resumed its usual appearance of security, having suffered but little damage save the scorching of its outer wall. Poor old Ralph, however, was found dead in the dungeon, probably stifled by the smoke. But it is not with the inmates of Leslie that we have now to do.

As may be imagined, directly the coast was clear, Maxwell lost no time in slipping out of the tree. With a fervent thanksgiving in his heart, he dropped upon the sward, and ran as hard as his legs could carry him in the direction of the open country. Yet, even now, his situation was one of no ordinary hazard and embarrassment. He was unarmed; he was in an enemy's country; he might meet, at any moment, with retainers of Lord Rothes, who would recognise him at once for an escaped prisoner. Moreover, he was weaker than ordinary, from his long confinement, and, even had it been otherwise, he could not expect to reach Perth on foot in time to warn the Queen of the plot laid against her person; and how was he to procure a horse? Cogitating these matters with considerable anxiety, he hurried on nevertheless, and was dismayed to find limbs and breath failing him as he ran.

To add to his discomfiture he heard footsteps approaching rapidly from behind. Turning his head, he espied the countryman whom he had already observed in the garden, nearing him with every stride. Maxwell would have given ten years of his life ungrudgingly to have had as many inches of steel in his belt.

''Od sake, man, ye can run as weel as fight!' exclaimed a familiar voice close to him, as the fugitive slackened speed to collect his strength for the desperate struggle he anticipated. 'Keep wast, hinny! keep wast! down yon burnie-side. I can hear "Wanton Willie" nickerin' at us the noo!'

Though they still kept on at a rapid pace, between running and walking, Maxwell's hand was fast locked in that of 'Dick-o'-the-Cleugh,' whilst the borderer, pointing to a neighbouring brake in which a confederate, with two led horses, was concealed, in a tone of suppressed triumph assured his friend that he was safe.

It took but little time to mount 'Wanton Willie,' the redoubtable bay that Dick affirmed was the pride of his lord's stable, and less to inform the borderer of the plot against Her Majesty, and the necessity for reaching Perth with the utmost speed they could command. As they swung along at a hand-gallop, Dick, with many a smothered laugh and quaint allusion, for he looked on the whole performance, from first to last, as an unparalleled jest, detailed to his companion the measures he had adopted to effect his delivery.

Translated from his own vernacular, the borderer's account was as follows:—After his interview with the Queen and her ladies in Edinburgh, he had ridden on to Leslie with the intention of rescuing Walter with the strong hand; but on arriving in Fife he found that country in so alarmed a state, and Leslie House itself so securely watched and strongly garrisoned, that such a project was utterly impracticable. His predatory habits had taught Dick, long ago, that where force was useless, resort must be had to stratagem, and he set about his task with all the quiet energy of his character and the craft of his profession.

In the first place it was necessary to diminish his retinue, in order to avoid suspicion. 'Lang Willie' and 'Jock-o'-the-Hope' accordingly were despatched back to Hermitage, leaving one of their horses for the use of the prisoner, and Ralph Armstrong, a sedate and cautious old jackman, remained at a considerable distance from Leslie with the three horses, which he kept well exercised, and fit for a trial of speed and endurance at any moment.

Dick then disguising himself like a countryman, applied for a day's work or two in the gardens and pleasure-grounds of Leslie, and ere long his great strength and inexhaustible good-humour so won upon the gardener, that he was installed as a regular labourer about the place. Here he soon made himself acquainted with the passages and entrances of the stronghold, more especially with the geography of the dungeon tower. Nevertheless, study it as he would, he could find no means of communicating with the captive, much less of liberating him from thraldom. A thick iron door between massive stone walls is no ineffectual barrier, if only it be kept locked.

Turning matters over and over in his own mind, while he worked away in the flower-garden, Dick had arrived at the conclusion that the shortest method would be to set the whole place on fire, seize his keys, after braining old Ralph the jailer in the confusion, and thus make his escape with the prisoner through the flames. To his great relief he had long since ascertained, amidst the gossip of the servants, that Maxwell was still alive.

It was necessary, however, to choose a judicious moment for this exploit, and Dick, understanding that the Lord Rothes and a large force were to move on the Sabbath from Leslie, had selected that day, when the house would be less strictly guarded than usual, for his undertaking. His plan was to fire the place about the hour of curfew, when the retainers were sauntering abroad in the summer evening, and were less easily collected than at any other hour; but as our borderer was a man of great rapidity in action, and kept himself ready at any moment to take an advantage, Armstrong had strict directions whenever, by day or night, he should see a wreath of smoke or a red glare above the old beeches, that instant the horses should be brought to a certain secluded coppice within half a mile of the castle.

Thus our friend laid his plans, and with equal judgment disposed his combustibles, straw by straw, as it were, and faggot by faggot, even as the bird of the air builds her nest, with secrecy and perseverance. Everything was ready, and the borderer went about his work in the garden, as he said to himself, 'with a clear conscience.' On this very afternoon, when Maxwell made his unaided escape from confinement, Dick had just returned from attending the three noblemen to their game at bowls—the very game which Maxwell had remarked unfinished as he crossed the green. It was with no small surprise that he saw the prisoner escaping across the garden which was his own peculiar charge.

The borderer was somewhat disconcerted; nevertheless, he reflected for a moment. 'If,' thought he, 'Mr Maxwell can surmount the outer wall he will but light down plump amongst the three earls who are walking in the avenue beyond; if he remain concealed here in the garden, he is sure to be missed when old Ralph visits the prison, discovered, and retaken; nay, if Rothes be the least out of humour, probably put to death. The faggots are all laid: I have a flint and steel in my belt; I had best set fire to the place at once, and have done with it.'

Moreover, Dick was not very sure on his own account that he might not be himself suspected. In getting the bowls ready for the three noblemen, Moray's piercing glance had not failed to detect a face he seemed to recognise. With a brief effort of memory the Earl recalled that thrust on the causeway of Edinburgh from mad Arran's blade, and the interposition of Earl Bothwell's henchman, which saved his own life.

'Good fellow,' said he, as Dick raised his face from setting 'the jack' in its place, 'I have seen you before; I owe you a debt for saving my life a while ago, during a brawl in the High Street.'

Argyle and Rothes were at the other end of the green, poising their bowls to begin; Dick answered hastily, and in a whisper—'I've been in trouble on the border; I'm in trouble yet; but I'm no kent in Fife. Your honour can best pay it by no lettin' on[15] that ye've ever seen me before!'

[15] "Lettin' on," Scottice for disclosing a secret.

Moray was a good-natured man enough; he nodded an understanding, and put a piece of gold in the gardener's hand; but, nevertheless, Dick felt none the more sanguine, after this recognition, for the success of his enterprise.

No sooner, however, had he seen Maxwell swing himself into the old beech tree, a gymnastic feat which called forth his warmest approval, than he hastened back to put his long-laid scheme in practice, with what success we have already learned; for the bloodhound's sagacity must unquestionably have led to a discovery of the fugitive, had it not been for the diversion occasioned by the fire.

'An' noo,' said the borderer, with a sad, wistful expression on his honest face, very different from the roguish humour with which he had narrated the detail of his adventure,—'an' noo, I'm easy in my mind, whichever way the bowl may rin. I've paid my debt, Maister Maxwell, ye ken; I'm thinking it'll no be lang or I get my quittance.'

Maxwell was somewhat puzzled; he could not quite fathom the meaning of his honest friend. Alas! ere a few hours were past he understood it but too well.

Time of course was the chief object with the three cavaliers; it was indispensable to arrive in Perth at as early an hour as possible, so as to warn the Queen of her danger, and to raise the country for the punishment of her foes. The party however were right well mounted; Dick had not selected the *worst* of Bothwell's horses for an expedition in which speed was so likely to be an essential element of success; and 'Wanton Willie,' once the property of Lord Scrope himself, and stolen from the English warden by a series of stratagems, remarkable alike for ingenuity and audacity, was an animal of extraordinary power, mettle, and endurance.

It was no ordinary sensation of delight that Maxwell experienced as he swept through the evening air borne onwards by the long untiring stride of the powerful bay stallion. It was like grasping the hand of an old friend to stroke and smooth that swelling crest as 'Wanton Willie' tossed his head and snorted, champing the bit and snatching playfully at the rein.

He had always loved a good horse well. Now with the fate of a kingdom dependent on his speed, he could not prize too highly the merits of his charger. Also Maxwell's heart was even yet sore and empty; it was soothing to rely on the honest fidelity of a brute. How many men are there who lavish on horse and hound the affections that were hoarded, it may be, long ago, elsewhere; given unreservedly, accepted with glee, and returned after a while to the dejected owner with the sap dried up, the core extracted, and the virtue gone! So he learns to content himself perforce with that which is real and substantial, at least as far as it goes; learns to thrill at the note of a hound, forget the past in the glowing excitement of a gallop; and the well-judging world opines that he has a grovelling soul which soars not above the stables and the kennel, and is fit for no better things.

The moon was coming up from the horizon, and still the three rode swiftly and steadily on. They were many miles from Leslie now, but, alas! they were not yet clear of Leslie's influence. At a small hamlet where they stopped to water and refresh their horses, Maxwell was recognised ere he touched the ground by a scion of the house of Rothes, even then on the march with a party of horse to join his kinsman's forces at the Paren-Well.

David Leslie started with surprise as the bay was pulled up at the stone trough before the village inn, but the young soldier was prompt in action and saw at a glance he had but three men to deal with, and one of those unarmed. His own retainers were numerous and on the spot.

'Walter Maxwell!' he exclaimed, seizing 'Wanton Willie' at the same instant by the bridle, 'you are my prisoner! Ho! a Leslie! a Leslie! to the rescue!'

His men came pouring out at the well-known cry. Stout troopers all of them, and armed besides to the teeth. There was nothing for it but a quick and determined resistance.

Dick spurred his horse without hesitation against the assailant on foot, dealing him at the same moment a heavy buffet with his gauntleted hand, for he had no time to draw his sword. Armstrong protected Maxwell's other flank. There were several fierce oaths, a pistol-shot, a smothered groan, much trampling of hoofs, a plunge or two, and Maxwell found himself again careering along between his two defenders over the open plain at a pace that set pursuit at defiance.

'Well out of that, Dick!' said he cheerily, as they pulled their horses at last into a trot, and listened for the enemy who came not. 'Well out of that! we'll win the race and be home now before midnight, I expect. These are rare stuff, these Border nags of yours; it's no wonder men should be tempted to steal such cattle as we are riding to-night!'

But Dick answered nothing, only he seemed to hold his horse in a rigid immovable grasp, and the three broke into a gallop even swifter than before. The moon was up now, riding clear and high in the mid-heaven. Was it only her light that made the borderer's face so pale? Dick spoke at last in a thick, hoarse voice, and the others pulled up simultaneously as he did so.

'I'll light doun, I'm thinkin,' said he. 'Ride *you* on, Maister Maxwell! I'll just bide where I am awee. It's a kin' o' dwam[16]-like that's come over me.'

[16] Dwam—a swoon.

He dismounted while he spoke. He was scarce clear of the saddle ere he staggered and fell heavily to the ground. Armstrong unbuckled his corslet and opened the buff jerkin beneath. It was light enough for Maxwell to see the little round mark that soldiers know so well. Large drops were standing on the borderer's forehead, and his lips were turning white. Maxwell took his hand, and the dying man smiled a feeble, ghastly smile, as he returned the grasp.

'I'll no win back to Liddesdale,' said he, faintly. 'I'll no get the length o' Perth the nicht. I'll be meat for the corbies[17] the morn. Gude speed ye, my canny lad! Pit yer foot intill the stirrup again. A Queen's errans munna stan' still for the like o' me!'

[17] Corbies—crows.

Maxwell's tears fell thick and fast. While Armstrong held the horses, he propped the borderer's head upon his knee, and whispered a few broken words, he knew not what, of grief and hope, that seemed a mockery even then.

The mossy turf on which they rested was not more clammy than the pale forehead in its damps of death; he was bleeding inwardly, and every breath he drew exhausted more and more the shallow stream of vitality that was left.

'Ride *you* on,' he whispered, 'ride *you* on! leave Ralph wi' *me*, I'll no keep him lang. Ye'll win to the Court the morn, lad, an' ye'll see bonny Mistress Seton, an' ye'll tell her frae me — —'

He was getting very weak now; twice or thrice he strove to speak, but no sound came. Maxwell bent over him, and held his breath to catch the sacred accents of the dying man.

He raised himself a little with an effort, and his voice was stronger now.

'Tell her,' said he, 'that if ever she can win to Liddesdale, she maun walk afoot through the bonny glens, and hearken to the lilt of the lavrock, an' pu' a sprig o' the red heather, just to mind her o' "Dick-o'-the-Cleugh" — rough, rantin' Dick, that wadna ha' evened himself to kiss the very ground beneath her feet. Eh! lad, an' she hadna been a born leddy, I wad hae lo'ed yon lassie weel!'

Then Dick's head sank lower and lower; nor, although he lived for a short space afterwards, was he heard to speak again. Maxwell was forced to leave him, however loth, in charge of his comrade; his own duty would admit of no delay. Sadly and slowly he mounted 'Wanton Willie' once more; sadly and slowly he loitered away at a foot's pace, turning his head often to gaze wistfully back where Ralph Armstrong was stooping in the moonlight over the long prostrate figure of the henchman. At last he saw Ralph lay the head gently down upon the sward, and walk a few paces away. Then he knew that it was over, and galloped on towards Perth with wet eyes and a heavy heart.

CHAPTER XXXVIII

'For though her smiles were sad and faint,
And though her voice was low,
She never murmured a complaint,
Nor hinted at her woe,
Nor harboured in her gentle breast
The lightest thought of ill;
Giving all, forgiving all,
Pure and perfect still,

'Confiding when the world was hard,
And kind when it was cold,
What wealth of Love was stored and barred
Within that Heart of Gold!
Exulting every grief to share,
And every task fulfil;
Giving all, forgiving all,
Fond and faithful still.

'And when upon that patient brow
The storm had broke at last,
And all her pride was shatter'd now,
And all her power was past,
She meekly kissed the hand that smote,
And yielded to its will;
Giving all, forgiving all,
True and tender still.'

'Happy's the wooing that's not long of doing,' says a hopeful Scottish proverb. 'Marry in haste, and repent at leisure,' is a wholesome English warning, that may be considered the converse of the above.

'Some, by construction, deem these words misplaced,

At leisure marry, and repent in haste,'

quoth Congreve, or one of the old dramatists. We may take our choice of maxims on the important topic of wedlock, satisfied that, ponder on it as we may, it is a matter in which blind fortune concerns herself more than in any other of our human affairs. Yes, 'your marriage goes by destiny,' no doubt, and sometimes the fates draw you off nectar, and sometimes wholesome bitters, and sometimes weak, insipid, flat, and stale small beer. Under any circumstances it is better not to pull a wry face at the draught. If the fairest woman the earth ever saw could not make sure of conjugal happiness, who has a right to complain?

Darnley was now Duke of Albany—the handsomest Duke in Christendom—and on the evening before her nuptials his affianced bride had somewhat prematurely caused him to be proclaimed King of Scotland. Two religions had prepared to consecrate the tie; the Pope's dispensation, inasmuch as the lovers were blood relations, had been obtained from Rome, and the banns by which, according to the Reformed Persuasion 'Harry Duke of Albany and Earl of Ross should be united to Mary, by the grace of God, Queen of Scots, and Sovereign of the Realm,' had been proclaimed in the Parish Church of the Canongate.

The Queen had escaped the plot laid against her by her enemies at Leslie House, and, it is needless to say, how royal favour and ladies' smiles were showered upon the daring rider who foundered 'Wanton Willie' for ever by the speed with which he brought his timely intelligence to Perth, a speed that enabled the Queen to sweep down to her capital with a strong, well-mounted escort, in advance of all the preparations made for her capture. She had quelled an insurrection at St Leonard's Craigs since then; she had strengthened her party by all the means at her disposal, and even striven hard to listen without anger to the ill-timed remonstrances of Elizabeth, forwarded through Randolph, who, somewhat to his dismay, and much, to his disgust, found his importance waning, hour by hour, at the Scottish Court.

Everything a woman *could* do by persuasion, by policy, by forbearance, by her own intrinsic fascination, Mary had done to attain, if possible, a few months or even weeks of repose for the enjoyment of the present; happy, as she fancied herself, in her love, and willing to be at peace with all the world.

And while the young Queen looked about her for friends and partisans in every direction, was it likely that she would forget her stout champion on the border, the warlike Earl of Bothwell? It may be that she had long sought an excuse to pardon him; it may be that, like the rest of her sex, though prone to commit it in haste, her heart smote her sore, after awhile, for an act of injustice. She recalled him, she forgave him, she brought him back to her dangerous presence, and the flame that was consuming this wild and tameless heart, only burned all the fiercer that he must stifle it for awhile.

Moray kept aloof from the sister whom he had deceived, and the Queen against whom he had conspired. Accustomed as Mary had been for so long to depend upon her brother whenever she needed counsel or assistance, no doubt she felt his estrangement very keenly; but even Moray, notwithstanding all his offences, she would have received once more with open arms, had he abjured his devotion to the interests of the astute Elizabeth, and returned to his natural duty and allegiance.

The fairest daughter of the Stuarts was always, alas! more of the woman than the Queen. Had she been less frank, less trusting, less kindly, less affectionate, above all, less beautiful, the crown of Scotland would have sat more firm upon her head, the head itself would not at last have been severed by the cruel axe at Fotheringay.

But that dainty head never looked more nobly than to-day. With the glory of love and happiness shining round it; with the royal diadem resting on the white and gentle brow; with the soft rich hair gathered into such a coronet of splendour as no other princess, as no other *woman* in Europe, could boast; with a majestic form set off by the sweeping robes of *black* in which, as a royal widow, *étiquette* bade her approach the altar; above all with the atmosphere of beauty that surrounded Mary as with a charm, Old Thomas the Rhymer had never such a vision of the Fairy Queen herself as burst upon the sight of loyal Lennox and devoted Athol, when she emerged from her chamber and suffered them to conduct her to the Chapel Royal of Holyrood, at six of the clock on the summer Sabbath morning that smiled with such well-omened brilliancy upon the bride.

Could black fate be hovering over that gay and sparkling throng, marking them out, as it were, one by one, for her future shafts? There they stood—so many of them; the brave, the beautiful, the loyal, the gentle and the true, glowing in youth and health, towering in the pride of manhood and the pride of place; radiant in silks and velvets, blazing with gold and gems; and the red mark scored in the book of destiny against two out of every three illustrious names, and the little cloud, though still below the horizon, yet waiting none the less surely to break in fatal tempest over the proud unconscious brows, and shatter the guilty and the innocent in one indiscriminate ruin to the dust.

Even crook-backed Riccio could not forbear an exultant song of rejoicing when the ceremony was concluded, that gave his indulgent mistress to the handsome, petulant boy she had chosen for her lord.

'Glory to God!' exclaimed the secretary, in his deep, rich tones, as the rites were finished with a burst of chanted thanksgiving. How long was it ere those same lips, writhing in their death-pang, were gasping for mercy in hoarse, gurgling whispers choked in blood? In the meantime, the Queen is conducted back from the Chapel to the Palace, and the ceremony takes place of unrobing Her Majesty, who is now no longer a widow, but a bride, with all the established jests and noisy glee such an occasion is calculated to call forth.

First Darnley takes out a pin, then Athol, then Lennox, then each of the gentlemen of the household as he can approach the royal person, while her ladies like a guard of Amazons close round her more and more as the spoliation proceeds. The process, as is natural, soon degenerates into something like a romp, and Walter Maxwell, with a heavy heart, finds himself, to his own dismay, mixed up with such merry fooleries.

While Her Majesty proceeds with a few of her tiring-women into another chamber, whence she will presently reappear in dazzling apparel suited to the occasion, we will return to the humbler personages of the scene, who may now, like the supernumeraries in a theatre, come up to the foot-lights and display their antics, whilst their betters are off the stage.

To begin with the Maries, whom we have too much neglected whilst taken up with ruder and less engaging natures.

Those young ladies, by the very act to which they have even now been lending their assistance, have become freed from their self-imposed obligations of celibacy, and might marry, if it so pleased them, one and all to-morrow. To the philosopher who fancies he understands the nature of the sex, it will not appear surprising that at this juncture none of them should show the slightest disposition for entering that holy state, from which it has hitherto been considered such an extreme hardship they should be debarred. Hilarious, as it was their duty to appear during the performance of Her Majesty's nuptials—hilarious, of course, be it understood, with the proper admixture of tears—for ladies esteem a wedding to be essentially an April performance of showers and sunshine—yet no sooner was the principal excitement over, no sooner were the four young beauties released from their respective attitudes of attention, and at liberty to receive the compliments and reply to the bantering congratulations of the courtiers, than a cloud seemed to come over each of them, and they looked far less inclined to laugh than to cry.

Mary Beton, perhaps, kept her spirits up with more determination and a greater show of indifference than either of her sisters in sorrow; nevertheless, Mary Beton, while she certainly enjoyed an advantage over the others, was in an uncomfortable state of uncertainty and transition.

Although it is doubtless a wise and wholesome precaution for a lady to have two strings to her bow, yet the instrument is apt to get somewhat warped and out of order in the process of taking off the old and fitting on the new. There is something softening as well as soothing in the attentions of the recent capture, and they remind us rather touchingly at times of those other looks and tones which made such fools of us not so long ago. We cannot do the same things, say the same words, go through the same exercises (and in truth there is, we believe, but little variety in the drill by which the human heart is disciplined), without experiencing very much the same kind of sensations as heretofore, and it is not always easy to distinguish between the old feelings and the new. The former come over us with an overwhelming rush when we least expect them, and our only chance is to credit the fresh account with as much of the balance as we can. That same tenant-right is a very difficult matter to get rid of when once it has been firmly established in the breast.

Mary Beton had broken with her old lover for good and all. She had convicted him of treason to her Queen; and although this offence she might possibly have forgiven, she had found him out in treachery to herself. It is needless to say that she would have nothing more to do with Randolph, and was prepared to listen with no unwilling ear to the suit of Alexander Ogilvy. But the latter was distant and offended still. He had not forgotten certain rebuffs, certain black looks and cold answers, that had piqued and irritated him long ago. He loved her indeed very dearly, therefore he did not mean to hold out for any great length of time, but still it was *his* turn now, and he could not be expected to forego his share of advantage in the merciless game. It is an old saying that 'many a heart is caught on the rebound,' and perhaps he was sure of his prey, and content to wait a little and enjoy the excitement of the capture.

Proud Mistress Beton, too, had become far more docile and womanly of late. Pained and humbled by the treatment she had experienced from Randolph, it would have been inexpressibly soothing and delightful to encourage and return an attachment she could trust, and on which she could lean, so to speak, without fear of mortification. Great liberties are sometimes taken, great risks run, in these affairs. Tempers that are imperturbable on all other topics, blaze up with reckless violence against the nearest and dearest. When the wild bird has ruffled her plumes in anger, and broken her jesses in pique, the observant fowler, who watches his opportunity, finds every facility afforded for his lure. There is no time at which the human heart is so susceptible to kindness as when writhing under a sense of injustice and ill-treatment which it has not deserved.

So Mary Beton was less haughty, less overbearing, and consequently looked ten times lovelier than usual on her mistress's wedding-day.

She stands now nearest the door, waiting for the Queen, and whispers gently and lovingly to Mary Seton, who seems to cling to her senior as to an elder sister, and whose fair face has of late assumed a sad and thoughtful expression very different from that which it used to wear.

The arch looks are downcast now, and the merry voice is hushed and low. The girl is not unhappy, only grave and saddened perhaps a little by her experiences. She has bid Walter tell her over and over again how poor Dick Rutherford laid him down to die in the moonlight and spoke of her—of *her*, the vain, frivolous girl!—with the last breath he ever drew. What had she done to win so entirely the devotion of that great honest heart? Had she suspected it? Had she triumphed in it? Had she prized it? Ah! never so much as now, when all the wishing in the world would fail to bring the trusting kindly nature back to her feet.

She was a noble damsel, and Dick but the mere retainer of a warlike lord, ranking scarce above a man-at-arms. And yet it was something, surely, to have been so loved by any one human heart: to have taken everything and given nothing in return. She could weep now to think that never— never would she be able to make him amends.

Ay, he was a *man* that was brave and strong and single-minded, daring, patient, resolute, fearing nothing under heaven, humble and child-like only with *her*. How often might she unwittingly have wrung the gentle, uncomplaining heart; how often purposely, just to essay and feel her power! She could hate herself to think of a hundred trifles now! Ah! too late—too late! He was gone where neither foeman's lance nor lady's look could reach; where cold words and bare steel were alike powerless to wound. Gone— gone altogether, and she would *never* see him more.

It seemed to Mary Seton, as she stood there and looked at her comrades, that she alone would fulfil that vow of celibacy from which to-day's festival had enfranchised the Queen's Maries. Where could she expect to find hereafter such an affection as she had neglected and lost? No; henceforth she would devote herself heart and hand to the service of her mistress; cling to the Queen through rain and shine, calm and storm, good and evil. If prosperity blessed her dear mistress, she would rejoice; if adversity frowned, she would console her; if danger or calamity came, she would share it. Let the others marry, an' they must; for her, she would belong to her Queen! And nobly, in after years, Mary Seton redeemed her vow.

But there was one of the maids-of-honour whose wedding was indeed to succeed Her Majesty's, who looked forward to its arrival with more than maidenly longing; who hoped for it, and relied on it with more than a woman's trust. Mary Hamilton, with her pale face and wasted form, had continued her service with the Queen, silent and uncomplaining, never unbosoming herself to her companions, not even confiding her sorrows to her mistress until now. To-morrow she would be free; to-morrow would be the day of her espousals, and the poor weary head would lay itself to rest, the poor sore heart find comfort and relief at last. It was for this she had been waiting so patiently, for this she had borne her burden so uncomplainingly. To-morrow she would become the Bride of Heaven, and the veil she would then put on must never be taken off again this side the grave!

In her cell (so her religion taught her, hopeful even in death), in her cell she could pray for the soul of him she had loved so fondly; could believe, when his fiery sufferings and her own prayers and tears had obliterated his crimes, she would meet him, never again to part, on the shining hills beyond the dark shadowy valley that she feared no whit, nay, that she only longed to tread.

Mary Hamilton took the vows on the day subsequent to the Queen's marriage, at the bright midsummer season, when the blooming world should have looked fairest and most captivating to her who turned her back upon it so willingly for evermore. During a twelvemonth, so the Romish Church enforced, she must make trial of her new profession, and at the expiration of that period, should she continue in the same mind, the novice was to become a nun.

There is little doubt she would have fulfilled her intention had the occasion ever arrived.

It was an early harvest that year in Scotland, but ere the barley was white, Mary Hamilton had done with nuns and nunneries, vows and ceremonies, withered hopes and mortal sorrows, and had gone to that place where the weary heart can alone find the rest it had so longed for at last.

There is but one more of the Maries with whom we have to do: Mistress Carmichael must speak for herself in another chapter.

CHAPTER XXXIX

'For love will wear through shine and shower,
And love can bear to bide its time;
Unwearied at the vesper hour,
As when the matins chime.

'And love can strive against a host,
Can watch and wait and suffer long;
Still daring more when fearing most,
In very weakness strong.

'Though bruised and sore, it never dies,
Though faint and weary, standing fast;
It never fails, and thus the prize
Is won by *love* at last.'

Perhaps of the four young ladies who had thus devoted themselves to the service of the Queen, Mary Carmichael was the least changed in demeanour and outward appearance at the auspicious period which gave them their freedom, and entitled them to assume that temporary dominion over the other sex which is a woman's birthright. She was still beautiful as ever; her sorrows, if she had any, did not veil an atom of brilliancy in her eye, or take a shade of colour from her cheek; her figure was no less rounded and symmetrical in its full flowing lines, her step no less firm and haughty, her manner, if anything, colder and more self-reliant. If there was any change observable in Mary Carmichael, it was that she seemed to become harder, prouder, less sympathising and less womanly day by day.

On some natures anxiety and distress produce a bracing, and as it were a petrifying effect; they will not have it thought that they can be affected by such morbid influences as the feelings. There are women of ice and women of fire, women of wax and women of marble. It is possible that, if the truth were known, these strong beauties suffer as much as their more impressionable sisters, and yet the proud face never falls, the hard eyes never soften. Try her with words that ought to stab, each of them, to the quick; if she winces you never know it, for the white bosom heaves no higher, the colour neither fades nor deepens on the fair, provoking cheek. It is maddening to the assailant; perhaps also the one attacked is not quite so comfortable as she looks; perhaps if you were to alter your tactics, to change your mood, and take up the cool, indifferent line yourself, she might be goaded out of this unnatural calm into a tempest that, if it did break out, would probably be very terrible. It is better not to try. 'Touch not the cat but a glove,' says the motto of a noble Scottish family; 'Never drive a woman into a corner,' is the maxim of every philosopher who would escape scaithless from those contests in which the rougher and honester nature is almost sure to come by the worst.

Walter Maxwell was not the man to persevere in a wooing that he once had reason to believe was unwelcome; he, too, could hide a warm, loving heart, under a grave, impenetrable brow—could bear the pain of seeing the idol of his fancy day by day more and more estranged, yet never wince nor writhe under the torture, far less upbraid or complain. For weeks he had been habitually in her society, himself the hero of the hour, the man whom the Queen favoured as her deliverer, whom lords and ladies greeted as her champion, yet never hazarded a word nor look that could lead Mary Carmichael to believe he still cared for her, far less sought an interview, as doubtless she often hoped he would, that should bring about reproaches, tears, a quarrel, an explanation, and a reconciliation.

These two proud dispositions were like the parallel lines which, similar in all their properties, are for that reason incapable of meeting. How the woman's heart swelled and ached when she watched him always so calm, so courteous, so impassible, so indifferent; how she longed for him to be rude, fierce, angry, even unjust and unreasonable! she would rather he had *struck* her than thus passed her by with that studiously gentle manner, that hateful iron smile. Oh! it was hard to bear—hard to bear; and yet she *must* bear it, and none must know her weakness or her sufferings.

And he, too, longing only to forgive everything in which he felt himself aggrieved, believing he could be quite content now if they were but *friends* and nothing more, thirsting for one kind look from her eyes, one cordial word from her lips, felt bound perforce to treat her with the calm, courteous, defiant bearing of those who are enemies to the death.

Ludicrous as it might have been to the bystanders, it was an uncomfortable state of things to the performers themselves in the little drama,—tragedy, comedy, farce, call it what you will, and your nomenclature will probably depend upon your time of life: lovers' quarrels look so different as the decades roll by. An uncomfortable state of things, doubtless, and it might have gone on for a lifetime but for one of those accidents to which such sufferers are peculiarly susceptible.

Accidents, like the fresh breeze that springs up on a sultry summer's day. The heavens are dark and lowering, there is an oppressive weight in the atmosphere, the very birds sit hushed and sullen behind the motionless leaves, and the earth looks saddened and weary, mourning as if she had made up her mind that the sun was never to shine again. Suddenly the breeze wakes up and comes laughing out of the west; the clouds fly scattered before him, the young leaves flicker in the golden sunshine, the birds burst forth in those joyous strains which, to do them justice, they are ever ready to strike up on the slightest provocation, and the whole landscape shines and smiles and quivers in life and light once more.

When the Queen emerged from her tiring-room in the magnificent apparel best befitting such a bride, another courtier, in addition to the party that had thronged the Chapel, entered the royal circle to tender his homage as in duty bound, and congratulate Her Majesty on her nuptials.

This new arrival was a tall, handsome man of middle age, perhaps a little past that delusive epoch, yet still bearing the traces of considerable beauty of feature, and distinguished for peculiar fascination of manner and grace of bearing. He was dressed, too, with the utmost splendour, and obviously in the very latest fashion of the French Court. Several of the Queen's immediate attendants seemed to know him well, and greeted him with a warm assumption of cordiality and interest, although in the outer circle, so to speak, inquiring glances were shot at the welcome stranger, and whispers of 'Who is he? who is he?' passed unanswered from mouth to mouth.

It was chiefly among the younger courtiers and those whose rank did not entitle them to share the secret councils of Her Majesty that this curiosity was observed to manifest itself. Two or three of the seniors accosted him with obviously suppressed warmth and mirthful looks that denoted a world of intelligence only known to themselves, but Mary Carmichael's eyes rested on the distinguished stranger with an expression of the utmost love and confidence those very expressive eyes could convey. Had it not been for this, Maxwell might never have remarked the late addition to the royal circle, so absent was he and preoccupied, truth to say, so utterly weary and sick at heart. Watching, however, as he had accustomed himself to do, by stealth, the direction of his mistress's glances, he could not but be aware of the stranger's presence, and it needed no second look to satisfy him that this was the identical cavalier whom he had seen that starlight night in the

Abbey-garden, whose face and figure he was not likely to forget should he live for a hundred years. On that memorable occasion he remembered to have experienced a vague and puzzling sensation that he had met his rival before. To-day, in the Queen's presence-chamber, it came back again; but he was in no mood now to speculate on such random fancies and probabilities.

No, in five seconds of time he had made up his mind to the worst, and had resolved upon the line of conduct he should adopt.

Of course it was all over at last. Never till this moment, when it crumbled and fell to ashes, had he been aware how much of hope there was mingled with his suspicions and his pique. Hope! the word itself seemed an absurdity now. Nevertheless, there is no such utter composure as a brave mind borrows from the total annihilation of all it has loved and cherished most. Men *can* have no anxieties when there is nothing left to lose, and even a coward will sometimes die gracefully enough if there be an obvious impossibility of escape.

The most accomplished gallant of the French Court could not have moved through the circle of ladies that crowded the Queen's ante-room with a more assured air than did Walter Maxwell; the most consummate fop could not have shown less agitation than was betrayed in the few words he addressed then and there to Mistress Carmichael.

'We were old friends once,' said he, 'though now we seldom even speak. Shall I find you in the gallery before the banquet. I should like to be friends again once for all.'

He might have been criticising the pattern of her dress, so cold and quiet were his tones. The lady did not show quite so much self-command. She turned very pale, and her lip trembled so that she did not dare trust her voice; but she bowed her head in the affirmative, and was glad to screen herself from observation meanwhile amongst the ample dresses of her companions.

You see she had by no means made up her mind that all *was* over; perhaps, too, a horrible misgiving came across her that she might have driven him too far.

While the rest of the household were preparing for the banquet, they had the gallery to themselves. Strange to say, the lady reached the trysting-place first. Though the colour deepened on her cheek when she heard his step, she never turned her head till he came close to her, and by that time she had recovered her self-command. They were standing on the very spot where she had dropped the roses long ago. If this coincidence occurred to her, be sure she did not think it worth while to mention it.

He spoke first, very gravely and kindly, in the tone of a man who feels he has a reparation to make.

'Mistress Carmichael,' said he, 'I have treated you unfairly and unlike a friend. I may have thought I had a right to be angry with you; now I know for certain that is all over. I am no longer angry. I ask you to forgive me, and to shake hands before we part.'

She scarcely dared look at him, standing there tall and manly before her, with his kind eyes, and bold, frank brow. No fopling lover to be given up lightly and at a moment's notice, forsooth? Over, was it? Perhaps she did not see it at all in that light!

'What do you mean?' she gasped, trying hard not to tremble, nor to laugh, nor indeed to cry.

'I am reconciled to it all,' was his answer, 'because I see you love him, and that you are happy. It is but a selfish affection that cannot rejoice in the welfare of its object. To-day,' he added, with rather a sad smile, 'the maiden's vow is at an end. Never mind what follies may have once crossed my brain. Prove to me that you forgive them by confiding in me as if I was your brother.'

She looked up at him with a quick, searching glance.

'You mean you think I am going to be married?' said she, 'and you are wishing me joy?'

'I am indeed,' he replied, with another smile yet sadder than the last. 'Somewhat awkwardly, I fear, yet none the less honestly for that. Listen! I shall never tell you so again. I loved you as dearly as it is possible for man to love woman; so dearly that even now I can rejoice that you are happy. I can give you up to one you love. I can ask you now at this moment, when everything is at an end between us except friendship, the purest and most loyal, to let me serve you all my life; though it will be years before I shall have courage to look on your face again.'

The last sentence came out in spite of him. It spoke volumes to a woman's perceptions. Perhaps she liked that involuntary confession of weakness better than all the strength and self-denial she had so admired a while ago.

'You do *really* love me,' said she, trembling indeed still, but pale no longer, 'so well, that for my happiness you would give up everything, even myself?'

'Had it not been so,' he answered, 'do you think I should have been so angry with you for what I saw in the Abbey-garden? Well, he may claim you now before them all. God bless you and *him*! Farewell! Will you not give me your hand once more for the last time?'

She must have been a strangely unfeeling lady, Mistress Mary Carmichael, to resist such an appeal, and yet the tears were brimming in her eyes despite of a roguish, happy smile on her red lips. She withheld her hand, however. Perhaps she did not wish to part quite so abruptly.

'You are generous,' said she, between tears and laughter, 'and you used to be obedient—at least sometimes. Wilful always, you know, or I should not have had to chide you so often. Will you shake my—my future husband by the hand, and assure him of your good-will?'

He thought she might have spared him this, but he assented cordially. What mattered it, a little suffering, more or less? At least it would put off the parting for a few minutes.

'Wait here an instant while I bring him!' said she, and darted off, leaving Walter in that frame of mind which is best described by the metaphor of 'not knowing whether he stood on his head or his heels.'

He had not long to wait, though in truth he kept no account of time. A light hurrying footstep trod the gallery once more, followed by a heavier and manlier stride. Maxwell turned round to confront his lost love, closely followed by the individual she had promised to bring.

'Tis strange how a vague, misty idea, that has puzzled us for long, will sometimes shine out on a sudden as clear as day. There was a frank, joyous expression on the stranger's brow, a sparkle of excitement in his eye, that brought back to Maxwell's recollection for the first time where he had seen him before the well-remembered night in the Abbey-garden. It was the same tall cavalier who had spurred his horse so gallantly into the skirmish near Hermitage, shouting his war-cry the while. It was a kinsman, then, whom she was going to marry after all.

Mary Carmichael stood silent for an instant looking from one to the other. Then she spoke out very quick, as if anxious to tell her story while she could.

'Farewell, Master Maxwell! farewell, if indeed you mean to leave us all at such short notice. You shall not go, however without knowing my father, my dear father, who has never dared show himself openly in Scotland till to-day. And none of you ever found him out—not even you, with your sharp, suspicious eyes,' here she began to laugh; 'and—and—*Walter*, if I have seemed unkind to you, I am sorry for it now,' here she began to cry, 'and I hope you will forgive me, and love my father as well as I do. My dear, dear father, who has got home safe at last!'

And then she flung herself on the paternal breast and hid her face there, laughing and crying together, in a strange, wild mood, very unlike the proud, self-reliant Mary Carmichael whose tears Walter had so often wished he had the power to call forth, if only for the pleasure of drying them; but then these natures, like frozen streams melting in the sun, are proof against everything but the warmth of a great happiness.

Sir Patrick Carmichael, for such was the name of Mary's adventurous father, had probably some inkling of how matters stood. Whether she had explained to him that she had a slight regard for this loyal servant of the Queen, or whether, as is more likely, she had confined herself to talking of him on all occasions, and constantly finding fault with him most unjustly rather than not mention his name, is matter for conjecture; but Sir Patrick, grasping Maxwell warmly by the hand, assured him of his own good feelings towards him, and his sincere respect for so brave and devoted an adherent of their Sovereign.

It was this latter quality that had won its way so triumphantly into Sir Patrick's heart. A staunch Catholic himself, Walter Maxwell was probably the only Protestant in Scotland to whom he would have intrusted the happiness of his daughter, but the stout Queen's-man was only bigoted in his loyalty, and he could have refused nothing to the man who saved Mary Stuart from the treachery of her intriguing brother, and the violence of her own subjects.

He had himself been carrying on a secret correspondence with the Guises on the part of his Sovereign for years, a correspondence that involved continual disguises and many hair-breadth 'scapes from the emissaries of those unscrupulous statesmen, who would not have hesitated for an instant to take his life. Such an exploit as the attempt to rob Randolph of his dispatches was but an amusing interlude in a career like his, but it was seldom indeed Sir Patrick could enjoy a ride, either for sport or strife, in the society of his own countrymen.

His daily existence was one of imminent peril, only warded off by constant vigilance and acuteness: his only pleasures, and even these were subservient to political purposes, the stolen visits to his daughter, which had so excited Maxwell's jealousy and distrust. He was a bold, nay, a reckless man enough, but he loved that daughter in the corner of his fearless heart better than anything on earth, *except* the cause of his Queen; also, Sir Patrick was a person of delicacy and kind feeling withal, owning that sympathy for a love affair which those cannot but entertain who have themselves passed, more or less scorched, through the fire.

So he left his daughter and Maxwell together in the gallery, and when they all met at the Queen's table an hour afterwards, he observed that the pair never exchanged a word, but looked as if they had some mutual understanding nevertheless, and were so happy they could neither eat, nor drink, nor converse rationally, nor sit still.

CHAPTER XL

'I watched her in the morning hour,
So pure and fresh and fair;
A blossom bursting into flower
To gladden all the air.

'I marked her shedding sweets around
Beneath the noontide ray;
The glory of the garden ground,
And the pride of the summer's day.

'But long before that daylight's close
The southern blast awoke,
And crushed and tore the queenly rose
Beneath its pelting stroke.

'Alas! her petals strew the bower;
Yet mangled tho' she lie,
The fragrance of the perished flower
Floats upward to the sky.'

So the Maries were disposed of at last. The roses were unbound from the chaplet and set free. Two of the flowers bloomed happy and beautiful on the manly breasts in which they had not spared on occasion to drive their thorns; one clung obstinately to the person of her Queen; and one, perhaps not the least fragrant and fair of the posy, drooped in a cloister, and so withered untimely away.

Mary Hamilton went peacefully to her rest. Mary Seton vowed eternal constancy to her Sovereign, and wished for nothing better than to live and die a maiden in the Queen's service. Mary Beton took her loyal soldier at last, and made him amends, doubtless, for the pains he had inflicted during his probation. Randolph, a little disgusted and a good deal amused, drank a posset to the health of the newly-wedded pair, and even addressed a neatly-turned compliment to the bride, which met with a colder reception that its ingenuity deserved; but then the diplomatist consoled himself by reflecting that a continuance of his attentions to 'worthy Mistress Beton,' as he called her, would be a sad waste of time when she ceased to furnish him with the intelligence he required; and as for marrying her himself, why that of course was out of the question. Ambition is a bride who brooks no rival, and, in good truth, her worshippers cannot have too few ties connecting them with their kind, for they must turn their hands to strange jobs on occasion. Altogether he was well satisfied to see her so comfortably disposed; for Randolph, as has already been stated, was a good-natured man.

Having got over all their differences before marriage, Walter Maxwell and his Mary quarrelled but little after that welcome event. Tried, as their affection had been, in the fire, and proved through so many years of anxiety, sorrow, and estrangement, it would have been unreasonable to doubt it, and madness indeed to hazard such a treasure for the sake of a light word or a moment's discontent. So they went on caring for each other as fondly, though not so uncomfortably, as before. Neither of them were people to make much demonstration of their feelings, but a calm happiness of repose to which it had long been a stranger seemed to have settled on the husband's brow, and the love-light still shown soft and lambent in the wife's blue eyes when they turned upon the man she had trusted so long and so feared to lose at last.

Their time, too, was fully occupied. Plenty to do at home; troubles and strife and stirring news day by day abroad; constant anxiety for the beloved mistress, whom they were still prepared to serve with zealous loyalty; and no small share of ill-will to sustain from the many disaffected and intriguing, who were never quiet for a day throughout the length and breadth of the land. Nevertheless, of all the Maries, perhaps Walter Maxwell's bride flourished the happiest and the best-cared for of the blooming cluster.

But what of the Queen of the Roses, the Mary of Maries, the noblest princess in Europe, the loveliest woman in the world? Alas for the fairest flower in the garden! rain or shine, storm or calm, there was to be no domestic peace, no permanent repose for her. The man who should have tended and cherished her to the death, proved but a selfish profligate, and left her to pine and languish, weary, sorrowing, and alone. The man who would once have shed his heart's blood freely to shield her from the slightest injury, goaded into madness, ere long snatched wildly at her beauty, soiling her petals with unknightly hand, and dragging the beloved one with him ruthlessly and shamelessly to the dust.

Yet still the stately flower bloomed on, fair and fragrant under the pure air of heaven, fair and fragrant in the close confinement and the darkened daylight of a prison-house.

But the storm was brewing the while low down in the southern sky; the storm that was about to gather so dark and pitiless, to burst at last in its fury over the Queen of the Roses, and lay that lovely head upon the cold earth, beautiful and majestic even in the pale agony of death.